COPPER FOR THE COUNTESS

COPPER FOR THE
COUNTESS

HEARTS OF ARIZONA BOOK 2

SALLY BRITTON

Published by Pink Citrus Books
Edited by Jenny Proctor of Midnight Owl Editors
Proofread by Emily Poole of Midnight Owl Editors
Cover design by Blue Water Books
Illustrations by Melanie Bateman

Sally Britton
www.authorsallybritton.com

First Printing: October 2021

For Sallie Britton Lary,
And All the Women Who Came Before

CHAPTER ONE

AUGUST 25TH, 1895

KB Ranch, Arizona Territory

The harsh afternoon sun baked the desert earth until it cracked, but the grass resisted giving in to the arid climate. That was something Chris Morgan appreciated about desert plants and wildlife. No matter what the wind and sun did, no matter how harsh the weather, the plants hung on to life, and the animals just kept going about their business.

"Frosty," one of the new hands, known by the name Whiskers to most, called from behind.

Chris turned in his saddle at the shout, his horse not breaking stride. They had just passed under the iron sign that welcomed them home after every cattle drive and foray into the rest of the wide world. KB Ranch, a stylized sun setting atop King Bolton's initials.

Chris had won his cowboy christening, *Frosty*, for two reasons. His cold blue eyes that made his men shudder when he leveled them with a glare, and his apparent aloofness toward others. Somehow, his dislike of idle chatter had granted him the status of a man who held himself apart. His brusque, direct instructions to his men added to the idea of a taciturn nature. As

1

a foreman, his name added to his perfect reputation of obeying orders and keeping his men in line.

Whiskers pointed to the road behind them. Toward Sonoita. No one could even call the small collection of buildings that made up the nearest settlement a town. A familiar wagon bounced along the road, coming toward them.

He didn't let his shoulders sag. Not so much as a twitch of muscle betrayed his disappointment and annoyance. As much as he wanted to get back to his house, the newest structure on the ranch, it'd be a mite rude to make Holloway come all the way down to the house if Chris could intercept him on the road. Most likely, the old farmer had a batch of mail to deliver up from Tombstone.

As the foreman, he could've sent one of the cowboys up the road. But Chris preferred to lead by example. That meant greeting the farmer himself.

Six cowboys and a wagon driven by their cook passed him by on their way to the bunkhouse and much-needed baths. They'd driven the cattle to the Tucson station rather than Benson, getting the last of their beef animals on their way for the year.

One rider stopped near him, watching Holloway approach.

Duke, an Englishman who'd married into the Bolton family, pushed his hat up his forehead. "Want me to wait with you, Frosty?"

Chris raised his eyebrows at his friend, and technically one of his bosses given his stake in the ranch. "You got a wife waiting on you."

The Englishman's eyes darted toward the ranch buildings, his entire body leaning that direction. He hadn't been married to the rancher's daughter long, and only the lure of taking part in his first cattle drive had pulled him away from his bride.

"She won't mind a few more minutes," Duke answered, focusing his gaze on Chris once more. He turned his horse around toward the road, as did Chris.

There wasn't anyone waiting for Chris to return. Just an

empty house that still smelled like fresh-cut timber. He hadn't even needed the house, but King Bolton, owner of the ranch, had insisted that his foreman couldn't keep living in the bunkhouse with the rest of the hands.

"It's a benefit to your position," King had insisted. "And it gives you room to stretch out a bit. Maybe start a family."

Chris hadn't deigned to respond to that idea.

The privacy of his own house had appealed to him, though, along with more room for putting up shelves for his books. Keeping them in a crate under his bunk wasn't ideal. So he'd agreed to the house.

They passed under the sign again, just as it caught a touch of wind that made it swing above their heads. The breeze, warm as it was, felt good across Chris's forehead and exposed neck. Grit from the trail had worked its way beneath his collar, despite his care with his bandana.

Holloway was nearly to the turnoff in the lane, his mules walking with their heads hung sulkily. They likely hadn't wanted to pass by the entrance to their home and barn without stopping, as Holloway had to do to deliver the mail. He was their settlement's registered postal carrier with Western Union. Once a month he went to Tombstone, the county seat, to gather up mail and bring it back to the people who called Sonoita and its surrounding farms and ranches home.

"Mr. Holloway," Duke called out loud enough to be heard over the tramp of hooves. "Good afternoon."

"Duke. Frosty. Mighty glad to see you had a successful trip." The man's tone and the solemn look on his face were at odds with his normally jovial personality. Chris frowned, already expecting bad news. But for whom?

Holloway pulled the mules to a stop, then looked back into the bed of his wagon. His shoulders slumped. "Frosty, I've got a couple of special deliveries for you. They were waiting when I got to town today."

Though he hadn't been expecting anything, he didn't say as

much. Chris nudged his horse to move the gelding alongside the wagon bed and looked down.

Two pairs of dark eyes peered back up at him, from two little faces streaked with dirt and tears. A girl sat in the wagon, against the backboard, with her arm around a boy smaller and younger than she was. They both wore straw hats and dark clothes. The boy had a piece of paper pinned to the strap of his overalls.

To Chris Morgan

KB Ranch

Sonoita, Arizona Territory

Someone had sent him children. By mail. Someone who knew his proper name rather than the one his fellow cowboys had christened him with. His stomach sank like a stone through cold water.

Not two girls. His sister in Missouri had three little girls. They weren't Susan's children.

The little boy ducked his head, but the girl lifted her chin higher. "Are you our daddy's cousin? Chris?"

Cousin.

He looked up at Holloway, who'd turned to watch the reunion. The man had made a telegram and sealed envelope appear from nowhere and held them out to Chris. "The telegram came three days ago, but no one brought it out to us. The letter came with them."

Chris looked at the children, then took the paper. He read the telegram first.

To Chris Morgan. Cousin William Ashford and wife Maria dead. Morgan declared guardian of children in last will. Children arriving August 24, 5 o'clock stage. Regards, Leman Rutherford at Law.

So few words, yet they altered everything if they were true. He looked up at the little girl. "William Ashford is your dad?"

Her chin trembled. "He was."

William and Chris had been inseparable as young boys. Their kinship had come through their mothers. William had nearly traveled west with Chris when life in the city became too stifling for the boy set on finding adventure and wide-open spaces. "Breathing room," William had called it. But there had been a girl. Maria Larsen. And William had fallen in love.

They'd written from time to time. At least twice a year. They'd filled pages and pages with their doings, with mutual friends and relatives, and Chris had kept every letter he could as a reminder that he had people out in the wide world who cared about him.

It still took a moment for Chris to remember the names of the children. When he hit upon them at last, he breathed them out loud. "Laura and Ben."

The boy looked up at that, his eyes pained. How old were they? Chris didn't know enough about children to make an educated guess.

He looked up at Holloway. "This says they arrived the twenty-fourth. Yesterday."

Holloway nodded. "The general store clerk put them up for the night. His wife fed them. They were getting ready to come looking for us when I showed up to collect the mail."

Duke approached, looking at the children for a moment before addressing Chris. "I'm sorry for your loss, Frosty."

It hadn't sunk in yet that William was gone. That his daughter and son were all that remained of the lively young man with a perpetual grin. Chris gave himself a mental shake. He could read the letter and figure out what had happened later. Right now, he needed to worry about the children.

Did they know how to ride a horse? No reason to make them uncomfortable, really, if they didn't like being atop the tall animals. He looked up at Holloway. "D'you mind bringing them all the way to the house?"

Holloway clicked his tongue. "Not at all." He gave the mules a command and snapped the leads above their rumps. The mules protested with a couple of brays but obeyed.

Chris followed with his eyes on the children, and they gazed back at him without blinking.

Duke rode alongside him, the gesture one of friendship and

support. Chris wanted to thank him but didn't know exactly what to say in the moment. He looked down at the envelope crushed in his hand, recognizing his name written across the front, even though the handwriting appeared unstable. Shaky. Hardly familiar. But he knew William's writing.

A hard lump formed in Chris's throat. It took the entire distance from road to ranch for him to rid himself of it well enough to talk. Duke dismounted first, and everything blurred together after that. The women, all three of them, appeared and found the children. They clucked over them, embraced them, took the children into the main ranch house with promises of food and baths.

Duke explained to whomever else remained what he knew. Holloway filled in gaps.

Chris dismounted, handed the reins to someone. He didn't care who. Then he walked away. Beyond the main house, toward one of the windmills that marked a well and cistern on the property.

He leaned against the windmill's supports and opened the envelope. The letter was brief. The handwriting inside as miserable as on the envelope.

Chris,

Maria passed three days ago. Diphtheria and Influenza. We got the kids out of the house as soon as we knew how bad off she was. I'm sick now, too. If you're reading this, the worst has happened. I contacted lawyers and told them where to find you. I made it legal. Laura and Ben will be in good hands. Tell them I love them, and so does their mother. Raise them like we were raised. I don't trust anyone else the way I trust you. I know you'll do right by them.

See you on the other side.

-Will

His fist crumpled the letter, pain ricocheting in his chest like a bullet in an iron stove, making it hard to breathe.

Will was gone.

And Chris knew nothing about raising children.

CHAPTER TWO

SEPTEMBER 9TH, 1895

Bisbee, Arizona Territory

E velyn hadn't been born into nobility, but she still knew how to carry herself like the lady she had become. When she drifted into the management offices of the Copper Queen Mine, people stopped to stare, just as they had in London. The society papers had called her many unflattering things over the years, but her first nickname had held even when her popularity fell. *The Red-Headed Venus.*

The beauty that had inspired the name—along with the jealous looks, the cruel gossip—she wore like a suit of armor. It protected her. Insulated her from the rest of the world. Today, however, she needed to wear the armor with confidence and grace. Her daughter depended on it.

Evelyn stopped in front of the largest desk in the room, and the clerk behind it jumped to his feet so fast, he knocked over the chair behind him.

"Ma'am," he squeaked, then cleared his throat and deepened his voice as he continued. "Good afternoon. What may I do for you?"

She didn't turn her full smile on the young man because she

didn't need to. His ears turned red before she spoke a single word. "I hope you can direct me to someone in charge. I have come a very long way, and my need is quite urgent."

Uncertainty tinted his eyes. "Do you have an appointment?"

She hated this. Evelyn's mother had once said, *"Women have precious few advantages in the world. The Good Lord saw fit to give you one with your looks. Use it."* She hadn't wanted to do as her mother said. But when she'd lost her mother and stability, she'd needed protection. Then she'd lost her first husband, the provider of that protection, and had a daughter. With that beauty, Evelyn had secured a second husband as quickly as she could.

The London gossip rags had called her a siren, and at every event she attended, she heard worse whispered about her from behind fans and elegantly gloved hands.

Evelyn's daughter depended upon her now just as she had in their unlucky past.

"I do not have an appointment." She held the portfolio in her hand tighter to her side. "This is a matter of expediency, however. Here." She withdrew one of her calling cards from a fold in the leather and handed it to him, allowing some of her desperation to show through her wide eyes.

She watched his lips form the words that her late husband had insisted be printed in gold script on the expensive paper. *Lady Evelyn Lyon, Countess of Tyneham, Dorset.* The London address printed below no longer belonged to her, nor would she ever set foot upon that street again.

Her late husband's heir had made certain of that.

"Of course, Countess. I'll tell the manager at once. One moment. Mr. Douglas is in his office." The clerk's eyes had gone large, though his address to her proved once again that most Americans did not know how to address someone holding a title.

It was quite refreshing.

The clerk disappeared through a door behind his desk, big and dark, the frame embellished with woodcarving that looked like something one would find in a castle in England rather than an office in the midst of desert mountains. The wealth of the mining company was on full display in this building. The wood was rich and dark, the chairs of even the lowliest clerks were fine leather, and there were expensive carpets covering the floor.

This was a place where money came out of the ground every second of every day. The Copper Queen Mining Company made sure everyone knew it, too.

She took a steadying breath, her back to the rest of the room. She hoped the tremble in her legs went unnoticed. That the quiet complaint of her empty stomach passed unheard.

The door opened, and the clerk came out, holding it open and bowing awkwardly. "Mr. Douglas says please come in." He gestured broadly with one hand, as though to sweep her inside. Evelyn smiled at his enthusiasm, and for a moment she felt lighter.

She entered the office to find a large desk near tall windows, with a man standing at the corner. He approached her, his expression curious.

"My lady, it is a pleasure to meet you." He held his hand out, and Evelyn placed her hand in his. He bowed over it politely, then gestured for her to sit in a chair in front of his desk.

"Thank you for seeing me on such short notice, Mr. Douglas. This is a very important matter, and I appreciate your time." She lowered herself to the chair and placed the folder upon her lap, keeping her posture perfect and her chin tilted upward. She smiled, as her late husband had always commanded her to when he presented her to his associates.

Mr. Douglas returned the expression. "I am happy to be of service however I can. How can we of the Copper Queen Mining Company be of assistance? Do you wish to learn more about our operation? Perhaps invest with us?"

"I am already an investor." She laid her hand flat upon the leather folder. "Or at least, my late husband, the Earl of Tyneham, held stock in the company. He died recently and left the stock certificates to me. I have come to discover what they are worth."

9

She couldn't help but glance around the office building with renewed hope. The mines obviously produced wealth. Perhaps the stocks she now owned would be worth enough for her to settle somewhere safe and comfortable with Madeline. That's all she wanted; Madeline deserved a stable home and an education.

"An English earl?" Mr. Douglas held his hand out. "I cannot recall seeing that name in our books, but if you would allow me to examine the certificates?"

"Yes, of course." She held the folder out to him, ignoring the way her empty stomach twisted itself into knots. "Thank you."

He walked behind his desk and seated himself, then put the folder on the table and flipped it open. The moment his eyes fell upon the first certificate, his brow creased. Deeply.

Mr. Douglas turned the first document over, sat it aside, and inspected the next. He did this several times, and with each page his frown grew deeper. Finally, he closed the portfolio, then looked up to meet her gaze. "You are from England? Did your husband ever visit Bisbee? Or send a representative here?"

Something was wrong. Evelyn forced herself to smile. "He met with a representative seeking investors in London, some four years ago, I think."

Mr. Douglas heaved a sigh, focusing his gaze on the paper in front of him again. Then he bent and opened a drawer on his side of the desk and withdrew an enormous book. He opened it, then spun the book around and pushed it to her side of the desk. "These are what our stock certificates look like, Lady Tyneham."

She forced herself to remain calm as she leaned forward, peering at the document. The certificates were inked in black, with golden borders dotted with five-pointed stars. At the top of the certificate, in artful lettering, was the name of the company and an image depicting miners with raised pickaxes and lanterns in a cave.

They looked nothing like the red-and-black inked certificates she had spent weeks holding close to her chest. Nothing about the documents, except the fact that they all bore the name of the mine, looked the same.

Her heart clenched and her throat turned dry. She looked up at Mr. Douglas, whose expression had softened with pity. "The papers you have here...they are counterfeit. And not even particularly good counterfeits."

She swallowed, attempted to smile, and failed. The room grew dark around the edges. "There must be some mistake. My husband guarded these papers closely—he said they were worth a small fortune."

The man across from her slowly shook his head, closed her folder, and handed it back to her. "No, Lady Tyneham. They are not. Someone duped your husband, and I am most sorry for it."

She took the folder back, looked down at it, uncomprehending. "Are you certain? Perhaps they are merely old—"

"I have been a part of this company since it first came to Bisbee," he told her, tone gentle, as though he spoke to a child of a simple matter. "We have never issued stock certificates like those, and we are the only mining operation in Bisbee. Your papers are worthless."

"Can't you check—there must be records..." Her voice trailed away as he heaved a sigh and rose. He went to a bookcase filled with documents and large leather-bound volumes. He took out two.

"Lyon, and Tyneham," he muttered, bringing them back to the desk. He thumbed through pages on one, then the other, and pushed the books across the desk. "See for yourself. The name doesn't appear in our records."

She looked at the neat rows of alphabetically arranged surnames. The late earl's title and surname were missing.

The black at the corner of her vision deepened and stretched, and she stood mechanically. There was no use in arguing when she could see the truth with her own eyes. She held the folder against her chest and spoke without quite knowing what she said.

"I thank you for your time, Mr. Douglas. I am sorry to have interrupted your work. Good day."

He rose, too, and looked at her with some concern. "Will you be all right, ma'am? Do you need something to drink? You've gone pale. Here, sit again." He came toward her.

Evelyn took a quick step back and shook her head, trying to stave off panic long enough to get out of his sight. "N-no. Thank you. I am well enough." She turned and hurried to the door, throwing it open despite hearing him call to her again.

She marched out the way she had come, her head held high, and her tears kept at bay. She kept a smile on her face all the way out into the sunshine.

She turned and walked up the steep hill, the dust from the streets billowing up around horses as they passed, stinging at her eyes. She went in the direction of the boarding house, where she had taken a small room with a single bed the evening before. She'd paid for two nights, thinking it might take a day or two to arrange the liquidation of the stocks. Meals for one had come with that meager investment, and Evelyn had turned her breakfast that morning over to her daughter without hesitation. Trusting that they would be eating well that very night.

Her knees buckled, and she stumbled against the wall of the building as she passed. Spots appeared in her vision. The former countess blinked rapidly until she made out a bench only a few steps away. She kept her hand against the wall to maintain her balance until she could make it to the bench and lower herself to its rough wooden planks.

People passed by her without saying a word. Without looking at her. Trousers and shined shoes, buttoned heels, boots. She kept her gaze to the ground and watched them all, without really looking.

The purse dangling from her wrist was empty except for a clean handkerchief and her last calling card. The leather portfolio on the bench beside her was worthless. The fine dress she wore, an entire year out of season in England.

She had nothing left. And after that night, there wouldn't even be a roof over her head. Or Madeline's.

Gripping the edge of the bench, Evelyn tried to think of something—anything—she might do to spare her daughter from the knowledge that they had nothing. She could sell every article of clothing she owned—though she hadn't been able to bring much with her in the single trunk she had shared with Madeline on their ocean crossing. She had sold as much of her personal possessions as she could in England, then more in New York City, her hope fixed on the idea of owning stock in a lucrative copper mine in the Arizona Territory.

Her late husband, the earl, had promised to leave her and Madeline something in his will, even though Evelyn was his third wife. And Madeline a child of Evelyn's first marriage.

He had promised that all she had to do was behave as a proper English countess and she would be well looked after. But mere hours after his unexpected death, his abrupt passing in the middle of the night, his eldest son and heir—a man her own age —had turned her out of the house.

He'd accused her of trapping the earl in marriage, of seeking to use the earl's wealth and position in society to raise herself up its rungs. And he'd said even worse things to her, calling her every vile name a woman could be called.

She'd never liked the earl's oldest son, nor the way his eyes followed her across the room when he visited his father's London house. She'd always felt sick when he came near. Evelyn had taken Madeline and fled the house with almost nothing rather than attempt to reason with him.

The solicitor hadn't been pleased when Evelyn had arrived at his door in London. He'd wasted no time to inform Evelyn that the late earl had *not* changed his will since marrying her.

There was no legal way for her to claim any part of the estate.

Her second marriage had ended the same as the first. A dead husband she felt no inclination to mourn, her daughter's hand in hers, and not a penny to her name.

A pair of pointed women's shoes walked by. The shining shoes of a child skipped along behind. Then came a man's dusty boots. As she watched the boots stand a moment, toes pointed away from her, a penny fell onto the boardwalk with a quiet little "clack." It spun for a moment, then fell onto its side between the heels of the boots.

Evelyn watched the penny, fascinated by its bright gleam in the late afternoon sun.

The man in the boots stepped away, leaving the bright piece of copper behind.

Evelyn rose from the bench, the useless folder left behind, and bent to retrieve the coin. She stood and looked up, her eyes finding the boots and their owner a few steps away.

"Sir?" The word came out as a whisper. Evelyn forced herself to speak louder, though why it mattered she didn't know. "Sir? Pardon me, but you dropped this."

The man paused, and when he turned, she took in several things at once. He was tall. He wore a stern expression, as though displeased with the day and everything in it. And his features were chiseled roughly, making her think he might well be made of stone.

He looked like the unruly cowboys she had seen outside her window the night before—the same type of hat, dust-covered trousers, and broad shoulders. She'd woken when a group of rowdy men had stumbled down the street, singing raucously and using the worst sort of language.

She'd shuddered and pulled the drapes closed, reflecting on how different this dirty mining town was from everything she had known in England.

She swallowed her discomfort as the man looked from the penny in her hand slowly upward to meet her gaze.

A shock went through her, as though she'd fallen through ice and into frigid water. Never had she seen such clear blue eyes. Given the heat of the day, the cold sensation wasn't entirely unpleasant. One of his dark brown eyebrows raised.

"Ma'am? Were you speaking to me?" He didn't sound as heartless as he looked.

The ground shifted, returning beneath her feet to hold her up. As it solidified once more, she held her hand out further, palm-up, with the penny in its center. "I believe you dropped this coin."

He blinked, then approached slowly. Until he stood only a foot away, and her head tipped back just enough to keep her eyes upon his. She was tall, by English standards. He was tall by any standards. His gaze dropped to her glove, and his hand reached into his pocket. She heard the jingle of metal against metal before he pulled out a handful of coins and looked at them.

"Hm. You might be right." He offered her the barest of smiles, and that changed everything about his appearance. Quite suddenly, the stone face became kind. "But I can't be sure. Maybe you'd better hang on to it. In these parts, a penny found can bring good luck."

Evelyn looked down at the penny in her hand, noting the dirt on the tips of her gloves where they had scraped the ground to lift the coin.

And she burst into tears.

CHAPTER THREE

C hris hadn't been around many women of late, other than the married ladies on the ranch where he worked, but he didn't think he'd grown uncouth enough to make a woman cry just by speaking to her. And the way the beautiful woman standing in front of him started crying, as though she bore as much pain as sorrow, immediately split his heart in two.

No one should cry like that. He hadn't been able to bear it when his little sister cried, either. He'd given her anything she'd wanted to make her smile again.

What could he possibly do for this copper-haired, green-eyed stranger who looked like she belonged in a big city opera house rather than the streets of Bisbee?

Chris took her by the elbow, as gently as he could, and walked her to the bench where she'd been sitting before. Yes, he'd noticed her there. Just in passing. He doubted a man could walk by someone like her without taking a second look.

He sat, lowering her down to the bench with him. She had closed her hand into a fist around the coin, and as soon as she sat, she curled herself forward, her body stiff and shaking.

He knew he ought to say something, offer some sort of reassurance, but his mind went completely blank. By rights, he couldn't even touch her to offer any kind of comfort. Not unless he wanted a hard slap across his face.

What could he say, not knowing what had sent her into such heart-wrenching sobs? He glanced up once, looking around to see if there might be a husband or a friend coming to the woman's aid. There was no one. Just a few strangers who slanted him an uncomfortable look before picking up their speed, walking away. Determined not to get involved.

Chris wasn't any good with this sort of thing.

Laura cried sometimes, and he didn't know what to do for the little girl, either. He'd hold her when she'd let him and kept his distance when she'd pushed him away. Ben was almost worse, given how often he looked near to tears, but never said a single word. Hardly made a sound. He'd just stare at Chris, heart in his eyes, as though he waited for Chris to understand what to do to fix things.

But how did he fix a little boy's broken heart?

So, he just sat there, like he did for the children. Waiting.

The woman's sobs abated, turning into softer sniffles. She worked at the strings of the purse dangling from her wrist, penny still clutched in her hand, and pulled out a white handkerchief edged in delicate lace.

"I'm terribly sorry," she said, her words as elegantly accented as the cloth in her hand. "Forgive me. I did not mean to turn into a watering pot."

He wished he knew how to help her banish those tears. "I think I ought to apologize, ma'am. You were fine until I opened my mouth." He offered what he hoped was a reassuring smile.

"Oh, it wasn't you." She sniffed, her lovely eyes now rimmed in red, and looked up at him again.

Despite the crying, she was one of the prettiest ladies he'd ever seen. Everything from her fair skin to the dark leather of her shoes spoke of a life far from the desert wind and sun.

"Truly, sir. You are very kind. Thank you for attending to me. I am well enough now. You may continue on about your business."

He hadn't been busy, exactly. Mr. Bolton and his wife had come to Bisbee to hear some politician give a speech the day before, and he'd accompanied them to provide extra protection on the road and visit the bookseller to see about collecting more children's books. Laura and Ben hadn't seemed interested in much, but he'd seen them eyeing his books frequently in the two weeks they'd been with him.

Chris leaned away from her enough to take in the whole of her appearance again. The woman wore a hat and dress finer than anything he'd ever seen, and he knew she had to come from the same side of the Atlantic as Duke. She was British, and most likely born to a higher station in life than he could imagine.

She wasn't his problem. And he had plenty of his own to deal with.

He stayed on the bench next to her. "I can't leave you here like this. Not unless it's to find someone else to help you. Do you have a husband or someone I can fetch?"

To his dismay, her eyes started watering again. "No husband. Not anymore." She put a hand to forehead, then looked up the street in the direction he'd been headed. "Only my daughter, and I cannot let her see me like this."

A woman alone with her daughter, in a desert town like Bisbee—especially a woman like her—meant trouble. Though the town had made progress toward respectability, roughnecked miners still made up most of the population.

Why was she without protection or companionship?

Chris studied her profile, noting her still swollen eyes and reddened nose with concern. That kind of crying didn't usually happen over something small. This woman needed help, and it didn't sound like any was coming.

"We best cheer you up before you see her, then." He gestured across the dusty street, where a small shop had a sign offering up coffee, soup, and a sandwich for a nickel. "I haven't had lunch yet. Would you join me for a bite to eat?"

"Oh, no. Thank you. You have already done enough." She pulled herself upright, and her deep green eyes widened. Maybe in England men didn't invite women they'd just met to lunch. She gathered up a folder he hadn't noticed on the bench.

Then an all too familiar sound bubbled up from somewhere inside the lady—a growl of hunger his own stomach had made more times than he could count. Her cheeks went pink as her gaze darted away from his. Seemed she hadn't had lunch yet, either.

"I have a friend from your part of the world, ma'am. In these situations, he always gets his way by saying just two words. Hope you don't mind me trying them on for size." He stood and extended his hand out to her. "I insist." Those words always worked when Duke was determined to do something kind for anyone, especially when their pride got in his way.

"I suppose... if you insist." Though her smile wavered, it had at least appeared.

The woman put her hand in his, the cream color of her glove contrasting with his calloused, sun-bronzed skin. After she stood, he stole another of Duke's easy gestures and settled her hand on his forearm, as though he meant to escort her to a ball rather than across a dusty road. Once there was a break in traffic, he took her across to the little restaurant.

"My name's Chris Morgan," he told her, figuring she'd prefer calling him something more traditional-sounding than *Frosty*. "I'm the foreman at a ranch north of here."

And he was supposed to meet up with his employer in less than an hour to make the return trip to that ranch.

They had attained the other side of the road when she responded, almost too quiet for him to hear. "I'm Lady Tyneham. My late husband was the Earl of Tyneham." She winced and turned her face away. "I suppose that doesn't matter here, though."

So she was a widow. An English widow, unaccompanied by anyone but a daughter. Despite knowing it wasn't his business, Chris couldn't help being intrigued.

"If it's who you are, it matters," he said, trying to reassure her. Whether or not it was the right thing to say, he didn't know. He settled her at the table beneath the awning and went to find the proprietor. He ordered two sandwiches and two coffees, then went back to join her.

She sat as still as a statue, her gaze directed up the street, though he doubted she was actually looking at anything. More likely, her thoughts had drawn her gaze inward. When he sat down, she blinked and turned to face him. A smile touched her lips, but not her eyes.

"I'm terribly sorry, Mr. Morgan. Please, don't feel obligated to buy me refreshment. I have no wish to inconvenience you."

Chris sat back in his chair and removed his hat, then ran a hand through his hair in hopes of giving it some semblance of tidiness. He put the hat in an empty chair next to their table.

"Buying a sandwich and coffee for a lady isn't an inconvenience. Besides, my mother raised me to know when people need looking after." It was the best excuse he could give for wanting to offer help.

"She sounds kind," the English woman said, voice low and expression soft. "Thank you, Mr. Morgan."

A young woman came out carrying a tray laden with two mugs, two plates, and sandwiches on thickly cut bread. She put each item on the table, one at a time, and sent a flirtatious smile Chris's direction before disappearing back inside the eatery.

Lady Tyneham put her folder in her lap, then removed her gloves and put them to the side. Then she sat a moment staring at the large sandwich as though uncertain how to approach eating it. Chris doubted she'd ever eaten such simplistic food. He'd heard that the wealthy ate things they called *finger sandwiches*, laden with cucumber and tomatoes rather than the hearty stuffings found in most of the food to which he was accustomed.

He picked up his sandwich in one hand, his coffee in the other, and started eating in silence. She'd figure it out.

She took up the coffee first, inhaling deeply before sipping at it as daintily as if it were in a teacup made of fine china. She closed her eyes as she drank, and Chris couldn't help but smile. He'd done the right thing, based on how pleased the simple offering made her.

She didn't catch him looking, thankfully, as she turned her attention to her sandwich and took it up in both hands. She held it gingerly, examined the bread and trimmings from all sides, then tried to open her mouth wide enough to take a bite of all the layers at once.

Chris had to take a large bite of his own food to keep from chuckling. Though it couldn't be easy, she somehow maintained her dignity and delicate appearance while she ate. And it didn't take her long to polish off the last bite.

Maybe she hadn't had breakfast, either.

With some food in her, maybe she'd share more of her story. Why he felt the tug to hear the whole of it, Chris couldn't say. Nor did he think too much about it. The fact was, if he could help her, he needed to. He could feel it.

"Thank you again," she said, patting at her lips with her handkerchief. "I am most grateful, Mr. Morgan."

He folded his arms and leaned against the table. He fixed her with the stern look he'd give a young cowboy whose hat couldn't carry water. The one that got him confessions of foolish mistakes and promises to do better.

"Ma'am, I know we've barely met. You've got no reason to explain yourself to me. But if you'd tell me what's troubling you, I can promise I'll do my best to help or find someone who can. I've got a sister and a little girl under my care, and if someone found them crying all alone in a strange town, I'd hope that person would help."

She didn't shift or shy away from the question. Chris watched as she folded her gloveless hands upon the table, and he heard the deep breath she took before she answered. "Normally, sir, I would refuse to impart such personal information to a stranger. But my position is such that I have few options, and nowhere to go for help." Her gaze stayed upon her hands, the table, not looking at him at all. "You said you are friends with an Englishman?"

"Yup. He lives on the same ranch that I do. He used to be an English lord." She raised her eyebrows at that, and he shrugged. "It's true. His brother paid us a call not too long ago, too."

"Then perhaps you know a little of what it is like in England for someone like me." She nibbled at her bottom lip, then her shoulders slumped. "I was not the earl's first wife. He'd been married before and already produced an heir and several other children. We married recently, after my first husband passed away." She winced, and he saw the tension in her fingers—her knuckles whitening—as she continued. "My first husband left us with nothing. The earl knew this, and he promised he would take care of my daughter and me. But after he died, his eldest son wasted no time in removing me from my home, taking away most of my things, and leaving me on the streets. The earl never changed his will. He left my daughter and me with nothing. Again."

She looked across the street, her eyebrows furrowing. "Except for a portfolio full of stock certificates for a mine in this dirty little town. I sold my clothing. My wedding ring. We came so far..."

Chris looked down the street. "I could take you to the mining office—"

"The certificates aren't real."

His mouth clicked shut, and he frowned at her. "Not real? You got fake stock certificates for a territory mine all the way over in England?"

She nodded, her expression miserable and her eyes growing damp again. "The Copper Queen Mine has never heard of my husband, and their certificates look nothing like the ones I brought with me."

He rubbed at the back of his neck, his thoughts circling the problem the way a cattle dog circled a herd, trying to make order out of chaos. "You don't have any friends here?"

"We know no one in the United States." She raised her gaze to his at last. "And after tonight, we will have nowhere to stay, unless the woman who owns the boarding house takes pity on us. Perhaps...perhaps I could find work..." Her voice shrank as she spoke, dwindling to almost nothing when she added, "Though I don't know what I might do."

This wasn't a woman who knew how to take on a position she might find in Bisbee. Her fair hands looked smooth and soft. She held herself like a queen. Chris knew well enough that people who had worked all their lives were impatient with those who had not.

And she was alone. In a mining town. Without protection of husband, family, or friends. In a territory where folks could be sweet as honey or mean as hornets.

She couldn't stay in Bisbee.

"How old is your little girl?" he asked.

Though she didn't quite smile, her expression lightened. "Madeline is ten years old."

"That's my niece's age." Chris saw her eyebrows raise. "I'm her guardian. Her and her brother. It's not always easy with kids, is it?" He saw her expression change, growing thoughtful. He didn't have any care to discuss his particular situation, though, so he hurried the conversation along. "Where's your daughter right now?"

"The woman who runs the boarding house promised to keep an eye on her, but I left Madeline with a book in our room." She put her fingers to her head and massaged her temple, her gaze losing focus. "We're staying at the Little Blue Boarding House."

"Ma'am, I'm here in town with my boss and his wife. Maybe the four of us might come up with a solution to keep you and your daughter safe. May I bring them back to your board-inghouse?"

She tilted her head to the side. "You would do that, for a stranger? It's too much trouble—"

"Not at all. I'll round them up and meet you there in half an hour or less." He grabbed his hat and put it on as he came to his feet. "Between the four of us, we'll figure it out. I'm sure of it." She came to her feet slowly, her eyebrows drawing together. Maybe she didn't believe him, or perhaps she wondered if she could trust him.

Mrs. Bolton would set her at ease. She mothered everyone, and this English woman with her dark green eyes and uncertain smile would be no exception to that. Before she could thank him again, he gave her a deep nod and hurried on his way to the hotel across the street from the post office, where Mr. Bolton and his wife would be waiting.

EVELYN WATCHED THE COWBOY STRIDE AWAY, WITH PURPOSE IN HIS every footstep. Did he even see the two dusty miners who stepped aside to let him pass? He was the sort who didn't let people get in his way, and others likely sensed it when they saw him coming.

She had moved with that kind of confidence once, certain of her path and where she wished to go. She had cut through ballrooms, and women in brightly hued gowns had parted in a sea of silk rather than stall her progress across the floor.

Where Evelyn had fought to convey herself with poise, Mr. Morgan had an easiness of movement that made her think that nothing he did was an act.

She tugged her gloves back into place, and she returned her handkerchief to her otherwise empty reticule—except it wasn't totally empty. Her gloved hand brushed the edge of the coin, a penny she'd only meant to return to a stranger and which had instead brought her to someone who might help her.

A stranger. She shook her head at her own foolishness. She had given away too much of herself to someone she had no reason to trust. Except—he had stopped to sit with her while she cried. Had anyone ever done that for her before?

Pulling the strings of her purse tight, Evelyn tucked the folder against her side, and she rose from the table. The whole town felt like one steep hill which she had to climb to get back to Madeline.

Bisbee was a strange place. As she walked up the hill, she found her eyes traveling upward on either side of the road. The town wasn't conventional, but it looked as though someone had poured buildings and houses into the crack between two red-tinted mountains. The buildings pressed together, every inch of space filled, all the way up to the tops of the mountains on either side. Houses had two corners against the rocks and the other two resting on stilts, propping the buildings up against the solid, steep ground.

How did people live this way, atop one another, tucked into stone?

She shuddered and stopped before the small blue building where she had purchased two nights of safety. Inside, Madeline waited for her in a room with a single narrow bed pushed against a wall and a chair in one corner. Madeline had slept in the bed, and Evelyn had reassured her several times that the chair was best for her own rest.

Mrs. Parker sat on a chair that barely fit on the narrow-boarded porch. She peeled potatoes, her hands as brown as the vegetables in her basket. She sniffed and wiped her forehead with the back of her arm.

"How is Madeline?" Evelyn asked.

"Hasn't made a peep. Your business go well?" The older woman went back to her potatoes, her disinterest in Evelyn something that felt merciful rather than dismissive.

Evelyn didn't answer the question as she stepped onto the porch and through the door. "Thank you for minding her, Mrs. Parker."

The front room of the boarding house was smaller than

Evelyn's closet had been, back when she'd been a person of importance. A faded blue settee and two wooden chairs were the only furnishings inside the formal room. The stairs going up to the four tiny rooms above were narrow, the wood worn smooth in the center of each step.

Evelyn came to the door and pushed it open, her heart in her throat.

Madeline lay across the bed on her stomach, book in hand, a bored expression on her face. She looked up at the same moment Evelyn released a relieved sigh.

"Mama." Madeline squirmed off the bed, fluffed the skirt of her blue traveling dress, and came two steps closer. "Can we explore the town now?"

"Not just yet, dear." Evelyn bent to kiss her daughter's head, then smoothed a curl behind Madeline's ear. "I have guests coming to discuss business before we decide on our next act."

The little girl's shoulders slumped, and she picked up the book again, then sat down in the chair near the window. "Mrs. Parker says there isn't anything to see here but dusty miners and chipped paint."

"I cannot entirely disagree with Mrs. Parker." Rickety buildings, splintering windowpanes, and dirty covered windows were all she had seen when she'd allowed herself to notice on the way to the mining offices. Stepping inside that office, wood gleaming with polish and wealth, she had felt more at home than she had since they'd left New York City.

Evelyn went to the window that faced the barren side of the mountain. Plants with more prickles than an African porcupine grew between the red rocks, and grass that appeared warped and dry rustled in the infrequent breeze.

The train ride across the country had been dusty, smoky, and dirty. The landscape out their window had changed from green to brown so subtly, she couldn't be certain when all the color had vanished from the world, only that it had. Then they had boarded the stagecoach that brought them from the train station in Tucson down to Bisbee. Evelyn had spent most of that trip clutching Madeline to her side and keeping her mouth covered with a handkerchief. That piece of flimsy, lacey fabric had ended the trip streaked with dust, and Evelyn had stowed it away in the trunk that held what was left of their worldly possessions.

The trunk contained Madeline's favorite book, Evelyn's photograph of her parents, another of Madeline's father, and what remained of their clothing. The documents in the folder, along with the fake stock certificates, were of the sort to prove her identity and her child's. A birth certificate and copy of the church register, a wedding certificate, and a letter of introduction from the otherwise unhelpful solicitor of the late earl.

Little enough from their lives remained that Evelyn feared they would both vanish altogether.

"What did the men at the mine say?" Madeline asked, her innocent question tugging Evelyn out of her thoughts rather abruptly.

"Not the mine, dear. The mining offices." She forced a smile as she moved to stand beside Madeline's chair. "I am afraid the stock certificates are not worth what I had hoped."

Madeline turned somewhat pale as she lifted her face to search her mother's gaze. "But that is all right, isn't it? We still have some money, don't we?"

Despite trying to hide their circumstances from her daughter, Evelyn knew the clever little girl had picked up on much of the situation. She had to know why they could not afford the sleeper car on the train. Why they had such light meals, and Evelyn proclaimed herself not hungry at least twice a day while still encouraging Madeline to eat her bread and butter.

"Never you fret." Evelyn bent and kissed Madeline on the forehead. "Go on and read your book. I must wait for my guests in Mrs. Parker's front room." She brushed the back of her hand against Madeline's cheek. "I will be up again soon."

As Evelyn descended the steps, she fought against the vise-like feeling tightening around her chest and heart. If she had been in New York when this discovery occurred, perhaps she could have found a sympathetic member of Society to lean upon. Or she could have applied to a service for companions or governesses—despite her lack of experience teaching, she had an education of her own—or to a girls' school.

No one in this dried-up town, or even in the whole of the Territory, would see any need for the type of training she possessed. Which meant having to earn an entirely new education. Something more practical.

But what?

CHAPTER FOUR

When Evelyn spied Mr. Morgan in front of the boarding house, two people with him, she had to blink in some surprise. Did everyone in Arizona grow to such unmatched heights? The older gentleman wore a fine black suit and a black felt hat, and his well-weathered face boasted a rather impressive mustache. At his side was a woman nearly his equal in years, and easily the same height as Evelyn. She had a motherly look about her as she peered at the boarding house from beneath a purple bonnet.

Evelyn kept watch from behind the faded curtains, sick with anticipation and dread all at the same time.

Mr. Morgan led the older couple, a determined expression upon his face, up to the porch where Mrs. Parker still worked with her vegetables.

The walls were thin enough for Evelyn to hear when he asked, "Is Lady Tyneham staying here?"

"If you mean that English woman and her kid, then yes." Mrs. Parker didn't sound at all gracious. In fact, she was downright suspicious. "What business do you'uns have with her?"

The other man came forward and doffed his hat. "We're here to conduct some private business, ma'am. My name is King

Bolton, and this is my wife, Mrs. Bolton. We have a ranch a day's ride north of here."

The ranch owner and his wife appeared perfectly respectable. Evelyn leaned closer to the window—and Mr. Morgan's stare caught her there, his blue eyes bright beneath the brim of his hat. She swallowed, then dropped the edge of the curtain and hurried to the door. There was no use delaying any longer. Either these people could be of help to her, or she and Madeline were on their own once more.

At the door, she brushed her full skirts most ineffectually. The dust clung to her no matter what she did. She stiffened her spine, squared her shoulders, and opened the door wearing her most lady-like smile—small, demure, unassuming.

"Thank you, Mrs. Parker. I'll see my guests inside." She opened the door wider and gestured for the three people on the street to enter the house. "Please, let me take your hats, gentlemen." She had never taken a man's hat before. There had always been footmen or maids to do that task. But there was a hat tree in the tiny entry, and she meant to make use of it.

The older of the two men towered over her, but he handed her the hat with a kindly smile. Then he led his wife into the sitting room with its two chairs and faded settee. They took the settee. Mr. Morgan handed her his hat, too, and offered her a reassuring tilt of his head before he went in to take one of the chairs.

That left Evelyn to follow after them, and she realized somewhat belatedly that she had nothing to offer them. A trickle of shame fell down her spine, and she looked to the back of the house, wondering if she dared try to find something in the kitchen.

"May I offer anyone...anything?" she asked weakly, then bit the insides of her cheeks. She was too old to exhibit social uncertainty.

The matronly woman took charge at once, her expression gentle and kind. "We're fine, dear. Please, let me introduce myself.

I am Mrs. Beth Bolton, and this is my husband, King Bolton. Frosty works for my husband, and he told us all about your plight."

Evelyn darted a glance toward the now-silent cowboy. Frosty? What a strange name. Then she gave her full attention to the married couple. "I am terribly sorry to cause you any trouble, Mrs. Bolton. Mr. Morgan found me in an awkward position. He was kind, and he seemed to think that you might know how to help me. Though my father was fond of saying that God helps those who help themselves." She felt her cheeks coloring.

The earl had insisted she learn how to speak more like a noblewoman instead of like a "middle-class spinster." But she hadn't been brought up to live in that world. It had taken time to learn that one didn't mention God in casual conversation.

She was equally ill-equipped for the position she found herself in at that moment.

"True enough," Mr. Bolton rumbled from where he sat, lines appearing in his forehead as he considered her. "But sometimes that same God sends along a good Samaritan or two."

His wife beamed at him and put her hand upon his arm. "Precisely my thought." She turned her cheerful expression to Evelyn. "Frosty said that you haven't any friends in our country, and no place to go after tonight. Is that correct?"

"I am afraid so." Evelyn hadn't any friends anywhere. She threaded her fingers together and looked down at her lap, the streaks of dust on her dress reminding her of how low she had fallen. "I am uncertain what a woman in my position ought to do this far from home."

"I don't know what you'd do about the situation in England," Mr. Bolton said with a grumbly sort of tone. "Out here, we try to look after one another. You're a woman with a child, alone in a strange place. My wife and I would like to open our home to you and your daughter."

Evelyn had to stare a moment, uncertain of what she'd heard.

She looked to Mr. Morgan, who silently cocked an eyebrow at her, and then to Mrs. Bolton.

The woman's expression, gentle and sincere, set Evelyn at ease even before she spoke. "You are welcome to stay with us as long as necessary, my dear. I promise I will look after you, and you'll find your feet again in no time."

Tears prickled at Evelyn's eyes, and her throat tightened. She waited a moment to answer, trusting when no feeling of dread came that this would be the right direction to go. For the time being.

If only she'd trusted that feeling when the Earl of Tyneham had proposed their arrangement.

"You are most kind, Mrs. Bolton, Mr. Bolton. I did not look for such compassion from strangers."

Mr. Bolton stood and gave his hand to his wife to assist her to her feet. "We had planned to leave this afternoon, but if that isn't to your liking, my lady—"

"Please." Evelyn rose too and put her hand over her heart. "Titles do not matter in this country. Mrs. Lyon will do." Perhaps forgetting she had once been a countess was for the best, too. She looked toward the stairs, where Madeline waited for her. "We will be ready to leave in less than a quarter of an hour."

"Wonderful." Mrs. Bolton smiled broadly. "Everything will turn out all right, my dear. You'll see."

After Evelyn showed them to the door and Mr. and Mrs. Bolton had stepped out into the sunshine again, Mr. Morgan hesitated within the doorway. "The ranch has most of what we need to get along. Food and supplies and such. If you and Madeline need anything else..."

"I haven't the slightest idea what we could need," she admitted. "But I am certain we will get by well enough with what we have. Thank you, Mr. Morgan. I will never forget your kindness."

He nodded once, placed his hat upon his head, and took himself down the narrow porch steps, following after his employers.

Mrs. Parker dropped her knife into the pot, then stood and wiped her hands on her apron. "What was that all about?" she asked, removing a pipe from her pocket to stick it in her mouth. "Ain't never seen those folks before."

Evelyn squared her shoulders and smiled at her temporary landlady. "They are friends of mine, and I have been invited to stay with them for a time. Madeline and I will be leaving today. There is no need for you to worry over feeding us dinner."

The older woman squinted. "No refunds on your room."

That didn't surprise Evelyn in the slightest.

As she walked up the narrow staircase to tell Madeline her news, Evelyn didn't despair in the loss of the life she had known before. Ballgowns and carriages were all well and good, but the trappings of her second-husband's wealth had never made her happy. Though she had depended upon his title and money for Madeline's future, the silks and jewelry had felt like a costume. And made her feel like a fraud.

Perhaps here, in a new world, she had a chance at happiness.

CHRIS CHECKED THE LINES ON THE MULES AGAIN WHILE MR. Bolton helped his wife into the wagon. They'd decided that Mrs. Bolton would drive the wagon, Chris would ride his horse, and Mr. Bolton would ride the new horse he'd purchased from the livery. The planned purchase certainly worked in their favor, given that their two additional passengers needed the wagon.

"I'm not letting a countess ride in the back of a wagon like a sack of potatoes." King had declared when they'd left the little boarding house. "That woman likely hasn't ever ridden behind a pair of mules, and there's no use shocking her by adding to that with a ride in the back of a buckboard. She can have my seat on the wagon."

Mrs. Bolton, Mrs. Perkins until quite recently, had heartily agreed. She could handle the animals easily enough. "I think it will make her more comfortable to sit with another woman for the trip. We can get to know each other."

Chris didn't share his thoughts one way or the other. They didn't matter. He'd done his part. He'd found a way to help a distraught woman and her child. Now he turned his mind back to his own concerns.

Laura and Ben.

He mounted his horse to ride behind the wagon to the little boarding house, his mind on the children under his care. The kids still looked at him like he was a stranger, and they couldn't be sure if he was worth trusting. They'd lived with him for a few weeks, yet every word he said made them eye him with skepticism. It was their way of defending themselves, he well knew, and he couldn't blame them after what they'd been through. Losing parents and being thrown into a stranger's hands would rattle anyone.

Yet he wondered, as he watched the countess descend the steps, leading her daughter by the hand, why a woman so new to the territory had been quick to take him up on his offer of help.

Her daughter was the mother in miniature, he realized. The child looked wide-eyed at the mules, then up at him with equal wonderment. Her mouth popped open.

Chris had to smile at that, and he tipped his hat to her before climbing down from his horse. A small trunk sat on the porch where the landlady had been before, along with a single-handled traveling bag. It wasn't much for two people who'd traveled halfway across the world.

The Englishwoman helped her daughter up into the back of the wagon, and Mrs. Bolton spoke kindly as the mother situated her child.

The countess turned as he approached with the bag stacked on top of the trunk. "Oh—thank you." The weariness he'd seen in her eyes still lingered, and he didn't blame her one bit for looking as though she'd like to sleep for a solid week before facing the world again.

"My pleasure, ma'am." He hefted her luggage into the back of the wagon next to her daughter.

Mrs. Bolton, meanwhile, was asking the child, "Might you be Miss Madeline? Or is it Lady Madeline?"

The girl blinked at him with eyes that matched her mother's. "Miss Allen," she said quietly. Then she looked to Chris. "Are you a real cowboy?"

He gave her a serious nod. "Sure am. I chase cows all day long." Then he glanced at Lady Tyneham.

Mrs. Bolton frowned. "I am terribly sorry. Did I get the titles wrong somewhere?" Duke had explained the English way of addressing people born to nobility more than once to the people of the ranch, and while it sounded more confusing than a bag full of snakes, Mrs. Bolton had been one of his best pupils.

The countess's cheeks turned as pink and she looked from him to the child, then back up to Mrs. Bolton. "Madeline is an Allen. That was my first husband's surname."

"Land sakes, you poor darling," Mrs. Bolton broke in from her place in the driver's seat. "It's not uncommon around here to meet someone widowed more than once, but it still hurts my heart to hear it. My first husband passed not long after our marriage." She reached out her hand. "Here, let me help you up. We can trade stories on the road."

Though the lady appeared taken aback a moment, her slight smile reappeared as she put one gloved hand in Mrs. Bolton's and the other on the seat, ready to lever herself upward.

She'd never get in that way, though. Not without stepping up on the spokes of the wheel, which she didn't seem to know.

Chris didn't really think about what he needed to do—he just did it. He put both hands on her waist and lifted her up into the seat. She squeaked just before landing on the springboard, then looked over her shoulder at him with wide eyes.

"Thank you, Mr. Morgan."

He nodded. "Ma'am." Then he went back to his horse and swung up into the saddle.

For a woman as tall as she was, the countess didn't seem to weigh enough. The hollows in her cheeks had given him pause, especially when he saw how she'd devoured the sandwich and coffee he'd bought her.

The woman had no place to go. No friends. No money. How long had she gone without a decent meal?

King led the way on his horse, and once the wagon started forward, Chris tried to brush the concern out of his head. Again. He didn't need to worry his head over the lady when Mrs. Bolton had things well in hand.

Better to think on how he'd get Ben talking.

Not that there was anything wrong with being silent from time to time, but he hadn't heard the boy utter more than a few sentences since his arrival. The kid let his big sister do all his talking for him, even though it plainly exasperated her.

Dannie Rounsevell, wife to Duke and daughter to King Bolton, had tried to take the children under her wing. She'd fed them a few meals at her table, given them rides on her horse, and introduced them to the growing litter of puppies that needed new homes. The kids didn't seem to mind her, but that wasn't the same as forming a connection.

They climbed up to the Old Divide, a pass that always had strangers gasping for breath and holding onto wagons for dear life. But Mrs. Bolton kept a steady conversation going as she expertly guided the mules upward, and though Chris saw well enough the way the Englishwoman held onto her seat, he didn't detect any change in her demeanor otherwise. A mark in her favor.

The little girl clung tightly to the side of the wagon, and her eyes went wide as the back of the wagon tilted downward. Chris caught her eye and grinned at her, hoping to coax a smile back. He got one, though it was wobbly.

That was something else that bothered him with the two children in his charge. They didn't smile much. Or laugh. Ruthie— wife to the former-foreman-and-now-partner, Abram Steele, had suggested they come over to her house and get their schooling done alongside her grandson. When Chris had asked the children what they thought about that, they hadn't seemed excited.

He had almost asked if their reluctance was due to Ruthie and Lee's skin color. There were too many people in the world who would look at kind-hearted Ruthie and see only a Black woman. Ruthie had told him she didn't think that was the trouble.

"Let them mourn a bit more, Frosty," she'd said when he'd broached the subject with her. "Their hearts are still broken. They'll want to learn soon enough. Give them ways to keep their minds sharp. They'll do all right."

Since she'd been a mother and grandmother, he'd trusted her judgement. And now he had a saddlebag full of children's books for them to read.

Fifteen days. He'd had the children in his life a mere fifteen days, and already Chris couldn't get them out of his head. Couldn't get the worry out of his heart. What had his cousin been thinking, sending his kids out to Arizona to live with a bachelor cow puncher? Maybe it had been a matter of trust. But there had to be someone better suited to raising them. Someone married. With children of their own.

They were going down the other side of the Mules—the small mountains and foothills that sheltered Bisbee from the rest of the world—when Chris saw the Englishwoman turn in her seat and bend down to speak to her daughter. The mother put her hand on the child's shoulder, and though her hat blocked most of her expression from view, he could see the gentleness in the way she spoke to the child. The girl's smile reappeared, bright as the afternoon sun, and he heard her laugh over the rumble of the wagon wheels.

He'd give just about anything to hear Laura and Ben laugh like that.

If only he knew more about raising children. There had to be a secret to it—a secret someone like him had no hope of learning anytime soon.

CHAPTER FIVE

The sun gave a last kiss to the tops of the mountains as the wagon turned down a lane, going beneath an arch and iron sign that didn't swing in the barely existent breeze. Evelyn looked back again into the bed of the wagon, not in the least surprised to see Madeline sound asleep, head resting against a sack of flour.

Her heart twisted within her breast. A year previous, her daughter had ridden in the finest carriage through London, head high and face pressed to the glass window. But everything had changed. For both of them.

"Your daughter is a real sweetheart," Mrs. Bolton said with a pleasant lilt to her voice. "I imagine she's been through a lot recently."

"We both have," Evelyn acknowledged softly. "I think she is far more resilient than I am, to be truthful."

"Children surprise us that way, don't they?" Mrs. Bolton shook her head, a sad look coming into her eyes. "When I first came out West as a housekeeper, I was also the one looking after King's children. They'd lost their mother not long before. They had tender hearts but were so eager to love and be loved. That's what I keep telling Frosty."

"He mentioned he has children under his care." Evelyn's mind flooded with questions at the recollection. She hadn't thought much on the cowboy's circumstances as she'd been too preoccupied with her own.

Before she could ask Mrs. Bolton about Mr. Morgan's situation, he rode up alongside the wagon, and his employer did the same on the opposite side. Evelyn lifted her gaze to the somber-faced cowboy.

Mr. Morgan glanced at her daughter, and Evelyn clearly saw the way his eyes softened at the sight of the little girl sleeping so soundly, despite the bumps and jostles of the wagon.

One could tell a lot about a person by the way they acted around children. Mr. Morgan had proven himself in possession of a kind soul by seeing to Evelyn's distress, and now she glimpsed yet more of his gentle heart. Perhaps some would call her foolish to trust these strangers—but beyond the fact that she had few options, Evelyn trusted her intuition in this matter.

It wasn't the cowboy who spoke to her, though.

"We're nearly there, ma'am," Mr. Bolton said. "We'll have you and your little one fed and snug in bed in no time. I figure the serious talk can keep until you're rested."

Gratitude pressed her heart and made tears prickle at her eyes. "Thank you. That is most kind."

Evelyn's mother hadn't brought her daughter up in a religious household, so they said prayers naught but high and holy days. But Evelyn had done a great deal of hoping and lifting her eyes to heaven on the way out west. Maybe her intuition, in this case at least, had a little help from Someone Else.

She'd made a choice to come with the Boltons and Mr. Morgan. Time would prove if it had been the correct one to make. Even if some of her choices had proven rather terrible. The choice to marry Madeline's father? She could never regret that—because that marriage had given her Madeline. But the choice to wed the late earl? To travel west?

If Evelyn was honest with herself, she hadn't felt like there were alternatives. Not when she had Madeline under her protection. Her parents had both long-since died, her other relatives were distant on the branches of the family tree and in their hearts. Her few friends proved false without the earl's money to cushion her fall. She had no one to turn to, and no other options.

As they rounded a rise in the ground, a series of buildings came into view. Structures with purposes she couldn't hope to name were pressed near one large house, but it looked almost like a small village rather than a single homestead. Everything was constructed of either whitewashed wood or the strange reddish adobe brick she'd asked a woman about while on the stagecoach to Bisbee.

"We'll pull up at the house. King, can you send one of the boys to the front to help with our guests' things?" Mrs. Bolton released the reins with one hand to pat Evelyn on the arm. "No use dragging you through the rear entrance. Half a dozen people back there, and twice as many animals." She clicked her tongue.

Mr. Bolton and Mr. Morgan tipped their hats, then rode ahead, making for another building entirely.

"The house isn't connected to the adobe buildings," Mrs. Bolton explained, not in any hurry despite how near they drew to her home. "Not directly. There's fencing that goes from one to the other, then to the stable and barn. In the early days of the ranch, King and his partner would drive their animals into the paddock through the bunkhouse corridor. A *zaguán*, it's called. It kept the animals safer, because no one could drive them out without first passing right by the men.'

"It sounds as though it is a courtyard, of sorts?" Evelyn hadn't any idea what to expect from a ranch, though she had glimpsed a few during her journey west. Seeing something from the distance while on a moving train hadn't quite prepared her.

"I wouldn't use that word to describe it." Mrs. Bolton pursed her lips as she thought. "It's more barnyard than courtyard, for cattle and horses and men come and go. You'll see it tomorrow."

Madeline sat up, rubbing at her eyes. "Mama? Are we almost there?"

"We are arriving now." Evelyn reached back to smooth a curl behind her daughter's ear. "Take a look around, darling. This is a real cowboy ranch."

Madeline shuffled to the side of the wagon, hands going to the wooden side to support herself as she leaned up on her knees. Evelyn looked, too, at the long grasses rolling away from the house into the distance, where mountains formed a wall, as though protecting the valley from the world outside of it.

The sun had disappeared, but a little light remained as the wagon stopped near the porch. A lone, large tree stood sentinel before the structure that was smaller than any English house Evelyn had lived in since her first marriage. The windows glowed with light behind white curtains, and smoke curled up from the chimney. Despite the humble size, a spirit of warmth and welcome lingered about the doorstep.

The front door opened, and a boy came out, holding a lantern over his head. "Mom? Dad says you've got visitors for us."

Mrs. Bolton climbed down from the wagon without waiting for help, and she took the lantern from the boy. "Sure do. Clark, this here is Mrs. Lyon. She's from England. This is her daughter, Madeline. Would you get their things and take them up to my old room?"

"Yes, ma'am." The young man grinned at Evelyn and offered her his hand to help her down, which she took gratefully. He couldn't be more than fifteen or sixteen years old. Someone had raised him to be a gentleman. He leaned over the side of the wagon. "Howdy, Miss Madeline. You have a pleasant ride in the back of the wagon?"

Madeline stood, wobbly on her legs. Before Evelyn could reach for her, the boy had his hands on her waist and was lifting her down without effort. The little girl dusted herself off. "It was fun. Even if it was bumpy."

Clark chuckled. "That's riding in a wagon for you." He fetched the carpet bag first and held it out to Madeline, who took it with a frown. Then he lifted their one and only trunk. "Follow me, Maddie. I'll show you to your room."

When her daughter looked to her for approval, Evelyn had to bite back a smile as she nodded. "Go ahead, darling."

Another boy appeared on the porch as Clark and Madeline went inside. He came down the steps and went to Mrs. Bolton, giving her a kiss on the cheek. "Welcome back, Mom."

"Travis," she said with a mother's pride. Both boys had to be from Mr. Bolton's first marriage, given their age and Mrs. Bolton's newlywed status. That they both called her "Mom" struck Evelyn as uniquely sweet. "This is Mrs. Lyon, and you passed Madeline on the way inside. They're staying with us for a bit."

"Nice to meet you, ma'am." Travis reached his hand out and Evelyn put hers in his, receiving his handshake with some amusement. This certainly wasn't how men and women greeted each other in England, with such casual familiarity. "I'll take care of the mules for you. Ruthie kept back some dinner for anyone still hungry, and there's coffee on the stove."

"Thank you, Travis." Mrs. Bolton gestured to the door. "Come on inside, Mrs. Lyon. We'd normally all have dinner together, but we're later getting home than expected. Now, don't you go apologizing—" Evelyn had opened her mouth to do just that, but snapped it closed again. "—we get delayed all the time. Let's see what Ruthie left, and we'll have a bite to eat before we get you settled for the night."

Evelyn entered the house and noticed an immediate difference in temperature from the outdoors. The windows were all open, she realized, creating a cross breeze through the building. A long hall went from the front door to the back, where she saw another that opened and closed as people came and went from the rear of the house. That must be the kitchen. On her right was an open doorway, no lights inside, and she saw a desk and bookshelves. An office or study, perhaps? To her left was a room with fine furniture, lit oil lamps, and a small fire in the hearth. A parlor. A little way down the hall, a staircase on her left went to the second floor.

Madeline appeared at the top of the steps. "Mama, we have the prettiest quilt on our bed." She came down with a lightness in her step, and the boy named Clark came behind, hands in his pockets.

"I cannot wait to see it for myself." Evelyn reached for Madeline's hand and gave it a squeeze. "Would you like some dinner?"

"Yes, please." She came along with Evelyn into the kitchen— which seemed to take up the back half of the house, with all the necessary cabinets and equipment for cooking on one side of the room and a long table on the other, with chairs lined up on every side.

"Go on and take a seat," Mrs. Bolton said, wrapping an apron around her middle. "It looks like we've got fresh biscuits and jam, some beef stew, and sugared strawberries. Would you like some buttermilk, Miss Madeline?"

"I've never had buttermilk." Madeline's eyebrows went up. "Is it good?"

Evelyn sat in a chair at the middle of the table, and Madeline joined her. "I've had it. It's delicious."

"All right. Then yes, please." Madeline folded her hands in her lap, peering about with interest. Pots and pans hung above a large wood-block table on the other side of the room. An iron stove was in the corner. There was a pump-sink and tall cabinets, which Mrs. Bolton opened and shut as she went about her work.

The kitchen door leading outside opened, and in came Mr. Bolton. "Ruthie said she made plenty, so Frosty's coming to grab a plate before he goes in for the night." He dropped his hat at the head of the table before taking his seat there. "I told our friend Duke—Mr. Rounsevell—about y'all. He said he'll come introduce himself properly in the morning. I imagine it'll be nice to talk to someone from home."

Evelyn nodded graciously. "I look forward to meeting him."

Mr. Bolton brought coffee and three cups to the table, filling each with the hot, dark liquid, then he kissed his wife on the cheek. "I'll go clean up real quick."

"No hurry, darlin'." Mrs. Bolton's affectionate smile made something in Evelyn's heart twist. Seeing happily married people —though a rarity in her set in England—always made her feel as though she had missed out on something. Or perhaps done something wrong in her own marriages.

In another minute, the door opened again, and Mr. Morgan entered. He swept his hat off before the screened-in door shut behind him. He nodded to Evelyn, then went over to Mrs. Bolton. "Ma'am, I don't want to intrude. If I can borrow a plate, I'll bring it back tomorrow."

"How are Ben and Laura?" Mrs. Bolton asked as she filled a deep plate made of metal. "They do all right with Ruthie and Dannie?"

"They seem about the same as always," he said, his voice going softer.

Ben and Laura must be his children. Evelyn lowered her gaze to her daughter, the weight of responsibilities and love upon her shoulders as heavy as ever. How was she going to look after Madeline? She had found them a haven for another night, amid kind strangers, but what about tomorrow? And the next day? And the week after that?

She took in a shaky breath and replaced her usual cheerful mask. When she looked up, it was just in time to see Mr. Morgan walk out the door, his mouth turned down at the corners.

Knowing she wasn't the only one in the world with problems didn't exactly help, but it reminded her to count her blessings.

"That poor man. Had fatherhood thrust on him all at once." Mrs. Bolton put full plates in front of Evelyn and Madeline, then went back to fetch a cup and a pitcher. "Here's your buttermilk, Miss Madeline. Have as much as you like—or tell me if you don't like it, and we'll get you something else."

"Who doesn't like buttermilk?" Clark asked, sauntering in with a book in hand. He took a chair across the table from Evelyn.

"I have never had it before," Madeline said, then glanced quickly at Evelyn. She smiled, and her daughter continued her explanation. Madeline hadn't been used to being allowed to speak in her late stepfather's home. "I do not yet know if I like it or not."

The boy appeared amused, but he didn't say anything else. Just cracked open his book and started reading. Evelyn glanced at the spine, then raised her eyebrows higher.

A History of Art by the European Masters.

"Are you an artist, Clark?" she asked, somewhat curious.

"No, ma'am." He looked up from his book with a crooked tilt to his smile. "But everyone at Baylor University has to take a few classes related to the arts. I'm mostly interested in the agricultural and political courses. Travis and I are going to university together, next fall, if we both pass the admissions test."

Two boys working a ranch had university aspirations? And, apparently, the ability to ready their minds for the coursework. Evelyn hadn't thought upon the education of the people in Arizona Territory, but as she listened to the young man, she realized she'd been guilty of assuming it to be inferior to her own upbringing. Her mother had been her primary educator, and the occasional governesses of her distant cousins when she and her mother were permitted a place in their homes. Going from one relative to another, never quite sure of her welcome, had led Evelyn to seeking both comfort and companionship from books.

Her first husband had scoffed at her enjoyment of reading. Her second had warned her to only read the books he prescribed. The memories of their two dark frowns made a shudder pass through her.

"A marvelous and admirable objective," she said at last when she realized Clark still watched her. "When do you take your test?"

"January." He turned a page in his book. "We go in to Tombstone so one of the school teachers there can act as the exam proctor."

"We're all mighty proud of the boys." Mrs. Bolton settled the last of the dishes at the table for herself and her husband, then took her seat at the other end of the table. Mr. Bolton came in at the same time and settled in his chair.

"Beth, will you say grace tonight?" he asked in his rumbly voice.

Mrs. Bolton lowered her head, and Evelyn gave a quick glance to her daughter before she did the same. The prayer was brief, but made tears prickle at Evelyn's eyes nonetheless.

"Thank you, Father, for the bounty you provide. Thank you for guiding us to Mrs. Lyon and her daughter. Please let a spirit of rest be upon them, that they may find peace and direction while in our home. Amen."

Evelyn murmured her amen, too, then started nibbling at her food. Manners alone kept her from using the fork as a spade to devour everything on her plate. Though the sandwich Mr. Morgan provided had filled her for a time, she'd had too many days of eating like a mouse, and her stomach demanded filling now that the opportunity to do so was before her.

Madeline wasn't nearly so ravenous, but she drained her cup of buttermilk quickly, and then she politely asked for more.

The other Bolton son returned, and the four of them spoke of ranch matters. Evelyn remained quiet, listening to the easy conversation and noting the affection the people at the table had for one another. It was an easy thing with them, and comfortable, like a well-worn pair of shoes.

Before long, her eyes grew heavy, and Mrs. Bolton announced it was time for everyone to turn in.

As Evelyn tucked herself into bed next to her daughter, who fell asleep within moments, she couldn't help but wonder if that dinner prayer would be of any use. She felt the peace around her, but it didn't penetrate her heavy heart. Or the fog of anxieties in her mind. She had nothing. Knew no one.

She needed guidance and direction. Maybe the Englishman coming the next day would have some thoughts on the matter. As Evelyn drifted off to sleep, answers remained out of her reach.

CHAPTER SIX

The eggs weren't burned, but Chris had managed to make the toast darker than either of the children liked. Not that they said anything about it when he put their plates of food in front of them that morning. They never complained. But he saw it in the way they winced after taking a bite.

He sat at the small square table in his house—the foreman's house of KB Ranch—across from the two of them. He ate while he pretended to take no notice of them, but he stole glimpses of Laura and Ben as often as he could.

He was doing everything wrong. Chris knew that. But he also knew he could learn if they'd just give him something to go on other than their single-syllable answers to his questions.

"How'd you sleep?" he asked every morning.

"Fine," Laura would say. Ben would nod his agreement to his sister's answer.

"What are y'all doing today?" Chris would ask. They'd usually shrug in unison.

Today, the answers had been the same. They ate silently. Drank their milk. Then cleared their plates away and washed everything at the sink.

Maybe most men would call it good enough to have respectful and responsible children under their care, but Chris couldn't make do with that. Children ought to laugh more. They ought to chatter and giggle and have excitement for the day ahead. They should play and get into scrapes. Frosty always had, along with his sister and his cousin.

He opened his mouth to tell them about the books he'd brought back with them, still in his saddlebag slung over the back of an empty chair, but a knock at their front door stopped him. Both children looked over their shoulders from the sink with identical expressions of surprise.

Chris went to the door and opened it, certain one of the hands needed direction on a project or had a bone to pick with him.

Instead of a dusty cowboy, Duke and Dannie stood on his narrow front porch. They were both dressed for a day of working outdoors but looked far too cheerful, if that's what they were anticipating. The two of them always looked that way, these days. Marriage suited them.

"Good morning, Frosty." Duke tilted his hat in greeting. It had taken the Englishman time to learn the right amount of head-nodding and hat-tipping it took to say hello and goodbye to friends. He still carried himself more like a lord than a cowboy.

"We're on our way to meet Mrs. Lyon," Dannie said, hitching her thumb over her shoulder toward the main house. Dannie and Duke lived in their own newly constructed house. Their house, his, and the main house would form a triangle, if not for all the outbuildings scattered between them.

"All right," Chris said, looking between them with some confusion.

Dannie squinted at him. "Are you bringing Laura? And Ben? Since Mrs. Lyon has a little girl, we thought you'd want to introduce her to your two kids."

He blinked. That was a sound idea. Maybe even a good one. "Sure. On our way." He turned around to find the two children already right behind him, as solemn-faced as ever. Seemed they wouldn't mind a change in routine too much. "Let me get my hat." He went to grab it off the hook on the wall made especially for his working hat, then went out the door.

Duke and Dannie had waited, and Dannie took a hand of each child and walked ahead with them. The men followed behind.

"What did you think about this Mrs. Lyon?" Duke asked as they walked. "King didn't say much—just that she was a countess from England. Do you think that's true?"

"Yep." Chris kept his eyes on the children as they walked. "Lady Tyneham was the title she gave."

"Tyneham? That's a familiar name. He and my father were in the same circles. I've eaten dinner at the same table as the earl on more than one occasion." Duke's less than enthusiastic tone made Chris turn to look at him. Duke's forehead wrinkled, and his mouth formed a hard line.

"You didn't like him?" Chris didn't know why he asked. It was neither here nor there, whatever Duke's opinion, given that the earl was dead. Leaving his widow with nothing. Chris certainly didn't hold a high opinion of a man who'd do such a thing.

"I didn't know him well," Duke hedged, meeting Chris's eyes. "He had a reputation for being a man who always got what he wanted. He collected things. Artwork. Gems. Historical artifacts."

And pretty wives, apparently. Though the thought wasn't charitable, Chris felt in his bones it was a true assessment. "How old was he?"

"Older than my father. I'd heard about him getting married again, before I left. He kept a mistress—a lot of English lords do. So it surprised my sister-in-law he felt any need for another wife." He nodded slowly, his eyes dimming as he stretched back in his memory. "She had some choice words to say on the subject."

Chris rubbed the knuckles of his fist against his thigh as they walked through the *zaguán* to get to the kitchen door at the main house. "Lady Tyneham is lost and alone," he said, voice lowered, as they came out on the other side of the corridor. "She needs friends."

Duke strode up the steps of the kitchen porch behind his wife, who'd already entered with the children in tow. He held the door open for Chris. "I should imagine so, if she finds herself this far from home. I doubt her late husband's family were friendly. Never fear, Frosty. I'll be a perfect gentleman."

Although he hadn't intended to pay a visit to the main house that morning, given that he had plenty of work to catch up on from being gone two days, Chris entered the kitchen without pause. He needed to know that their guest was safe. That everyone treated her well.

The Englishwoman stood at the table, an empty plate in front of her from her breakfast, with one arm around her daughter. Today she wore a white blouse, with sleeves about four times as puffed up as he'd ever seen, and a long gray skirt that still looked elegant despite its simple cut.

Dannie was making introductions. "It's wonderful to meet you, Mrs. Lyon. This is my husband, Evan Rounsevell. You know Frosty, of course. And these two are Frosty's niece and nephew, Laura and Ben Ashford. They're ten and eight years old."

"It is a pleasure to make your acquaintance," Mrs. Lyon said, and her daughter dipped a curtsy. "This is my daughter, Madeline. She is ten years old, too."

"Wonderful. Why don't you children go play on the front porch?" Dannie suggested.

Madeline looked up at her mother, who dipped her head in permission, then the child skirted the table. She stopped in front of Laura and Ben, a winsome smile on her face. "Will you show me everything? I've never been on a ranch before."

"Sure." Laura turned at the same time she uttered the word, then walked through the house to the front door. Ben and Madeline followed, and Madeline started chatting the way a little girl should.

"Mama says there are cowboys who work here. I have never seen a real cowboy before this week. We don't have them in England. Mostly, we have sheep." Her cheerful voice receded along with the children's footsteps.

"Your daughter is sweet." Dannie pulled a chair out and sat. and that's when Mrs. Bolton came away from the stove with a large pot of coffee.

"Everyone sit on down. If we're going to talk, might as well be comfortable. Coffee, Frosty?" Mrs. Bolton gave him that same motherly smile she shared with everyone. He'd had some, but it hadn't been his best, so he nodded and made to get up for a cup. Mrs. Bolton waved him back to his seat. "I'll get you a mug." She went back to the cupboards.

"Lady Tyneham, it is a pleasure to meet you. I haven't heard another English accent in weeks. My father is the Marquess of Whittenbury." Duke settled next to Dannie and took her hand, holding it right there on the table. "I was acquainted with your late husband. I am sorry for your loss."

Mrs. Lyon lowered her eyes briefly, but nothing in her expression spoke of grief. "That is kind of you to say." Huh. Neither did her tone or choice of words. "I am afraid becoming a widow again has cast me adrift." Here she winced. "I am fortunate that Mr. Morgan took notice of me yesterday. I am not sure what I would have done upon waking this morning, without the ability to so much as pay for another night in a rented room."

Once everyone had a steaming cup in front of them and Mrs. Bolton had settled herself in her usual chair, the conversation around him began in earnest. He listened, not saying a word as Mrs. Lyon—Lady Tyneham—told her story again for Duke and Dannie's benefit. She'd left her home with next to no money, traveled over ocean and land, all the way to the dusty town of Bisbee. Only to find, upon her arrival, that the stock certificates she held were worthless.

"I am at a loss for what to do now," she confessed, her gaze trained on the cup she held but did not drink. "I am certain you know something of how unprepared I find myself for this situation, Lord Evan."

"Just Evan is fine," Duke said with a wave of his hand.

She raised her eyes, and Chris watched her tight expression soften the slightest bit. "Thank you. You must call me Evelyn." She looked around the table, and her gaze settled on Chris last as she spoke. "All of you, please. I don't feel that I was married long enough to really be Mrs. Lyon, let alone a countess."

Evelyn—Chris could call her that easily enough. The pretty name suited her.

"What do you mean, that you're unprepared?" Mrs. Bolton asked.

Evelyn's cheeks darkened. "I do not have what one might call employable skills."

"You were raised to marry well," Dannie said with a sympathetic smile. "I knew a lot of girls like that at my school in Boston." She looked at Evelyn, then addressed her comments to Mrs. Bolton. "There were girls who didn't know how to cook or sew a shirt, but they could preside over ballrooms and embroider cushions. Play piano, sing, but didn't know how to wash dishes. Is that the kind of thing you mean?"

The meek way Evelyn bowed her head made a pang of sympathy shoot straight to Chris's heart. He knew how she felt. He'd had to teach himself everything about caring for horses and cattle. He hadn't been raised to life on a ranch. The work had called to him, though, and he'd applied himself with vigor to learn everything he could. Just about wore himself out, those first years, doing everything in his power to prove himself to the drovers and ranchers he worked with.

"I thought I might try to get a job." Evelyn lowered her hands into her lap. "If I were in England, I would go to an employment agency. Perhaps I would apply to be a companion or governess, but there are few who would take me on, with a daughter. A housekeeper, perhaps?"

"Being a former countess would also be a problem back

home," Duke put in, wincing. "Not many would eagerly hire you since it would cast them in a poor light for putting a peeress into a position of servitude."

"That's not the only problem," Mrs. Bolton said, shaking her head with a rueful smile. "I came out here as a housekeeper and didn't worry myself too much about it, because I'm a plain looking gal. Always have been."

"Mother Beth," Dannie protested. "You're the kindest, sweetest, most patient woman I know! And we all think you're lovely."

Mrs. Bolton touched Dannie's shoulder. "Thank you, dear. But y'all know what I mean. One look at Evelyn and a number of women would turn her away—for any sort of job. Excuse me for saying it, dear, but you're far too pretty. Most would think you a temptation in their household."

Evelyn's cheeks flared up again, and Chris privately agreed with every word Mrs. Bolton said. The Englishwoman, despite having a ten-year-old child, wasn't just pretty. She was beautiful. Her maturity only added to the elegance of her face and form. The copper-colored braids twisted up at the back of her head like a crown made her look all the more queenly.

The thought of her working in a place where a man would take advantage of her, just based on her beauty—it made his stomach turn.

"Perhaps a school for girls. America has finishing schools, does it not?" She looked to Dannie. "That is the sort of school you attended in Boston."

"I can't imagine them turning you away, given your title." Dannie looked up at her husband. "What do you think? A school would love to claim they had a real English countess on their staff."

"It could be worth writing a letter of inquiry." Duke appeared thoughtful. "If they took on younger students, they might allow your daughter to accompany you, too."

Chris's coffee cup was empty, yet he lingered at the table. Unable to do more than listen as they proposed ideas for the displaced Englishwoman. Letter-writing seemed to be the favored answer. Duke offered to write a letter of introduction. The biggest obstacle they could think of was that any prospective school would want proof of her claim to the nobility, which would require more letters from England and more time.

"My late husband's solicitor could provide all the proof anyone would need." She looked to Mrs. Bolton. "But all of this would take time. Months, perhaps, to receive the letters and find a position. I cannot possibly trespass on your generosity for such a length of time, Mrs. Bolton."

"Nonsense. What does the Good Lord mean for us to do on this earth, if not help one another?" Mrs. Bolton rose to fetch the coffee pot and went around refilling cups—including Chris's. "What do you think, Frosty? You've been awful quiet sitting here."

"That's not unusual for him." Dannie flashed him a grin. He'd always liked the girl. She was whip-smart and spoke her mind. He'd trade any two cowboys for Dannie as a worker, too.

"Yes, Mr. Morgan. What do you think?" Evelyn peered at him over the rim of her cup.

He shuffled through the conversation in his mind, ruminating a moment before offering a shrug. "I don't think my opinion matters much. You could go East. Get a job teaching. But what is it you want to accomplish? I doubt teachers are paid all that well, even if they have a title attached to their name. And your daughter—if she grew up in a school like that, what would she be prepared to do after?"

"She'd have all the necessary skills to be a wife to someone important," Dannie said, speaking slowly. "But no money or connections to back it up."

Chris nodded. "Or she'd maybe become a teacher herself. Eventually." He squared his gaze with Evelyn's. "Is that what you want?"

She opened her mouth and closed it again without speaking, her eyes growing wider in the silence before she spoke. "I don't suppose I want that for her. Her options would be quite limited.

But then, I suppose it would depend on the salary...." Her voice trailed away, uncertain.

"Might as well give it a try," Mrs. Bolton encouraged, shooting Chris a glare. "It's not as though Frosty knows much about girls' schools."

"He has a point, though," Duke put in, and then received a glare of his own from the matron. "Forgive me, Beth. But it is a good question to ask. What do you want to accomplish for yourself, Evelyn? And for Madeline?"

She rested a hand on the table, the tip of one long, elegant finger tracing the woodgrain whorls beneath it. "I certainly want her to be better prepared for life than I have been. I want her to be able to care for herself, whether she has a husband or not. Or loses him. That means having the skills needed to find a job. To provide her own meals. I want her to be able to marry a man of her choosing, not just the man with the most to offer." She winced as she said that, and her shoulders pulled tight. "But I can't give her any of that without having employment."

"You write some letters, dear." Mrs. Bolton stood and started to tidy up. "We'll keep talking. Things like this have a way of falling into place."

Chris felt for Evelyn Lyon's plight. She appeared as lost at that table as she had in Bisbee when he'd first laid eyes on her. Pretty as a picture, sad as a saint. His heart tugged at him to do something more for her, but what? He'd already done his part. He'd gotten her to the ranch, to a place of safety where people would look after her.

"I cannot simply live upon your charity, Mrs. Bolton." Evelyn rose and gathered up dishes of her own. "A perpetual guest is of no use to anyone."

"Write your letters," Dannie advised, rising as well. Duke and Chris came to their feet and picked up their hats. "Then we'll put you to work, sure enough, if that's what you want."

"I'd best tell Laura and Ben it's time to get to Ruthie's house." Chris made his way to the hall.

"Oh, leave 'em be today, Frosty." Mrs. Bolton waved her dish-cloth at him. "Let them make Madeline feel welcome. I'll feed them lunch and send them home after that for a rest."

Chris gave a sharp nod and changed direction, going for the back door instead. As he brushed by Evelyn, she put her hand out to stop him, her touch light upon his wrist. He froze and looked down at her, eyebrows raised.

"Thank you, Mr. Morgan," she said, her voice quiet in the noise from the sink and the other women already striking up a conversation.

His stomach twisted again with her deep green eyes upon him, the shine in them full of all her worries. He hitched up one side of his mouth in a smile, feeling about as helpless as she probably did. "I didn't do much, ma'am."

"You saved me," she insisted as she withdrew her hand. "I'll never be able to repay you for that."

He didn't want her beholden to him. His hold on his hat tightened. "Like Mrs. Bolton said—people oughtta help each other." Then he left, uncertain what else to say. He slid his hat onto his head as he walked down the steps, seeing Duke waiting for him.

"Do you remember when I first arrived here?" Duke asked as they walked toward the barn and a full day's work.

"Couldn't forget it," Chris said, still thinking on those sad green eyes rimmed by copper lashes. "You were as green as they came."

"I cannot help but think it is ten times more difficult for a woman to be in such a situation." Duke shook his head. "A man doesn't need to depend upon anyone but himself for protection. Lady Tyneham doesn't have that luxury. Nor is she as prepared as I was, with at least some knowledge of what life is like out here."

"It doesn't sound like she intends to remain in the Territory." Chris ignored the jab in his gut that came with those words, that truth, and tried to focus on the task at hand, saddling up a horse to ride the fences.

Duke went through the same motions of getting saddle and

tack. Their horses were in the corral next to the barn. "I wonder if that would be a mistake, to go back East. I know the Arizona deserts aren't everyone's dream, but I found happiness here, in a life and place completely different from what I was used to living. It doesn't seem as though she has fond memories of where and what she was before."

Chris kept his mouth shut. Evelyn's future wasn't his business. Speculating on what she did or did not do would only take up space in his thoughts when he needed to see to his job.

Ride the fences. Check on the stock. Check on the men assigned to camp out with the stock at the far north end of the ranch. Come back in time to make dinner for the children. Try to get them to talk to him. Try to find a way to bring some cheer back into their lives and exchange smiles for their somber expressions.

That's where his thoughts needed to stay. On his own business.

Yet as he went through the work that day, riding along the quiet trails crisscrossing the KB Ranch property, he couldn't help but wonder what the former countess was up to. Writing letters all day long? Or would Dannie find another way to keep her busy?

And for some strange reason, he couldn't resist the notion that Evelyn would look mighty pretty wearing split skirts and sitting on the back of a horse.

CHAPTER SEVEN

E velyn first wrote a letter of inquiry to the school Daniella Bolton had attended. Dannie promised to write one to go with it, as an introduction of sorts. If required, she could send proof of her identity with the help of a lawyer in Tombstone. Thankfully, she had all the documents proving who she and her daughter were. She could offer that reassurance to any prospective employer.

Yet with every word she penned, sitting in the parlor at a small desk, Mr. Morgan's words came back to her.

What *did* she want most for Madeline? Evelyn didn't worry over herself. She was too late to accomplish any of her own dreams, whatever they had been or might be. She had given up her right to anything other than insuring her daughter's future against calamity.

Madeline shouldn't have to marry someone merely because they had money or position. Not like what had happened to Evelyn.

She put down the pen and rubbed at her eyes, then looked out the parlor window to see that the children no longer sat on the porch talking. Another boy had arrived—he couldn't be too much older than Madeline and Laura. He was dressed similarly to the men and boys Evelyn had already seen on the ranch. He brought puppies with him, several of them following him like chicks would follow their mother hen.

The boy sat under the tree with the other children, all of them letting the round-bellied puppies climb all over. Madeline didn't hesitate to speak to the new child, which made Evelyn relax. Madeline hadn't had friends with dark skin before. Children, of course, accepted such differences more easily than adults.

The boy laughed, and Evelyn caught the two quieter children giggling and smiling, too. A mother dog arrived—at least, Evelyn assumed that's who the black, tan, and white dog must be. The adult creature climbed onto the porch, met Evelyn's eyes through the window. Like one mother acknowledging another. Then the dog turned to sit and watch the goings-on, too.

If only life could always be so simple. Puppies and children beneath the shade of a tree.

Evelyn hadn't had a childhood with much laughter or leisure. Her father, an accountant with less than a modest estate and finances, had died while she was young. His estate had been sold to pay off his debts, leaving Evelyn and her mother to depend upon relatives for their upkeep. They'd gone from house to house, living with cousins and aunts, and Evelyn had worn cast-off dresses while her mother bitterly swore to find a wealthy husband for her.

Mother had died, still angry at her lot in life, three short weeks after arranging for Evelyn to marry the second son of a baronet. Thus, Evelyn had no title but ought to have had some stability.

Except her first husband, Theodore Allen, had been a solicitor. The Earl of Tyneham's solicitor, in fact. The earl had invited them to dinner shortly after Evelyn and Theodore had wed. Perhaps the old earl had wanted her for himself even then. He'd certainly made enough comments that night, and every time he had been in Evelyn's presence after, about her looks.

When Mr. Allen had succumbed to a complaint of the lungs, Evelyn had barely put on her black clothing before the earl had swooped in with an offer of marriage and a promise to look after both Evelyn and Madeline so long as Evelyn conducted herself as an English peeress.

A puppy leapt onto Madeline, knocking her backward. Evelyn stood, ready to go out and rescue her daughter, but then she laughed more while the puppy bathed her face with its tongue.

"Lee is keeping an eye on things." Mrs. Bolton entered the room, drying her hands on a small towel. "He won't let the puppies nibble at the children too much."

"Lee? Is that the little boy?"

Mrs. Bolton came into the room and sat down. "Lee Steele. He's the grandson of one of my husband's partners, Abram Steele. His grandmother, Ruthie, usually keeps charge of the children in the mornings. Though I don't know where she finds the energy to keep up with them. She's a few years older than I am. Fiercely determined to see to it her grandson has an excellent education. When Frosty's niece and nephew arrived, she offered to teach them, too."

"She sounds very kind. Will I get to meet her?" Evelyn left the finished letters folded on the desk and went to sit on the couch near Mrs. Bolton. "Does she live nearby?"

"They have a house on the other side of our courtyard, as you call it." Mrs. Bolton settled back in her chair. "I imagine she'll be over with a welcome treat for you. Ruthie's pies are legendary in these parts."

"I'll hope for a pie, then." Evelyn folded her hands in her lap and looked about the comfortable room. "This is a beautiful house. I cannot say I knew what to expect for homes out here in the middle of nowhere."

Mrs. Bolton's eyes twinkled mischievously. "We do our best to be civilized. But I know just what you mean. I came from Oklahoma—it's a territory, too, but a bit more established in terms of towns and travel. My family settled there when I was a little girl —what an adventure that was! Coming out west has been more of the same."

"Do you ever miss your home?" Evelyn plucked up a small cushion, running her fingers over the embroidered roses along its edges. "Is Oklahoma like this?"

"Heavens, no. Where I lived, lakes and ponds surrounded us. Water everywhere—and the spring rains nearly flooded out our crops on plenty of occasions. It's much greener." She didn't sound wistful, necessarily, only thoughtful. "Maybe that's why I like it here so much. I didn't at first. The desert has to find its place in your heart. We're lucky with this land. It's not quite as barren or dry as some stretches of Arizona. We even have a few springs on our property. It's different, but any place can be home when you're with the right people."

Evelyn stilled, thinking on her mother again. On her own life. Had she ever felt like that...anywhere? There had never been time to grow attached to a place, in her childhood, and then she had worried more over pleasing first one husband and then the other than she had about her surroundings.

"Madeline has been my home," she murmured, almost without meaning to. Then she looked up to find Mrs. Bolton watching her, and she hurriedly put the pillow aside. "As long as we are together, I think I will be happy anywhere."

The truth of that statement settled in her heart and provided comfort she didn't expect.

The kitchen door opened and closed, heralding a newcomer to the house. "Beth? Is our new friend ready for another visitor?"

Mrs. Bolton's expression brightened. "Come on into the parlor, Ruthie, and sit a spell. We're watching the children and having a chat."

"Don't mind if I do." A moment later, a handsome Black woman with silver-threaded hair came into the room, wearing yellow-checkered calico and a broad smile. Evelyn rose as the woman held both hands out, enveloping one of Evelyn's in her own. "I'm Ruthie Steele. You must be Mrs. Lyon." Her grasp was firm, her hands warm and smooth.

"Please, call me Evelyn." The words slipped from her quite naturally, and she immediately relaxed upon saying them. Her late husbands—both of them—and her mother would have been shocked at how casually she was behaving around strangers. Strangers of such different backgrounds than herself, too.

"Ruthie." The woman looked deeply into her eyes, then released her hand. "Are we making a habit out of giving homes to English folks?"

Mrs. Bolton laughed, and Evelyn answered with a smile. "Likely only the strays, like myself and the man you call Duke."

"Oh, and did he fight that nickname." Ruthie chuckled and took a seat on the couch, too. "Kept on telling us how much his people wouldn't like it, where he came from. I understand you have a title of your own."

"She's a countess," Mrs. Bolton answered with a tilt to her head. "So I say if we keep collecting people from England, we have standards. Titled lords and ladies only. Maybe a prince or princess, too."

Ruthie's warm chuckle settled into a kindly smile. "How's your little girl getting on?" Ruthie asked, making herself comfortable.

Evelyn looked out the window again, seeing her daughter stand and race away with puppies trailing after her. "Madeline is a resilient child. I think she trusts me to take care of her, so she hasn't any concerns. This has all been an adventure for her." She looked to Mrs. Bolton as she spoke, her eyebrows raising.

Mrs. Bolton settled more comfortably in her seat. "As I said about my own childhood in the wilds of a new place. Children take to changes easier than adults do. Most of the time."

"True enough. My Lee's the same. He's been with us since he was a tiny thing." Ruthie's expression took on a look of old mourning—a soft sadness that was well worn and didn't hurt as much as it used to. "His mother died giving birth to him at Fort

Huachuca. Our son wasn't too keen on being a cowboy and wanted to give army life a try, like his pa had. Annalise sent for me to help with the birth." She looked Evelyn in the eye. "The doctor at the fort claimed he had no time to play at being a midwife."

"The fool shouldn't have claimed to be a doctor, either," Mrs. Bolton said with real heat in her tone. "I still can't stand to think about it, and I didn't even know you at the time."

Ruthie lifted one shoulder in a shrug, then leaned closer to Evelyn as though to impart a confidence. "He didn't want to help a Black woman have a baby. Pure and simple. I got there later than I would've liked. Annalise had lost too much blood. The doctor probably couldn't've helped, as things were. I did everything I knew to do."

Evelyn felt the blood drain from her face, and her hands went cold. Every woman she knew lived in fear of what might happen if things went wrong in labor. For themselves, for their sisters and friends.

"Ruthie is a skilled midwife," Mrs. Bolton put in. "She's delivered most of the babies within ten miles of here. Saved a few lives, too."

"Thank you, Beth." Ruthie folded her hands in her lap. "Our son, Lincoln, reacted poorly. He left Lee to our care and transferred to a new unit. In New Mexico." She shook her head, sad and slow. "Then he left there and went up north. Four years ago, we found out he passed from an infectious fever."

A mother's heart always turned tender at such stories, knowing well enough how much the teller had suffered. The loss of a child was like losing a piece of one's own soul. "Oh, I am sorry." Evelyn tentatively put her hand out to cover Ruthie's. "That is dreadful, Ruthie."

"It is, isn't it?" Ruthie's eyes were bright with tears, but then her smile reappeared. "I don't know that it'll ever stop hurting. But having Lee with us, getting to watch him grow up, has been a balm to my soul. I might've curled up and died at the news if I didn't have Lee to help me find hope in each new day."

"Children are a wonder at that," Mrs. Bolton remarked, watching the children out the window as they played some sort of tag that involved dodging the energetic dogs. "I wasn't privileged to bear children of my own, but I've loved the Boltons as the children of my heart almost since I arrived here."

Evelyn felt the quiet settle around the three of them, a peaceful and calm blanket of understanding. Three women of such different backgrounds, with such different stories to tell, yet they all understood one another. They all understood the love of a mother for her children.

Had Evelyn ever felt such immediate acceptance in her life? Or such a feeling as the one that pressed upon her heart in that moment?

What was this strange place, this ranch and this house, that made her feel as though she'd never been safer or more protected in her life? Something here was different. Something about this place made her heart settle, despite the uncertainties of her future.

Like finding harbor in a storm, she imagined. Or shelter in the rain.

Or an oasis in the desert.

HOURS LATER, EVELYN ASSISTED IN MAKING LUNCH FOR THE LADIES and the children. The job assigned to her had been to set the table and slice bread. She managed those two things easily enough. Ruthie had brought dessert, too, and everyone received a thick slice of the peach pie with their sandwiches of ham and cheese—cheese from the dairy cows the ranch kept. Madeline drank two more cups of buttermilk, too.

After lunch, the Morgan children were expected to go home

and do their chores, then amuse themselves until their guardian returned home.

At the door of the kitchen, with hands tucked behind her back and chin ducked, Laura made a quiet request. "Could Maddie come to our house? I told her she could meet my doll."

The way Mrs. Bolton started bobbing her head rapidly, widening her eyes at Evelyn, meant she didn't hesitate. "Oh, of course, dear. Madeline, would you like to go?"

"Yes, please." Madeline stood from the table. "I can even help with your chores, Laura, if you tell me what to do."

Ruthie and Lee had already taken their leave, with Ruthie telling her grandson it was time for him to see to his chores and schoolwork.

"You go on with them, Evelyn." Mrs. Bolton was already tying on her apron again. "You'll feel easier about Maddie playing over there if you see the house for yourself. Though don't expect much —Frosty is a bachelor, after all." She raised her eyes heavenward and muttered to herself. "A bachelor with a couple of children. Lord have mercy on him."

Evelyn smiled at the exasperated tone of her hostess. She'd seen and heard enough to know Mrs. Bolton had affectionate feelings toward the ranch foreman—she likely mothered him the way she had mothered everyone else since Evelyn had met her.

Following the children out back, she looked about her with interest. The patch of dirt and gravel in the middle of ranch house, paddock, adobe bunkhouse, and barn certainly couldn't be called a courtyard. There wasn't anything growing, but there was a lot of coming and going. Or at least, there had been before the men working nearby caught sight of her.

Two men holding boxes of tools stopped where they stood in the open barn door, staring at her with slack jaws. She saw another man coming through the *zaguán* stutter to a stop in his walk, leading a horse behind him. A horse in the paddock appeared to be training, attached to a long lead gripped in the hand of another cowboy. That man stopped what he was doing too, until the horse nearly yanked the rope out of his hands.

Color climbed into her cheeks, but she refused to acknowledge the stares. At least they weren't hostile or calculating, as they'd been in England. These men were only surprised. Maybe curious.

"Ben," she said to the little boy, waiting next to the girls at the bottom of the porch. "Won't you tell me what all the buildings are for while we walk to your house?" She held her hand out to him.

The child looked first at his sister, who was already holding Maddie's hand, then up to Evelyn. "Yes, ma'am." He took her hand and tugged her down the last porch step.

As they walked, the men went back to work, and Evelyn tried to relax. The boy pointed as they went. "The barn is for the special horses and dairy cows. That there's the hay barn, it's where they put the hay for winter. That's Lee's house. That's the laundry shed. Blacksmith shed." He pointed everything out dutifully, including a windmill and cistern of water. They left the main ranch buildings behind, a field of grass with well-worn tracks on the other side of the foreman's house before them. "That's Dannie's house." The boy pointed to the left at a house a hundred paces from where they stood. "That's Frosty's house." He pointed to a house on the right at a similar distance.

Evelyn looked down at the serious little face, tanned from time in the sun, as the boy looked up at her, his brown eyes warm and soft. "It's your house too, isn't it?"

He shrugged. "I guess."

Poor soul. She understood his uncertainty.

They reached the house and climbed the two steps up to the narrow porch. There wasn't as much room on this one as the porch at the main house, but a couple of chairs could easily fit between window and rail. When they walked inside, Evelyn looked about with greater interest. How precisely did a bachelor live in the desert?

A large rectangular room, well-lit by the large windows facing north, met her eyes. There were three bookcases at the back wall and several dozen books within them. Along with small boxes here and there on the same shelves. She spied a collection of glass jars, too, that held an assortment of objects.

There was a long wooden bench, a rocking chair, and another wooden chair. One sofa. One soft chair. A small table set between rocking chair and sofa. There was a trunk next to a stone hearth. Upon the rough-hewn mantel were two framed photographs and a clock. She went closer to study the photographs.

One photograph featured Laura and Ben, with a pair of adults who had to be their parents. Her heart softened. Mr. Morgan had done the right thing, putting that picture up where the children could see it every day and remember their mother and father.

The other photograph was older, less clear, but she still recognized Mr. Morgan as a ganglier version of himself in a suit that looked a little too small, given the way his wrists protruded from the sleeves. He stood with two older people—his parents, of course—and a girl not much older than he was. His sister.

She withdrew from the mantel as the girls went to one of the doors. There were three leading from the room. One at the back wall, one on the same wall as the hearth, another on the opposite.

"This is my room," Laura said, sounding less enthusiastic than before.

Evelyn followed to look inside after the girls and Ben had entered. The room had one bed, suitable for a growing girl, tucked beneath the window. A chest of drawers against the opposite wall completed the furniture. Then there was a crate beside the bed that appeared to hold a few toys, and a doll rested on the child's pillow. The room was humble. And small. And there weren't any curtains or a rug to add warmth to the empty walls and floor.

Evelyn pursed her lips and looked down at Ben, who stood near the door. "Would you like to show me your room, Ben?"

The boy nodded once and took her hand again, leading her

back across the long room to the opposite door. Far from his sister. He opened it and went inside. No curtains or rug here, either. But another bed that matched the first, with warm blankets and a pillow. A stuffed horse, made of fabric and likely filled with sawdust, rested on the boy's pillow. Aside from the chest of drawers and a few hooks on the walls, there wasn't much else to the room. Another crate with a few toys beside the bed. That was all.

The children hadn't been in the house long, she knew. That they had what they did was a testament to their guardian *trying* to do right by them. Who knew but that he had more plans already in the works? Or perhaps needed more funds before making the house more comfortable for its new occupants?

"Where does Mr. Morgan sleep?" she asked, looking over her shoulder.

The boy took her hand and walked out again, closing his door behind him, and drew her through the last door into the kitchen. This room looked a lot like the one at the main house—it was long, one side filled with a stove, an oven, and cupboards, and the other holding a square table with four chairs surrounding it. A door went out the back of the house, and windows were over the sink and table. No curtains.

Evelyn looked behind her at the wall separating the kitchen from the main room. A ladder went up the wall at an angle. Ben stared up at the opening in the ceiling.

"He sleeps up there?" Evelyn narrowed her eyes and looked up. "Is that even a room?"

Ben shrugged. "Two rooms. I think."

"Oh." She itched to climb the ladder and look upward, but immediately rebuked herself for even thinking such a thing. Her curiosity was most ungrateful. The man had done her a kindness, and she would not betray his privacy as a reward for that.

Instead, she looked about the kitchen a bit more. "It seems very nice. What are your chores today?"

He went to the longest cupboard and opened it up, taking a broom out. "Sweeping up the downstairs."

"Wonderful. You know, I have never swept *anything*?"

The boy's eyebrows came down, and his response came out most skeptical. "Never?"

"Never. Would you show me how it's done?" she asked, folding her arms and fixing him with what she hoped was an enthusiastic smile. "I should like to learn."

He regarded her with misgiving, but finally nodded and began to demonstrate the process. After a few swipes with the straw broom, Evelyn asked to try. Sweeping wasn't difficult. She'd seen it done, even if her mother had never permitted Evelyn to take up a broom. The two of them took turns first in the kitchen, then in the main room. Ben saw to his room on his own, and by that time Laura had produced cloths for dusting the windows for herself and Madeline.

Evelyn volunteered to dust the bookshelves, and she took extra time to examine the titles of the books as well as the contents of the jars. One jar had arrowheads. Another contained a variety of buttons and small spools of thread. The last had small rocks of strange hues. She didn't peek in the boxes.

The book titles were rather surprising. Many of them she had heard of or seen in London bookshops and libraries. Though none of the volumes she'd seen before looked as worn or weather-beaten as the books in Mr. Morgan's care. He had a shelf with several volumes of poetry, including Tennyson—England's poet laureate. He had Victor Hugo's *Les Misérables*, and the Scot, Robert Louis Stevenson's *Strange Case of Dr Jekyll and Mr. Hyde.* American titles and authors greeted her, too. Mark Twain's *Adventures of Tom Sawyer* and *Adventures of Huckleberry Finn* sat together, as the two friends ought.

Evelyn started when a soft voice spoke at her elbow. Laura had crept up on her. "You can read them, if you want." The girl's wide brown eyes were captivating, truly. "That's what Frosty always says. He says books are meant to be read, and we could read them, too. But most of these are too big for me. I don't know all the words."

"Really? Let me see if I can find one you might like." She ran her fingers along a few titles and settled on *Treasure Island*. Though she wished something by Lewis Carroll or perhaps *Black Beauty* had been on the shelves instead.

She settled on the couch, and Madeline took the rocking chair with something like glee. Laura sat on Evelyn's right, and after she began reading, Ben came to perch at her left. As she read the opening paragraphs, Evelyn's mind transported her back to her childhood. To the books that had been her only escape from her mother's lessons and lamentations. This one hadn't been published until nearer her first marriage, but she'd still read it with all the glee of a child throwing off her responsibilities.

"'Fifteen men on the dead man's chest— Yo-ho-ho, and a bottle of rum!'" she sang in as gruff a voice as she could, which only made Ben giggle. She didn't stop to think if a tale of pirates might be too frightening for young children. Instead, she thought about the adventure ready to befall them.

CHAPTER EIGHT

Hot and tired from riding the property, and annoyed at the questions the men at the bunkhouse had lobbed at him when he arrived to check in with them, Chris dunked his head in the cistern near the house before going in for the evening. The men had asked him about the Englishwoman in their midst. Apparently, several of them had caught sight of her earlier that day.

They'd been respectful, but far too nosy about Evelyn's circumstances.

The sun was still out, which usually meant more work, but having two children dependent on him changed things. His work ended earlier so he could tend to them.

Chris scrubbed at the dirt behind his neck and on his face, then replaced his hat. Laura and Ben deserved him at his best, even if he wanted nothing more than to drop into his bed and sleep until dawn the next day. The water helped cool his irritation, and he entered through the kitchen door with a cheerful greeting on his lips—

It died the moment he heard laughter from the front room. Children's laughter.

"Say it again," said an eager young voice that sounded startlingly like Ben's.

"If you insist." *Evelyn.* What was she doing in his house? He experienced a moment of panic, then sheer confusion when her voice sounded ragged and unpleasantly high-pitched. "'*Pieces of eight! Pieces of eight! Pieces of eight!*'"

The children roared with laughter again, and Evelyn's deeper laugh joined them.

"Stop," Laura cried, still giggling. "We'll never finish the story if we keep hearing the parrot!"

"But I *like* the parrot," Ben insisted.

"We are nearly to the end of the chapter, and there I think we must pause." Evelyn cleared her throat. "And a good thing, too. I will have no voice at all if I read much more."

Three young voices groaned before Madeline made herself heard. "We can make more tea."

"Tea won't be enough this time, dear. I'll need to rest my voice. Perhaps we can continue tomorrow?" Evelyn offered, sounding as eager as the children. "And you want me to finish the chapter, don't you?"

"Yes," they chorused together.

Chris didn't dare move as he listened, though he felt like an intruder in his own home. Evelyn kept reading *Treasure Island,* and he recognized where they were in the story. A man had gone overboard, and the ship was moving along without the unfortunate soul. Jim Hawkins, the intrepid cabin boy, crawled into a barrel of apples to have a snack, not realizing he was about to overhear plans for mutiny, and worse.

When Evelyn read the last words, crafted in such a way that a reader would want to turn the page to immediately find out what happened next, he heard the book snap closed. More groans followed.

Chris opened and shut the kitchen door again, announcing his presence as though he'd just arrived.

"Frosty's home," Laura said.

He walked through the door, and his eyes beheld an incredible sight. Evelyn sat on the couch, looking over her shoulder at him, and all three children sat with her, the two girls pressed up on one side, Ben on the other. They had all turned around to peer at him, and Laura wore a wide grin.

"You should've been here," she said happily. "We've been reading *Treasure Island*."

"It has pirates," Ben added.

Chris's throat tightened when he saw the little boy's eyes bright and lively for the first time since he'd met the child. Evelyn had done more than read a book. How long had she been in his house? The four of them appeared quite cozy.

"I hope you don't mind," Evelyn said, gently disentangling herself from the children and standing. "We did the chores first, of course."

"You did?" he asked, still standing in the doorway, afraid to step further into the homey scene in front of him. Uncertain he belonged there. "You didn't have to—"

"It was my pleasure to help. Then we read some, and had tea, and we just finished chapter ten." She pulled the book to her chest and held it there, her sharp green eyes watching him carefully. "Why do you have tea? I thought Americans preferred coffee."

"Medicinal purposes," he mumbled, rubbing at the back of his neck with one hand. His quick wash in the cistern didn't feel like enough anymore. Not that he needed to impress Evelyn, or anything—but she *was* a countess, and he probably smelled of horse and dirt. It didn't seem right. "Glad you found it. And liked it?"

She nodded when his words came out as a question. "Very much, thank you. I am afraid we ate the biscuits, too."

"Cookies," Ben corrected. "Ginger cookies."

"Oh, yes. Thank you." Evelyn answered the boy quite seriously before sharing a good-humored glance with him. "The children have also been teaching Madeline and me *American*. Did you know I say 'tomato' entirely wrong?"

He huffed a laugh and looked at the children. "It's a good thing you've got a couple of Americans to teach you proper, then."

"Indeed." Evelyn handed the book to Ben. "Will you hold on to that for later?"

The boy nodded rapidly, then jumped up and ran to his room, likely to put the book away.

Evelyn took her daughter's hand. "I think we had best return to the Boltons' house now. I am sure you're eager to rest after a day of work."

She was leaving already? Why did that disappoint him so much? Maybe because he wanted to watch her with the children. See the miracle for himself and figure out how to perform it later. Instead of protesting, though, he looked to Laura.

"Why don't you set the table for dinner? I'll walk Mrs. Lyon and Madeline back to the main house."

"Yes, sir." Laura stood, clasped Madeline to her in a quick hug, then skipped back to the kitchen singing over her shoulder. "I'll see you tomorrow, Maddie!"

Chris opened the front door and followed the English ladies out, then kept his pace matched to Evelyn's as they walked. "How did you do that?" he asked without preamble.

"Do what?" She turned her head just enough to look at him from the corner of her eye. Madeline walked a few steps ahead, humming to herself. "Read aloud to children?"

"Not that. Not *just* that." He had left his hat on the hook in the kitchen, so he pushed his hand through his still damp hair as he tried to put the question into better words. "I haven't heard more than a handful of words from Ben since the day he arrived. I've never heard either of those kids laugh."

She narrowed her eyes at him and stopped walking abruptly. "How long were you in that kitchen before you came out?"

Ducking his head a bit, the admission left him a little sheepishly. "From when you imitated a parrot."

Instead of taking offense or acting embarrassed, she laughed, then covered it quickly with one hand. It alarmed him that he liked the sound of her amusement. "I have heard a parrot before. They're rather dreadful. Have *you* ever heard a parrot?" She squared her shoulders and affected a haughty glare.

He raised both hands as though to ward her off while trying to ignore the way his heart flipped. "No, ma'am, and I'm not saying anything against your imitations."

"Good. It would be terribly rude of you." She started walking again, her eyes finding her daughter along the well-worn path from one house to the other. "As to your question, Mr. Morgan—"

"Frosty."

She blinked and looked up at him. "That isn't your name, though."

He shrugged. "It's good enough, isn't it?"

She pursed her lips. "It's strange to call people things other than proper names. Is Chris your Christian—I mean, is it your given name?"

It was the shortened version, but he wasn't about to tell her the whole of it. "Chris is good enough for me."

"Chris." She pronounced the single syllable with all the care of one trying out a foreign word. No one had said his name out loud in a long time. He liked it. "So, it is short for something?"

"Yep." He averted his gaze from her. "About that question...."

"Oh, yes. Of course. The children. I find them absolutely delightful, and I promise I did nothing extraordinary. Merely kept them company for the day. I talked to them about whatever they wished to talk about."

It wasn't the secret he'd been hoping for, then. He released an exasperated breath. "That's all the rest of us have been doing."

"I imagine everyone has been kind to them. Perhaps treading lightly?" she ventured, her voice gentle. He nodded. "I cannot say I understand it, but perhaps that is what made the difference. When one is mourning, and everyone around them knows it, it is most difficult to act normal again. People mean well, but they treat you like you're about to shatter if they say the wrong word. In my experience, at least, I started to feel that they were right. That I would break into a thousand pieces."

"You felt that way when your husband died?" he dared to ask, somewhat surprised.

"When my father died. I was a little older than Laura and Madeline." The admission surprised him, as did her candid way of speaking. She waved a hand before her, as though to clear her words from the air. "I think you still ought to be tender with them, in those moments you can see they are struggling. But otherwise, why not treat them like you would any child? That will give them permission to behave as you'd expect a happy child to behave."

The idea, so simple and obvious now that she'd spoken it, worked its way through him. Chris found himself looking over his shoulder at his house, seeing a lamp had been lit and put in the window for him. A thoughtful thing for a child to do. "I suppose it's worth a try."

He walked her all the way to the porch, coming to the steps moments after Madeline had disappeared inside. They could both hear the people within greeting the little girl, and Evelyn hesitated, a smile lingering upon her lips.

"Is everyone here always so kind?" She looked at him, her expression innocently surprised.

"Sometimes we get ornery, I guess. When times are hard." He rubbed the back of his neck, thinking on the spring when he'd been laid up with a broken leg and none of them had known if the ranch could hold together another year. Things had turned around since then, thanks to Duke. Life on the ranch was better than it had been since '91, before the droughts hit. "Evelyn."

Her gaze snapped to his at the sound of her name, and her chin came up the slightest bit. "Yes?"

"Would you mind coming by the house again tomorrow afternoon?"

Her smile reappeared. "I already told the children that I would."

"I know, but—" He cleared his throat, and he almost said more. Almost asked if she'd stick around after he returned, too. But that would be mighty presumptuous of him. And might make her uncomfortable. He didn't have any reason to want to be around her, either. "Just making sure," he finished, knowing the words lacked conviction. "Good evening, then."

"Good evening, Chris."

As he walked back to his house, Chris ruminated on his situation. He didn't know how to raise two kids. He'd learn, and the women of the ranch had promised their help. Yet at the end of the day, when the sun went down and the stars came out, it was just him. Just him tucking Ben into bed with his sawdust horse. Just him to listen at the door when Laura cried herself to sleep. Him feeling helpless when the children had nightmares.

When he'd left them with Ruthie for the first time after they arrived, to get back to work, Ben had stared up at Chris with fear. As though Chris planned to abandon them rather than return at the end of a long day.

That evening, when he climbed the porch steps and entered the house again, he heard the children in the kitchen. Talking to each other about pirates. Their voices didn't fade when he entered the kitchen, either. In fact, Ben jumped up from his chair. "Have you read *Treasure Island,* Frosty?"

Somehow, Chris spoke around the lump in his throat. "Sure have. Who's your favorite character in the book so far?"

"Oh, Jim Hawkins." The boy's little chest puffed out. "He's brave."

"I like Long John Silver. He's tricky, though." Laura tucked a strand of hair back behind her ear. Her long day had loosened the braid she'd put her hair in that morning, and every morning since they'd arrived. He'd been relieved she knew how to take care of her hair—he hadn't the first idea how women twisted their slippery locks into any kind of submission.

"The tricky characters are the most fun to read about," Chris agreed, turning to give attention to getting dinner on the table. "But they don't make the best neighbors." He'd had too much experience with cruel-hearted people to wish it on anyone.

"Pirates are outlaws, right?" Laura waited for him to give a nod before she started chattering on about all the outlaws she'd ever heard of in her young life. She knew a mix of stories, from Robin Hood to Billy the Kid, and had a whole host of opinions on why someone would be an outlaw in the first place.

Ben didn't share much more at the dinner table, but he swung his feet beneath his chair and listened to his sister with rapt attention.

When Chris tucked Ben in that night, he had hope for the future. The children had arrived with broken hearts and wounded souls. And Chris didn't have the necessary knowledge or tools to start repairs. But Evelyn did.

In the dark hours before dawn, Chris woke with an uneasy clench in his gut. He stayed still, listening, until he identified the sound that had crept into his sleep. He hadn't slept deeply since the children came. Since he'd moved his few possessions up into the unfinished second floor of the house. He had to remain alert, had to be ready in case they needed him.

Another quiet sob echoed through the house. Chris threw off his blankets and pulled on a pair of pants, stumbling toward the ladder. A little boy needed help, and Chris gave that help the best he could.

He sat on the floor by Ben's bed, crooning to the boy the way he would to a skittish colt. "Easy there, Ben. I'm here. You're safe." He laid his hand on Ben's back, surprised anew at how small and fragile the child felt.

Evelyn's words came back to him. *"People mean well, but they treat you like you're about to shatter if they say the wrong word."*

Maybe she'd know what to do in a situation like this one, too. Ben's sobs quieted after a time, and Chris allowed himself to close his eyes. He leaned his head back against the bedpost. He'd ask Evelyn the next time he saw her.

A pair of sparkling green eyes beneath a halo of copper braids lingered in his mind as his last thought before he drifted into an uncomfortable sleep.

CHAPTER NINE

W hen Evelyn woke, she discovered the other half of the bed she shared with Madeline empty. Her daughter had already risen and disappeared from the room. With a wince, Evelyn looked to the small clock on the bureau. She'd overslept. Something she'd promised herself she wouldn't do while staying with the Boltons. The day before, she hadn't much contributed to the household, but she refused to be a burden on anyone.

"I'll do my fair share," she said firmly, climbing from the comfortable bed. She washed her face in the basin of water on the low table, dried off with a small towel, and then went to work on her hair. She'd braided it the night before, and she almost wanted to leave it that way rather than bother with a more formal style. The braid felt more practical. Instead, she started looping it about her head and securing the coils with pins. Not at all fashionable, but it was quick.

Then she slipped into the same clothes she had removed the day before. The blouse and gray skirt were her only option unless she wanted to put on her stiff traveling skirt and the blouse she'd worn beneath its matching coat. That clothing needed a good brushing first, given the amount of dust streaked along its seams.

Maybe she'd request a tutorial on laundry from one of the other women.

She went down the stairs, her high-buttoned shoes clicking on the wood. The fashionable footwear didn't seem at all practical, either. She'd noticed the other women wore boots with flatter soles.

When she reached the ground floor, Evelyn heard sounds of laughter in the parlor and went to investigate there first. She found Madeline, Laura, and Ben playing with jacks and a rubber ball. Content that her daughter hadn't suffered for lack of a mother that morning, Evelyn withdrew before she called attention to herself. She went to the kitchen in search of Mrs. Bolton.

"That blue would look lovely on her, I think." Dannie's voice drifted out the doorway.

"The red checkered cloth is pretty, too. Though maybe a bit light for the coming weather." That was Ruthie.

Practical Mrs. Bolton spoke with the air of a queen making a decree. "We'll put long sleeves on it and make sure she has a flannel petticoat on when she wears it." The murmured responses were in favor of the idea.

Evelyn stepped into the kitchen and froze in the doorway, realizing all at once what they were talking about. Yards of fabric, folded and rolled and spread out, covered the long table. Dannie sat on one side looking at a pattern book while Ruthie sipped at a cup of coffee on the other, running her thumb across a bright yellow gingham fabric.

Mrs. Bolton saw Evelyn first. "There you are, Evelyn. At last. Here, come get some flapjacks. We'll get you fed before we take your measurements." She retrieved a plate from one of the countertops and bustled forward, snatching a fork as she came. "Eat up."

Evelyn accepted the plate and fork, then looked dumbly at the fabric. "My measurements? You cannot mean to create a new wardrobe for me, surely." She tried to laugh at the idea, but the sound came out weaker than she expected.

"The clothes won't be too fancy," Dannie said with a single shoulder shrug and a broad grin. "But they'll be serviceable and pretty enough. And with all of us working, we'll get you in a new dress before dinner."

Tears pricked at her eyes, and Evelyn tried to shake her head. "It's too much. All your lovely fabric—and I do not truly *need* the clothing."

Ruthie rose and put her hand on Evelyn's elbow, gently guiding her to the table. Evelyn towered over the more diminutive woman, but she allowed herself to be led and sat when Ruthie pointed to a chair. "You listen here, Evelyn. You're going to accept our friendship, and our kindness. Maybe someday, you'll be able to do the same for someone else. But you need to know that in these parts we help one another. If we didn't, there's not a ranch or farm within twenty miles that would still be working today."

"It's true." Mrs. Bolton went to a sewing basket on the table and brought out a measuring tape. "Besides, you've given us an opportunity to do nothing but sit around and talk all morning."

Dannie folded her arms up and tipped her head back, amusement dancing in her eyes. "Which freed all the children from their schoolwork, too."

All the children? "I didn't see Lee in the parlor." Evelyn popped two little pancake squares into her mouth and nearly closed her eyes as she savored the sweet taste. She could get used to breakfast like this. Simpler than what she'd found at her late husband's table every day, but certainly delicious.

"Travis, Clark, and Lee are helping with fence repairs, out with the men." Mrs. Bolton spoke almost brusquely, which had Evelyn checking the matron's expression. A wrinkle had appeared in her brow.

"Is there something wrong with the fences?" Evelyn's ignorance of the matter didn't forestall the question. Mrs. Bolton seemed...concerned.

"Someone cut the fence line in a few places," Dannie

answered, her voice low and solemn. "It's been a problem since the spring. We had new hands come on a few months ago, and it stopped for a while, but now we're finding evidence of cattle leaving through the damaged wires."

Evelyn looked from one woman's solemn face to another. "That sounds quite serious. What do you do about it? Does the military help with such matters?"

Ruthie snorted. "Nope. County Sheriff can't do much, either. By the time we report anything, the rustlers are long gone."

"We'd have to catch them in the act—or close to it— ourselves. Then maybe get our neighbors and cowboys to help us put a stop to it." Dannie rose to clear away her own breakfast things. "It's a dangerous business, rustling. For everyone involved."

"The men already have camps they take turns sleeping at," Ruthie went on to explain. "But it's not enough. There's too much ground to cover, and the cattle tend to scatter as they feed on what's left of the autumn grass."

"It'll be easier during winter. We bring them in closer to home every night by putting hay out for them." Dannie settled back in her seat.

Evelyn finished off her plate, which Mrs. Bolton swiped away at the same moment she handed Ruthie the measuring tape. "Let's get started. Daylight's a-wasting."

The conversation didn't go back to cattle thieves again, but focused more on matters of underthings, buttons, hems, and all the important details of a woman's dress. "We won't have the fabric to spare for those leg-o-lamb sleeves." Ruthie sounded somewhat regretful as she noted this lack.

"I truly don't mind." The more experienced ladies had tasked Evelyn with cutting fabric first, along the chalked lines Dannie had measured out. "They're certainly fashionable, especially in London circles, but they're not exactly useful. Do you know, I went to a ball in London where a lady had such large satin sleeves that she had to turn nearly sideways to slip through the door without crushing them?"

Mrs. Bolton clicked her tongue to the roof of her mouth. "Lands, what women do for fashion. My mother had a photograph of herself in one of those enormous hooped skirts held out like an upside-down punch bowl."

They all laughed, and Evelyn settled happily to her task.

After lunch and near to dinner time, they'd done as promised. Evelyn had one new dress to wear. They'd decided on using the red and white gingham on a day dress. It was long-waisted, with buttons going up the front. Ruthie made surprisingly quick work on the buttonholes. The dress fell nearly to the floor without more than one petticoat beneath it. Their only concessions to fashion were the pleats put in at the waist of the skirt and a few more at the shoulders to make the slightest of feminine puffs.

"We'll have more soon," Mrs. Bolton promised, eyeing the dress critically. "This one isn't fit for any kind of outdoor work, of course. You could wear it to church, though."

"It's quite beautiful." Evelyn didn't voice her only concern, which was trivial and vain. As a woman with red hair, she hadn't worn many red dresses in her life. Her mother had always insisted it made Evelyn look like a cherry from top to bottom. "I cannot begin to thank all of you for this."

"Never you mind about that." Ruthie had folded up the cloth. "I've got baking to do tomorrow, but I'll cut a few pieces while the bread rises and bakes."

Dannie had her own armful of fabric. "It's laundry day for us, so I'll work on a petticoat or two after I get my mending done."

"I suppose I had best take the Ashford children home." Evelyn had checked on her daughter and the other two children throughout the day. They'd been content to play together in the house, with old toys leftover from when the Bolton children were young. She'd heard Madeline chattering happily throughout the afternoon. "I promised they'd be back in time to do their chores, and we have some reading to do."

"With the men working all day in this sun, I doubt Frosty will want to put together a fine supper." Mrs. Bolton shuffled to the stove and a large iron pot that had been simmering with vegetables and beef stock. "Think you could carry a pot of this stew all that way?"

"Of course. I'm stronger than I look." Evelyn lifted her chin with false bravado. "I've carried a full tea service without breaking any cups."

"I don't doubt you one bit, dear." Mrs. Bolton chuckled and started ladling soup from the large pot into a smaller one. "It's a baking day for us tomorrow, too. Remind Frosty so he can put in his requests, will you?"

"Certainly." Evelyn called to the children to ready themselves for departure. They were out the door before she was, patiently waiting for her to come with the handle of the pot grasped tightly in both hands. It wasn't too heavy. If she didn't have to hold it for long.

After getting the pot safely up on Chris's stove, Evelyn took up the broom to sweep the kitchen. Madeline and Laura disappeared to collect eggs. Ben gathered up laundry into a large woven basket.

"Is tomorrow your laundry day, too?" Evelyn asked as he dropped the clothing basket beneath the loft door.

"Yep. Frosty does the laundry when he gets back at night. He says we're too little to be around the boiling pot and the lye without him." The boy climbed up the ladder and a moment later tossed down shirts and trousers into the basket below.

After a long day of work, the man still did laundry for himself and the children?

She pursed her lips. Maybe she could learn a bit of baking *and* how to do laundry, if Dannie didn't mind giving Evelyn that lesson. Evelyn had Madeline's clothing to care for, too.

Before long, they were all settled on the couch again with *Treasure Island* spread open in Evelyn's lap. The children stilled, though their anticipation filled the room with energy. With a full heart, Evelyn read aloud as Jim Hawkins discovered Long John Silver wasn't the friend he'd hoped for.

THOUGH CHRIS DIDN'T TAKE ANY MORE TIME THAN NORMAL TO wash up before going home for the night, he did a more thorough job of it. The other men around the cistern were silent, too tired from their day in the sun fixing fences to jaw about it. Except for Ed. The half-Cherokee, half-Mexican cowboy never ran out of good cheer or things to say.

"You're washing up like you're going to church," Ed said, not quite loud enough for anyone else to hear. He mopped at the back of his neck with his wet bandana slowly, like he wanted to enjoy the leisure of cool water on his skin.

Chris cut him a glance of irritation but didn't say a word. It was easier to offer no explanation than to try and say anything that made sense. Ed had a way of getting things out of people they'd rather keep to themselves.

"Cook said he thought he saw you walkin' with your new friend last night," Ed continued, a sly look in his eye. "Think she'll need an escort tonight, too?"

Unwilling to rise to his friend's bait, Chris put his head in the water and scrubbed a bit harder than before. But when he came up for air, Ed was still there, waiting with arms folded and eyebrows raised. Chris sighed and glanced at the other men, then jerked his head to indicate Ed should walk with him toward the ranch buildings.

"Ben and Laura like Mrs. Lyon and her daughter. A lot. Mrs. Lyon agreed to spend time with them this afternoon. If she's still at my house, I'd rather not smell like a mule when I walk in."

Ed walked with the same swagger most cowboys had, but he added something all his own to the set of his head and shoulders. Chris had always thought it was the Indian in his friend that made him move like a hawk rather than a strutting rooster.

"That's good for the kids. But what does it matter how you look or smell, *amigo*? You're not trying to impress anyone, are you?"

If he hadn't been a touch sunburned, Chris likely would've felt a bit of heat on the back of his neck from considering that question. "No." He turned it over a little more. "I know I'm not much to look at. But she's used to finer things than what we've got out here. I figure I don't need to make things worse by giving her cause to hold her nose when we're in company together."

Ed's boots scuffed to a stop. "In company together?" he repeated, somewhat incredulously. "You sound like a man going courting."

Before Chris could deny it or take exception to that remark, a hand slapped him on the shoulder. Chris nearly jumped out of his skin—he hadn't heard anyone come up on them. What was the matter with him? That kind of lapse in attention could cost a life out in the desert.

Ed's eyes twinkled knowingly, but Duke didn't seem to realize he'd done the impossible by surprising the ranch's foreman. "Frosty, before you go home for the night, I wonder if I could have a word?"

"Sure." Chris sent one more irritated glare Ed's way before the bronze-skinned cowboy chuckled and made for the barn, whistling a popular love song they'd heard at the last town dance.

Chris glowered at his friend's retreating back, then settled that glare on Duke. "What's on your mind?"

"Dannie's birthday."

An actual groan escaped Chris's mouth. "No. I'm not getting involved in any of that. She's your wife. You figure out a present for her."

"I have," Duke insisted. "I want to find a stud to match with Wisteria."

Wisteria was a prized Palomino, a new breed gaining popularity in the Territory. Dannie's favorite horse was a prime specimen of the prototype breed. Its coat was tawny, a golden brown, and she had a buttermilk-colored mane. A beautiful horse, and intelligent enough for riding herd as well as cutting cattle.

"You want to get your wife, a rancher's daughter, a horse." Chris blinked at his friend.

"Not just any horse. A match to her favorite horse." Duke puffed his chest out and his eyes glowed. "Wisteria is ten years old. She won't be around forever, and getting a few pretty foals out of her that carry her looks and capabilities would make Dannie happy. I'm sure of it."

Given that the ranch had been the center of Dannie's world her whole life until the Englishman came along, he was probably right. The gift seemed perfect for her.

"I'll put the word out that we're looking for a stud horse with the right look, but I can't promise anything." Chris had more contacts in the Territory than Duke at this point, but that would change before long given Duke's determination to rise in the ranching world.

"Thank you." Duke looked somewhat relieved. "She means the world to me. I couldn't be happy with giving her a trinket."

Chris looked Duke up and down. They were of similar height. Duke had an inch on Chris. Maybe two. But they also turned out to have a similar work ethic and way of thinking, from time to time. "What do you think about Evelyn's problem?" he asked somewhat abruptly.

Duke's expression turned immediately from that of a pleased husband to a concerned English lord. His head and shoulders tilted a bit differently, and he answered with an extra kick to his accent. "I cannot say what is best for her, of course, but I am concerned. She's a woman alone, vulnerable, and having a daughter with her makes her twice as likely to be a target for people who would take advantage—whether it's a school docking her wages in order to enroll her daughter, or a man making promises he doesn't mean to keep. If she goes back east, she might find friends, or she might not."

With a nod of agreement, Chris shifted his stance and tapped his hat against his thigh. "That's what I keep thinking. I wouldn't want any woman I know to be in her position."

"Dannie seemed to think that Mrs. Lyon is a bit—well—naive." Duke winced as he said the words, and Chris didn't blame him. Everyone knew Dannie spoke her mind, and sometimes what came out wasn't all that flattering to others. "But I don't see how a woman who's been married twice, to men of such poor character, could possibly be innocent to the idea of people taking advantage of her."

"And she made it here, on her own, all the way from England." Chris glanced toward his house. The sky grew darker, and he could see a lamp already waiting in the window for him. "You know from experience how difficult a journey that is."

"True enough." Duke settled his hat upon his head. "Whatever happens, I hope it's for the best. I almost hate to see Mrs. Lyon leave without any kind of protector. Though I don't suppose there's much we can do."

"Right." The agreement fell easily from his lips, but Chris kept brooding over the troubling situation. "Good night, Duke."

"Good evening, Frosty." Duke strode off in the direction of his own house, the windows lit from within by his bride. Someone who loved him, waiting on him.

Chris bit the insides of his cheeks, rolling ideas around and casting them away when they didn't solve the problem of Evelyn and Madeline striking out alone to who knew what kind of future. He walked up the porch steps to his house, deciding to enter through the front door this time. When he opened the door, he caught sight of a scene similar to the evening before, only sweeter.

Ben had fallen asleep with his head on Evelyn's shoulder. Madeline lay on a quilt someone had spread across the floor, stacking blocks as she listened to the story. Laura held her doll and leaned into Evelyn's other side, her eyes upon the page.

He only had a split second to see it all, to take in the moment's gentleness, before three sets of feminine eyes rose to see him there. Evelyn smiled a greeting at him, but she kept reading to the end of the paragraph. He came all the way into the room, closing the door quietly behind him.

Then she placed a ribbon in the book and closed it, careful not to jostle the sleeping boy.

Laura came up from the couch. "Frosty, you're home so late." She pointed to the kitchen. "We already had dinner, but we saved you some."

"Thank you. I appreciate that." He stayed where he was, not making his way to the kitchen or any closer to the domestic tableau before him. "Looks like it's a good thing you already ate, with Ben sleeping."

Evelyn's warm, rich voice answered him. "He's had a long day."

He put his hat on a hook near the door, then crossed the room to stand in front of the couch. He looked down into Evelyn's gem-green eyes. He wished he knew exactly what they reminded him of. He didn't think he'd ever seen that shade of green before meeting her.

"I'll put him to bed." He bent to scoop up the little boy, and his hands brushed the fabric of Evelyn's gown as he did so. Only then did he take note of the dress she wore, the fabric different from what he'd seen her in before. She looked at home in red and white gingham. Just like she looked at home there on his couch.

The dangerous idea stayed at the forefront of his mind as he carried Ben to his room, laying him on the bed with care. He took off the boy's shoes and socks, then covered him with a light blanket. The little fellow mumbled in his sleep and turned onto his side. Chris looked around for the horse, then stilled when a shadow fell across the doorway.

"Does he need this?" Evelyn whispered, and he turned to see her holding the sawdust horse out to him. "He seems quite attached to it."

Chris took the two steps needed to accept the toy animal, trying not to let his fingers brush hers. Being near her muddied his thoughts. "It's the only toy he brought with him." Then he took the toy back to the bed and tucked it beneath Ben's hand. He brushed the boy's hair away from his eyes, realizing the kid probably needed a haircut to keep it out of his face while he played.

How did boys get their hair cut? His father had taken Chris to a barber next door to the family business when he was a boy. It was a monthly ritual. Now, he tended to hand over a pair of scissors to one of the hands to shorten his own locks.

When he turned to leave the room, he saw Evelyn still there, watching him. She stepped back when he came out and shut the door behind him.

"Would you mind staying a minute to talk?" Chris asked and realized he'd spoken without warning when she blinked up at him. But not too far up. Her height and the shoes she wore brought her closer to his eye level than most women.

"Certainly. Perhaps while we eat?" She gestured to the kitchen. "I fed the children, of course, but neglected to eat anything myself. I thought it best to read aloud while they enjoyed their stew." Her expression brightened. "I don't believe I've ever had stew before."

Her easy smile, the way her green eyes stayed wide and hopeful, might be marks of naivety in others. But that wasn't the case with Evelyn. In fact, if he had to lay a wager on it, he'd say her cheery attitude had more to do with a false front for her daughter than her real thoughts on her situation.

He'd put up enough of those the last few weeks for the benefit of the children in his life. That's how he recognized the chipper mask. But she needn't wear it for him.

"Laura? You can take the jars down, if you want, and show Maddie the arrowheads or buttons."

Laura jumped up from the floor and went to fetch the jars while Chris gestured for Evelyn to precede him into the kitchen. Without meaning for it to happen, his gaze dropped to the sway of her hips below the curve of her waist. Beneath his sunburn, his cheeks grew warmer as he snapped his gaze upward again.

What was wrong with him?

Ogling at a pretty woman would've gotten him a stern lecture from his mother and a hard glare from his sister during his youth. He had better manners than that. It didn't matter that Evelyn had one of the prettiest faces he'd ever seen, and a graceful way of walking that made him wonder if it was practiced or came naturally to her.

He entered the kitchen a few steps behind, thanks to the lecture he'd given himself. She stood at the stove already, a shallow bowl in hand, spooning out stew. As he approached, she turned and held the bowl out to him with both hands.

He paused, less than a step away from her. "You're the guest, ma'am. I need to serve you."

"That's silly. You've been away all day, and I already served the children. Here." She held it out a little more.

He felt that tug again, deep in his chest, and the only way to ease it seemed to be to give in to her with a smile. "I guess I know better than to argue with a woman holding my dinner." He put both hands around the bowl, unable to avoid the way his fingertips grazed hers. He backed away, going to the table.

This is what came of him thinking. He got trapped in his ideas until he started feeling things that he shouldn't feel just to justify the pattern of his thoughts. Because when he'd walked in that door, seen Evelyn surrounded by children in his home, he'd come up with an outrageous plan to keep her and her daughter safe and cared for.

A plan that would likely have the other three women on the ranch ready to strangle him if he spoke it out loud.

Because they wouldn't want their newfound friend to solve her problems by marrying for a third time. Even if Chris was the one proposing that marriage to Evelyn. Even if he had the best of intentions.

When she sat down at the table across from him, spoon in hand and green eyes upon him, Chris had to swallow back more words than he'd probably said all year.

"You wanted to speak to me about something?" she ventured politely, holding her spoon in a way that emphasized her elegance. The world she came from was so different from his. But Duke had learned, hadn't he? He'd even said he preferred life on a ranch to life in English Society.

But what could Chris offer her that would be any better than what she might find out on her own? Or at least better than what any other man might give her? She had been an English countess —still was, technically. He was the son of a restaurant owner, a drover and foreman without much of an education.

"Sure did," he said at last, realizing she still waited for him to speak. Instead, he took a bite of stew. "Mm. This is good." At least he had the wits to chew and swallow before speaking.

"Mrs. Bolton told me everything she put into it this afternoon. I had no idea so much went into a simple meal. Oh, that reminds me. Baking day is tomorrow. I'm to take your requests back with me tonight, to make certain you get all the baked goods you need for the week." Her bites were much smaller than his, which meant he'd finish his meal before her and have nothing left to do but talk.

Which he wasn't the best at.

"The children minded you all right?" He made the statement into a question, lowering his gaze to his food.

"Perfect angels, of course. I thought they would grow bored, given that they were in the house all day while we sewed."

"Did you make that dress?" he asked, letting his eyes fall on the fabric at her shoulders but not daring to look directly at her again. Not yet.

"The other ladies did most of the sewing. But I do hope to learn." She leaned a bit toward him. "As I am a quick study, I'm certain to be a seamstress in no time." Her lips tilted upward in one of her charming smiles.

"I'm sure you will." He ate another bite of stew.

Being attracted to Evelyn couldn't be the whole of his reason for offering her marriage. If he decided to do so. Though it certainly helped matters. The main thing was that she was an incredible mother. He saw evidence of that in the way she put her daughter first, and how she interacted with Laura and Ben. The children responded well to her, too.

"Thank you for keeping an eye on the kids."

"I enjoy them," she said with easy honesty. "Ben seemed particularly tired tonight. Is that normal for him?"

"It's hard to say what's normal." He put down his spoon in the empty bowl and rubbed his palms along his thighs. "They haven't been with me long enough. But—" He leaned back in his chair and squared his gaze with hers at last. He saw her concern in the way her eyebrows drew together, in the slight purse of her lips. "He has nightmares, and last night he didn't sleep much."

"Oh. The poor little chap." Evelyn put her spoon down, too. "Do you know what is bothering him? What he's dreaming about?"

Chris shook his head. "He won't talk about it. Sometimes, he mumbles a bit in his sleep, but it's never anything I can make out." And he felt like a failure every time the boy woke up in fear or sorrow.

Her expression softened. "Bless him. And you, too. This cannot be easy, having fatherhood thrust upon you all at once."

"Fatherhood." He shook his head a little, the word strange. "I don't know if I've thought about it like that."

"Even if they never call you father, you are standing in his stead. That's your role for Ben and Laura from now on." She wrapped her arms around herself, her gaze intent. "They are affectionate children. I have seen it in the two days I've been with them. They have a foundation of love that their parents gave them. That means things will get better, in time, so long as you build upon what's already there."

He ran a hand through his hair, then dropped it to tap his knuckles against the table. A nervous tick. "I'm not sure I know how. I haven't even been around kids much."

Her smile reappeared, somewhat teasing. "They aren't too

difficult. I promise." Then she leaned forward, her hand covering his before he knew what to expect from the movement. "You are doing a splendid job. Don't give up."

He didn't so much as glance at their hands, not wanting to bring her attention to it, even though his whole body grew immediately attuned to her touch. Her hands were soft, the pads of her fingers smooth where they touched his knuckles. Her palms were small, too, and her fingers long and trim. If he covered her hand with his, it would disappear entirely in his larger grasp.

"Thanks," he managed to choke out, sounding somewhat natural. "That means a lot."

She gave a succinct nod and withdrew her hand. "I had better return to the Boltons'. Oh, do you know what you need from baking day? I don't think you ever said."

"Same as last time is fine," he said, not moving his hand an inch.

"Of course. Let me see if Madeline is ready to leave." She exited the kitchen, and Chris exhaled sharply before drawing in a deep breath to settle himself.

He couldn't tell her his idea yet. Not until he had all the details ironed out. Presenting a plan half-formed from desperation and partly mixed with his sudden attraction toward her, would lead to a quick refusal of his offer. He knew this with certainty.

If Chris got his plan in order, and if Evelyn saw the merit of his idea, they could get married in Tombstone before the month was out. Then Evelyn's future would be settled and safeguarded, and he would secure a nurturing mother for Laura and Ben.

He had a lot of work to do.

CHAPTER TEN

Saturday morning at the table, Mrs. Bolton explained their Sunday rituals to Evelyn as they rolled out bread dough. Visitors came to the ranch on Sunday, or the people of the ranch went visiting when there wasn't a man to preside over the congregation at the little church in Sonoita.

"We plan to stay home tomorrow," Mrs. Bolton added. "You're more than welcome to join us in the parlor to meet our neighbors, or if that's too much for you, you can keep back. I imagine people will have heard about you by now."

Evelyn paused in the work to wipe her brow with the back of her wrist. Kneading and rolling out dough took muscles she hadn't used much in the past. Her upper arms would certainly ache the next day. Today she wore a borrowed blouse from Mrs. Bolton with sleeves only to her elbows, and her brushed-out gray skirt.

"Does news travel fast in your community?" She hadn't seen many houses when they'd come closer to the ranch, though there had been paths turning off the main dirt road. People seemed too far apart to exchange information easily.

"Oh, sure. One of our cowboys is friends with the Masons, and Travis is sweet on a Harper girl. There's comings and goings all the time. Meetings over fence posts, an errand to borrow a particular tool or even sugar." She brushed her hands off on her apron. "I think we can put that one in a pan and let it rise a bit." She nodded at Evelyn's pile of dough.

"What would be best? Should I be here to satisfy curiosity?" Evelyn lifted the pan of dough and moved it nearer the stove on a set of wooden shelves built up next to the oven. Made especially for baking day. "I am rather used to being on display."

Mrs. Bolton paused in her work, that crease in her forehead appearing. "How do you mean?"

Evelyn poured herself a cup of cooling tea—an herbal concoction she wasn't familiar with, but Mrs. Bolton had sweetened it with wild honey. It made for a refreshing drink, even if the taste was odd. "In English high society, a woman is an accessory to her husband. My duty at events my husband attended involved wearing the best clothes and jewels, the most sophisticated hair styles. In short, my appearance was a reflection upon his status." She knew how it sounded, what a practical woman living the way Mrs. Bolton lived must think of such things. Evelyn kept her voice light. As though she didn't care what anyone thought. "That is merely how it was."

With a click of her tongue, Mrs. Bolton put her hands on her hips. "Mercy. Treated like a doll, or an ornament. I can't imagine. I'm all for a woman putting her best foot forward, and I like pretty things as much as the next gal, but if King even tried such a thing—"

"What am I trying?" the deep voice of the rancher interrupted the tirade as he sauntered in from the hall. He'd been in his offices that morning with his son-in-law, going over contracts. The Englishman followed in behind him.

When Mr. Bolton reached his fingers toward the dough, his wife playfully smacked his hand away. "No pinches of bread dough. It's not good for you to eat it like that."

He sighed as though put-upon, then gestured to Evan. "Duke here says they're bringing pie to Sunday dinner."

"Lovely. We're having potatoes and roast, Duke. Make sure Dannie knows."

"Yes, ma'am." Hearing the slight Southern drawl attempted by an Englishman made Evelyn smile.

Evelyn took her seat again at the table. "Evan, do you think I ought to meet the neighbors tomorrow?"

His expression clouded as he answered. "I doubt it would prove harmful, though I feel I must warn you, Evelyn. I know our hands are already speaking about you with interest. You will excuse me for saying so, but it is rare that a woman deemed as attractive as you are visits this area."

Heat bloomed in her cheeks. Besides the tell-tale blush, she was too well practiced to squirm in her seat or let anyone see how uncomfortable the idea made her. As she had told Mrs. Bolton, she was quite used to people staring. "I cannot be of too much interest to anyone, given that I'm a widow and only a temporary guest."

Mrs. Bolton and Mr. Bolton exchanged a glance that Evelyn read easily enough. They expected the opposite of her statement to hold true.

The family matriarch's expression smoothed, and her warm, motherly manner returned. "We just want to make sure you're comfortable. If you don't mind meeting new people and swapping a few stories, we're happy to have you meet our friends."

"If it gets to be too much, you can always make a run for it," Mr. Bolton added, and his wife laughed.

More than ready to change the subject, Evelyn met her fellow countryman's eye. She tried to sound excited rather than nervous. "Evan? Do you think Dannie would mind if I asked for a laundry lesson?"

A smile she didn't quite understand appeared on his face. "I'm sure she won't mind. We did our laundry this morning, so our things are probably near ready to come down from the line."

We? Did he participate in the chore? How odd. She couldn't think of any Englishman she knew who would be willing to admit to even knowing how one performed the chore of washing one's clothes.

"Oh. I was hoping I could join her, so as not to put her out."

"It won't be any trouble at all." Evan gestured to the back door. "I can walk you over to our house right now, if you'd like. You can ask her yourself."

Evelyn looked to Mrs. Bolton, who immediately waved her away. "Go on now. Don't forget to take your things that need washing, so you needn't make another trip."

In due course, Evelyn soon stood at the laundry shed. Sturdy poles with thick twine stretched away from the small, three-walled building. An immense cauldron of water boiled, filled with Evelyn and Madeline's underthings and white clothing. Evelyn poked at them with a long wooden oar.

"Not nearly so complex as you thought, is it?" Dannie asked from her place at the scrubbing board and cool bucket of water. "The hot water gets everything loosened up, the board gets the stubborn bits out, then we put it through the wringer."

"And then pin the clothes to the line." Evelyn used a large pair of tongs to transfer clothing from the hot tub into the cooler tub. "Not so difficult, in concept, but I can see how a woman would grow weary of it. In London, we sent our clothing out. At the country estate, there were paid laundresses."

"Wouldn't that be something?" Dannie chuckled and stepped aside. "You want to try the board?"

"Of course." Evelyn set to work cleaning the soiled hem of a petticoat. "I thought after I completed my wash, since there is so little of it, that I might gather the laundry from Mr. Morgan's house. As a way of saying thank you to them for their kindness." She held up the hem, amazed to see the ivory-colored fabric as clean as ever.

A buzz of pride made her grin. She had done that.

She put it through the wringer next, turning the crank with relish. It wasn't necessarily important work, but for one who had never done the job before, it was astounding.

"You want to do Frosty's laundry?" Dannie sounded highly skeptical. "I can't imagine voluntarily cleaning up after an extra cowboy. I suppose it would be a nice thing to do. Maybe have the kids help, so you don't get tuckered out."

"An excellent idea. After my things are on the clothesline, I'll fetch the children." Evelyn put the last shirtwaist through the wringer. "I suppose we have to iron everything out, too."

"That comes later, though." Dannie followed Evelyn to the clothesline and helped pin everything in place. "Things dry up fast, too. One of the few perks to an arid desert. The real problem is remembering to get things down quick enough that the sun doesn't bleach out the colors like old cow bones." She looked down the line, which only had a third of the space taken up by the few things Evelyn and Madeline owned.

"I had best hurry and gather the rest of the laundry. If you have other things you need to do, I am certain I'll be fine now."

"Send someone to fetch me if you need any help, though." Dannie waved over her shoulder as she strode away.

"Of course." Evelyn went back to the Morgan house, where Madeline had gone to help with chores again. The children had started their day in the barn, but they were playing a game with the buttons when Evelyn arrived at the house. When Evelyn announced her idea, they were all quick to agree to help.

"So long as you'll promise to read to us again, after." Laura delivered the ultimatum with all the gravitas of a lawyer. "We need to know what happens next in the story."

"We must limit ourselves to one chapter today," Evelyn warned, trying to hide her pleasure. "I'm trying to make myself useful to the adult population of the ranch, you know."

"Is that why we're doing this for Frosty?" Ben asked. He held open the front door for the girls and Evelyn to walk out.

Rebalancing the basket of clothing on her hip, Evelyn waited for Ben to fall into step beside her to answer. The girls skipped ahead, apparently racing to the laundry shed. "It isn't the whole reason, but yes. I want to show him that I'm grateful for what he did, bringing Madeline and me here where we are safe."

"Oh." Ben stuck his hands into the pockets of his faded denim trousers. "I think he likes you. He asked a lot of questions about you."

"Did he?" Evelyn tried to ignore the twist of nerves that statement caused.

"Yep. Laura told him she liked you." He spoke with as unhurried a manner as his guardian had ever used. The boy's drawl sounded well-practiced, but his somewhat indifferent tone didn't fool Evelyn.

"I'm pleased to hear that."

"Yep." The boy walked silently the next few steps, then heaved an enormous sigh. "I told him I liked you, too. I guess."

The anxious feeling dissipated, replaced by a satisfactory warmth at the child's words. "Thank you. I rather like you, Ben."

His succinct nod was his answer—and the end to that conversation. They'd arrived at the laundry shed. Evelyn set the basket down and looked at the still-bubbling hot water. "Right. Let's see if I remember how to do this." Chin lifted and shoulders back, she began her work.

CLEARING BRUSH FROM WATERING HOLES, BOTH NATURAL AND manmade, took a full day of hard work. The only thing Chris enjoyed about that kind of work was the ability it gave him to think. Though he and Ed worked side by side for hours in the sun, they didn't say much to one another. They kept their shirtsleeves rolled down to avoid the burrs and thorns of the brush, and old leather gloves protected their fingers from most of the harmful bits of the nuisance plants.

But they still ended the day with scratches along their forearms and faces, and stubborn prickers that would need plucking out by hand. They tossed shovels into the back of a buckboard wagon, and the pickaxes they'd used for the more stubbornly rooted desert plants. Gus, the shepherd dog, had sat beneath the wagon for most of the day, enjoying the shade.

"He gets the easy job," Ed said, taking off his gloves and tossing them in the back too. "Next time, Gus, I'll be on the lookout for snakes and puma. You can dig up roots."

Gus's tongue lolled out, and his canine teeth flashed white in a dog grin.

Chris removed his gloves and bent to scratch Gus behind the ears. "He pulls his weight. Don't you, boy?" Chris gave a pat to the small ladder built to lean against the cistern. They'd put the A-frame ladder in to help critters who got in the cistern on accident to get out again.

The dog obeyed the silent command, jumping up on the ladder and dipping his head down to take a drink before they headed back to the ranch. Ed drank from a canteen and tossed Chris one to drink out of, too. Once they'd all been refreshed, Chris climbed up into the wagon and Gus jumped into the back.

"I'm washing up and going to turn in early tonight." Ed rubbed at the scruff on his chin. "And taking my day off tomorrow to go to Tombstone for a barber. You coming?"

"Sunday tomorrow." Chris kept his eyes on the mules that pulled the wagon. "I figured I'd stick around here."

Ed went to church when the preacher came around, but on certain days, he'd make the trip nearly to Tucson, to an old Catholic mission called San Xavier. Chris hadn't asked, nor did he care, whether Ed felt one way of worship was better than the other. A man didn't stick his nose into another man's business without invitation.

Maybe it was just another one of those things that Ed had to deal with, given that he straddled more than one line when it came to his personal history. His mother's family had lived in Texas since it had been under Spanish rule and had fought alongside transplanted Americans to gain independence and vote themselves into statehood. Ed's father had an even deeper claim to the land as a Cherokee. Ed's family had moved to Indian Territory, now swallowed up in Oklahoma Territory.

"I can't wait for the winter to get here so we can complain about bitter winds rather than the blazing sun," Ed muttered, looking up at the cloudless sky. Mid-September meant cooler weather most days, but the work didn't get easier.

Chris gave Ed a narrow-eyed look and spoke without heat to his words. "Doesn't help much. Complaining."

Ed snorted, which made one of the mules toss its head irritably. Ed leaned back, with his forearms braced on the buckboard's short backrest. "I guess kickin' up a fuss doesn't get you anywhere unless you're a mule."

"True enough."

Chris made out the homestead buildings in the distance. Everyone who'd worked away from the ranch would be coming in about then, looking for food and chores closer to their bunks. The newer hands were an interesting lot, but Chris hadn't made an effort to get to know much about them outside of their work ethics. Things would come out, from time to time, as they had with Ed.

Ed had left home years before, claiming more interest in chasing cattle than farming his father's orchards on land granted to the family by the United States government. Then there'd been other conversations. Conversations that made Chris wonder if Ed had left home for family reasons. He didn't talk much about the people he'd left behind. Yet whenever a letter came for him, maybe four times a year, he'd take it out into the middle of nowhere to read it.

Not like the other men who read snatches of their letters aloud, merely for the enjoyment of sharing gossip with others.

No one gossiped quite the way men in a bunkhouse did.

Which might've contributed to Chris's reputation for keeping his mouth closed on most subjects. He'd always planned to be a foreman, maybe eventually work his way up to partner at a ranch or start a spread of his own. So he'd never given anyone ammunition to use against him—better to keep his head down and do the job his bosses had hired him to do.

A drawback to that attitude meant he didn't have many people to confide in, though. Especially about the somewhat crazy plan he'd concocted regarding Evelyn Lyon. Which left him to stew about it all on his own.

As though he'd read Chris's mind, Ed tilted his hat back and fixed him with a hard stare. "You're quieter than normal. Something eating up at you on the inside?"

Chris hunkered down, elbows on his knees. "Thinking about something I'd rather not have all the men jawing about."

"Have you ever known me to go around spreading people's secrets?" Ed tilted his head toward the dog. "Gus is more likely to share anything you'd feel like saying."

Ed had a point. The two of them had worked together for the last five years at the Bolton spread. In that time, Chris had felt more than once that Ed would stand by him come heck or high water. They'd stood up for each other on more than one occasion.

"I'm thinking of getting married."

Ed's head jerked to the side hard, his jaw falling open. "You what now?"

"I've got two kids to care for, and I need some help." Chris relaxed once he'd said the words out loud. His grip on the leads softened up. "I figure I'm not too bad a catch, either. I have a steady job that pays well. A house. I don't drink or gamble."

"You live out in the middle of nowhere," Ed added, a crooked grin appearing on his face. "How do you figure to meet someone? I thought none of the girls around here were of interest to you. They're all a mite young, even if they've been bred to life in the Territory."

Chris pulled in a slow breath, then let it out again as he measured his next words. "I've been thinking about the countess. Maybe marrying her."

Ed sat up and held a hand out. "Gimme the reins."

"What?" Chris looked down at the thick strips of leather in his hands. "Why?"

"Because I'm not about to let a man crazy as a cat in a sack drive me another inch." Despite what he said, he threw both his hands in the air. "Frosty, that'd be like marrying a coyote to a lapdog. It's the biggest mismatch I've ever heard of—like ducks and hawks getting along. Or a zebra and a lion."

"Can we leave the animal kingdom out of it?" Chris asked, slumping down again. Dejected. "I didn't think it was that far-fetched."

"Well, it is. It's plumb *loco*." Ed crossed his arms and resumed his slouching. "You're right that you need a woman. Those kids of yours could use a mother, and you were lonely enough before they showed up. But an English lady?"

"Dannie married an Englishman." Chris didn't exactly regret telling Ed his thoughts, but the end of the conversation couldn't come soon enough for him. They were getting closer to the barn.

"That's different. Duke *wanted* to live in Arizona. Seems like the countess wound up here on accident. She's a lost sheep, not a maverick looking for a herd." Ed squinted at Chris one last time. "Is it just because she's pretty?"

Though a silent admirer of Evelyn's beauty, Chris could at least shake his head in the negative to that. "It's because of the kids. You should see them with her. She's got Ben talking and Laura smiling like she's got hope again."

Silence followed that comment. Ed knew enough about the situation with the children to understand what those seemingly small things meant to Chris. They were near the entrance of the *zaguán* when Ed finally heaved a sigh. "I guess you could always ask her what she thinks. Worst thing she could say is no. Worst thing she could do is laugh at you."

"My thoughts exactly." Chris's words echoed in the corridor, and the conversation ended with that. Together they saw to the comfort of the mules and the proper care of the wagon. Chris fed Gus and left the dog to the barn.

He walked to his house, hat pulled low against the evening rays of sun. The days were growing shorter and shorter, but the work never lessened. The laundry still waited for him.

Chris entered through the kitchen door, figuring the kids would've left the basket of soiled clothing in the kitchen as they had the last time. He hadn't bothered to wash up, either. Wasn't much point when he was about to sweat over a vat of soiled clothing.

Which made him that much more surprised when he found Evelyn sitting at his kitchen table with stacks of clothing folded up in front of her. She looked up as the screen door sprung closed, an expression he could only call guilty on her face. She bit her bottom lip, and he could've sworn there were tears in her eyes.

His heart squeezed tight. "Are the kids all right?" he asked, since he didn't see them in the room with her. Why else would she look ready to dissolve into tears?

She nodded. "Everyone is fine. But—but not every*thing*. Oh, Chris. I'm so sorry." She picked up a stack of clothing several inches thick. "I didn't mean for this to happen. I promise, I was trying to help. But a red bandana fell into the pot with some of your things."

He took the clothes from her and finally looked down at them. He owned a few lighter-colored shirts. Nothing white, except one shirt for Sundays that still hung on a peg in his loft. But he had light blue shirts, a few tan shirts, and canvas-colored pants.

Except now all those lighter hued clothes were tinged pink.

He blinked and shuffled the top shirt to the bottom, looking at another, then another. Then he raised his gaze slowly to Evelyn's.

Her bottom lip trembled. When she spoke, her voice came out a touch higher than normal. "I'm so sorry. I've ruined them."

And all at once, relief bubbled up in his chest. Relief, and a bit of laughter. He tried to bite back the latter, but some of the amusement inched out in his voice. "It's just a few shirts, Evelyn. No harm done." He waved a hand to the rest of the short, neat stacks of clothing on the table. "You didn't have to do this, but I sure appreciate it."

The men might side-eye him a bit, but a benefit to being foreman is that they wouldn't laugh. Much.

"You are merely being kind." She sniffled and took a step back from him.

Chris caught her hand before she made it far, giving it a gentle squeeze. "I wasn't looking forward to another hour or two of work. You've saved me that."

Her eyes brightened somewhat, and she tilted her head to one side with a skeptical little smile upon her lips. "I'll ask Mrs. Bolton or Ruthie if they know how to fix the shirts. Maybe I can set them to rights."

"Mighty thoughtful of you." He put the clothes down and swiped off his hat, dropping it onto one of the chairs. "Where are the kids?"

"Oh, Lee and Clark came by with those puppies and asked if they wanted to watch some training at the front of the house." She waved in that direction. "They'll be back soon, I imagine. Looking for dinner."

"Right." He rubbed his hands along his thighs. "Weren't you baking at the big house today? Hope your good deed didn't interfere with those plans."

"Oh, not at all. I went back and forth between the two things." As she spoke, a bright red curl of hair bobbed a bit in front of her ear. She tucked it back. "I'd be happy to bring your loaves over, if you like, or I can send them home with the children if I leave now."

"I'll walk with you to the Bolton house and bring them—the kids and the bread—back with me." He gestured to the front door. "Does that suit you, ma'am?"

"Yes, perfectly. It's an ideal solution." She led the way through the house, and once they were both out the door, she tucked her hand through his arm. Then immediately pulled it back. "Oh, I'm terribly sorry. I didn't mean to be overly familiar—I am only used to—"

"Evelyn." He said her name with an easy smile tugging at his lips. "I don't mind. So long as you're on the left side." He briefly patted the holster on his right. "That leaves me free to draw out if we come across any mean critters." Then he held his left elbow out, a clear invitation.

She wrinkled her nose. "You are kind to humor me." Then she put her hand through the crook of his arm, and Chris's heart flipped with all the enthusiasm of a child turning handsprings.

"A lady never goes anywhere in England unless she is on a man's arm or accompanied by a chaperone."

"Sounds a bit limiting." Chris concentrated on the path, watching their steps to keep them both safe from the unexpected. "I s'pose it makes sense, especially if London's as large a city as Duke says."

She tucked her free hand in a large pocket of the apron she wore around her waist and looked at him from the side of her eye. "Do you always carry a weapon?"

"Most of the time. While the wildlife tends to shy away from the homestead, you get the occasional young coyote sniffing around, or a snake cutting through on its way to better hunting. A rifle is better, out riding the spread, for bigger predators. But a pistol is smart when you're walking from building to building, especially at dusk."

"I will keep that in mind." Her cheerful expression faded as she surveyed the grass on either side of them. "I understand tomorrow the ranch is expecting visitors. Mrs. Bolton has invited me to meet the neighbors."

He'd already heard about it. "I hope that goes well."

She gave a tight nod. "As do I. Who knows how long my daughter and I will linger here? We need all the friends we can possibly find." She tilted her head up toward him, a pleasant smile nearly covering the concern in her expression. "Of course, I will always count you the first of our friends, Chris."

"That means a lot to me, ma'am."

She raised her eyebrows. "A few minutes ago, it was Evelyn, and now I'm back to ma'am?" She shifted her hold on his arm.

"*Ma'am* is just a show of respect around these parts." He kept his gaze forward. They had circled the barn to come to the front of the main house, where Chris already heard laughter and the yips of happy pups. "But if you'd prefer I didn't use—"

"I don't mind." Then she gave his arm a gentle pat before she withdrew her hand. "Thank you for walking me back to the house."

"My pleasure."

He stopped where he was at the corner of the house, watching as Evelyn called to the children for their attention. In seconds, she had his two kids running back to him, Lee and Clark rounding up puppies with Fable's help, and her own daughter climbing the porch steps to wash up for dinner. As the screen door shut behind Evelyn and Laura took Chris's hand, the rightness of his decision settled more firmly in his chest.

The worst Evelyn could say was no.

CHAPTER ELEVEN

Plaiting her daughter's hair hadn't ever been permitted in Evelyn's old life. "That's what the nanny is for," her second husband had insisted. "I don't need a wife who pretends to be a hairdresser for infants."

Since the earl's heir had ousted Evelyn and Madeline from the London townhouse, Evelyn had combed and brushed her daughter's hair every night and every morning. Madeline's hair, long and the color of gold, curled at the ends and felt soft as silk. And how the little girl could talk while her mother saw to her hair! It had become the highlight of Evelyn's day.

That morning, as Evelyn twisted strands of hair back and forth to form a lovely braid, Madeline spoke of all the fun she anticipated the day would bring. "Laura said the barn cat had three kittens, and they're nearly all grown up now, but they still like to play and don't hide when you go into the barn."

"I'd prefer you stay out of the barn today, Madeline. You're wearing the new dress Mrs. Rounsevell made for you." The soft blue plaid might've been meant for a man's shirt, but it made a lovely gown for blonde-haired, blue-eyed Madeline. "Barns are dirty places."

Madeline looked over her shoulder, just the barest peek. "I

could put on a different dress. The brown one. It won't show any dirt."

"It isn't just the dirt I'm concerned about." Evelyn tied off the braid with a small piece of ribbon. "Tomorrow, you can go kitten hunting. Today, I'd like you to behave like a lady. We want Mr. and Mrs. Bolton's neighbors to see that English girls have proper manners."

"Yes, Mama." She tugged the toe of her stockinged foot across the woven rug on the floor. "Do you think Laura has proper manners?"

"Yes, of course." Evelyn rose and went to the mirror above the chest of drawers. She undid her own nighttime braid. "She is a very polite young lady."

Madeline took hold of the bed post and twisted herself around it until she sat on the double bed they shared. "Do you think Mr. Morgan braids her hair every day?"

Evelyn's hands slowed, the brush mid-way through her hair. "I don't know." When she thought on it, she couldn't recall thinking the other little girl's hair required additional grooming. But it was difficult to imagine the cowboy with his big, rough hands handling a hairbrush and the thin ribbons Laura always wore.

"Laura says that Mr. Morgan said that she and Ben could call him Frosty. Do you think that means I can call him that?"

"Heavens, no. You may call him Mr. Morgan. He's their kin, and their guardian." She turned to look at her daughter. "We call people by their proper names, unless invited to do otherwise."

The girl heaved a sigh and stood, then she went to work straightening the edges of the quilt on their bed. "Mama? Do you think we're going to go back to England?"

A swirl of whispered insults and criticisms threatened to overtake Evelyn's thoughts, but she swiftly shook her head. "I cannot say for certain, darling. There isn't anyone there who would welcome us, at present." Then she put her brush down on the dresser and gently took Madeline's shoulders in her hands, turning the girl around to face her. "Do you miss England? Do you want to go back?"

Madeline immediately ducked her head, and Evelyn put a hand beneath her daughter's chin to lift her gaze again. "Madeline. You can tell me. I can't promise it will change anything, but I would like to know how you feel about that idea."

The little girl shook her head, and her cheeks turned pink. "I don't ever want to go back. People were mean there. Not like here, where it doesn't matter who my real papa was."

An icy bolt shot through Evelyn's heart. "People were unkind to *you* in England?" Evelyn had made certain to surround her daughter with the best people, children from the best families, a well-paid nursemaid, and a highly recommended governess. How could a child as protected and loved as Madeline have been treated poorly?

Madeline bit her lip and looked down, and this time Evelyn let her. "I heard Nanny Mary and Miss Hartfield talking once, about the scandal of the earl marrying you and taking care of me. And some of the girls used to tease me about not being a nobleman's real daughter."

Evelyn slowly sat on the foot of the bed, and she tugged her daughter to sit beside her. "They teased you?"

"And sometimes played jokes." Madeline leaned into Evelyn's shoulder. "When we played games, they said I had to be the maid. Then they'd pretend I wasn't there, or they'd tell me what to do. It was just a game."

But it hadn't been just a game. Evelyn sensed a great deal of hurt beneath the surface of her daughter's words. How had she missed this? Lord Tyneham had kept her quite busy, of course. Her wifely duties had been numerous, especially in London, where she'd had to accompany him to every social event. She'd had to be seen at all the fashionable teas and salons. Had gone to dress fittings every other week. Then there were the earl's more personal demands on her person—no, she wouldn't dwell on the past.

She had let her daughter down. Trusting too many strangers with Madeline's happiness had been a serious mistake.

"My dearest little girl." Evelyn wrapped both arms around Madeline and pulled her into a warm, firm embrace. "You have a kind and loving heart. Those children were wrong to treat you so, and the adults even more so for gossiping about something that was absolutely none of their business." She kissed Madeline's forehead. "You will find cruel people wherever you go. In England, France, Australia, and even here in Arizona. Just as you will find those who are kind. We have only had better luck here, thus far. The truly important thing is that *you* are kind to others."

Madeline relaxed in her arms. "I'm sorry you weren't lucky before, Mama. People weren't nice to you, either."

"No. But then, I never had much opportunity to search out the good people in English Society." Evelyn considered her daughter's words, then cleared her throat. "Why don't you go see if Mrs. Bolton needs any help preparing for her guests? I'll finish with my hair and join you shortly."

"Yes, Mama." Madeline rose, then giggled and dropped a quick curtsey. Something she hadn't done since their arrival in America, when sharing a hotel room every time they stopped for rest had also meant sharing a bed. There had been no leave-taking. No morning presentation of her own child to her for inspection.

Evelyn rather liked it. She watched Madeline with a grin as the little girl skipped out the door.

"Clark," Madeline's voice said clearly from the hall. "Are we going to play with the puppies again today?"

"If we're lucky, Maddie-girl." The boy's voice, starting to deepen, answered cheerfully. "But first we have to take care of some things...." His voice trailed away as the two of them went downstairs.

Evelyn went back to the mirror and started twisting and tucking her hair into a low chignon. She wore her gray skirt and a long-sleeved shirtwaist made from the same fabric as Madeline's dress. She stared at herself in the mirror, studying her red hair with disfavor.

"Oh well." She tucked a loose curl tightly behind one of the many pins in her hair. People had commented often enough on the bold color of her hair in unfavorable terms, but Evelyn tried to remember the handful of compliments she had received over the years. Her first husband had thought her hair "charmingly unique," and her second had called it, "as striking as a flame."

Not that their opinions mattered. Not anymore.

She took it down again, determined to do something with it to please herself.

A soft knock on the door surprised her, and she turned with a pin held between her lips. "Who is it?" she asked, teeth holding the pin in place while her hands held the loose hair up.

"It's only me." Mrs. Bolton cracked the door open when Evelyn bid her come inside. "I came to see if you needed any help."

Evelyn smiled and removed the pin from her teeth to gesture at her hair. "I am rather struggling with this mess this morning."

"Your hair is such a lovely color, my dear. Reminds me of the trees back east, when all the forests are clothed in their autumn glory." She came forward and held out her hand for the brush. "Let me see what I can do. You sit on down in this chair."

Evelyn obeyed, and for a time both women were silent. It felt lovely to have someone administer to her hair, for the first time since she'd left her late husband's home. Not that she needed a maid. She had done well enough without one. But to have someone else show her such care made the conversation she'd had with her daughter stand out even more in her mind.

Mrs. Bolton twisted a few strands of hair into braids, pulling some back and using pins to tuck curls here and there. "I think that should do it," she said, her voice softer than when she'd entered the room. She sounded almost sad.

Coming out of her own thoughts, Evelyn looked up and caught a strange expression on her friend's face. She didn't wear her usual smile or seem to hold her usual energy. "Mrs. Bolton? Is something wrong?"

For a long moment, Mrs. Bolton said nothing. She turned the brush she held over and over in her hands, then released a sigh. "Do you know how old I am?"

"No." Evelyn tilted her head to the side. "Somewhere about forty, perhaps."

"I am forty-three. And I've been with the family since Dannie was only ten years old. Nearly thirteen years." She lowered the brush onto the dresser and stepped back until she sank onto the edge of Evelyn's bed.

"You've been part of this family for a long time." Evelyn leaned against the wall near her open window, grateful for the gentle breeze that entered the room. "It's no wonder they accepted your marriage so quickly."

Rather than appearing pleased, Mrs. Bolton winced and looked down at her hands. "I never thought I would marry a second time. My first husband died shortly after our marriage, and I moved home. I have sisters. All younger. Prettier than I thought myself. Everyone said the same thing about me, growing up. That I was sturdy. Hearty. Made to work. When my sisters were all married and having families of their own, I couldn't stand it any longer. I found an advertisement for a housekeeper in Arizona Territory for a widower and his children. So I came here, where I wouldn't be reminded of all the things my sisters had that I never would."

The knowledge weighed on Evelyn's heart. "Oh, Mrs. Bolton. I'm sorry you went through that."

The older woman waved a hand dismissively. "That is all in the past. When I started to fall in love with King, I hid it. For a long time. Until he said he loved me, too. That was the most terrifying moment in my life. He is older than me, you know. He's fifty-five." She smiled a little. "He's made me feel more beautiful than I ever have in my life."

Evelyn's heart went out to her new friend, grateful that she had somehow merited enough trust in the compassionate woman to be taken into her confidence.

"All his children are nearly grown, and since I've had a hand in raising them, I was perfectly content with that. At my age, most women have at least a grandchild or two." Beth settled one hand over her stomach and met Evelyn's eyes, alarming Evelyn when she saw tears gathering in Mrs. Bolton's. "I'm pregnant, Evelyn. And I don't know what to do."

Though Evelyn's mouth dropped open in shock, she knelt by her friend and took up her hands. "But this is wonderful news, surely. Oh, King must be so happy."

"He doesn't know." Mrs. Bolton's eyes filled with tears. "I only confirmed it myself this morning, though I suspected something was wrong when my courses stopped. I'm not so foolish as to think it couldn't happen at all, but with my age and how things have been...." Her tears started flowing down her cheeks. "His oldest child is *married*. And here I am, ready to announce a pregnancy before Dannie does. And what will this do to the ranch?" She sniffled, and Evelyn hurried to offer up a clean handkerchief to her friend.

"Dannie will be thrilled for you," Evelyn said fervently, unable to imagine anything else. The young woman had shown herself to be both practical and kind in all her interactions with Evelyn. "She is a good woman, as *you* raised her to be. King, too. How could he not be? I imagine the ranch is big enough to accommodate another little one, don't you? Everyone will adore your baby and be eager to congratulate you." She squeezed the hand she still held tighter.

Mrs. Bolton wiped at her eyes, and a trembly smile turned up the corners of her mouth. "I want this to be true. I can't help but feel...like I've tricked everyone, somehow. I was only supposed to be a wife. Not a mother. Not so late in life." She sniffled again. "I don't know why I'm burdening you with my troubles."

"Oh, Mrs. Bolton, do stop being hard on yourself. You have let me into your home, despite my situation, and offered my daughter and me safety." Evelyn rose from her knees and kissed Mrs. Bolton on the cheek. "You are perfectly capable of being a mother. I've known women who have had children late. Think of this as a surprise gift. You're going to have a baby. You must tell King, and soon. And Ruthie! You haven't told her yet, either, have you?"

Ducking her head, appearing shy for the first time since they met, Mrs. Bolton shook her head. "I cannot imagine what Ruthie will say. At my age, being surprised by a pregnancy."

"She will say everything I've said," Evelyn insisted. "And then she'll likely give you a thousand things to do to prepare for your baby. And offer good advice, too." Evelyn laughed and hugged her friend around the neck. "I'm so happy for you, Mrs. Bolton."

The woman returned the embrace, chuckling despite her happy tears. "After this chat, you must call me Beth. We are friends now."

"So we are." Evelyn stepped back and smiled broadly at Beth. "Thank you for confiding in me, Beth. I don't know that I deserve it. But I am honored you told me about the baby and what's in your heart."

"I could hardly hide it from you long." Beth wiped at her eyes again. "I imagine you would recognize the signs, as the only other woman living in this house right along with me." She put a hand over her abdomen. "Though you're right. I need to tell King and the rest of the family. There will be a great many changes ahead."

And though Beth smiled happily, appearing comforted as she left the room, Evelyn's thoughts turned uncomfortably inward. With the Boltons expecting an infant, that made her position as a guest turn tenuous.

Evelyn left her room, feeling less prepared than before for whatever the day and the neighbors might bring.

WAGON AFTER WAGON CAME AND WENT FROM THE MAIN HOUSE, starting almost as soon as folks considered the hour decent for visiting. The Sonoita community wasn't large. Seven ranching families made up the principal citizenry, and with their cowboys and ranch hands added to that, it made about eighty people within easy reach of one another. A bit further out, and there were farmers scattered here and there. If everyone who considered Sonoita a place to gather in times of need, worship, or for entertainment came together on the same day, there might be around a hundred adults present. Then the passels of children.

Chris leaned back in his chair on the porch, arms crossed, watching the road that led to the main house. It felt like everyone in twenty miles were trying to come to the ranch at the same time. All because they were curious about the new person in their midst.

Ben sat on the steps, reading the children's primer that Chris had bought for them. "Jane and Bill aren't very smart," he said, his nose wrinkled at the illustration of two children staring down at a dog. "They followed that dog into the woods and got lost. Now they have to wait for Youncil Fred—"

"Youncil?" Chris repeated the unfamiliar word and looked down at the book again, trying to find the combination of letters that had confused the boy. "Oh. *Uncle* Fred. The 'u' doesn't stretch out long in that word."

The boy wrinkled his nose. "Uncle?"

"Yep. Funny word, isn't it?" Chris looked up again as another wagon left the house. Evelyn and everyone else would be tuckered out after answering the same intrusive questions over and over again. And he'd noticed that some wagons stayed parked longer than others. Namely those that came with unattached men between the ages of twenty and fifty.

He scowled at that thought and pulled his hat down a little farther.

Laura came out the door and put her hands on her hips. "You

ready to go over there or not, Ben?" she asked, her tone bossier than a broody hen's. Reminding Chris of his own sister.

"I already said I'm not going." Ben's chin came out, but Chris noted the boy's eyes had widened briefly in alarm.

This wasn't the first time Laura had asked if Ben would go over to the house with her to meet more of the area's children as they came and went with their families. But Ben had firmly declared he didn't feel like meeting anyone new. And Laura wouldn't leave her little brother behind. The two hadn't left each other's company since their arrival at the ranch.

Chris suspected they were afraid if they were out of each other's sight for anything less than sleeping, they might not see each other again. No way around that fear except to get through it.

"All right. That's enough of that." Chris put his feet firmly on the ground and stood. He stretched his hands over his head and looked the kids over. They were both wearing their best clothes. Something Ruthie had suggested, to keep them trained up about what Sunday meant.

"Let's walk on over and see who might be on the front porch. You can be neighborly, Ben. Won't hurt you any."

Ben's little chin quivered a moment, but he snapped the book closed and stood. Then he held the dark blue covered primer against his chest like a shield. "If you're coming, Frosty, I guess it's fine."

They started walking. At least, Chris supposed, some might call their different ranges of motion walking. Laura skipped. Ben drug his feet. Chris ambled. Somehow, they made it around to the front of the big house.

A few children played beneath the shade of the Boltons' one and only tree. Laura squealed with delight and ran forward, and a moment later, Madeline stood up and held her arms out to catch the other girl in an embrace. The enthusiasm of the greeting made it look like they'd been apart for years rather than hours.

Ben looked up at Chris and heaved a sigh. "*Girls.*"

Chris chuckled and ruffled the boy's hair. "Go say hello. The Mason boys are over there. They're close to your age."

The boy gave a tight nod, squared his shoulders, and approached the group of children as though he went to the gallows. The kid just didn't seem to like people. Maybe all that quiet of his before had been because he hadn't liked Chris, either.

Chris glanced at the porch, not surprised to see Jessica Harper and Travis Bolton on the bench, with Clark leaning against the rail talking to the two of them. The two Masons that were near Clark's age were with them, all of them just shooting the breeze full of word-shaped holes.

Though his eyes flicked to the front door, Chris didn't approach. He had no intention of going in. While a foreman rated higher than a cowboy, employees of the ranches and farms knew that intruding on the family's get-togethers wasn't polite.

A cowboy or a foreman from another ranch might swing by for a visit without appearing rude. But it was rare. Except for today. Today, Chris counted four horses tied up to posts that he knew for a fact belonged to drovers on the Harper spread.

The front door opened, and Dannie came out on the arm of her husband. The two of them sauntered down the steps, Dannie shaking her head while her English husband appeared less than cheerful. They spotted Chris at the corner of the house, and Dannie shifted their path toward him.

"Frosty. Good afternoon." Duke's expression brightened somewhat. "I'm surprised you didn't venture over here earlier in the day."

"I don't usually intrude on the family's Sunday." Chris shrugged, then took his hat off to address Dannie. "Afternoon, Mrs. Rounsevell."

For a moment, she appeared pleased. "Are you trying to butter me up, Frosty? You know that's my favorite name."

"I figured as much." He made eye contact with Duke. The newlyweds were head-over-heels for one another. There likely wasn't a faster way to cheer Dannie up than to remind her she'd married the choice of her heart. "I don't think the dust on the road settled once this morning, with all the coming and going."

"Oh—Evan. Frosty can help." Dannie gave her husband's arm a quick shake, as though to emphasize her words.

"Help with what?" Chris replaced his hat, trying not to sound too suspicious.

Duke looked from his wife to Chris, his expression changing from surprised to thoughtful. "You might be right. Frosty, how would you like to rescue a damsel in distress?"

Chris blinked. "A what now?"

"Evelyn." Dannie's eyes narrowed to dangerous slits, like a rattler's about to strike. "The Masons' cowboys have her practically shoved in a corner, talking her ear off. She looks tired, too. Like she's ready to fall over."

"I find it hard to believe Evelyn—Mrs. Lyon, that is—would let anyone run roughshod over her." Chris looked to Duke for confirmation, but the man shook his head.

"I am afraid she's exceedingly polite. Evelyn is following all the rules of English socializing, but she's the only one in there who is. I've tried to free her twice, but she gets drawn right back in."

"We even invited her to come home with us." Dannie appeared somewhat pained. "But I didn't have much of a reason that required any get-up-and-go. So she stayed sitting where she was."

"Maybe she's enjoying the visit?" Chris hedged, glancing to where the kids were happily playing some kind of rock-stacking game in the shade.

The married couple exchanged a glance. "Doubtful," Dannie said at last. "Dad is in his study talking to the married men, and Beth disappeared a few minutes ago to show Mrs. Mason a new recipe in the kitchen."

"And then *you* abandoned her?" Chris looked at the door to the house. "Who's left in there with her?"

"Felicity, Robert, and Patrick Mason. And those cowboys."

Dannie released her husband and turned around. "Ugh, we gotta go back. Even if we look plumb foolish. Felicity's brothers are nearly as bad as the cow punchers."

Chris raised his hand to stop her. "I've got an idea. Pretty much the only thing that'll worry that lady more than being polite is her daughter." He went over to where Madeline and Laura were playing, and he crouched next to them.

"What's this you two made?" he asked, looking at the scattering of rocks.

"I'm trying to show Laura what the Tower of London castle looks like. I've been twice." Madeline huffed and adjusted a squared stone at one corner. "But I'm having trouble remembering things."

"Do you think your mother would know?" Chris asked.

"Oh, yes. Mother knows everything about London." Madeline looked over her shoulder at the house. "But she's busy right now."

Chris looked up at Dannie, who had stopped a few feet away. Then he pushed his hat up his forehead a bit and looked at Laura. "I bet she's not too busy to come help her daughter. Laura, would you go get Mrs. Lyon? Tell her Madeline needs her help for just a minute or two."

Laura didn't need to be asked twice. The natural obedience of children raised on farms and ranches was deeply ingrained. They had to listen, every time, because some things became a matter of life, death, or injury. The child jumped to her feet and dashed off into the house.

Madeline's eyes widened. "Oh, no." Her cheeks reddened as she looked up at Chris. "I used to get in terrible trouble for interrupting Mama. Children are supposed to be seen, not heard."

A frown tugged Chris's lips downward, but before he could remark on that bit of adult wisdom he'd heard a time or two in life, the front door opened again, and Laura came out holding Evelyn's hand.

"Madeline? Is something wrong?" The Englishwoman moved at a quick pace, though when she caught Chris's eye, she didn't look worried. Only curious. "Laura says you needed my help?"

He stood and gestured down. "We need your help with a map-making project." He looked over her shoulder, where he could see a couple of masculine faces pressed against the parlor window. Irritation made him bristle up. "In fact, I think we ought to find pencil and paper and do this properly. Don't you, Maddie?"

The little girl immediately abandoned her rocks, coming to her feet with a flounce of her skirts. "That's a splendid idea, Mr. Morgan."

"I have some. No use interrupting the Boltons to ask for theirs. Why don't we go back to my house?"

Ben was suddenly beside him, book still in hand. "I want to come, too." The kid had apparently had enough socializing.

"Sure thing. Mrs. Lyon?" He offered her his arm, trying not to smile too broadly. There wasn't anything subtle about this ploy, and it was completely up to Evelyn if she accepted the escape he offered.

She nibbled at her bottom lip, then took a quick glance toward the windows. She must've seen those eager faces watching, because she immediately took his arm. "That sounds lovely. Dannie, Evan, will you two join us?"

Chris had almost forgotten the couple still stood there, each of them grinning.

"Delighted to, Evelyn." Dannie looped her arm through her husband's. "Better walk fast, though, and get out of this heat." She made a show of fanning herself with her hand.

And just like that, Chris had company at his house for Sunday afternoon.

CHAPTER TWELVE

Duke and Dannie had left Chris's house half an hour ago, but Evelyn and Madeline remained sitting in his front room. The children had begged for more *Treasure Island*, and they had nearly come to the end of the book. Chris sat in the rocking chair, pretending to read a novel, but in reality, he listened to every word Evelyn read aloud.

She spoke with different voices, even different accents, for all the characters in the book. She read as though she performed the whole of it on a stage rather than before three children. It was no wonder they loved listening to her read. Chris did, too.

When she came to the last word of the second-to-last chapter, Evelyn closed the book. "There. We must save the very end for later."

A few groans met that statement, and Madeline slumped down where she sat.

"Now what do we do?" Ben asked.

Before Evelyn could answer and likely suggest she and Madeline return to the Bolton house, Chris spoke. "What about those cookies you wanted to make, Laura?"

The little girl straightened up. "Oh, yes! We've got everything to make them. Ruthie even wrote out the recipe. Do you want to bake with me and Ben?" She turned to Madeline and held her hands out, imploring her friend to say yes. "We can take a few to Abram and Ruthie to say thanks, too."

Madeline, perhaps sensing her mother's intention to leave, was on her feet instantly. "That is a lovely idea. I've never made biscuits before."

"Cookies," Ben corrected politely, also rushing to his feet. "I want to put in the raisins!" With that, all three children were gone before Evelyn could form any sort of argument against the idea.

The gleam in her eye said well-enough that she knew what he'd done with his simple suggestion. "Why are you so determined to have the children bake?"

"Laura's pretty good at cookies, if I get the oven temperature right." He grinned at her, not precisely answering her question. "Why don't I go do that? I'll be right back." He didn't spend long starting the fire in the small brick oven. The children didn't even acknowledge him. They were too busy piling ingredients onto the table. As soon as he'd done the job, he returned to the parlor.

Evelyn had risen from her chair to explore his bookshelves again. She ran one finger along the spines, her lips forming the words as she read the titles. He leaned a shoulder against the wall near the bookcase, folding his arms as he watched her.

"You have an impressive collection. I never thought to find some of these titles so far from civilization." The crooked smile she sent his way made his heart stutter.

It was time to ask Evelyn to marry him. He felt it in his gut. The proposal didn't need to be romantic, just practical. Given that they'd passed an easy afternoon together with the children, in exactly the circumstances that he hoped for should they wed, it presented him the best possible example to explain how it would be.

Baking had distracted the children in the kitchen. He could hear their voices as they worked together to measure out the ingredients. They wouldn't interrupt. And Evelyn appeared relaxed.

But he felt like a man springing a trap rather than attempting to put forth a practical solution to both their problems.

"Oh dear. I cannot say I like the cloud overshadowing your expression." Evelyn stepped nearer, making him blink back into the present. A smile teased at her lips. "Have I insulted you terribly?"

"Nope." He shifted his weight, standing to his full height. "Just thinking." He needed to start talking, though, before he lost his nerve. "I actually have something I'd like to speak to you about. Ask you about. If you'd like to sit down?" He gestured to the couch.

"Of course." Evelyn returned to the couch, fluffed her skirts, and sat so they settled gracefully around her. All her movements were like that—graceful, and naturally so. That made him feel all the more like an awkward, long-legged colt when he lowered himself to the couch next to her, a good foot of empty air between them.

"I suppose the first thing I should say is that I'm well-aware this is going to take you by surprise, but please know I've been thinking on the subject for some time. You're an intelligent woman, Evelyn, and I respect what you've been through and what you're trying to do for yourself and your daughter."

For the first time, her smile faltered. "This does sound serious." She folded her hands together in her lap and angled her body to face him more fully. "You have my full attention. I'm listening, Chris."

He waited for a sick feeling to overcome him, for any kind of premonition or even a warning from on High that this was a terrible idea. Lightning strikes or indigestion would work as a sign. Instead, a calmness settled upon him, with the same soothing weight of a warm quilt on a cold winter's night.

"I've never felt as lost as I did when Laura and Ben showed up." His throat closed over the words, and he had to clear it before speaking again. "I don't know how to be a father. I'm determined to try, though. I want to provide them with everything they need for a happy childhood. I want to prepare them to go into the world, too, and accomplish whatever it is they set out to accomplish."

He waited for her nod. Her lovely eyes had softened, too. Then Chris went on. "When you came into my house that first time, you changed everything. Ben barely spoke before. Laura didn't smile at all. You have a way about you—it's more than being a mother yourself, I can tell. It's something unique to you, Evelyn. You're gifted with children. Probably with most people, too."

Her cheeks reddened and she lowered her eyes. "I only read a story to them, Chris."

How could he explain that he'd seen more than that? "I've seen your kindness to them. Even though you're as lost as I was about what comes next, you're still compassionate and gentle. You're reaching out to make a difference to others." He was talking too much. Drifting from the purpose at hand.

The fewer the words the better.

"I was thinking we could help each other. That instead of going back east to start over with strangers, for your daughter to live at a school, you two could stay here." He held his breath and watched her carefully, certain her initial reaction couldn't and wouldn't be favorable. "Instead of leaving, you could marry me."

EVELYN HAD RIDDEN ON A TRAIN WITH HER FATHER AS A YOUNG girl. She'd watched the countryside go by from the window, amazed at the speed of their travel. Then, without warning, the conductor had put on the brakes. The whole train had jolted, slowed, and jolted again—and Evelyn had been knocked out of her seat onto the floor. Along with most of the other passengers.

Frosty's suggestion gave her that same feeling of being thrown from her seat—a shock that left her momentarily speechless.

Though she certainly remained still as a statue on his couch and outwardly calm.

She needed to say something. Anything.

"You barely know me," she said, voice low so as not to carry farther than his ears. "I'm a stranger to you. To this place."

A third marriage proposal. Had she even dreamed such a thing possible? No. Of course not. And, just as the first two times men had asked her to wed, marrying would solve several of her problems. Except she hadn't ever wanted to rely on a man, no matter how kindly intentioned, to provide for her future again.

He gave one slow nod. "And yet you're managing just fine. You haven't complained about learning new things. You volunteered to do my laundry."

"And turned everything pink," she reminded him, feeling her cheeks warm. "Surely, if it's a wife you need, there are women more suited to life on a ranch."

Her first husband had saved her from living as a pauper with relatives who didn't want the burden of keeping her. He'd promised to care for her for the rest of her life. The earl had saved Evelyn and Madeline from destitution, and he had promised Madeline would have an education and dowry to ensure her future. That both men died without fulfilling their promises haunted her, impacting every breath she took.

Chris watched her with those calm blue eyes of his. "You're the one who helped Ben and Laura, not anyone else. And Madeline has made a difference, too."

He sounded as though he saw value in her as a person. Of course, most men of Evelyn's acquaintance had made it quite clear she held the same appeal to them as any pretty bauble would. They wanted her as they wanted something shiny to set upon a shelf or hang upon their watch-chain. An attractive wife had been all any of the others had wanted.

Yet Chris had never, even once, made her feel like her looks mattered. He'd hardly seemed to notice them, truth be told. He spoke to her, to Dannie, to Mrs. Bolton, all with the same respect.

As though he'd heard her thoughts, Chris tapped his fingers on the arm of the couch. "I know I'm not much to look at, and I'm not wealthy like an English lord or gentleman. But I've been putting money aside since I was a boy running errands for my parents' restaurant, saving for the future. Foremen aren't paid poorly, either." He didn't quite smile, but she heard the pride in his voice as he spoke. "I can swear that if anything ever happened to you, I'd raise Maddie the way you wanted, too. Because life isn't predictable out here."

The children laughed in the kitchen, their youthful voices bursting with glee. A strange contrast to the seriousness of Chris's proposal.

Evelyn had momentarily forgotten that the three of them were in the next room.

"I've had men make promises to me before," she whispered as she clasped her hands tightly together. Why was she still sitting here? Why hadn't she told him off and left?

Evelyn looked out the window of the front room, the slight swells of desert hills covered in long dry grass the only sight from her vantage point. She'd been silent too long. Yet Chris didn't seem in any kind of rush. He wasn't pressing her for an answer like her first husband had, nor had he smugly assumed she would say yes, the way the earl had.

His proposal wasn't at all romantic. But it wasn't as business-like as the previous two had been, either. In fact, Chris made it sound as though *he* needed *her* as much, if not more, than she needed him.

Chris studied her, his expression earnest and his posture relaxed. "If it's my character you're worried about, you can ask anyone you want about me. Write my family back in Missouri. Find out if I'm a man of my word. I don't gamble. I don't drink. I'm not a womanizer. I go to church when the preacher's in town. I even read my bible most nights." Here his voice lowered, his gaze becoming more intense. "I want you to think about it as long as you need to. It's a big decision."

Her past suffocated her with memories of broken promises and indifference, cold silences, and arrogant smirks. An answer rose to the tip of her tongue—a harsh one.

Madeline appeared in the doorway with a swirl of a borrowed apron and skirts. "Mama, come see the cookies! We made faces with the raisins." She giggled and turned around again without waiting for a response.

Chris looked over his shoulder at the kitchen doorway, then to Evelyn, and he stood up. His movement broke through the cold spell that had seized control of Evelyn's thoughts. "Guess we'd better go admire their efforts." He held his hand out to her.

Evelyn looked down at his palm, noting the callouses on his fingers and the sun-bronzed tan below his wrist. She slid her hand into his. And despite the work-roughened texture of his skin, the strength in his hands, his grip was gentle. His hand was warm. The touch dispelled the last of the past's grip upon her. He helped her up from the couch, then immediately released her and gestured for her to lead the way to the kitchen.

Despite the turmoil within her mind and the building worry in her heart, Evelyn smiled brightly at the three children as they showed how they'd pressed the raisins into the dough to form eyes, noses, and mouths. Or made stripes and other patterns. They'd used twice as many raisins as the cookies needed, too.

Chris slid the trays of cookies into the oven, closing the door carefully. Then he checked his watch and announced they'd come back to see how the cookies were doing in a few minutes.

"Until then, I'm challenging Ben to a game of marbles. You ladies want to play?"

"How do you play a game with marbles?" Madeline asked.

Laura hurried back into the front of the house, calling over her shoulder, "We'll teach you."

Somehow, Evelyn was swept along to the front room again. Laura and Chris made a circle on the floor with a thin piece of thread. Evelyn sat on the couch and pretended to watch the game, and though her eyes were on the four of them sitting and lying on the ground to shoot marbles, her mind was on Chris. On his offer.

He'd pushed up his shirtsleeves to his elbows and settled on the rug, laying on his chest with his long legs stretched out behind him. He didn't seem to mind playing on the floor with the children. He patiently instructed Madeline on the game's rules. He helped Ben line up most of his shots. For all that he said he didn't know what he was doing or how to act as a father, Evelyn thought he had a better handle on what the job entailed than either of the men she'd married before.

CHAPTER THIRTEEN

"**I**s Chris Morgan a good man?"

Mrs. Bolton didn't even flinch when Evelyn threw the question at her the next morning over their sewing. Ruthie raised her eyebrows, but her fingers kept flying down the hem of a dress for Madeline. It was Dannie who spoke first.

"I knew you were bursting to ask a question as soon as those kids went out the door. I can't say I expected that one."

Mrs. Bolton adjusted the spectacles on her nose and inspected the cuff of one of her husband's shirts. "I can't say I'm entirely surprised. You've spent nearly as much time at Frosty's house as you have in this one since your arrival."

"Sounds like you ought to have your own opinion by now," Ruthie said, leaning back in the comfortable parlor chair. She folded her arms over her chest and settled her gaze on Evelyn.

"Perhaps. Yet a fortnight is hardly enough time to *know* a man, isn't it? All of you have the benefit of having known him for several years." Evelyn looked at each of them feeling almost desperate in her need for more information.

She blamed her lack of subtlety on her lack of sleep the night before. She'd lain awake for hours in bed, thinking through Chris's proposal. She'd compared it to the others she had received in her life, turning each word over carefully. Inspecting them all for some hidden meaning. Yet he'd spoken plainly enough that she found nothing nefarious in his words. As she'd rehearsed to herself all the reasons marrying again would be an exceptionally poor idea, she couldn't help considering all the good points to the idea.

Mrs. Bolton put the infant gown she worked on in her lap. It seemed she'd told the family. Given the way Dannie kept glancing her direction with a gentle smile, the woman didn't mind her stepmother's pregnancy in the slightest. "I've known him since he started working here as a hand, when Abram still worked as the foreman. What is it you want to know, Evelyn?"

"Does he have a history of kindness? Honesty?" She had dozens of questions, but how many could she ask before she would need to confess the reason behind her inquiry?

Ruthie put her work aside, too. "I've never known him to so much as stretch a tale." She pointed one finger at Evelyn. "As to kindness, you know well enough his good nature brought you here."

"I do. I'm most grateful, too. For all of you showing us compassion." Evelyn's smile felt weak to her. Perhaps she should simply tell them what he had proposed.

Evelyn hesitated, though. She wanted to make her own decision. Yet despite that desire, certain truths remained inescapable.

The world they inhabited meant men had more rights and privileges than a woman. It didn't matter that a queen ruled England, or that women had started voicing their opinions in newspapers around the world. The law favored men in every way. Society favored men. As a lone woman with a daughter and no male protector, the world became not only uncomfortable but exponentially more dangerous.

"Frosty's a good man," Dannie reiterated. "He's quiet. But he's thoughtful when he's quiet. He doesn't rush to say whatever he's thinking. He takes his time. I've heard cowboys say enough foolishness to fill a library full of books. But not Frosty." She lifted one shoulder and jabbed a needle through the stiff cloth they'd chosen to make Evelyn a split skirt.

Evelyn lowered her gaze to her work once more. Did she tell them? Would that be fair to Chris, to share their business before she had made up her mind? If she said no, she didn't want him to lose face. She didn't want the women who had been so friendly to her to turn against her, either, if they thought so highly of Chris and she rejected him.

Ruthie chuckled to herself, her gaze traveling to the window. "First time they rode together, Abram in the chuck wagon of course, he told me that Frosty put his nose into a book every time the men stopped moving. Abram thought he was shy or didn't get on well with the others. But when Frosty opened his mouth, everyone listened."

Though Evelyn's own experience with Chris had proven he spoke well, his reticence to speak made her wonder what all he thought and *didn't* say.

"That reminds me," Evelyn said, sensing an opportunity to change the subject that she had introduced with a lack of fore-thought. "We are going to start reading Lewis Carrol's *Through the Looking Glass*. Would Lee like to come over before dinner to listen with the other children?"

Evelyn bit her tongue, realizing the invitation she'd extended to a house not her own sounded entirely too familiar, even if it felt completely natural. Perhaps that ought to mean something.

Ruthie gave the question a moment of consideration. "He might enjoy that. I know he loves the way you talk, Evelyn. He follows Duke around from time to time, just to listen to him."

Dannie grinned outright. "I have to admit, sometimes I do the same thing." All the ladies laughed, and the conversation mean-dered in a different direction.

"Have you ever met the queen?" Mrs. Bolton asked. "Duke has told us a bit about her, but as a man, he didn't notice some of the details I'd be interested in knowing."

Evelyn's smile tightened. "I met her once, after my second

marriage. Due to my husband's title, it was expected that I be formally introduced. I only received a moment with Her Majesty." And a cold moment it had been. Gossip had obviously reached the court before Evelyn had. Everyone knew the queen's stance on morality and marriage. Evelyn had married almost exactly one year after her first husband's death—and had been accused of using feminine wiles to tempt the earl into a proposal. "There isn't much I can tell you."

The other women picked up on her reluctance to discuss the queen, and Ruthie clicked her tongue against the roof of her mouth. "Can you imagine if every important person had to go to the White House and be introduced to the President? Or the First Lady?"

"We need more important people in Arizona going to the capitol," Mrs. Bolton said. "It'd be nice to be a state instead of a territory. We could get more of a voice in politics. Maybe even the right to vote."

The other two nodded as though this opinion was well understood by them. Evelyn remained quiet. She tucked a pleat and pinned it into place. Mrs. Bolton had a treadle sewing machine to finish the dress. It made the work go easier, to do the cutting and piecing, all the pinning, first and then run things through the machine after. Evelyn hadn't ever seen a machine like that at work until the previous week when she'd watched Mrs. Bolton feed yard after yard beneath the pulsing needle.

"After we finish putting together a suitable rancher's wardrobe for Evelyn," Dannie said, a wide grin on her face, "we need to piece a quilt for the new Bolton baby."

Beth blushed, despite her age, and lowered her eyes to the small garment in her hands. "I was thinking about how lovely it would be to make new blankets and such for the baby. I've always been partial to yellows in a nursery."

A nursery. A new baby. A sliver of worry went through Evelyn's heart. In a few months' time, Beth would be a mother. A very special time in any woman's life, but likely more so considering how long she'd had to wait for that blessed event.

Despite being welcomed into the home, Evelyn and Madeline would be intruders at such an important time for the family. She took up a room, and took up time, of a woman who had more than enough to worry about without having a perpetual guest living in her home.

Evelyn had already learned so much. Washing clothes, baking bread, preparing vegetables for a stew, and sewing clothes rather than embroidering useless frippery had made her feel acutely the uselessness of her life before.

Now she had a growing desire, a hunger, for keeping herself useful. Spending hours sitting with a group of ladies discussing fashion or tittering over who had worn what to a ball or dinner the evening before had always felt like a waste of energy to her. What purpose did it serve to fill the hours and minutes of the day with talk of things that wouldn't matter when the next ball or dinner provided entirely new fodder for gossip?

If she went in search of a teaching position, perhaps that would fill her need to be useful. Training girls in the gentle graces of womanhood would surely provide her a sense of achievement. Except. Except that position meant preparing the next generation of ladies to sit about in parlors, embroidering cushions, speaking ill of their neighbors in French, and finding the pinnacle of their achievement in marrying a man whose social status was equal to or better than their own.

"...isn't that right, Evelyn?" Dannie's question interrupted Evelyn's horrid line of thought.

Evelyn felt heat seep into her cheeks. "I beg your pardon, my mind wandered away. What did you ask?"

Beth adjusted the spectacles on her nose. "Evelyn, dear, you look as though you've just faced some sort of disappointment. Is something the matter?"

The front door opened, saving Evelyn from an immediate answer, and Madeline came hurrying into the room. A reminder to walk like a lady rose to the tip of Evelyn's tongue, but her daughter's excited smile froze the words before they escaped her.

"Mama, Mr. Morgan said the kittens in the hayloft are old enough for us to visit them now. May we go to the barn and play with them? Please?" Madeline danced from foot to foot.

"I don't know." Evelyn looked to Beth. "Is it safe?"

"Quite safe. But we can ask Clark to go with them, if that makes you feel better." She raised her voice so it would carry to the study. "Clark?"

In seconds the boy appeared at the doorway. "Yes, ma'am?"

"Could you take a break from your studies and take the little ones to the barn? They want to play with the kittens in the loft." Beth asked kindly, no hint of demand in her tone. Clark could obviously deny the request.

"I'm at a good point to do that. Just finished biology for the day." He grinned and went to the mirrored hat tree on the wall. He selected a wide-brimmed straw hat. "C'mon, Maddie. Let's go find us some cats."

She went through the front door ahead of him, already talking with great excitement about the number of kittens.

"Clark is a good-natured boy," Evelyn remarked, leaning back a little in her chair. "What is it he hopes to do after university?"

"He's talked about helping with the ranch," Dannie answered, putting aside her things. "The three of us Bolton kids each inherit a share, and Lee will, too, if he wants it. Duke has a smaller percentage that we're considering selling to Frosty. That would keep the two of us from having a controlling share, which I know makes Travis a bit uncomfortable."

"Your father is willing to divide the inheritance?" Evelyn blinked rapidly. She hadn't heard of this plan yet. She had assumed that Travis, the eldest son, would inherit everything. He had an obvious love for the land, and that was the way of things in England.

"Why wouldn't he?" Ruthie looked up at Dannie. "If you're about to get lemonade, I wouldn't say no to some."

146

Dannie chuckled. "You know me too well. Beth? Evelyn? Would either of you like a glass of lemonade?"

Beth accepted with a nod, and Evelyn responded, "That would be lovely, thank you."

Evelyn turned her attention to Ruthie's question. "In England, only the eldest son inherits. Most of the time. In rare cases, daughters receive estates or money, but usually they only have their dowry to recommend them before their parents' death, and after, they receive only the money their parents thought to put aside for them."

"Women here can inherit anything," Ruthie said evenly. "I don't think King would feel right, just handing Dannie a purse of money and nothing else. She's been raised on the ranch, same as those boys of his. And Abram took financial risk as a partner early on. If Lee wants to ranch, he'll get his stake when he's old enough."

If only Madeline had been given even half as much—by her father or stepfather.

Evelyn cleared her throat and tried to rejoin the conversation. "Will Lee go to university, too?" Evelyn asked his grandmother.

Ruthie lifted her chin, the fiery pride in her eyes. "That he will, God willing. Abram has subscribed to university papers and journals for years, to find the right fit. There is a Black professor at the Tuskegee Institute in Alabama who has been so kind to answer our questions about what to teach our boy to prepare him. Professor Du Bois. He has suggested we prepare Lee for the University of Pennsylvania."

"Lee is exceptionally bright," Mrs. Bolton put in. "He'll do real well for himself. Travis and Clark have promised to tutor him when they come home from Baylor for holidays."

Dannie reentered the room, carrying a tray of lemonade glasses and a crystal pitcher filled with more. "Sometimes, I think I disappointed Daddy a bit by not going from finishing school to a college of some sort." She handed a glass to each of them and caught Evelyn's surprised expression. "Do women not go to college in England? I felt sure they did."

"Well, yes. Some do. But the general opinion is that only those with no hope of a good marriage would spend time on obtaining a degree." Evelyn sipped at the lemonade; immediately pleased with the taste, she took a bigger swallow.

"That's how a few people see it here, too." Dannie retook her seat and swirled her glass in one hand, a grin on her face. "Daddy wanted all of us to get the most education we could. But I hated being away from home. It wasn't for me. And the University of Arizona, in Tucson, is still too new for Daddy to trust what they teach."

"Your father isn't the least bit disappointed in you, Dannie. How could he be? You're smart as a whip and as capable of running this ranch as any man working it today." Beth gave an approving nod to her stepdaughter. "I've heard your father say so." She turned to Evelyn. "Would you want Madeline to go to a university?"

"I have never considered that option." Evelyn looked down into the yellow-tinted water in her glass. She turned the idea over in her mind, thinking of Madeline's cleverness with a new swell of hope. Maybe...maybe in this place where women could dream of such a thing, she could find a way for Madeline to obtain an education of that sort. "If that's what she wanted. Someday. Perhaps."

Would that path be available to her daughter on a teacher's small salary? A finishing school might be the right place to prepare to find a husband. But would it do for a girl who might have other dreams to chase? Likely not.

Evelyn looked at the women sitting around her, taking in their pleasant expressions, their friendly way of talking, and their perfectly fine manners. They didn't gossip about their neighbors. They spoke intelligently of the world around them and their hopes for the future. They never boasted about the men in their lives. The contentedness with which they faced their chores each day, and their kindness to a stranger in their midst, filled an ache in Evelyn's heart she hadn't allowed herself to notice before.

And she wanted more of this. For herself and for Madeline. She could have it, too. If she accepted Chris's proposal. She could learn from these women. Make room for new hopes and dreams for Madeline's future.

Evelyn hadn't ever believed in fate. Perhaps it was time she believed in something else, though. And that Something had guided her to this place, to show her what her life had lacked, and to give her the opportunity to provide her daughter with something better.

Chris enjoyed sitting on the rocking chair on his porch, watching the sky as the sun set behind the house. Arizona sunsets were always beautiful in a way he didn't think he had the words to explain. Dannie Bolton had once told him no one back east believed the sky could turn a hundred shades of purple and orange in the minutes before darkness overtook the night sky. He didn't blame them. He wouldn't believe it if he hadn't seen it a thousand times himself.

Tonight, he'd opted to watch the stars appear rather than the sun's brilliant disappearance. So he faced east, watching the sky darken to a blue-black that he didn't have a name for, and the stars appeared first one at a time and then with greater speed. It was half past six, and he could hear Laura and Ben in the room behind him laughing as they played marbles. He smiled to himself, tilted back in his chair with his boots kicked up on the railing.

The children still had long stretches of silence, and he'd seen flashes of pain and loneliness in their eyes, but there were more smiles. A lot more smiles. Whether Evelyn could see it or not, she'd wrought a miracle for those kids just by being present in their lives. Maybe she could do the same for *him*, too.

Not that he'd let himself dwell on that aspect of a marriage too much. No need to get his hopes up, or to start thinking about the beautiful Englishwoman in anything more than a friendly way. Not unless she said yes. Because if she said yes, if she agreed to be his wife, that would change everything.

Yes, she possessed a stunning beauty. He'd never seen her equal, with that blazing coppery hair and her eyes that shone like emeralds. She looked like an angel, but not the sort that sat idly playing a harp. He could picture her holding a shield and sword or pointing at some poor misguided soul and calling upon them to change their ways. That imagined scene came from the iron he sensed in her soul and the strength he'd seen in her character.

He admired her. But he had to leave it there. At least for now.

A swinging light caught the corner of his eye, coming from the direction of the main house. He turned his head, wondering who was coming his direction when all the chores were done, and the main house folks would likely be sitting down to dinner.

Then his boots hit the porch with a thud.

He knew that tall, slender form quite well by now. The shine of red hair reflecting the lantern light only reaffirmed his recognition. Evelyn Lyon walked toward him, lantern held high, head tilted down to watch her step in the dark grass.

Chris rose from his chair and stepped down from the porch. Then he waited.

As she neared, Evelyn looked up, and he saw the hesitant smile form upon her lovely face. When she was only a few feet away, she at last spoke. "Good evening, Chris." Did he imagine the slight tremble in her voice when she said his name?

"Evening, Evelyn." Chris held his hand out for her lantern, which she gave to him without hesitation. He turned and hung it upon a small hook at the porch's support beam. "What brings you out here after dark?" he asked, taking his time in turning back around. "Come to see the kids?"

"No, actually." She clasped her hands before her, tight against her waist. Today she wore the red and white gingham again, with a dark gray shawl around her shoulders against the cooling night air. "I came to see you."

His stomach flipped, and his heart gave an insistent thump against his chest before beating at a faster tempo. "Would you care to sit down?" He gestured to the porch, rocking chair and stools in place behind the railing.

"No. I wouldn't want the children to see and come out to interrupt. Not this evening." She looked from the soft light coming from the window back to him.

"Sounds serious." Chris realized he still wore his hat. He took it off and tossed it to the rocking chair, then faced her with what he hoped was an encouraging smile, despite his uncertainty.

Evelyn twisted her fingers together, but her eyes stayed upon him. "I've come to discuss your proposal. So, yes. It is quite serious."

He cleared his throat and stepped closer. He had to make sure she understood his feelings on the matter. He couldn't have her deciding out of pity or some misguided gratitude for what little he'd done to show her kindness.

"Listen, before you say anything, I want you to know something important. Just in case I didn't make myself clear before. I respect you, Evelyn. What you've already done for Laura and Ben, for me, is enough that I'll be a friend to you for life. You don't have to worry about hurting my feelings any. As much as I think we could be good for the three kids together, maybe even good for each other, I'd never want you to do something that makes you unhappy."

And how could she really be happy in the desert, given that she'd been in the finest houses in England? The doubts swarmed in his head like horseflies, irritating him, making him twitch, but he couldn't banish them.

She tilted that graceful chin of hers up. "You sound as though you think I'm here to say no."

He forced out a sound that was somewhere between a laugh and a groan. "Aren't you?" Despite going over all the reasons his offer had made sense, he'd not let himself hope for a positive answer from her.

Evelyn stopped fidgeting with her hands, dropping them to her side and balling both into fists. Her eyes gleamed in the lantern light, and she took a step closer. They were only a foot apart now. She didn't have to raise her head much to meet his eyes, and he liked that. Had from the first time they'd stood looking at each other in Bisbee.

"I've given the matter a lot of thought. I have an answer for you."

It had only been a *day*. He'd fully expected her to take a week or more to consider marrying him. The fact that she'd arrived at a conclusion so early had to mean she'd decided to say no.

"Though the answer is conditional..." His heart flipped. Something he'd never thought the word *conditional* might do. "I am saying yes to your proposal. I'll marry you."

And just like that, a dam he'd built up around his thoughts and feelings regarding Evelyn Lyon, Countess of Tyneham, burst open. He'd not let himself admire more than her mind. He'd not let himself think of her as more than a guest at the ranch. A friend. But here, at this sudden alteration in their future relationship, everything changed.

Evelyn ducked her head, and in the low light of the lantern, he detected the faintest color appearing in her cheeks. Maybe he should've held back his grin, which stretched his cheeks wider than he'd been accustomed to of late. There hadn't been much to smile about before now.

He lowered his voice, willing her to hear the sincerity behind his words. "Thank you, Evelyn. I promise, I'll do everything in my power to make you and Madeline happy and comfortable."

She gave a sharp nod and didn't quite meet his eyes again when she spoke. "I thought you should know. It didn't seem right to keep you waiting. We can discuss more details tomorrow. Good night." She turned away and started walking.

"Evelyn," Chris called, taking the lantern down again and

following her. "You forgot something." He held the lantern out. He wanted to walk her back, see her safely onto the porch and through the door of the Bolton house. But she seemed to want to get away from him as fast as possible.

The pink in her cheeks was even darker as she accepted the lantern, her fingers brushing his as she took the loop at the top of the light in her grasp. "Thank you."

"Of course. Can we speak tomorrow morning?"

Her gaze darted up to his. "What about your ranch duties?"

"They'll keep, and an advantage to being foreman is that I can delegate a few of them." He put his hands in his pockets, watching her with interest and admiration. She'd said *yes*. The astoundingly beautiful and entirely captivating woman had said yes, when by rights she belonged in a castle somewhere across the ocean.

"Very well. I'll be over directly after breakfast." She took a backward step. "Good night, Chris."

"Good night, Evelyn."

She spun on her heel and hurried away, the lantern swinging before her with her haste. He smiled to himself, then heaved a sigh of relief. He wouldn't be alone anymore. Not to raise the children on his own, not to pass the days and nights without a partner. And the woman who'd agreed to be that partner—she had impossibly agreed to be his wife.

Chris retraced his steps to the porch, fetched his hat, and took one last look at the stars. It was dark enough now that the wide path cut through the sky by the Milky Way was within sight. A river of stars flowing through the heavens, the sight had always tugged a sense of reverence from his heart. He looked toward the main ranch house, and he saw that lantern bobbing nearer the porch. He watched until the distant door opened and shut, and then he relaxed.

Evelyn had made it back safely.

He walked into his own house, a lightness in his heart as he knelt to join Laura and Ben at their game. They welcomed him more easily now than they would've even a week before. Soon enough, they'd spend their evenings with Madeline and Evelyn, too. All five of them. As a family.

He didn't give much thought to Evelyn's mysterious conditions. Whatever it was she wanted, he'd do his best to give it to her.

CHAPTER FOURTEEN

Evelyn sat at Chris Morgan's table the next morning, her hands folded upon the table. "It's about the children," she said with hesitation. "I have been thinking about Madeline's future, and I want to be certain you understand how important that is to me. After we marry, I'll feel the same about Laura, too. I'm sure you've got ideas for Ben. Especially if you get a stake in this ranch or someday have one of your own. But I want both of us to promise we will give the children every opportunity to advance in this life. Even the girls." She pulled in a deep breath.

Chris folded his arms across his chest and considered her with a puzzled expression. "I'm not sure I understand what it is you're saying, Evelyn."

"College," she blurted out at last. "For all three, if they want it. And...and any others that may come along." Her cheeks burned, and she suspected every one of her freckles had vanished beneath her blush. "No one ever expected me to want or need more education. But if we can find a way to provide it for the children—boys and girls both—I would be grateful."

"I barely finished the eighth grade."

Her gaze snapped up to his again. Did this mean he didn't see a reason for greater education? Her insides twisted.

"I'll send every kid who wants to go to a university, Evelyn. I can promise you that." The firmness of his answer surprised her, and the doubt slipped away again. "You have my word."

Madeline could go to college. A university, perhaps.

Evelyn lowered her gaze to her lap, overcome with relief. Despite the generosity of the Boltons and the others who lived on the ranch, she had known her position as a guest couldn't last forever. All she could do was hope someone would take her on as a teacher, allowing her to keep her daughter with her. Each day that passed was another day of her being a burden upon people who had taken her in out of kindness, a kindness that was impossible for her ever to repay.

As a wife, she could work and earn her child a place in the world in a different way. Chris had promised. And that meant everything to her.

Chris covered the hand she'd left upon the table with his own. His hand was much larger than hers. Stronger. She could feel the callouses on the edges of his fingers where they rested atop her skin, and they served as reminders that he was a far different man from any she had known before. He worked with his hands, his labor physically taxing, to provide for himself and anyone under his care.

His already deep voice went an octave lower, his declarations weighed with earnest intent. "I promise to take care of all of you, Evelyn. You and the children. You're my family from here on out."

She choked out a soft laugh. "I only hope you aren't too disappointed with the little that I bring to this arrangement. I've never been a housekeeper before. There's so much I need to learn."

His hand squeezed hers gently. "You're an intelligent lady, Evie. You'll learn what you need to learn."

Evie. Had anyone ever called her that before? Not that she could recall. And something about the way he said it...something about it struck her as familiar, right. "Evie?" she repeated aloud.

"Do you mind?" His deep voice went soft, as did her heart. Which was dangerous. One ought not to allow one's heart into an arrangement like this. It could only lead to trouble.

He drew her hand a little closer to him, prompting her to lock up and meet the smile in his eyes. "You're bringing a whole lot to this arrangement. You're bringing yourself. And Maddie. Your mothering and the understanding that they desperately need."

Watching him carefully, letting his words sink into her heart, Evelyn allowed him to reassure her. She nodded, pulling in a deep breath and releasing it shakily. "Thank you, Chris." Evelyn needed to clear the air around them. Everything had grown too heavy. Too emotionally charged. She leaned closer to him, not taking her hand back yet. "Do you think you could tell me your secret, now?"

His eyebrows lowered and he frowned. "Secret? I don't have any—"

"Your name." Evelyn grinned when his eyes widened with realization, and she had the pleasure of watching him falter for a moment. "You wouldn't tell me before. Only that Chris is short for something else. I'll find out soon, you realize, given that your legal name will be on our marriage license."

"I guess you'll find out when we get married, then." He released her hand and pushed away from the table. "Coffee?"

Whatever could his Christian name be, that he would put off telling her? She let the matter rest, relieved that the question had done as she'd intended, and brought them out of the emotional depths of their conversation. She accepted coffee with grace, and Chris returned to the table with the more businesslike question of when they would go to Tombstone to see to their courtroom marriage.

"Will we bring the children with us, or leave them here?" Evelyn asked between sips of her coffee.

Chris retook his seat at the table, leaning back a little in his chair. "It's a long trip, even if we can do both ways in a day. Doesn't seem fair to make the kids sit in the back of the wagon for hours on end. But we'll do as you think is best."

While the idea of bringing the children tempted Evelyn, she thought of that long wagon ride from Bisbee to the ranch. Asking children to make a similar journey, then sit still in law offices and a courtroom, didn't seem all that fair. It certainly wouldn't be exciting for them so much as it would be a chore. Evelyn nodded at last. "You're right. I think they should stay here. I can ask Ruthie or Dannie to keep an eye on them."

A long moment of silence passed as Evelyn realized that there were conversations of an important nature in her future. "How will we tell everyone?" she asked, lowering her cup to the table. "And what will they think?" Because that mattered to her.

Beth, Ruthie, and Dannie had become her friends. They knew some of the less savory details of her previous marriages. Would they think her a weakling to choose marriage a third time to get herself out of trouble?

"I'm betting they'll be pleased you'll be around for the long term." That's when she caught the way one corner of his mouth tugged upward, the not-quite-smile lessening the weight of the topic.

"Of course." She put her hands in her lap, holding them together as tightly as she held herself. Would Chris think it cowardly for her to ask that they present the news together? Evelyn tucked a loose strand of hair behind her ear, meeting Chris's gaze. "Still. I wouldn't want to explain things the wrong way. They need to know that this is an arrangement of mutual benefit and agreement. Not something...something that it isn't." She had almost said the word *romantic*.

Evelyn had long since given up on ever having anything that resembled a romance. Or a love story. No, she had a far more practical frame of mind. One could hardly concern herself over flowers and chocolates when daily survival was a legitimate concern.

"Do you want me to come to the Bolton house tonight, to tell everyone?" Chris lowered his chair back down to all four legs. "That'll give you time to think on it. Change your mind, maybe." Though he said it with a self-depreciating sort of smile, Evelyn saw the caution in his clear blue eyes.

Why would he worry? She knew as well as he did that marriage to one another was the best option. So long as he kept his word.

"Yes, I think that would be best. That will give me time to explain to Madeline, too." Evelyn took a last sip of her cooling drink, then stood up. "Thank you, Chris. For everything. I'll see you this evening?"

"Yes, ma'am." He had come to his feet when she had, that uncertain look gone from his expression. "At six, if that's all right."

"Of course. I'll mind the children until you're done with work." She went to the door to the front room. The children were all playing in Laura's room.

"Evelyn?"

She turned and looked over her shoulder at him, pausing where she stepped but not turning.

"Thank you for saying yes." With that, he gave her a smile that made her stomach drop. It wasn't like any expression she'd seen him wear before. This one had an effortless charm to it, a gentle confidence that transformed the cowboy's normally serious countenance into something much more striking. He scooped up his hat and went out the back door before she could form any sort of response.

Evelyn put a hand to her chest and reminded herself to breathe.

The rest of the day, she kept her attention on the children. They followed her from one small chore to another. She had framed their day as an opportunity for the children to teach her how to wash windows, beat a rug, and gather eggs from the ranch's impressive chicken flock. The brown dress she wore was one of Beth's old housekeeping gowns that they'd taken in at the waist for Evelyn. She was grateful for the cloth's drab brown color by the time evening approached.

Grateful and exhausted, she left Laura and Ben as soon as she saw the bulk of the men leaving their work for the day, gathering as they did around one of the large water cisterns. Chris would be in soon, and she'd left a stew the children promised tasted and smelled just fine on the top of the stove for him.

She'd have to learn how to do more than boil meat and vegetables. A foreman's wife had to know how to cook. Clean. Mend. The list went on and on in her mind. Thankfully, she'd already begun to learn with the help of the ranch's women.

Evelyn held Madeline's hand as they walked out the kitchen door. More for her own comfort than any need her daughter might have for the gesture. Madeline had grown too old to want to hold hands with her mother, but they had relied upon only each other for so long that none of that mattered. So long as they were together, they were happy. Whatever came their way. Be it a stone-faced earl, a ship traveling across the Atlantic Ocean, or a handsome cowboy with a kind heart.

Yes, Chris was handsome. And young. Nearer her own age than either of the men she had married. That smile he had given her before he left had stayed with her throughout the day. And it promised more for her position as his wife than she felt ready for.

"Laura says that Mr. Morgan promised to build her a doll-house," Madeline said as she swung their joined hands back and forth. "Ten years old isn't too old for dolls, is it?"

"I shouldn't think so. Not if you enjoy them still." Evelyn looked down at her little girl with her golden braid bouncing against her back as she walked. Her daughter had a future on this ranch. Then she could search for more when she grew older. Chris had promised.

What would Madeline think when her mother married for a third time? Someday, Evelyn fully intended to explain her choices to her daughter—if only to spare the child from making so many horrid decisions of her own. Until then, she hoped her child trusted her to do what was best for them both.

Evelyn hadn't expected that marrying Chris Morgan would be for the best. The thought never would've occurred to her without him voicing it. Madeline would know that someday, too. But for now, Evelyn couldn't show her daughter her uncertainties. Instead, she had to present their new future with confidence.

When they entered their shared bedroom to wash up for dinner, Evelyn first sat on the bed next to her daughter. "Madeline, darling. We need to have a talk. A serious one." And one that would—she hoped—be enough to set both their minds at ease.

AFTER RECEIVING PROMISES FROM LAURA AND BEN THAT THEY'D BE all right on their own for a while, Chris left his house by way of the front porch. He saw Duke and Dannie leaving their porch and heading for the main house. He'd told Duke and Abram both that he needed to call a meeting to discuss something important, and that they'd best meet in the Boltons' parlor.

He pulled his hat down low on his forehead and flexed his hands at his side. The gun on his hip might've made him feel better about walking around in the desert, but it didn't give him any kind of courage when it came to sharing the news of his impending nuptials. Although Laura and Ben's enthusiastic acceptance of the idea had bolstered him somewhat. Their happiness mattered most, and the two children were full of excitement at the idea of Evelyn and Maddie becoming permanent members of their household.

Chris looked up at the evening sky. The sun hadn't started painting the blue canvas just yet, but the clear sky had its own kind of beauty, too. Just as the mountains in the distance offered a protective comfort and the rolling hills set his mind at ease. KB Ranch wasn't perfect, but it had long since become part of Chris's soul. Maybe, in time, Evelyn would feel the same way.

He hadn't missed her anxiety that morning when they'd spoken of things to come. Despite all his promises and reassurances, uncertainty of her choice lingered in her eyes and voice. Maybe her worrying only had to do with what others thought, but soothing her fears now fell to Chris.

As he passed by the adobe bunkhouse, he heard the laughter of the men inside. Not too long ago, he'd bunked in there with a handful of cowboys, thinking a wife and children were far in the future for him. If he'd have that kind of family life at all. But here he was, ready to marry and raise three children.

And any more that came.

Chris took his hat off as he climbed the steps of the front porch, and he knocked on the door. Important conversations like this one shouldn't begin by popping into the house through the kitchen. This was a front-door and front-room type of situation.

The door opened, and there stood Evelyn. Pretty as a picture. She'd changed into her gray skirt and a blue-plaid blouse. She looked as lovely and warm as a Spring morning. She wore her hair up and twisted back, only a few strands escaping to frame her face. A face that held a pensive expression, though she tried to smile upon seeing him.

His heart hung heavy in his chest. "Changed your mind already?" he asked, trying to sound teasing, though his voice came out huskier than he'd meant it to. Had she noticed? Evelyn didn't need their union the way he did. He knew that. With her education and elegance, she could likely find a place much better suited to what she was used to back in England. Surrounded by wealth and people to wait upon her needs.

"Oh, no. Not at all." The words came out almost breathless. Evelyn stepped aside to allow him into the house. "Merely nervous."

His first instinct was to reach for her hand and offer reassurance. Would that be too familiar? Sure, they were about to wed, and they'd certainly touched before—but the atmosphere felt as charged as the desert during a lightning storm. One wrong move on his part might cause an explosion.

He settled for leaning closer to her, keeping his gaze upon hers. "I'm nervous, too."

The tension around Evelyn's eyes eased. "That is most reassuring, actually." She led them into the parlor, where King and Beth Bolton waited, already chatting with Ruthie and Abram Steele. The Steeles sat on the couch next to one another, the Boltons in matching chairs on either side of the hearth. That left another set of matching chairs near the doorway, and two chairs borrowed from Mr. Bolton's study in front of the window.

Evelyn took one of the chairs from the study, and Chris followed suit.

King immediately addressed Chris, asking a series of questions about the work around the property. "Any new breaks in the fence?"

"None that I saw today, sir. We're keeping the men on a rotating schedule, riding along the fences and camping on top of Middle Canyon. Based on when we've found the fence line tampered with before, we're planning to put more men up there during the week of the full moon. I think they're coming in by night."

"That tells you something about them, doesn't it?" Abram shook his head. "They only snatch up a few cattle, and in the dead of night. These aren't men with a whole lot of experience. Sounds like younger fellas."

Sounded like young men who knew their way around the area. But every time Chris started to suspect one of his neighbors, he pushed the thought away. Thinking that way could tear apart a community. He'd seen it happen.

Duke had come through the front door midway through the conversation. "Is this what the meeting is about this evening? The cattle rustlers that have nipped at the herd since I joined up in May?" He and Dannie hung their hats on the mirrored hat tree and took the two remaining chairs.

King shook his head. "Nope. I doubt the ladies want to hear us bellyache even more about those fool-headed enough to go around the Territory stealing cattle. This here meeting was called by Frosty." King leaned back in his chair and puffed out his chest. "And I'm warning you now, cowboy, if you're about to say you're gonna quit, I'll have no choice but to raise your salary. Best foreman I've had in years."

Abram grunted. "Including me, King?"

"Especially you. There you are, with a wooden leg, showing up the younger cowboys—didn't do much good for morale." King chuckled, and an easy grin spread across Abram's lined face. They had worn that joke out to the point that only the two of them still had any pleasure in it, as was the way of things with old friends.

"Are you trying to quit, Frosty?" Dannie asked, moving to the end of her seat. "I can't imagine how this place would run without you."

The impact of King and Dannie's praise eased Chris's worries. He knew he wasn't family—not the way Abram and Ruthie were family, or even Duke having married into the ranch. But sometimes, they treated him like he was. Those were the moments he knew he could happily spend the rest of his life working for the KB Ranch.

"I don't intend to quit," he told them, keeping his voice steady. "But I've got a big change coming, and I wanted to make sure everyone understands why. I'd also like to know I have the support—" He took up Evelyn's hand that had rested on the arm of her chair, and she startled a bit. "—That *we* have the support of everyone on the ranch." He didn't look away from Evelyn, willing her to feel as confident as he did in that moment. "I've asked Evelyn to marry me, and she's said yes."

He heard the gasps, the exclamations of "Well, I'll be" and "Didn't see that comin'." But his attention stayed focused on the Englishwoman. She didn't flinch. Nor did she look at all uncertain. Instead, a pretty pink bloomed in her cheeks, and her eyes lifted slightly at the corners with her smile.

When she looked away, he took in the expressions of the others. They'd recovered from surprise quickly.

"Who'd have thought it? Can't say I saw this coming, Frosty." King slapped the arm of his chair. "But by thunder, it's a wonderful idea."

"Evelyn?" Mrs. Bolton's expression was difficult to read. "Are you certain this is what you want?"

Chris tried not to take that personally. Mrs. Bolton was a motherly sort. She'd want to be sure Evelyn was happy with her choice. The way the room grew still after the question told him everyone needed to hear from the bride-to-be before the rest of them weighed in on whether it was a good idea or not.

Evelyn hadn't released his hand yet, and her grip grew stronger as she spoke. "I am quite certain. Chris and I have discussed the arrangement at length, and I've pondered on what it would mean for Madeline and for me. Everyone here has been so kind, so accepting, and I cannot help but feel that there is a reason Chris is the one who found me in Bisbee. There's a reason I'm here. I've never felt so at home anywhere as I have at the ranch." She looked from Ruthie to Mrs. Bolton and then to Dannie. "We all know how difficult it is for a woman to make her way in the world alone. With a child in tow, it becomes even more so. Chris has offered me safety, protection, and provision. He's given me purpose, too."

"I think I'm benefiting from the arrangement, too," Chris put in, watching her profile as she spoke. "A cowboy bachelor raising two kids on his own is bound to run into more problems than he can handle. As helpful as y'all have been, I haven't seen Laura or Ben so happy as when Evelyn is with them."

Another moment of quiet followed, with the ladies looking from one another with expressions he couldn't read. There was a whole conversation happening in which he had no part and no interpreter to aid his understanding.

Then Mrs. Bolton stood, and all the men stood with her. "I think this calls for a toast, and then a serious planning meeting. As nice as Frosty's new house is, it's not set up for a family of five."

A family of five. Hearing someone say it aloud shifted his thoughts. That was the whole point of their marriage, really. The two of them joining up to raise three children in a happy home. They'd be his family. The center of his world.

Chris's chest grew warm, and something inside him went soft as a kitten.

Evelyn released his hand to put it in Duke's as he held it between both of his. "Congratulations, Lady Tyneham," he intoned formally, his English accent thick. "Mr. Morgan is a deserving gentleman, and I hope you find happiness together."

As Chris watched, Evelyn's posture changed. For a moment, he saw her stand as she must have when she walked through English ballrooms and gardens. Her chin tipped upward, the way she held her posture altered. "Thank you, my lord. We will certainly do our best." A knowing look passed between the Englishman and woman. Perhaps it had something to do with how they'd both exchanged one world for a new one.

Dannie stepped around her husband to offer Evelyn a hug, and at the same time a warning glare at Chris. When she stepped away from Evelyn, she shook a finger at him. "You treat her like a queen, Frosty."

Evelyn laughed before Chris could answer, and the light-hearted sound lifted some of the worry that had built in his chest. "I doubt many queens scrub floors or tend to laundry."

Abram had come forward to shake Chris's hand. His deep chuckle was a familiar, comforting sound. "Ruthie's a queen, and she does that kind of thing all the time."

"Flatterer," Ruthie accused her husband as she wrapped Evelyn in a warm embrace. Evelyn had to bend at the waist to accommodate Ruthie's slighter frame. The older woman placed her cheek against Evelyn's, and Chris heard her whisper. "He's a good one, Evie. But then, so are you. This'll all work out just fine."

Then Ruthie released Evelyn and motioned for Chris to lean down—far down—so she could place a kiss on his cheek. "You be good to her, you hear?"

After more well wishes, Mrs. Bolton returned with a bottle of wine kept aside for only the most special occasions. King poured it into teacups since the best crystal, brought by the first Mrs. Bolton from California, was stored in the attic. Chris and Evelyn stood shoulder to shoulder in front of the mantel, cups in hand, as the others toasted their impending union.

ONCE THE TOASTING WAS OVER, THE QUESTIONS BEGAN. EVELYN HAD avoided looking at Chris, with something like shyness. She'd meet Chris's eye and look away again. She'd known their announcement might unsettle the other members of the ranch family, but she hadn't expected the supportive reaction or the protectiveness of the other ladies.

"When are y'all planning on getting married? And how?" Beth had settled in her chair again, her eyes narrowed and her questions business-like.

"A courthouse wedding seems best," Chris said quietly, looking to Evelyn for her nod of confirmation. "And just as soon as we can. No use waiting."

Abram shook his head. "Need to get your house in order first, Son. Are you still sleeping upstairs on the floor?"

Evelyn gave him a startled glance. She hadn't ever gone up the ladder to see Chris's bedroom. Was that truly how he slept? The children both had sturdy wooden beds while he went without. She saw red creeping up the back of his neck.

"I am, but a bed's an easy enough thing to get."

"What about a wardrobe for your new missus?" Ruthie asked. "A place for her to hang her things?"

Shaking his head, Chris protested. "We can figure that out—"

"No woman wants to 'figure out' where she'll sleep at night, or where she'll hang her best dress." Dannie snorted. "Sounds like y'all need a little planning. Or a little shopping. If y'all are getting married in Tombstone, you can take a buckboard and bring back a few things."

Chris and Evelyn exchanged a glance, and Evelyn hurried to reassure him. "I need very little. I'm certain we can manage with however things at the house are at present."

"No." Chris surprised her by shaking his head. "There's no reason for you to make do and do without. Sounds like we might need to spend two days in Tombstone instead of the one."

Her cheeks warmed immediately, but Evelyn didn't voice her immediate concern. Of course, as a widow, it was perfectly acceptable for her to travel alone and take her own room at a hotel. She'd just never really done it before. Madeline had been with her. Not a man.

Chris looked at Mr. Bolton. "Sir, would you excuse me from my duties next Monday and Tuesday?" He looked back to her. "We can get rooms at a hotel and take care of a few things, then get married the next morning."

"I'll mind the children," Ruthie volunteered. "During the day. Dannie and Duke can have them at night." Her eyes glittered with humor as she looked to the young married couple. "They might as well get some practice in."

When everyone turned to look at Evan and Dannie, she was blushing, and he raised his hands palm out. "We're happy to take the evening shift, but we have nothing to announce on that front."

"Yet," Dannie added, wrinkling her nose up at her husband. "No need to sound so terrified, Evan." Everyone laughed, and the tension dissipated again.

King Bolton gazed at his wife a moment, his eyes twinkling. "I'd say there's no rush to starting a family, but I'm not exactly one to talk right now." His wife blushed and gave him a narrow-eyed look that wasn't even a bit disapproving. Then the rancher rose to his feet again. "I think it's time to adjourn this meeting.

We've all got chores early in the morning. Frosty and Evelyn, congratulations again. This is a big decision, and you're both mighty brave to make it." He shook Chris's hand again. Everyone left the parlor, with Dannie and Evan lingering a moment in the entryway to talk to King and Beth.

Evelyn followed after them but halted halfway across the room when Chris took her hand. She looked back at him to find his eyebrows furrowed.

"You can still say no, Evie. All the way up to the moment you say 'I do' in front of a Justice of the Peace. I'll not hold it against you. Nobody will."

Had he somehow sensed the building pressure within her chest? The way her lungs had tightened and her heart had thudded faster and faster as the conversation had gone on? Evelyn took in a shaky breath and fell back a step closer to him. "Chris. I'm a fully grown woman, completely capable of making up my mind. I meant what I said. I've given it all a lot of thought. And Madeline...' Here, at least, she relaxed. "She is quite thrilled with our plan. It is a good decision for us."

Evelyn gave his hand a squeeze. His expression didn't quite lighten, but that one corner of his mouth hitched upward again, like he wanted to smile.

"All right, then. If you're sure."

"I am quite certain." As Evelyn spoke those words, much of the nervousness from the evening dissipated. The truth of her conviction resettled, as it had that morning when she and Chris had spoken at length at the kitchen table in his house. His house where he didn't even have a proper bed, because he was too busy looking after everything and everyone else to bother taking care of himself.

The man needed a wife.

"Then I'll say goodnight." Chris hesitated, looking down at her with a puzzled expression on his face. Then, moving slowly enough that she should have realized what he meant to do, he bent forward and place a kiss on her cheek. A soft kiss, a brush of his lips so tentative that she barely felt it before he was walking away, not looking back.

She raised a hand to her cheek, covering the spot where his lips had touched her skin. The gesture had been sweet. Not possessive or demanding. Chris had seemed uncertain, too, making the gesture more endearing.

Yet as Evelyn climbed into bed next to a sleeping Madeline, her mind presented her with all the things being a wife—again— must mean. She shied away from those thoughts and the memories they conjured. Memories of what marriage had meant for her before, and how quickly she'd lost herself to the selfishness of the men who'd seen her as a possession and nothing more.

Chris is different, she thought, forcing away the remembrances that she wished she'd buried with both husbands. *This whole situation is dissimilar.* Everything would turn out all right.

And yet, she wasn't the least bit tempted to have a conversation with her soon-to-be-husband about anything to do with what she might expect on their wedding night. Or any of the nights thereafter. Because wifely duties weren't something a woman discussed with anyone. Not even her husband.

CHAPTER FIFTEEN

The days passed in a flurry of Chris's usual work supervising the drovers accompanied by the business of preparing his house for two new occupants.

Late Sunday evening, Abram and Whiskers helped him put beds together and moved into the right rooms. A cowboy, a *vaquero* they all called Dominó, was skilled with woodworking, too. He and Whiskers worked on the new bed for Madeline and carried it through to Laura's room. They also added two chairs and a small table to the girls' bedroom and put new pegs into the wall. They'd finished up in time for the kids to return from dinner with the Boltons, and Chris had tucked Laura into bed, trying to hide a smile at her obvious glee.

"I'll have a sister," Laura had whispered to him. He'd ruffled her hair and told her to get some rest, knowing her excitement would likely keep her awake for some time.

Abram and Chris worked on getting the upstairs in better shape. The wooden frame of a bed built for two hadn't been easy to haul up a ladder.

Abram had started measuring out a narrow staircase.

"I'd intended to put one in, eventually," Chris said sheepishly from the second floor while Abram took measurements below him. "It just didn't seem important when we were building the house."

"Didn't know you'd have kids coming to live the same week it was finished, did you?" Abram chuckled and rolled his measuring tape up. "Pretty sure you meant your upstairs to be nothing but empty for the next twenty years."

"I don't know if it would've taken that long to start a family," Chris muttered.

He rubbed the back of his neck and looked behind him at the master bedroom. The roof sloped downward on either side, but the principal part of the room was taller than him. Maybe Evelyn would think the gentle slope gave the room character.

When the men of the ranch had helped Chris build the foreman's house, they'd divided the whole upstairs into two rooms, with two open doorways. Only yesterday, they'd added a door to the bedroom side. A door made up of scrap wood sanded down and nailed together. It looked fine for a barn, Chris supposed, but wasn't as nice as what the Boltons had in their house.

Seeing that door open, leading into the room he'd worked on all day to make welcoming for Evelyn, Chris went somewhat weak in the knees. He leaned against the doorway, looking at the new bed with a new feather mattress—thanks to Ruthie and Beth. Ruthie had brought over quilts and bedding she'd kept in storage. Dannie had ordered two feather mattresses when she'd wed, intending to use one in a spare room of her new house. Instead, she gifted the mattress to Chris.

He'd thanked them both, but whether they sensed his embarrassment, he didn't know. How had he planned on getting married when he slept on a one-person sized mattress on the floor?

"You still awake up there, Frosty?" Abram called, and Chris looked down at the older man. "It's getting late. Aren't you planning to get an early start tomorrow?"

Chris climbed down the new stairs, ignoring the nervousness in his gut. "We're leaving at first light." He looked upward and shook his head. "One minute, I think this is the best idea I've ever had. The next, I'm sure it's a big mistake."

Abram limped over to a kitchen chair and settled in. This late at night, after a long day of work, his leg had to be sore where the wooden peg was secured by belts and buckles. "Why do you think it's a mistake?" Abram pulled out a red bandana and dabbed at his forehead. "She's a fine lady, isn't she?"

"That's just the thing." Chris walked the length of the kitchen wall, then turned and paced back. "She's a lady. A literal, English-born-and-bred lady. With a title. She's a *countess*. I'm a cowboy. And this—" He gestured with wide open arms. "This isn't a castle, Abram."

"It's not a sod house, either. But Ruthie married me when that's all I could afford to live in." Abram chuckled to himself. "You don't give that woman enough credit. Is she used to different things? Sure. But she said yes, didn't she? When she could've gone back east and found herself a school. Or become one of those fancy governesses people in California hire right and left for their kids. She chose you over anything else she might've tried. That counts for something."

"Maybe that's just it." Chris turned the idea over in his mind before he spoke it aloud. "Even if I can see the practical reasons for it, I can't help but wonder if this should be more than a business arrangement. Because that's what it feels like."

"So let it start out that way." Abram stood again, grunting as he put weight on his bad leg. "In all honesty, Ruthie and I talked about it after your announcement the other evening. You're both young and will make a handsome couple. We figure you're both used to being lonely, too. Good people like you, you're bound to get along and make life better for each other. Make life better for her in all the ways you can. Then, you'll see. The practical reasons won't be the only reasons this marriage works out."

Though Chris tucked the advice away, he couldn't help feeling just the same as he had before.

A short time later, when he faced that new bed in his room,

Chris stared down at the twin goose-down pillows for a long while. He questioned his sanity as he finally slipped beneath one of Ruthie's quilts. He folded his arms behind his head and stared up at the wood-planked ceiling, promising himself he'd finish it off with plaster and paint as soon as he had time and funds to spare. The planks were good enough for him, but after all Evelyn had known and been through, she deserved something finer.

For the next two days, it'd be just the two of them together. Driving the wagon to Tombstone. Sorting out business there. Marrying. Driving back.

At least she'd have a good stretch of time alone with him in case she wanted to change her mind.

~

EVELYN WOKE EARLIER THAN SHE MEANT TO ON MONDAY MORNING. She spent far too long lying in the Boltons' guest room, listening to her daughter's gentle breaths as the child slept next to her. It was the last morning she'd wake up in this bed, and her last day as a countess. Not that she'd felt much like a member of the peerage, even in the early days of her second marriage.

Now, she was about to enter a third marriage.

Maybe Chris should've thought it over a bit more before asking for her hand. Not only had she already given it twice, but having two dead husbands should've put him off. Wouldn't most men think twice before marrying a woman like that?

True, both men had been substantially older than she was. But maybe that should've been a mark against her, too. Why did he want to marry her? He was handsome, and he had a secure position at a well-known ranch. He could've had his pick of Territory women.

When Evelyn could stand it no longer, she rose and prepared for the day as quietly as she could. Madeline slept on, untroubled by her mother's fretting.

Evelyn dressed in the same traveling suit she'd worn during

her journey out west. She slid the single hatbox she owned out from under the bed and found the hat she'd kept clean and pretty to prepare for her meeting with the Copper Queen Mine manager. What a strange turn of events. She'd expected to find herself well-situated, thanks to those counterfeit stock certificates. Instead, she'd been penniless.

Penniless.

Evelyn went to the drawer where she'd dropped her small purse on their first day at the ranch. She hadn't touched the little bag since, but now she found it and drew it open. She reached in with her bare hand, and the cool touch of a metal coin met her fingertips.

She took the penny out and held it in her palm, her fingers closed around it. She hadn't left Bisbee empty handed that day, though she walked away with far less of a copper fortune than she thought she'd possess.

Evelyn tucked the penny back in her purse, along with her gloves, and tried to steady her nerves before she sat on the edge of the bed next to Madeline.

"Madeline, darling?" She stroked the child's back. "I'm leaving soon."

The little girl rolled over and blinked sleepily at her mother. "To get married?"

Heart gripped with concern, Evelyn nodded. "That's right. You, Laura, and Ben will need to be good for Mrs. Steele and Mrs. Rounsevell until I return with Mr. Morgan."

"Yes, Mama." She stretched. "Do you think Mr. Morgan will let me call him Papa?"

The unexpected question caught Evelyn by such surprise that she didn't immediately speak, though her mouth fell ajar. "I—I think—" She shook her head. "Do you want to call him Papa?"

"Yes." Madeline pushed herself up until she was sitting against the headboard. "Lord Tyneham said I mustn't call him Papa, because he wasn't that. He said I could call him 'my lord,' and 'the earl.'"

Evelyn sat back; this new information surprised her more than she liked. "I didn't know—did you ask Lord Tyneham...?" She couldn't quite form the words, already seeing from her daughter's downcast expression a new layer of hurt she hadn't expected.

"Once. He called me to his study when the governess said I had misbehaved. That's when I asked." Madeline scooted closer to Evelyn and leaned against her mother's shoulder. "I don't think he liked me very much."

Though a piece of her heart mourned the hurt of her daughter, Evelyn mustered up a cheerful tone. "It doesn't matter anymore, Maddie." The shortened form of her child's name fell easily from her lips. "Mr. Morgan—Chris—he is a kind and thoughtful man. He already likes you. So do Laura and Ben." She kissed Madeline's forehead. "I promise things will be better for us as part of their family."

"Mrs. Bolton says that everyone on the ranch is family." Madeline tilted her head back to smile up at Evelyn. "She says that we're family now, too."

The day hadn't even begun properly, and already Evelyn found herself wanting to curl back up in bed to have a good cry. The kindness of the people she'd found at the ranch contrasted so completely from what she'd experienced as an outsider in English Society. She hadn't been born for either place—not really, even though her mother had trained her to be an obedient wife.

Whatever Evelyn became, it was through her own determination and merit. That made her straighten her shoulders and stiffen her spine. She would become whatever the children and Chris needed her to be. She would prove that she and Madeline could be part of this place, and they would make their home here the same as the Boltons and Steeles had done years and years before.

CHAPTER SIXTEEN

T he ride to Tombstone, though not precisely uncomfortable, had been mostly quiet. When they had started out that morning, Evelyn stiff as a rattler in January, Chris had nearly panicked. Had she changed her mind? Was she afraid of being alone with him? Did he make her uncomfortable? Then she'd started in talking about the weather and he'd realized she had turned a little shy of him. Uncertain, perhaps, of how she ought to act with their relationship undergoing such rapid changes.

But being stuck in the same wagon with someone for a few hours was bound to mean thawing away any awkwardness, and they'd spent the time talking about their growing-up. Evelyn had asked dozens of questions about his life, past and present, and she'd obviously forgotten whatever it was that made her close up on herself in the first place.

When they finally arrived in town and Chris pulled up in front of a law office instead of a hotel, Evelyn looked at him with confusion in her gem-tinted eyes.

"Gerhart, Jones, & Abernathy Law Offices?" She read the sign aloud, as though it were a question.

"Yep." Chris climbed down from the wagon, then reached up

to help her down. "First thing's first. I've got a promise to keep to you."

Though she appeared puzzled, Evelyn didn't question him. She followed him inside, looking about with interest. "I thought you only meant to purchase household furnishings today. I hope I am not intruding on important ranch business."

Chris chuckled. "We're here on business for our family, Evie."

Once they were settled in Mr. Abernathy's office, it didn't take long for Chris to explain what he needed done. And though he glanced at Evelyn several times throughout the discussion, she wore such an expression of shock that he wondered if he had made a mess of everything.

"Marital contracts aren't precisely a regular part of our services," the lawyer said as he rose with the notes he had taken during Chris's explanation. "But I am quite familiar with drafting them. Just a few clarifying questions, and I'll have everything written up for you to sign tomorrow morning. Is that acceptable, Mr. Morgan? Mrs. Lyon?"

Evelyn nodded mutely, but the moment they walked out of the law offices, she took Chris by the arm and pulled him into the narrow, sunlit alley between the law office and the courthouse itself. "Chris. What—did you really mean all of that?" Her eyes brimmed with tears. "You do realize what you just agreed to?"

"Yes, to all of it, Evelyn." He lowered his gaze to where her hand rested on his arm. "You'll have full access to the bank account I keep in Tombstone, including all records of deposits and withdrawals. I never want you to worry about our money. How much we have or where it goes."

"*Our* money?" Evelyn repeated those two words with surprise.

"You'll have equal ownership in any investments I make from now on. Cattle. Stocks. Land." He tipped his hat back and met her eyes again. "From here on out, everything will be in both of our names."

A strange lightness entered her eyes with his declaration, and

Chris finally started to relax. He'd done the right thing. It had been just an idea, when she'd told him she had conditions for marrying him. But making it all legal, rather than just his word, proved the extra reassurance she needed. He'd heard all that she had said and come to understand a lot of what she didn't, about her previous husbands.

She blinked away the dampness gathering in her eyes. She swallowed, her words trembling as she spoke. "Thank you, Chris. I didn't expect anyone to comprehend what we've been through."

Chris glanced away, determined to keep hold of himself. What kind of heartless men had she known before, to think he'd not take steps to ensure her safety?

"When we met, you didn't know what the next day would bring for you or your daughter. What if I hadn't been there, Evelyn?" His jaw set, and he met her gaze again, willing her to feel his sincerity as he spoke. "I don't know much about the people who forced you into that position, but it's my responsibility to keep you from feeling helpless or alone ever again. That's why everything that's mine is now ours. If anything happens to me, you'll have what you need to make a new life for you and the children."

She nodded and squared her shoulders. He took that as a sign that it was time to see to their other errands and leave that conversation behind them. As they exited the alley, Evelyn looked up at the red-bricked and white-trimmed courthouse. Chris looked, too. The people of Cochise County were proud of that building, and it was barely a decade old. Columns supported a small balcony on the second floor and stood to either side of the double-door entrance. It wasn't as grand as courthouses back east and likely didn't hold a candle to important buildings in England, but it served the county well.

"I'm told we just need to go in and speak to a clerk in the courthouse," Chris said when Evelyn continued to stand and stare, her expression untroubled but also unreadable. "They'll make sure the Justice of the Peace is in his chambers when we need him to be."

"Then we had better go in and see to that, since we're here." With a small purse dangling upon her wrist and her gloves on, she looked exactly as she had the day he'd found her in Bisbee. Beautiful. A little out of place. Elegant.

Chris offered her his arm, and the accompanying burst of pleasure in his chest when she took it with a smile surprised him. This woman would grow to trust him. She'd soon be part of his life for as far into the future as he could imagine.

Their business at the courthouse didn't take long. They were asked to sign a marriage license to present to the judge and help the clerk prepare the marriage certificate. The clerk put the official-looking document on the counter in front of them, then excused himself to disappear back into an office to check the Justice's schedule.

Chris leaned against the counter, facing Evelyn. "Ladies first," he offered, gesturing to the pen the clerk had left behind.

"How very gallant of you," she responded with a dry smile. A wrinkle appeared in her nose as she read over the document.

Evelyn removed her glove, took up the pen with a light hand, and filled in all the information about herself. Her date of birth, *December 1st, 1867*. That meant her birthday was near his own. She'd turn twenty-eight years old this December. He had a year on her, almost exactly. Her place of birth, *Stratford, Essex, England*. Her parents' names. *Albert Harlow and Geraldine Claire*. And her full given name. *Evelyn Agnes Harlow*. She also had to write down both her previous married names and the death dates of her husbands. The first, Madeline's father, had died nine years after their marriage. The second, after barely a year.

She put the pen down and tugged her glove back into place. "I believe it's your turn, Mr. Morgan." She slid the paper toward him and then made a point of staring at him with her eyebrows arched. "I'll finally learn your Christian name."

Though Chris felt the usual rush of heat into the tips of his ears, he shrugged as though it didn't matter all that much to him. He filled out everything that she had. Birthdate, *December 24th, 1866.*

"You are jesting, surely." Evelyn leaned a little closer. "What are the chances of that, do you suppose?"

"Plenty of people are born in December." Chris shrugged and kept going. Birthplace, *St. Louis, St. Louis County, Missouri.* "I was born a year and a little after the surrender of the Confederate troops." He filled in his parents' names. *William Morgan, Elizabeth Noel Morgan.* "My mother used to say she didn't really feel like the war was over until I was born. I think it must've been difficult to see a future in a world where brother fought brother. But here I am. Proof that life goes on." He winked at Evelyn. He filled out every line necessary, leaving his name for last. Then he wrote with a flourish his full, legal name and pushed the paper back in her direction.

Evelyn lifted the paper and made a show of narrowing her eyes to read. A smile immediately burst across her lovely face, and her eyes glowed with surprise. She looked up at him. "No. Really?"

He kept his voice light, and he didn't giveaway how much grief his given name had caused him as a kid. "My mother was born in December, too. You noticed her middle name, didn't you? I think she wanted to start a family tradition. Too bad she couldn't ask my opinion on it."

"I think it's lovely." Evelyn put the paper down and tilted her head to the side. "Christmas William Morgan. Christmas Morgan." He caught the slightest hint of laughter in her voice, but she seemed delighted rather than amused. "Did she name you on Christmas morning? Did she realize how it sounded, all together like that?"

"She did, in fact, name me on December 25th." Chris rubbed the back of his neck, looking at the form. "I don't tell many people my full name. I'd appreciate it if you kept it between the two of us."

"As the future Mrs. Christmas Morgan, I see nothing wrong with it." She looped her hand through the crook of his arm. Their gazes met, and for a brief, blissful moment, he forgot all the reasons he didn't like his name. "Do you know, Christmas is actually my favorite day of the year? I've always loved it. We would go to services at St. Helen's Church. They kept a beautiful organ and choir. The music always thrilled me. It's full of such joy and hope."

"Really?" Chris stared down into her eyes, bright and shining like warm caramel. "The last couple of years, we've gone to Sonoita for Christmas. Everyone packs into the church and sings all the carols we can. There hasn't been a permanent preacher for a while, so that's usually the best we can do."

The clerk came through the door before Chris answered. "Everything looks to be in order for a ten o'clock wedding, if that suits you both?" The young man looked from one of them to the other.

"That will do just fine." Chris paid the record fee and then escorted Evelyn out.

Chris walked Evelyn to the hotel, pleased that the tension had left her eyes and she seemed far more relaxed than she had that morning. Making her happy and comfortable was his job, from here on out, and he meant to be good at his job.

CHAPTER SEVENTEEN

The return trip to the ranch took longer than their time spent going to Tombstone. The added weight of Evelyn's new furniture accounted for the change in pace. They crossed under the KB Ranch sign with dusk nearly upon them. The sun had disappeared behind the mountains already, and it wouldn't be long before it sunk below the horizon on the other side of those mountains, leaving the ranch to the night.

"I'll drop you off at the house," Chris told her. "And leave the wagon at the back door. We can unload tomorrow. I'll take the mules to the barn and round up the kids."

A straightforward plan didn't need much more than her agreement, though Evelyn's insides had started to twist again, making her want to wrap her arms around her middle to keep everything still. That, or she could leap from the wagon and bound like one of the American antelope across the desert, running from the energy building up within her.

She'd put aside thoughts of her wedding night since the moment she had agreed to marry Chris Morgan. But now here it was, practically upon her.

When she walked into the kitchen, carrying her valise while

he unhitched the mule team, Evelyn determined to put aside those thoughts again. There was plenty to do before everyone turned in for the night.

She walked to the square kitchen table and found several small crates upon it, along with a thick book and a torn piece of paper on top. She put her luggage on the ground, then found one of the kerosene lamps on the back of the kitchen countertops. She removed the glass chimney to light the wick and turned up the flame before reading. The sunlight had disappeared completely from the house.

Evelyn,

I brought you some vegetables from the garden to help get your kitchen started. We will work on preserving them later this week. Congratulations on your wedding, and good blessings to your marriage!

-Ruthie

Written beneath Ruthie's note was another from Dannie.

To the New Mrs. Morgan,

I found this book in my mother's things. It was written by a woman in England, so I thought it especially fitting to pass it on to you. I'm not sure how much of the advice will work for a household in the desert, but surely there will be something useful in these pages.

Congratulations!

-Dannie

Evelyn smiled at the table and carried the lamp to better read the title of the book. Then she laughed aloud. *Mrs. Beeton's Book of Household Management*, published in London. Even *her* mother had owned a copy, long ago, because every untitled woman in London had to at least have this homemaker's bible upon her shelves to show her friends. Maybe it would be useful.

She faced the doorway to the front of the house and paused when she saw the stairs. The wood was new, unstained and unpainted, but the workmanship looked quite fine. She held the lamp high as she examined the steps leading upward to the only part of the house she hadn't yet entered. Looking upward into the dark, Evelyn shivered and hurried away to the front room.

Wanting to dispel the darkness, she lit the lamp above the fireplace and another on a shelf on the other side of the room. The children needed to receive a warm and inviting welcome home.

Evelyn removed her hat and placed it on a table, then took off her traveling jacket and hung it on a decorative hook near the door. She would need to brush out the dust from the road in the morning.

Not quite knowing what else to do, she went looking for the broom. The dry desert air meant a great deal of dust settled on the floors. Sweeping, Ruthie had assured her, was an every-day necessity. So she swept. And waited. And tried very hard not to think about the new staircase or where it led.

CHRIS GOT THE MULES SETTLED INTO THEIR STALL, BRUSHED THEM down, and rewarded them for their work with a scoop of oats along with the cut grass in their feeding trough. He left the barn by way of the stable yard and slowed when he realized his feet were taking him straight for the bunkroom of the hands.

Nope. He had absolutely no need to check on them this evening, and even less desire to submit himself to them for any commentary on his marriage. Despite the warning he'd given, he didn't have any intention of providing them with a reason to talk to him about the trip to Tombstone. He turned on the heel of his boot and went to Ruthie's house to search out the children.

Light glowed from the single-story Steele home, the windows already covered with Ruthie's dark blue curtains. Chris knocked on the door and took a step back, removing his hat so there'd be no question of his identity. When the door swung open, Lee stood in the doorway, his eyes bright and a bedroll clutched in one arm.

"Frosty," he greeted cheerfully. "I'm on my way to Duke and Dannie's house." With no further explanation, he ducked around Chris and went out into the dark.

Ruthie came to the door, calling after him. "You watch where you step, young man. We don't need to deal with any snake or lizard bites tonight." She shook her head and smiled up at Chris, her affection for her grandson obvious in her dark eyes. "That boy has been talking about sleeping at Dannie's house with the others all day." She stepped aside. "Come on in, Frosty. I didn't expect to see you tonight. Everything all right?"

He hesitated in the doorway. "Sure. Everything's fine. I came looking for the children."

At that, the diminutive woman put her fists on her hips and fixed him with a suspicious frown. "Mr. Morgan." She never called him that. "You aren't planning on taking those children home with you tonight, are you?"

Chris's shoulders dropped. "I was, actually. We said we'd be back tonight—"

"It's your wedding night." Ruthie glowered at him. "Do you really want children underfoot? Things are already going to be difficult, with the nature of how this marriage got started."

Abram had been sitting in a chair near their fire, but he had risen and come closer as Ruthie spoke. "The man can take his kids home if he wants, Ruthie-dove."

She turned her glare to him. "No one says he can't. I'm just giving some important advice." She then shook a finger at Chris. "You listen here. That woman has already been through two husbands who treated her like a suit of their Sunday best. They only cared about her when they wanted to be seen, and they ignored her the rest of the time. You've gotta do better, Frosty."

He ducked his head, not even sure why his stomach sank with guilt. "I intend to, ma'am." He looked over his shoulder, across the grassy patch that separated the three smaller ranch houses. Steeles, Rounsevells, and Morgans. "The children are all looking forward to their night with the Rounsevells?"

"Dannie promised they'd make those itty-bitty pies with the new tins she bought." Ruthie shrugged. "And Duke was hinting he'd be telling some old ghost stories. They've been talking about it all day. Lee couldn't wait to get out the door, as you saw."

Chris stepped backward through the door. "I guess I'd better get along home, then, and tell Evelyn about the change in plans." And try his best not to redden up like a ripe tomato when he explained Ruthie's reasoning.

"Good. You do that." Ruthie finally relaxed her stand. "She's a fine lady, Frosty. You be a gentleman to her."

"And congratulations on your wedding," Abram said, sounding heartily amused by Frosty's situation. "I'll finish those stairs of yours later this week and count that as a wedding gift."

"Thanks." Chris settled his hat back on his head. "Good night to you both."

His walk back to his house stretched before him. And he meant to make it last as long as possible. Maybe most men would be in a hurry to make it back to their bride. But Chris's evening had undertaken a disconcerting turn. How did he explain the uncomfortable talk with Ruthie? Or her way of thinking to Evelyn?

He climbed the front steps, noting the light pouring out from the windows. They needed curtains. Like Ruthie's. Evelyn had bought yards of fabric with that very thing in mind, he knew. She had plans for turning the house he'd built as a bachelor into a home for the five of them. He'd been impressed as she'd talked through why she wanted rugs and curtains, why fabric for cushions would be a luxury they'd soon not want to live without, and she'd chose things she meant to turn into clothing for the girls and Ben, too.

Evelyn had a kind heart, putting the children's needs far above her own. He had a feeling she'd do the same with his needs, too. Which was why, he realized anew, Ruthie had cautioned him as much as she had.

Someone needed to put Evelyn first.

That someone was him.

~

EVELYN HAD FINISHED SWEEPING THE MAIN ROOM AND WAS HALFWAY finished with the kitchen when she heard the front door open. She leaned the broom against the wall and hurried out, ready to greet the children with a smile and an embrace, eager for them to distract her from her anxieties over what the night held for her.

Chris shut the door behind him as she entered the room, holding his hat in one hand. He wore an expression full of apprehension. "Evie." His voiced sounded an octave lower than normal. "I went to get the children from Ruthie's house, but it turns out they're all spending the night with Dannie and Duke. Baking treats and listening to ghost stories. Lee, too."

The nervous state of her mind meant she took a moment to understand what he was saying. "They-they aren't coming home tonight?" Goodness, why had she stuttered? She never stuttered!

A well-bred lady always speaks with clarity and purpose, her mother had said. Though why that bit of advice returned to her at this moment, she couldn't say. Unless it had something to do with another of her mother's bits of wisdom that had been haunting her all day long. *A wife submits to her husband.*

"If you want them home, I'll go get them." He didn't make a move to step any closer to her, worrying the brim of his hat in his large hands instead. "But Ruthie made it seem like they've got their hearts set on having an evening of fun. Lee nearly ran me over on his way to get there. I think Dannie and Ruthie must've planned it out this way from the beginning."

Her shoulders sank, and she wrapped one arm around her middle. "They knew we would return this evening."

He nodded, the movement slow and deliberate. "They knew."

Evelyn had depended upon the children to act as a buffer between her and her disquieting thoughts for a few more hours. Though she'd wrapped that truth in the more comfortable idea of all of them having their first night together as a family. But Ruthie, it seemed, had other plans. Did the older woman have any idea what kind of position she'd put Evelyn in?

Everyone knew what was supposed to happen on a woman's wedding night.

A wife submits to her husband.

"I hardly see how our wedding night is Ruthie's business to worry about." Her mouth snapped shut on the last word. Her voice trembled as she hurried to say, "I'm certain she meant well."

To Chris's credit, he appeared as uncomfortable by the situation as she did. Not eager or expectant. He twisted his hat over in his hands again, then turned around and hung it on its hook. He kept his back to her for longer than necessary, likely determining what to say next, just as she was.

Her eyes traveled across the breadth of his shoulders, the height of him from head to heel. As men went, he was tall and slim, but his shoulders and arms were taut with the muscles of a man who labored with his hands and body. She knew from experience that his knuckles were rough, the calloused on his hands firm, and his grip quite strong. In all ways, Chris Morgan was a fine specimen of a man.

That thought made her knees quake more. She leaned against the corner of the bookcase. She wasn't ready. No matter how attractive he was. She wasn't sure she'd ever be ready.

When Chris turned around, his blue eyes bright in the darkness and his expression serious, Evelyn panicked. She bolted away from the wall. "I had better take my things upstairs." She left the room before she'd even finished speaking, taking up her valise and charging up the steps to the second floor. Forgetting that the rooms above were as dark as the night outside.

She stumbled into a closed door, her hand finding the latch, and she opened it, slipping inside and closing it again behind her. Shaking. She leaned against it, her eyes struggling to adapt to the shadows, with no more than the faint light of a slim moon coming through the window.

Twice before, she'd waited for a husband to come to her on the night of their wedding. Many times she'd seen to her wifely duties. But with Chris, she felt skittish as a doe. Why? Why couldn't she take her mother's advice here, closing her eyes and pretending she was somewhere else entirely?

Maybe it was his eyes. Or the way he smiled. Maybe it was more difficult because—she surprised herself by admitting it—she *liked* it when he touched her. When he held her hand or helped her from the wagon. When he listened to her, quiet, as she spoke. More than once, she had felt that he valued her words and her thoughts.

Rather than make the prospect of sharing a bed with him easier, she felt much more afraid than she had before. Because what if what he made her feel wasn't real? She would know the instant he touched her. The disappointment that would inevitably follow would be deep, and it would change forever how she felt when Chris sent one of his crooked smiles her way.

Because what if he saw her just the same as the men who had come before? A pretty bauble. A doll for them to play with and cast aside when they wished. A *thing* meant to see to their desires, not allowed to have thoughts and feelings of her own.

Maybe she ought to have waited for that letter from Dannie's finishing school. Maybe they would have wanted her, and then she wouldn't be in this position.

The tears running down her cheeks surprised her, and Evelyn brushed them away with haste. What would Chris think when he saw her crying over the thought of their wedding night? The man had expectations. All men did. A weeping wife had frustrated the other men in her life, and she'd learned to keep her emotions in check when near them.

It was safer that way.

Chris might've seen her cry before, on the very day they'd met, but they hadn't been married then. Things changed once a man and woman married.

The scrape of a boot on a step reached her ears. Her body

went stiff, and she leaned heavily against the door. Another step. Another. Chris came up the stairs.

Light appeared on the ground, coming through the crack between the door and the floorboards. Her heart pounded against her chest as though warning her of what was to come. Urging her to flee. Or find a hammer and nails and seal the door shut.

A soft knock on the door made her jump away from it, twisting around to watch for Chris to come inside. Evelyn braced herself, tilting her chin upward and forcing a smile upon her face.

"Evelyn?" Her name came out with a rasp. Chris cleared his throat before speaking again while she remained mute. "May I come in?"

A wife submits to her husband. Those words had haunted her previous marriages. No matter how she had tried to find happiness, and eventually only some sort of understanding, within her last two marriages, she could never forget her duty as a wife.

She donned a smile the way another put on a mask, hoping to hide behind it, as she opened the door. "I forgot it would be dark inside."

He held aloft one of the lamps from downstairs. At her admission, he chuckled, the sound at odds with the twisted mess of worry inside her. "I figured. Now that you can see better, what do you think? Will it do?" He nodded into the room, but when she turned to survey it with a compliment rising on her lips, all she could see at first was one thing.

A bed the same size as the one she had shared with Madeline sat in the middle of the room, a slim headboard against the wall. A quilt in shades of blue and green had been smoothed over the mattress, and white fluffy pillows waited at the head. A small shelf on one side of the bed held several books, and she realized that side must be meant for Chris. The man had a love for the written word. The other side had a small table, and when Chris walked around her into the room, that was where he put the lamp.

Windows on either side of the room were partway open, allowing a breeze to pass through to stir the air. The upper floor of the house only covered half the lower floor, meaning the rooms were long and narrow.

Needing a breath of fresh air, and to move from the spot where she had nearly grown roots into the floorboards, Evelyn walked to the windows. She had to bend over a bit as the roof sloped downward. Then she looked out into the night toward Dannie and Duke's house. The windows were lit, and she saw shadows moving within.

The children were safe and looked after. That was what mattered most.

"It isn't much." Chris spoke quietly, standing by the bed and surveying the room. He pushed a hand through his hair, and his smile turned nervous. "We can change whatever you'd like, though."

She still hadn't told him what she thought of the room. And he wanted to please her with it. Enough to offer to change things to suit her. That had to count for something.

Get hold of yourself, she thought. Aloud she said, "I think it's lovely. I cannot think of anything I would change." She dropped her hands to her side and nervously held her skirt's fabric. She tried to find something else to say. A compliment. A concern. Anything.

Then Chris stepped toward her, and all of Evelyn's thoughts vanished like sparrows in the face of a coming storm. Chris only had to take three long strides to reach her. In another moment, he had her hands in his. She willed some life into them but saw how limp her fingers were in her grasp.

This was the moment, then. Wifely duties. They were a part of every marriage. Like it or not. Though she hadn't dared to hope that things would be different this time, her heart mourned that she once again was a doll in a man's hands.

Chris bent toward her, his blue eyes soft—and Evelyn flinched away just before his lips touched hers. Not much. She only moved an inch. Instinctually. Immediately her stomach dove, and her heartbeat doubled in speed.

But it was too late to recover.

Chris released her and stepped away, his posture suddenly rigid. His eyes cold and a dark frown on his face. He studied her face, and Evelyn stared back. Horrified at her reaction. Then he gave one deep nod, as though he understood, when he couldn't possibly know the torrent of thoughts and fears churning in her heart. "Good night, Evelyn."

Then he left. And she stood there alone, wondering where he had gone. Too humiliated and afraid to go looking.

CHRIS DIDN'T SLEEP MUCH. HE'D ROLLED OUT A FEW BLANKETS ON the floor of the other upstairs room—the one without a door. He'd kicked off his boots and removed his suspenders, but that was his only concession to comfort. And he'd listened. All night. To the silence across the narrow hallway.

And he couldn't help the anger growing in his heart toward the men who had come before him. The fear in his wife's eyes when he'd bent to offer her a kiss—their first, if you didn't count the peck he'd given her on the cheek the night they'd announced their plans—stayed at the forefront of his mind. That look of panic was one he had seen before. In the eyes of a woman whose husband was known to beat her. In the look of a child when an adult had raised their voice, and likely their hand, too many times to be trusted. It was the look of a creature used to enduring anguish.

Not the way a bride should look at her groom on their wedding night. Even in an arrangement such as theirs.

He'd always treated her gently. The number of small touches they'd shared through the day as he'd escorted her around Tombstone and helped her in and out of the wagon, the way she smiled at him with that hint of laughter in her eyes—all of it had made him think they could ease into things together. That their first night as husband and wife would be more of the same. Something tender.

He'd never forgive himself if he'd frightened Evelyn. Or made her think he would treat her the same way her previous husbands had. As a thing to be used rather than a woman to be cherished.

As a consequence of the weight on his mind, he gave up on sleep earlier than usual. He made his way to the kitchen as quietly as he could in his stocking feet.

He had breakfast ready before the sun was up. He even put the kettle on to make Evelyn tea. Evelyn had found a tin of tea she recognized in a Tombstone general store. Her enthusiasm as she told him how pleased she was had made him laugh at the time. Now, how grateful he was she had found something familiar in a place so far from where she'd come.

Chris sat at the kitchen table, staring out the window and sipping at his cup of coffee, when he heard the light tap of her feet upon the stairs. He released a slow breath on his coffee, sending the steam away in a puff. Then he came to his feet and turned to face her.

Evelyn wore one of her new cotton dresses, and her long red hair hung across her shoulder in a braid. Her green eyes met his stare, and he read so much within their depths. Fear. Hesitancy. Concern.

Chris looked down at his dusty boot tips and rubbed the back of his neck. They needed to talk about it. He *knew* they did. And he needed to talk first. "I made you some tea."

"Oh." Her voice was whisper-soft in the silence of the house. She took another tentative step down. "Thank you." And another step.

"Evie?"

She froze where she stood, her gaze on his. She didn't speak. But her cheeks lost their color.

It was a good thing her previous husbands were dead and buried. He'd be having more than words with them, if not.

The incongruity of that thought finally got him talking. "I need to say something, and then we don't have to talk about it again, unless you want to. But you need to know something right here and now." He kept his voice gentle, his stance wide and his hands open at his side. He spoke with sincerity. And brevity. "I have no idea what you've been through. But I'm guessing it hasn't been easy for you—as a woman and a wife. And you need to know, right now, that I won't ever approach you as a husband unless you want me to."

She swallowed thickly and lowered her eyes. "A wife doesn't usually have a choice, Chris."

The words hurt him, deeply, on her behalf. And confirmed what he suspected. "Evelyn." Her gaze came up, hesitantly. "I won't touch you unless you ask me to."

The silence stretched long between them. He could hear the tick of the mantel clock in the other room. Then he nodded once, confirming she'd heard him correctly, before he went to the stove and the kettle to make her tea. "I figure I'll get the kids for you before I see to my chores. You go ahead and enjoy breakfast. I'm bettin' you'll have a busy day ahead."

He'd spoken his piece. And he'd given his word. Reassuring her every moment they spent together that he'd keep it.

CHAPTER EIGHTEEN

The desert in the morning had a quality to it that Chris hadn't ever tried to explain, nor did he think he'd ever find the right words for it. The coolest hours of the day were those filled with the most life. The most birdsong, the most antelope leaping through grass and patches of thorns, and the most movement of the cattle. When noon came, and everything grew warm, things got quieter. You heard the insects more, maybe, but a lot of the beasts hunkered down in burrows and shade—where they could find it—to rest during the warmest part of the day.

Ed and Duke rode with Chris, checking the fences by the canyon where they'd found evidence of rustlers throughout the spring and summer. They hadn't had the manpower necessary to lay a trap or pursue the thieves. Not until recently.

This time, they rode outside the fence. As they approached the canyon, Ed gestured to the sheer walls on either side of the opening. "Dominó said he tracked in about a mile without any sign of a camp or even a good idea of how many horses there were. It's rained since then, so there's nothing to see there right now. But that's definitely the way they drive the cattle away. I bet they watch from the top." He pointed upward.

Duke leaned against the pommel of his saddle, taking in the area with a keen eye. The man hadn't been born to the work, like most of them, but he'd sure made up time fast in learning all he could. "How easily can someone navigate this canyon? Would they have to be familiar with the area to even find it?"

Chris nudged his horse forward. "Let's show you." Middle Canyon, running a short distance east and west, was so named because it connected a gulch on the ranch's property to a larger canyon that ran north and south, prone to flooding during monsoon season. At the moment, a stream no deeper than their ankles and no wider than five feet ran quietly along the bottom of the canyon.

Natural walls, carved out by the stream and weather over time, rose about fifteen feet on either side of them. All three men rode abreast, their horses' hooves splashing into the water with each step.

"It's like a funnel," Duke observed, his voice echoing off the stone. "Once they get the cattle in here, there's no place for them to go but straight. You wouldn't need many men to push them through.

Ed nodded his agreement, looking upward at the clear blue sky. "Two could do it, at this point. But they'd need a dog or another man, at least, once they come out on the other side. Into the mountains."

They rode quietly after that and, try as he might to concentrate on the task at hand, Chris kept thinking back to that morning. With Evie. She'd been quiet and cautious as they'd had breakfast together.

Though once she'd had the tea in her hands, she had returned almost to normal. Given the way Chris had heard Duke talk about a good cup of English tea, it did not surprise him that the drink held restorative properties for his English bride.

"Rattler."

The single word, uttered by Ed, pulled Chris back to the present. Slithering along one wall, the long snake with its beaded tail had pressed itself against the stone and was starting to curl up protectively. The horses shifted, nervous.

The men moved their horses to the other wall, going down single file and giving the snake a wide berth. Wasn't any reason to hurt it, but they'd have to watch for it on the way back. That reminded him. He needed to give Evelyn a few lessons on what to do if she came across a snake closer to home. He wasn't about to hand her a pistol. Not yet. But Ruthie made do by carrying a sharp hoe with her when she stepped outdoors. Many an ornery critter had met its end with that hoe.

Come to think of it, maybe Ruthie should give Evie some lessons on the effectiveness of that particular garden tool.

"Something amuse you, Frosty?" Duke asked, beside Chris once more.

Chris raised his eyebrows. "Nope. Why? You need some enter-tainment, Duke?"

Ed chuckled, the sound bouncing along the walls around them. "I'm betting he's thinking about his new missus. Because that's not a smile I've seen him wear before."

"Ah, I see. And you have known him a long time."

"Five years." Ed kept the reins in one hand and his other hand on the butt of his rifle where it waited in the sheath. Cougars, coyotes, javelina, and even jaguars could be a threat in places with water and shade in the desert. Though they hadn't seen a jaguar in years, it didn't mean there wasn't one stalking them at that very moment. "Come to think of it, I don't think Frosty's ever really been sweet on anyone during that time. How'd you go from a complete disinterest in women to having a wife, boss?"

Chris shrugged, but the prick of his horse's ears betrayed that he'd gone stiff all over. He hoped the other two didn't notice. "I've already explained it. Evelyn needs a safe place to raise her daugh-ter. I need help raising two kids of my own. It made sense."

"An abundance of sense," Duke murmured, but the begin-nings of a grin on his face warned Chris that more was coming.

"Though I'm certain it helps matters that she possesses exquisite features."

"Prettier than a Mexican blanket, as my *mamá* would say." Ed flashed a wide grin past Chris to Duke. "I guess if Frosty had to get hitched, he picked a good one. They're gonna start calling us the English Outfit, though, if we keep adding on folks from that part of the world."

"I don't think there's anything wrong with that." Duke grinned hugely. "Though I will say that I'm surprised Frosty's English bride let him leave her alone on the first day of their marriage."

"She's been alone at the house before," Chris muttered, not willing to admit she'd practically pushed him out the door once the children had arrived home from their night of fun. They'd all talked, of course, and he'd stayed long enough to give out the gifts he and Evelyn had bought in Tombstone, but then she'd raised those copper eyebrows at him and pointedly asked if he needed to see to any ranch work.

Duke gave an understanding nod. "I suppose starting out with three children makes for an interesting honeymoon."

Chris opted to say nothing more until they came to the fork in the canyon. "The northern way," he said for Duke's benefit, "goes up into the mountains. It's a wider path but doesn't have a place to break free of the canyon walls until you're nearly at the top of the first mountain. The southern path is narrower, but it has more places to climb back into the valley."

"Not to mention it points them toward Mexico." Ed sat back in his saddle. "If they're from the Territory, they'd know going across the border would keep them from the law here. Maybe they'd even sell the cattle over on that side, though the prices are better in California."

"It's possible they'd just sell to another outfit and let someone else deal with rebranding." Chris didn't like it, but he'd seen ranchers play dirty with each other before. That was part of the reason he'd enjoyed working for King so much. People in this part of the territory, tucked up into their valley, depended too much on one another to perform such a double-cross.

"You think it's someone you know?" Duke asked, his eyes darkening.

Chris huffed an impatient breath. "Like you were saying before, I don't think too many strangers would be familiar with the way this canyon leads from our back acres out to open country. It would've taken a heck of a lot of exploring to find it on their own."

Ed wheeled his horse around, and they followed suit. "If we hadn't been having problems before the new hands arrived, I'd be mighty suspicious of those fellows first and the other ranches after." He spread his hands wide, still holding the reins, and shrugged. "Times haven't been easy lately, and we've been having trouble since before the new men came to the ranch. Makes me lean toward a distant neighbor."

The idea that one of the ranching families they knew, a family that might've come by to meet Evelyn when she'd arrived, might be responsible for cut fences and missing cattle didn't sit right with Chris at all.

But what if it wasn't one of their kindly neighbors?

"Did you say Buck went on to California?" Chris asked, looking at Ed.

"Buck?" Duke's posture stiffened. "That cowboy who followed Dannie around all the time? I haven't heard his name since he left."

Ed shrugged. "He was arrogant. Hard to work with even before he got it in his head to court King's daughter." He met Chris's gaze and raised his dark eyebrows. "You think he was always part of the problem? Or maybe just since King dismissed him?"

Chris shook his head. He didn't know. Speculating wouldn't get them anywhere, either.

"We're going to bring the cattle in closer to home for a bit. Just a small drive, like we're moving them to greener pastures. Act like nothing's wrong. The moon is bright for the next three days. Something is bound to happen."

They made for the ranch, bypassing the same ornery rattler again, and came out of the canyon into the bright sunlight.

"You're not going out tonight, are you?" Ed asked, riding alongside Chris. "Being a newlywed and all."

Chris narrowed his eyes at his long-time friend. "It's my job to make sure the cattle are safe, Ed. We'll all be out there."

Ed shrugged. "Just saying, I think the men would understand." He grinned when all Chris did was glare at him. "D'you mind if I ride ahead? Whiskers wanted help in the smithy today, and I volunteered."

"Suits me fine. Sooner your yapping is outta my ear, the better," Chris grumbled, but Ed's smile didn't dim in the slightest. He waved over his shoulder and gave his horse's sides a sharp kick. He tore off across the patchy grass and sagebrush, a happy whoop drifting back to Duke and Chris as the younger cowboy went.

"He's always been a cheerful chap, hasn't he?" Duke chuckled and pulled his bandana up to protect his face from the dust that Ed had kicked up.

"Most of the time." Chris had seen Ed during some pretty low points in his life, too. "He's always eager to ride like he's got a calvary behind him, that's for sure."

"I'm a bit surprised that you're not as eager to return to the homestead." Duke kept his voice even, and with half his face covered, Chris couldn't really read his meaning in his expression. "Is married life what you hoped it would be?"

Not this again. Chris shrugged. Duke's position as a part-owner in the ranch, not to mention a son-in-law to Chris's boss, put him in a unique position. Chris couldn't boss him around quite the same. But then, maybe it wouldn't be so bad to talk to the man. He was English, like Evelyn, and newly married. Even if he was a year or two younger than Chris, Duke had a heap of experience that Chris didn't.

"I've only been married a day," Chris said, drawing the words out slowly. Thinking them through carefully. He had no intention of saying anything that would cause himself or Evelyn embarrassment. Some things had to stay private. "I know I've got my work cut out for me. I feel like I've done everything backwards."

"How so?" Duke asked, wisely keeping his eyes straight ahead.

Chris chewed on the explanation a bit before he let it out. "I had kids first, then got a wife I barely know. I don't know if I'll ever have what you and Dannie do. What I do know is that I want Evelyn to be happy. I don't want some cold, business-like relationship with her. Because it sure sounds like that's what her other marriages were, and she deserves more than that." He didn't like making long speeches about emotions, especially with his men. Duke felt safer, though. He'd certainly heard the Englishman wax eloquent on several subjects.

When Duke took his time answering, Chris appreciated the man all the more. Only an arrogant idiot would offer advice with the speed of a sharpshooter taking down a target.

"That you are concerned about such a thing indicates to me that you'll be well enough. Eventually." Duke tugged the bandana down at last and glanced Chris's way. "Dannie's been worried about Evelyn since you brought her to the ranch. I don't blame her. A woman like Evelyn is used to being treated like a commodity rather than a person. I think, if you keep making her feel the respect and admiration you have for her, you'll be well on your way to an affectionate relationship."

Chris moved his gaze forward, staring out at the land before them and noting where cattle dotted the landscape. Dark brown and black spots on gentle swells of pale green grasses. "Thanks. That means a lot, coming from you. I just wish I had more direction here. Ideas of how to speed things along."

"We cannot rush the best outcomes, especially when it comes to ladies. They take a lot of time and a lot of dedication." Duke chuckled. "Not to mention a gentle touch. Wooing Dannie wasn't the easiest thing I've ever done, though it certainly came natu-rally. It felt right to be near her."

Turning that over in his mind, Chris finally tucked the thought away to examine later. He'd had a similar experience or two with Evelyn. Sitting in his chair, listening to her read to the children, had felt more than right. It had felt familiar. Like some-thing he'd always done and longed to do forevermore.

A list of chores waited for him when he returned to the ranch, and he had to spend a fair amount of time checking in on his men. Before they gathered for dinner, he laid out the plan for them to make their way to the canyon that night and lie in wait for the rustlers. "I don't plan on there being any fighting. Men like this usually get frightened off at the first sign of trouble. But let's be sensible about it. And safe. We'll settle on shifts and ride out after everyone's had dinner. Bring a coat. It gets cold out there at night, and we're not risking any fires."

There hadn't been much grumbling from anyone other than the cook, and he got to stay behind anyway.

Finally, Chris turned his boots in the direction of his own house. The fact that he couldn't wait to walk in the door brought a surprised grin to his lips. Maybe he hadn't planned on getting a family anytime soon, but he certainly didn't mind having one now.

NOTHING HAD GONE RIGHT FOR EVELYN SINCE THE MOMENT CHRIS left the house. If Evelyn had been the type to believe in signs or auspicious occurrences, she'd likely have packed her bags and gone straight back to England. Thankfully, she had a good head on her shoulders and too much tenderness in her heart to let difficult moments weaken her resolve. At least, at first.

"What is that horrid smell?" she asked when she walked into the girls' bedroom shortly after breakfast. All three children were inside, sitting on the floor, and they looked up at her with wide and guilty eyes.

Madeline looked to Laura, who looked to Ben, who shook his head and bolted to his feet. "Uh-uh. I said this was a bad idea. I'm not getting in trouble for it." Then he took off running from the room, jamming his shoulder against the doorway on the way out. He'd yelped and then cried, rubbing at the spot that would most certainly be bruised.

Evelyn had taken time to see to Ben and left him sniffling in a chair while she went to speak to the girls. When she came back into the room, they were sitting on Madeline's bed, each with a kitten on her lap.

"Oh," Evelyn murmured, the strange odor making sense. "You brought the barn kittens inside. But how? I didn't see you with them this morning."

The girls exchanged looks, then Laura held her kitten close. "They were playing out back this morning at breakfast, and I didn't want a predator to get them. So we rescued them."

"When you brought in the eggs," Evelyn murmured, remembering the way the girls had hurried out of the kitchen the moment the egg basket was on the table.

Madeline continued to stroke the striped tabby in her lap. "In our apron pockets." Then her little nose wrinkled. "We've been playing in here, but a few minutes ago, one of them...well. They don't know they're not supposed to do that in the house."

"Because they are *barn* cats." Evelyn looked around the room. "Where is the mess?"

They both pointed to Laura's bed on the other side of the room.

"Then I suppose you two are going to help me with laundry, *after* you return the kittens to the barn."

"Yes, Mama."

"Yes, ma'am."

Evelyn went back to see to Ben but discovered he wasn't where she'd left him. She heard a sudden thump above her head.

With a frown, Evelyn went to the unfinished steps—they needed a rail, at the very least, she had decided. She climbed up and looked first in the room where Chris had slept the night before—mostly full of crates and tools, a storage room at present. She didn't see Ben in there. So she looked in the bedroom.

Ben sat on the edge of her bed, looking out the window. He grinned when he saw her come in. "This is much better than what it looked like when Frosty was the only one in here."

Evelyn felt her cheeks redden. "Thank you. But you shouldn't come in without permission in future, Ben."

"Oh." His face fell. "I just wanted to try out the stairs." He rose to leave.

"They are nice, aren't they?" Evelyn rubbed at her temple. "I don't mind that you're in here. It's important to ask first, is all." She held out her arms to him. "Let me see your shoulder. Does it still hurt?"

"It's sore." He shrugged. "Did the girls get in trouble?"

"The girls are returning the kittens to the barn, and then they're going to help with the laundry." Evelyn gave him a quick hug. "Why don't you help put away the books we brought back from Tombstone? I think Chris left the crate by the shelves."

"I can do that." He pulled away from her and rushed down the stairs at a speed that made her heart jump into her throat. Yes, they needed a rail.

She went to strip the sheets and quilt from Laura's bed, trying not to touch the soiled portion of fabric the kitten had left behind. "Bringing barn cats into the house," she muttered with a shake of her head. "If they want a pet cat, maybe Chris can help me figure out how to housebreak it."

Having a cat wouldn't be too terrible. She'd prefer a cat in the house to the possibility of finding mice in her kitchen. Evelyn stepped out of the bedroom with the bundle of bedding at the same moment Ben toppled one of Chris's glass jars off the shelf. Evelyn watched, unable to do anything to help, as the jar full of buttons tumbled to the floor and shattered.

Ben squeaked and hopped to one side, then screamed and lifted his stockinged foot.

He'd stepped on a piece of glass.

Evelyn dropped everything in her hands, thanked the Lord for the small mercy that she already wore a pair of shoes, and hurried to help Ben. She picked her way to him carefully while he sobbed, lifted him into her arms, and carried the surprisingly heavy little boy into the kitchen. He wailed and wept, clutching at his foot.

"Now, now. It's going to be all right." But the sock he wore was wet with blood, and she could see more leaking from the fabric. Her head went a little light, but she forced herself to sit down and examine the wound. "Let's take this sock off—"

That was met with a cry of alarm. "No! No, it hurts! Don't touch it!"

The front door opened. The girls had returned from their errand. Evelyn shouted, "Do not come in! Stay right where you are."

"Mama? Is something wrong?" Madeline called, sounding confused.

Laura's voice was more worried. "Is Ben hurt?"

"We broke some glass, and Ben stepped on a piece." What did she do? She didn't know the first thing about attending wounds. "Both of you, go tell Mrs. Steele what happened. See if she can come and help. If you can't find her, go to Mrs. Bolton's house."

The front door opened and banged closed again. Evelyn tried once more to reason with Ben about taking his sock off, but the boy screamed in horror and pulled away from her.

"All right. This is fine. Here. Let's do this." She hurried over to the tea kettle and poured everything in it in a bowl. The water had at least been boiled. She knew that was essential. Even if it did smell deliciously of cooling tea, Ben needed it more than she did.

She put the bowl under the chair. "Put your foot in that. It should help. I'll clean up the glass."

"You're leaving me?" he asked, hiccoughing through his tears. "Don't go."

"I am only stepping into the front room to sweep up so no one else gets hurt." This explanation did nothing to ease his mind, and in another moment, Evelyn found herself holding a sobbing Ben in her lap, the bowl of tea forgotten on the floor while he spent his miserable tears into her shoulder.

The back door opened next, and Ruthie came in with a small leather satchel. "I hear we need some doctorin' in this house." The girls came in behind her. "Have we seen to the glass yet?" she asked, though her tone indicated she knew the answer.

"Not yet." Evelyn ran her hand along Ben's back. "Ben needed me."

"Can't help that, can we?" She turned to the girls. "You two. Pick up all the big pieces of glass you can find and put them in one of those empty coffee tins." She pointed to a row of cans beneath the oven. "Then get the broom and do a good job sweeping everything together. When that's done, I'll slice a potato up for you to find the slivers."

"A potato?" Madeline and Evelyn said together.

"Sure. It's an old trick. You press the potato on the ground and even the tiniest pieces of glass attach to it. Then we just get rid of the potato." Ruthie sat in the chair Ben had occupied for a short time. "Let me see that foot, young man."

He buried his face in Evelyn's shoulder, but she maneuvered him so Ruthie could grab his foot and put it into her lap. She wore an old apron, thankfully, and didn't seem to mind the blood. Without asking, she took the boy's sock off, and he didn't make a sound.

"See," Evelyn murmured into his dark brown hair. "It didn't hurt, did it?"

"It will," Ruthie said quietly. "In just a moment."

The boy shuddered, and Evelyn looked at the older woman with some shock.

"No use sugar-coating it. It's better he knows what's coming and that he has to be brave." Ruthie gave the child a pat on his ankle. "It's a deep cut, Ben. We need to clean it up so you don't get infection or blood poisoning, then we've got to stitch and bandage it. Can you hold real still while we work on you?"

Ben gulped but nodded.

"Good. Evelyn, we need to clear the table. This will be easier if he's laying down where there's good light." Ruthie carefully lowered his foot and then looked strangely at the bowl of tea. "What's this?"

"Nothing." Evelyn helped Ben sit on the edge of the table, then swept the tea away. 'What do you need to clean the wound?"

"Iodine. I've got some in my doctorin' bag." Ruthie removed everything from the table—mostly the vegetables she'd left there the day before. Then she rolled up one of the coats she'd found hanging on a hook and put it down for Ben to rest his head on it. "And we need something for you to bite while we stitch. It helps." She found a wooden spoon.

Evelyn sat down next to Ben's injured foot, then stretched her arm up to hold his hand tight.

"Good news is that the glass doesn't appear to be in there still." Ruthie had cleaned out the tea kettle and set it atop the still-burning stove. She opened the kettle lid and dropped in a curved needle, long forceps, and a spool of thick, black cord. "Where's Frosty?"

It took Evelyn a moment to understand the sudden question, unrelated as it was to their circumstances. But in that same moment, she suddenly wished Chris was home. "Out working."

"Hm." Ruthie sounded entirely disapproving of this. "All right. Let's work on cleaning the wound while that water boils. I've already got some clean bandages. You know, Ben, you're going to have to keep off that foot for a while. No wearing boots or going outside."

The boy groaned, then sniffled more. "It was an accident."

"I know, Ben." Evelyn squeezed his hand again. "Accidents can happen to anyone."

Ben cried quietly when the iodine got into his wound, whispering, "It burns." All Evelyn could do was nod in sympathy and offer reassurances that it would be over soon.

When the water had boiled, and the girls had been given a slice of potato each to get up the last of the glass, Ruthie settled with a needle and the thick black cord—which turned out to be catgut. "As a midwife, I've got to be prepared for just about anything. I've stitched a few women up in my time. The ones that get impatient, usually." She smiled to herself. "Ben, hold still. Evie, you're going to have to help him. Put that wooden spoon in his mouth. Bite down hard when it hurts, son."

The next quarter hour seemed to last for days, and Evelyn had to release Ben's hand in order to hold down his foot with both hands and lean her weight onto him. The boy did his best, but he bucked upward a few times and hit the table with his fist. Tears leaked from his eyes as he gritted his teeth around the spoon.

"There, now. All finished." Ruthie wrapped his foot in pristine white cloth bandages. "We'll need to check on it again at bedtime, and in the morning. Watch for infection. It's best if you keep your foot propped up. Maybe put him in bed with a few cushions stacked beneath his ankle. A nap would help, too. A body needs rest to heal."

Evelyn nodded mutely, absorbing every word and piece of advice as Ruthie gave it. She carried Ben to his room while Ruthie cleaned up, and the little boy held tightly to her neck. The girls were sitting on the couch, heads bowed and eyes solemn. They still needed to do the laundry, and Evelyn already felt exhausted.

She tucked Ben into bed, propped his foot up with a thickly folded extra blanket, and handed him his sawdust-stuffed horse. "You just rest for a little while. Stay right here. I'll get you a book and some milk with honey to drink."

Ben sniffled. "Ma'am?" He hadn't quite settled on what to call her, though Evelyn had told both children they could call her

Aunt Evelyn if that was easiest, or Mrs. Morgan if that was more comfortable.

"Yes, Ben?"

"Th-thanks for taking care of me." He spoke with such an earnestness, despite the tremble in his voice.

"Of course, darling." She ruffled his hair. "I married Frosty so I could take care of you, you know."

"Really?" His smile returned, though it was somewhat wobbly. "You like us that much?"

"Yes. I adore you." She kissed his forehead. "And I'm certain your mother would want someone taking care of you. Like I would want someone to take care of Madeline. I think it must be a special thing that we mothers do." She sat on the edge of his bed, looking him in the eye. "I promise I will do everything I can for you, and love you, the way your mother would want."

He took in her expression, his dark eyes serious, before he finally nodded. Evelyn rose again and set about fulfilling that promise. After she had bid Ruthie farewell, seen to Ben's comfort, and searched the floor to make certain the girls had found all the glass, she packed up the bedding and took the girls out to the laundry shed.

The last time she had done laundry, she had used water and a fire someone else had prepared. This time, she had to figure everything out on her own. It didn't take long, but by the time she'd hauled water to the large iron pot and built up enough of a fire to heat it, sweat dripped down her back and fell into her eyes from her forehead. The girls had helped, of course, but it still made for back-aching work.

Once everything was washed and no longer smelled horrible, they clipped sheets and blankets to the line and went back to the house. Ben had fallen asleep, thankfully. Evelyn gave the girls Ben's former job of sorting out books and other Tombstone purchases, and she set herself to the task of rearranging her kitchen in a way that made sense to her.

Then she had to teach herself, with a little help from the book

Dannie had gifted her, how to clean and prepare potatoes and carrots for boiling. The girls happily helped—until Madeline gave herself a nasty scratch. Evelyn sent her to Ruthie to clean it and get a bandage.

Laura broke down into tears shortly after, wailing about how her brother had been hurt and it was somehow her fault for bringing the kittens into the house, which had led to him being alone at the bookshelf. "I'm the worst sister ever, and I'm supposed to take care of him."

"Oh, dear girl. Accidents are going to happen. It's all right. Ben will be fine, and it isn't at all your fault." Evelyn held Laura while she cried, for quite some time, and had the feeling the child mourned her lost parents more than she did her hurt brother. After some time, Evelyn took Laura to her room and insisted the little girl take a nap in Madeline's bed. The sheets on her own bed were still out drying.

Given the amount of carrying on, she wondered when exactly the children had slept—if they'd slept at all—the night before.

While Evelyn calmed Laura's worries, the fire went out in the oven. It had to be relit before she could get the potatoes cooking. There was bacon to cook—but the grease in the pan kept popping at Evelyn's hand. All the while, she tried to remain cheerful.

But the bacon burnt. The potatoes didn't seem to want to soften all that much in the boiling water. Ben woke up crying that his foot hurt. Laura seemed intent on punishing herself. And Madeline sat with wide eyes, watching all of it, clearly uncertain how to help.

"Why don't you go sit with Ben?" Evelyn offered her daughter at last. "If he's awake, you can help distract him by reading or playing something that will keep him in bed. If he's asleep, you can read in the parlor." Madeline slipped away with obvious relief. This was new to both of them. There weren't any servants about to fetch and carry. Food wouldn't simply appear in front of them on the table. And though Evelyn had been learning in her three weeks at the ranch, there had always been someone nearby to help. Ruthie, Mrs. Bolton, Dannie, or even Chris.

By the time Evelyn had dinner on the table, looking outside to watch for the darkening sky that would mean the men's work was done, she wanted nothing more than to climb in bed and give into a good cry herself.

She made a plate of food for Ben, after cutting off the burnt bits of bacon, and asked Laura to eat with him. The little girl brightened exceedingly at the idea of helping her brother in that small way. Madeline watched her go with a sigh, then pushed her food around her plate while Evelyn stood in the doorway or watched through the front window until she saw the familiar shape of a man striding toward the house.

When Chris heard about her day, would he regret marrying her? She'd done the best she could. But why had everything happened on the same day? The glass, the cut, a less than appetizing dinner, the kittens—

"Oh, no. I forgot Laura's bedding." Evelyn rushed to the front door and opened it at the same moment Chris stepped onto the porch. He rocked back on his heels, and a smile appeared on his face. Before he could say anything, she blurted out, "Pardon me, I forgot something." She hurried past him without another word.

She ran to the laundry shed, a three-walled building that stood between their home and the rest of the ranch, positioned to be of use by everyone. The clothing line stretched from the shed out to an empty field. Out of breath when she reached it, she hurried to pull the wooden pins from the first sheet. The sound of her heavy breathing and blood thrumming through her ears was all she could hear. Her face burned with humiliation.

She wasn't cut out to be a ranching wife. Surely, Chris would see that now.

Evelyn reached for the next peg—and another hand got there at the same time, covering hers. She jumped and turned her head, meeting Chris's concerned gaze. He stood so close that

Evelyn hadn't the slightest idea how she had missed him coming up beside her.

"You must think I've gone mad," she whispered, not moving her hand and clutching half a sheet against her chest.

"Nope." He squeezed her hand, then undid the wooden peg to let the other half of the sheet fall into his grasp. "You look about the way I felt when Ben and Laura first showed up."

A laugh that verged nearer a sob escaped her as she held the sun-warmed sheets against her chest. They smelled like fresh cotton and the desert wind. A scent she instantly realized she associated with the man in front of her. "I have had a formidable day."

"I'll bet." He undid the next sheet, bundling it up and adding it to what she already held. "Everyone all right?"

She stumbled after him, ready to accept the quilt, too. But when he had that down, he shifted the sheets from her arms to his. Evelyn stood still, watching his expression. "Mostly. Ben cut his foot on broken glass. Ruthie stitched him up and said he must stay off it for a while. A month or more."

Those normally light blue eyes of his went dark. "That sounds serious. How'd he cut it?"

They started walking back to the house, and Evelyn explained her day. Starting with Ben, and then summarizing everything else as simply as she could. "I am sorry," she said at the last, when they climbed the porch steps together. "You trusted me to keep everyone safe. I feel like the whole day has been one disaster after another."

Evelyn opened the door and hurried through, holding it wide for him. The moment he stepped inside, loud giggles erupted from Ben's room. Chris's smile reappeared, and softly he said, "That doesn't sound like a disaster to me." He took the bedding to the girls' room while Evelyn walked softly to Ben's door to peek in.

Ben was in bed, his foot still up, and the girls had two little dolls playing at nursing his horse back to health.

"He needs to drink lots of tea with lemon and honey," Madeline's little doll announced. "It will make him feel much better."

"How will tea and honey help a broken leg?" Laura asked in a high-pitched squeak of a doll's voice.

"It won't. But it will help him stop being a little *hoarse*."

Ben kept giggling. "But he's supposed to be a horse!"

Evelyn covered her smile with her fingertips and turned away from the door, looking across to the other room. Where Chris made Laura's bed. He hadn't just put everything down and left it for her or the girls. He was tucking sheets into place. She approached, watching him shake out the quilt before letting it fall onto Laura's bed. Then he smoothed out the wrinkles, his large sun-browned hand a light touch on the pink and yellow bedspread.

When she entered the room, Chris looked up. "They sound happy."

If only she could slide her arms around his waist and bury her face against his chest, the same way Ben had held her earlier that day. She had the same need for comfort and reassurance. But she had as good as pushed him away the night before. So instead, she came up as close as she dared and met his steady blue gaze squarely. "Thank you, Chris."

He hesitated, then opened his arms. As though he'd read her mind.

Evelyn didn't hesitate long. She stepped into his embrace. His strong arms wrapped around her immediately, holding her close against his warm chest. Desert wind, clean cotton, leather; all the scents mixed to make something uniquely Chris Morgan. He smelled wonderful. His arms around her felt even better than that. Evelyn relaxed into his hold, turning so her cheek pressed against his shoulder, her hand resting directly above his heart. It thrummed steadily against her palm.

He said nothing. Neither did she. They stood quietly, holding one another. For the first time in more than a decade, Evelyn wasn't alone.

CHAPTER NINETEEN

Chris sat at the table when Evelyn refused all his help with the meal. He glanced at the empty chair next to his and saw several sheets of paper. Listening as Evelyn spoke more about the pleasant parts of her day, he picked the papers up and thumbed through them. They were sketches.

He knew Evelyn had bought drawing supplies in Tombstone, but he hadn't had any idea how gifted she was. It looked like she'd been teaching the children. The first sketch he saw was of a bouquet of wildflowers. The same bouquet in a jug sitting on the windowsill behind the table. They were late-blooming marigolds from the main house's garden.

While the first sketch was beautiful and soft, the others of the flowers were decidedly more childlike. He put the papers down again when Evelyn brought him a cup of coffee.

Evelyn made several apologies for the state of the meal.

"Evie." He liked saying her name every chance he had. "You don't have to apologize. You've had a hard day. It'll be fine."

She blushed. "You might rethink your words after you taste everything."

"I've survived on cattle drives with nothing more than half-burned canned beans. Trust me. This is much better."

Sure, the potatoes and carrots were a little hard. Maybe the bacon was crispier than usual. But the meal filled and warmed him. That was all that mattered, considering the night he had ahead of him. The fact that Evie'd never cooked before she'd come to Arizona, coupled with her long day, made the whole thing too impressive for him to even think a complaint.

After he'd cleaned his plate, Chris explained he had to be away for the evening. "We're thinking, if the rustlers show, it'll be while the moon is at its brightest. That's what they've done the last couple of times."

Evelyn sat across the table from him, her posture like a soldier's and her hands tucked away. Her hair, which had been up in a twist when he'd left that morning, had several strands and curls falling loose from where she'd tucked and pinned it. She looked done in.

"Is it dangerous, to go after them at night?" she asked, her eyebrows pulling together tightly.

He hadn't considered what she'd make of that aspect of him being away. He'd never had to account to someone on a matter of safety before. King expected him to get a job done, and his men expected him to accept his orders in good faith.

Every man in the Territory carried a gun to protect themselves. Rustlers knew they'd most likely see jail time or meet their end at a noose if they'd committed the offense too many times. Horse and cattle thieves weren't tolerated in a world where a person's stock was all they had to depend upon.

Evelyn didn't need to know all the things that could go wrong. She just needed to have a little faith in him, in his promise to take care of her and the children.

"We'll be able to see clearly enough, and we know the land better than they do. I'm taking most of the men with me, and we'll take turns keeping watch so no one falls asleep on the job." He folded his arms and gave her a confident grin. "Rustlers are usually cowards. They're trying to make their money without doing any real work. They won't want to put up a fight. If anything, they'll cut and run when they realize we're there."

Her shoulders relaxed, as did that line across her forehead. "All right. When do you think you'll be home?"

"The moon sets after four in the morning. We'll make our way back then, so the men can catch a few hours of shuteye before we get on back to work." He finished his cup of coffee. "I'd better get my gear together."

"Can I pack you something to eat? We still have a few cookies. Maybe some biscuits." She bit her bottom lip and looked toward the cabinets, taking uncertain steps in that direction.

Chris caught her shoulder gently, and when she looked up at him, he smiled. "The Cook is putting together trail food for everyone, so you don't need to worry your head about me tonight. You just get some rest. You've had a long day, and I imagine tomorrow will have its own challenges."

Her eyebrows shot up, and a bemused tilt to her lips made his heart stutter. "Like keeping a little boy from running around with stitches in his foot?"

"Yep. Like that." Chris went up the stairs to find his bedroll and a coat. He came back down the stairs to find Evelyn cleaning up the dishes. She scrubbed at one harder than he had ever seen someone do the job, and he came up behind her with curiosity.

"Did that dish offend you, ma'am?"

She startled and turned around, water dripping from the plate to the floor. "Oh. This?" She looked down at it, then brushed back some hair with the back of her wrist. "No. I just... how do I know when it's really clean?" She shrugged. "I want to make certain I do this right."

"I don't think anyone can mess up washing dishes. In fact, that's a chore you should probably leave to the kids." Though he liked the way she looked, standing there with a damp apron and wisps of hair framing her cheeks and brushing her neck.

He took hold of himself with a stern, mental talking-to. *Get ahold of yourself, Chris. You're not supposed to even think about touching your pretty wife.*

"The girls are in with Ben. You should tell them goodnight before you leave." She bit her lip immediately after making the suggestion. "Not that I mean to tell you what to do—"

"I don't mind." He had his gear rolled up and tucked under one arm, his coat already on. But he came closer to her still, covering the last foot of distance between them. With his free hand, he tucked some of the hair back behind her ear and had the pleasure of watching her cheeks turn pink at his touch. "Don't forget that Abram and King are within shouting distance, and Cook and Whiskers are at the bunkhouse. Lock up the house." He considered her face a moment, watching the way her deep green eyes reflected the lamplight from above the sink. "I'll put Gus on the porch, too."

The cattle dog would give them all peace of mind, he figured. That dog wouldn't let anyone he didn't know cross his path. It wouldn't take Chris more than an extra few minutes to place the dog in a guard position.

"Thank you," she said softly. "It sounds like you're more concerned about my well-being than your own."

He chuckled. "That's likely true." How would she react if he bent and kissed her cheek, making it the second time his lips had touched her skin? He wouldn't, of course. Though he'd happily linger to drink in her scent and bask in the warmth of her smile. "Good night, Evie."

Her blush deepened, but she didn't shrink away. "Good night, Chris."

He went to Ben's bedroom, dropping his bundle on the floor. "What's going on in here? I hear we've set up a hospital." The children greeted him happily, explained Ben's injury, and then all three started talking about their game with the dolls and horse. He let them talk, liking the way their excited little voices washed over him. They were happy. That's all he'd wanted from the first moment he'd clapped eyes on Ben and Laura.

"Are you going someplace?" Laura finally asked, pointing to the bedroll. "Camping? Our daddy used to take us camping." Then she clamped her mouth shut and looked at Ben with big eyes.

Ben looked at the bedroll, too. "I liked it, because we'd build a fire and tell stories. Daddy would play the harmonica."

Chris's heart softened. He ruffled Ben's hair. "Your dad always had a harmonica on him, even when we were kids. He played music all the time."

Ben nodded, and Laura remained solemn. Chris cleared his throat and looked at the bundle on the ground. "I'm going out to watch the cattle tonight. It's not the fun kind of camping. But maybe, once your foot gets better, we can all go camping together."

"That'd be nice," Madeline said from her spot near the window. "I've never been."

"You've *never* been camping?" Ben asked, eyes huge. "Did you have any fun at all in England?"

Chris had to bite his lip to keep from laughing, and Madeline's nose scrunched up like her mother's did when she didn't wholly approve of something. Laura gave her brother's arm a pat. "Now, Ben, not everyone is as lucky as us."

"True enough," Chris said, coming to his feet. "You two tell Maddie all about camping. Then the three of you can plan our trip together. I know some great spots for a night under the stars." He stroked back Ben's hair again, gave Laura a kiss on the forehead, then turned to Maddie.

She didn't wait for him to decide how he'd take his leave of her. The little girl launched herself at him, wrapping her arms around his middle and giving him a fierce hug. "Goodnight, Papa. I hope you have fun camping."

His heart near exploded, and he nearly forgot to return her embrace. But when he did, she squeezed him just a little tighter. The little girl had a heart eager to love. She had to, accepting him as quickly as she had. It made him want to protect her, too. Wrap her up, keep her safe, and make certain she had a life full of happiness ahead of her.

When she released him from her hug, he gave her a kiss on the forehead, just like he had Laura. "Goodnight, Maddie."

Walking out of that bedroom, he found himself less eager to get on with the evening's work. Evelyn stood in the kitchen doorway, drying her hands on a kitchen towel. She smiled at him. "You needn't look so worried, Chris. We will be perfectly fine until your return."

"Do I look worried?" He chuckled. "Maybe that's what having kids does to a person." He shrugged away the thought and fetched his hat. He nodded to her from the front door. "I'll put Gus on the steps before I go."

"Thank you. Goodnight."

He nodded and let himself out, shutting the door behind him. Why, when things had started with him only taking care of Laura, Ben, and then Evelyn and Madeline, did he feel he'd left something essential behind him in that house? As though Chris needed *them* just as much as they needed him.

EVELYN WOKE WHILE IT WAS STILL DARK OUT. THE DOG HAD BARKED once, sharply, but had then fallen quiet. She listened, remaining perfectly still in her bed. Then she heard the front door open, and Chris's voice drifted up through the house.

"That's a good boy, Gus."

She relaxed and turned over, hugging herself. It had taken hours to fall asleep the first time, knowing Chris wasn't in the house. She'd felt exposed, somehow, without his presence in the room across the hall. It had taken her a while to realize that she'd never slept in a house in which she was the only adult present. There had been others, always, even if it was just a few servants in the attic.

Eventually, she'd snuck down the steps and found a poker for the fire, then brought it back up and leaned it against the wall. Perhaps it had been foolish, but she'd slept easier once she had the cast-iron rod within reach.

She didn't hear his boots cross the floor, though she listened intently for the clip-clop sound his steps usually made. It wasn't until she heard a light step outside her door, crossing into the other room, that she realized Chris must've removed his boots before entering the house.

With Chris safely returned, despite the approach of dawn, Evelyn easily returned to her dreams.

When she woke next, the sun shone brightly outside the windows. Which meant she had slept later than she liked. She heard voices coming from the kitchen. The children were trying to stay quiet for her. Evelyn threw back her blankets and hurried to get dressed. She looked at her hair in the mirror above the bureau and decided the single braid falling down her back would be enough for the moment. Fussing with her hair could wait.

She hurried downstairs, hand along the wall. "Good morning. I'm terribly sorry I overslept. Is everyone—" She stopped on the last step, seeing Chris push his chair back from the table. "—all right?" Heat seeped into her cheeks. Had he remained at home because she hadn't awoken?

The children looked up from their school slates, another Tombstone purchase, and said their good mornings without any ceremony before going back to whatever it was they worked on. Evelyn took the last step to the floor, meeting Chris's gaze.

"Good morning, Evie." He moved to the stove where a kettle waited, and he poured her a cup of tea. "Let me get you some breakfast."

"Thank you." She walked to the table and looked over Madeline and Ben's shoulders.

They were writing out lists of words with thin pieces of chalk. She read them out loud. "'Treasure, island, captain, global, Atlantic, freight.' Are we practicing our spelling?"

"Yep," Ben answered happily, grinning up at her. "Frosty says we need to start our schooling."

Chris and Ruthie had both mentioned that she taught Lee, and Evelyn had learned that Mrs. Bolton had taught Dannie, Travis, and Clark before they were old enough to work on their own to prepare for admittance to schools offering higher levels of education. But she and Chris hadn't spoken of what the three children under their care would do.

Evelyn sat in her usual chair, hand wrapped around her mug of tea. "I suppose he's right. Especially if any of you wish to go to university someday, like Travis and Clark, and Lee." She sipped at the tea, her gaze lowered as she thought. "I'm not entirely certain where we should begin with such work."

"We've got time to figure that out." Crossing the room, Chris put a plate of eggs and biscuits with jam in front of her. "Breakfast isn't much. There's some fried ham, but I've noticed you don't usually eat much of that. Do you want some?"

Ham tended to make her head ache. Evelyn shook her head. "This is perfectly adequate, thank you."

"Good. I hope you don't mind I stayed around this morning. Everyone who went out last night is getting some rest before starting up for the day, so there wasn't much for me to do yet." He dropped back into the chair across from her, his clear blue eyes taking her in while he wore a slight smile. "Ruthie came by earlier. She wants you to come work in the garden in about an hour. She said to bring the kids. Then you're going to spend the day canning vegetables over here. She talked like you knew the plan."

"Vaguely." Evelyn nibbled at her biscuit. "I'm going to learn how to garden in the desert and put up food for when the garden isn't producing. It sounds fascinating." She looked over to Ben and raised her chin. "I'm not sure how we'll get Ben over there, with his foot injured."

"I'll carry him, then he can hop around the Steeles' house on one foot. Can't you, Ben? That's how he got to the table today."

Ben grinned widely. "I'm really good at jumping on one foot. You wanna see, Evie?"

Madeline giggled. "Except when you hopped right into the table." Laura laughed, too, and Ben's little nose turned up at them both.

Evelyn ignored the teasing. "I'm certain I'll see plenty of your hopping over the next several weeks." She made eye contact with Chris. "We can leave as soon as you're ready."

He shrugged and tipped back in his chair. "I'm in no rush." He brushed his hand through his hair again, leaving it waving on top of his head. "I'm going to talk to Abram about getting crutches for Ben. That'll make it easier for him to get from one place to another, and get his usual chores done."

Ben sat up straight. "Chores? But, Frosty, I've got stitches!" The same protest had been on Evelyn's lips, and she nodded.

"I agree. He needs to rest."

Chris met Evelyn's eyes, and she saw what she'd call stubbornness in another man.

"Abram has a wooden leg," Chris drawled slowly, swinging his gaze to the boy. "He still manages to help out around the ranch."

Evelyn squirmed somewhat in her chair before finally speaking. The children were her responsibility, weren't they? Shouldn't her word count for something?

"Ben is a little boy. You cannot expect him to do much, especially with his injury." Then she braced herself as Chris's gaze settled again on her, his blue eyes the same shade as a frosted pond. She waited for a rebuke of some sort. Men didn't like when women, especially their wives, spoke against them.

"I agree that he's young, and his chores reflect that. Some things he certainly can't do. Sweeping would be hard on one foot, I'm betting." He shot a wink at Ben. "But other things, like helping his sisters gather eggs, checking on animals, cleaning up around the house, and doing his schoolwork are all manageable with a pair of good crutches."

Evelyn prepared to disagree again when she caught Madeline's bright smile. Only then did Evelyn realize what Chris had said. He'd spoken of her as Ben's sister.

Had Chris been intentional in his wording? It had seemed so natural that Evelyn almost didn't realize what he'd said. What it meant. Chris was treating them all like a family—like they had always been a family. Though her throat tightened, Evelyn forced her mind back to the matter at hand.

So she bit her tongue. Chris had disagreed with her in front of the children. And firmed up his point of view. Evelyn swallowed her embarrassment. Of course, Chris wouldn't expect the boy to do anything too arduous. He'd always been a kind man, not a demanding one.

"Did you know I broke my leg at the beginning of this year?" Chris asked, his eyes on Ben. Evelyn perked up. She hadn't heard this. "I still feel like limping from time to time. The leg's healed up, but something about the experience makes me want to treat it extra careful. It was hard, trying to be foreman on a ranch with a busted leg. And this was before Duke and most of the other hands came. It was just me, Ed, and another cowboy named Buck. Mr. Bolton was gettin' over a fight with pneumonia, too."

Laura pulled in a quick breath. "That sounds awful. How'd you get anything done?" She put her chalk down, and Evelyn noticed she'd drawn an ivy vine along the side of her spelling words. "Who took care of all the animals?"

"Mostly Ed, Dannie, and Travis. But I hobbled around on crutches, trying to boss everyone around." He chuckled and leaned forward, setting all four legs of his chair on the ground again. "I did my part, as best I could. Wound up cooking a lot, since that wasn't something that required two legs to do. I rode the wagon around the property, since I couldn't ride a horse."

"Didn't the doctor tell you to stay in bed?" Madeline asked, and Evelyn nodded along with the question.

"You mean Ruthie?" He grinned when Madeline and Evelyn both gasped. "She stitched up Ben all right, and she put my leg in a splint and plaster, too. Abram and Ed had to help set the bone, though."

Evelyn swallowed a far-too large a bite of eggs, then drank tea swiftly to help the lump of food go down. Coughing a bit, she was shaking her head. "You didn't have a doctor to set your leg, and you kept working?"

"There wasn't much of a choice," he answered with a nonchalant shrug, though his eyes darkened with concern as he watched her recover from her rather unfortunate bite. "And it'd be the same now, even with the extra men. A foreman isn't expendable on a ranch this size. Just as Ben has his chores to see to." He nodded to the boy, who sat up straighter under the scrutiny. "Just be smart about doing the work, so you don't hurt yourself more. We'll keep you off the foot a few more days while we get your crutches turned out. Then, it's back to work."

With her breakfast finished, Evelyn rose from the table with her plate. "Girls, help me tidy the kitchen. Then we will go see Ruthie's garden." The children were up and hurrying to the pump to start work on the dishes, but Chris stood as Evelyn walked by him.

"Evie?" He put his hand on her arm softly to gain her attention. He looked down into her eyes, his expression serious. "We need to talk."

Her stomach sank as she followed him into the front room. Now came the moment he'd rebuke her. She could only be thankful he'd wanted to do so away from the children. When they stood in the front room, he turned to face her. Before he could speak, she rushed to apologize. "I'm sorry I questioned you in front of the children. It wasn't my place."

He stared at her in silence. She fidgeted with her fingers behind her back, lowering her gaze to the floor. Waiting for him to speak.

Finally, he said, "I wanted to let you know that I'll make sure Ben is careful. I know you don't want him hurt."

She waited a moment for him to say more, to clarify his

words, to add a request for her not to question him in front of the children. But he didn't do any of that. He simply stood, waiting for her response. Finally, she spoke. "Thank you. I'm sorry I worried."

"Don't be. You married me because you care about those kids, right?" He extended his hand to her, and without thinking she put hers in his. Chris tangled his fingers with hers to offer a gentle squeeze of reassurance. "I don't know the first thing about being a father. You've got more experience than I do with parenthood. Don't ever hold back if you think I'm doing something wrong, Evie. We can always talk about it."

She gazed up at him, studying his expression closely. Finding no hint of irritation. "I am daily surprised by you, Chris Morgan."

He blinked at that, one side of his mouth going up while he furrowed up his forehead in confusion. "Really? Why?"

"You are more a gentleman than anyone I have ever met," she said firmly, and then dared to do something based solely on how right it felt in that moment. Evelyn tilted her chin up just enough to lean forward and place a kiss on his cheek. She didn't mean much by it. She needed him to understand her gratitude, though, and the sincerity of her compliment. Then she tugged her hand from his and marched back to the kitchen and the sink, speaking to the girls as she went. "Now then, how will we save this pan from the bits of egg still stuck to it? What do you think, Laura?"

She glanced over her shoulder as she put her arm around the girls, newly made sisters as far as this family was concerned. And she saw Chris still standing stock-still where she'd left him, his chin ducked, and a contented smile on his face.

CHAPTER TWENTY

When Ruthie Steele swung a hoe in a great arc, chopping viscously into a nettle-like plant that had taken up residence in her patch of garden, Evelyn wondered that anything would dare grow where the feisty woman hadn't put it.

"The roots of desert plants are the most infuriating thing." Ruthie bent down to grab the plant and pull it up from the thickly packed soil. "You can see how the roots are for this one. They go straight down a bit, wrapped in on themselves. This here is a brittlebush. Seeds probably brought in by a bird. They're pretty enough when they bloom in the spring, but they don't go in my garden."

Beth Bolton came over, thick canvas gloves upon her hands, and took the plant gently from Ruthie. "Which is why I'll plant it over by our road in front of the house. The bees like the flowers. They look a lot like daisies when they bloom."

"We try to keep the useful plants," Ruthie added, leaning against her hoe. "A roasted brittlebush twig does wonders for a toothache." She wiped at the sweat of her brow with the back of one hand. "Most green things have their uses, and we can't be too picky out here on our own."

Evelyn nodded her understanding, gripping the spade they'd handed her tightly in one hand. "I can understand that. Making do with what you already have is important."

"Precisely." Beth had deposited her plant into a wheelbarrow and now returned, brushing off her gloves. "Today, we're harvesting peppers and checking on our mousemelons."

"Mousemelons?" Laura asked from her place bent down by a green pepper plant. "Are they tiny watermelons?"

"Come see for yourself." Ruthie hefted her hoe and started walking down a row of plants. Her garden was planted on the northern side of her house, with rope strung up over the top so she could pull sheets of canvas to cover a small section of the garden when the most delicate plants needed more shade. Evelyn had studied the pulley system Abram had rigged up with wonder. At the moment, there wasn't any canvas covering. The season was late enough that the sun didn't do damage to the plants Ruthie cultivated.

When they arrived at several sticks with vines draped around them, the plant bush-like to Evie's untrained eye, she saw immediately what appeared to be tiny watermelons growing all over it.

"Try one," Ruthie said to Laura. Madeline had arrived, too, her small hands in a pair of too-large gloves. "Both of you."

The girls looked at each other, then popped off a single tiny melon each and put them in their mouths. The reaction was immediate. Laura squealed and wrinkled her nose, chewing faster and harder before swallowing. Madeline winced and kept chewing, then stuck out her tongue and groaned.

Beth removed one of the tiny melons and bit into it with a cheerful smile. "If you expect something sweet, then taste something sour, it's always a bit of a surprise."

"It's like a sour cucumber," Madeline said. She took another and stared at it, then nibbled off the end. This time, she appeared thoughtful as she chewed. "It has lots of little seeds, too."

"It certainly does." Ruthie nodded to Evelyn. "Would you like to try?"

Evelyn did, with the same experience as the girls. "What does one do with these mousemelons?"

"We pickle them," Ruthie explained. "Or chop them up and fry them, with onions and garlic, maybe a bit of beef."

"They add a delicious flavor to the meat." Beth chuckled and pointed to the short row of plants. "Girls, why don't you start picking them? If they have any yellow on them, leave those. Fill this pail." She nudged the tin pail with her foot. "And you needn't wear gloves for this one, Maddie dear. There aren't any thorns or prickles on this plant."

Ruthie took Evelyn down a few rows to the green peppers. After showing Evelyn how to pick the ripe peppers and leave the rest, Ruthie bent to work. She wore a wide-brimmed straw bonnet and had loaned Evelyn one of the same. The older woman talked while she worked, enumerating the various things one could do with green peppers. Drying them made them hotter, pickling them could make them sweeter, adding them to cornbread was a special treat, and frying them up in a potato hash sounded like a favorite way to eat them.

"Frosty loves green peppers in his eggs," Ruthie added. "And his chili. Come to think of it, I think that man likes the little green things in most foodstuff." Ruthie shook her head. "Abram is nearly the same. These menfolk can't stand for things to be boring, can they? Not even their food." She chuckled happily.

"I have heard it said that one of the reasons England goes about into foreign lands is to commandeer spices and save ourselves from bland food." Evelyn smirked, remembering the gentleman who had made that joke at her expense on the ocean crossing. "I suppose most English food would seem dull to people who put green peppers in everything."

Dropping peppers in her basket at twice the speed Evelyn managed, Ruthie still kept up with the conversation perfectly. "People like to judge what they don't know anything about. I'm betting English food is as tasty as anyone else's." They worked in silence for a few minutes, then Ruthie asked, "Is Frosty disappointed they didn't catch the rustlers last night?"

"I imagine so, though he didn't say directly." Evelyn examined the leaves of the little plant, noting with some surprise that they weren't overly dry or brittle, though they did seem somewhat wilted.

"You were certainly an understanding bride, letting him go off on a dangerous errand like that so soon after marriage." Ruthie shook her head. "Abram wanted to go, and I reminded him that he's too old for such foolishness."

Evelyn's hand stilled where she held it, just beneath a pepper, and she slowly closed her fingers over the green vegetable. "What do you mean? Chris didn't seem to think it was very dangerous. He made it sound like he has sprung such traps several times."

"That's a man for you." Ruthie knelt in the dirt, examining the base of a plant. "Needs a bit more water, I think. Maybe some eggshells, too," she murmured to herself. Then she looked up at Evelyn. "Of course he's going to make it sound like the easiest thing in the world. Probably trying to convince himself as much to reassure you, but I don't think that kind of yarn does anyone any favors. These rustlers have been slippery, and maybe Frosty has dealt with their kind before, but we haven't had problems like this in six years or more. Only desperate men turn to cattle-thieving. In the territory, it can still be a hanging offense."

A shiver went through Evelyn. Realizing she still held the same pepper, Evelyn hastily dropped it into the basket at her feet. Then she rubbed her hand along her apron, as though getting off dirt. "I don't imagine a rustler would want to be caught, then."

With a snort, Ruthie pulled herself to her feet, leaning on her hoe again. "Oh, they'll usually cut and run, but they'll also fight like their lives depend on it if they're cornered. Because getting caught means being branded a thief. Bringing shame to the family, too. If they have any." Ruthie looked over to where Laura had gone to the next row over, the girl looking at several long green, leafy plants.

"What are these?" Laura pointed.

"Radishes, dear. We can probably pick a few today, if you like." She looked at Evelyn and winked. "Not my favorite, but since they grow clear through April, they're a good crop to have."

Evelyn hefted up her basket of peppers and opened her mouth to ask a question when she spied movement from the corner of her eye, in the dirt on the same row she stood within. Some instinct she didn't know she possessed took hold, sealing away the scream her lungs had filled with. She remained perfectly still, instead. Then, in a whisper she hoped would carry, she said, "There's a snake here."

The serpent's long body was thick, making it appear larger than Evelyn would've guessed possible for such an animal. Its head was shaped like an arrowhead, a black forked tongue darting in and out of its mouth. Her eyes swept from the head to the tail and back again as she gulped with realization. The end of the tail looked rather like a group of beads woven tightly together.

A rattlesnake. Not three feet from her.

A flash of metal and wood arced between Evelyn and the snake, and the flat metal end of Ruthie's hoe made contact with snake and dirt, causing a loud thump that Evelyn would never forget. She jumped back, her eyes frantically searching beneath her.

Ruthie had cleaved the rattlesnake's head from the rest of its body, and Evelyn looked away rather than watch the twitch of the now dead animal. Bile rose in her throat, and she hurriedly backed away from the spot. Ruthie sighed deeply as she removed her tool and wiped it in the dirt.

"I hate doing that," she said, looking over her shoulder at the girls crowding up next to a concerned Beth. "You girls mark what I say. There's no good person who will kill an animal for just being what it is. You see a snake in the desert minding its own business? You leave it well enough alone. But when they come wandering in to where our little ones walk and we raise our food, you act fast so there's no call for a funeral by-and-by."

Beth nodded her agreement. "Amen to that." She rubbed the shoulders of the little girls on either side of her. "And we look where we're going and keep our boots on when we're outside, don't we?"

Madeline looked down at her once-fashionable shoes, then at Laura's sturdier footwear. "Mama. I think I want a pair of boots like Laura's."

The tension broke as the adults laughed at her assessment.

"We will get you a pair, dear. And some for me, too." Evelyn looked at the tip of her shoes. She wore the only comfortable pair she had, out of the two pairs she owned. Lower heeled, squarer toes, a little more practical than the fashionable button-up pair with the high heels and pointed ends.

"I never walk around the ranch without carrying my hoe," Ruthie said. "Unless one of the men is with me, and their gun is on their hip. You'd do well to do the same, Evelyn."

"You girls should always walk in pairs and be prepared to yell for help," Mrs. Bolton added. "There's enough coming and going on the ranch that not many wild animals come through, and snakes don't like the chickens or cats. But we still see the occasional critter that might make trouble."

Evelyn rubbed at the raised bumps on her arms. Sure, Chris had warned her about dangerous animals. Somehow, she'd thought he was being overly cautious. "I think I'd like to encourage some of those cats to make a home on our back porch."

Snakes and cattle rustlers. What else would she have to consider when she planned for the safety of her family? Teaching at an all-girls' school in the east would have been infinitely easier. Safer. For a moment, she thought again of the letter she had sent to Dannie's finishing school. But she wasn't there. She was here.

Lee appeared at Ruthie's back door and called out to them.

"Granny, there's a wagon coming down the path. Looks like it might be headed to the main house."

"I wasn't expecting company." Beth took her gloves off. "Why don't you girls come with me? If it's someone wanting a visit, I'll send you back to fetch Ruthie and Evelyn."

When both girls looked to Evelyn for permission, she gave them a quick nod. "That sounds like a good plan. Take your pails inside and put them on the table as you go."

She and Ruthie watched the girls disappear into the Steele house, Beth behind them. Then Evelyn turned to meet Ruthie's gaze, her insides tight with worry and her tone grim. "I think you had better teach me how to wield a garden tool the way you just did, Ruthie."

The older woman's wrinkles along her smile and the corners of her eyes deepened. "Absolutely." She held out the hoe. "It's all a matter of practice, and there isn't any place better for that than a garden."

Evelyn took the long handle in a firm grip. She wasn't going to let a snake get the better of her, or her children, again.

THE SUN HAD DIPPED LOW, PAINTING THE SKY IN PURPLES AND oranges, when Chris stepped onto his front porch. His hair dripped from his quick scrub at the cistern, but he wore a smile that Ed had teased him about not five minutes before. Chris's friend had called it a "mile-wide smile." Chris couldn't really help it. He'd been thinking about Evie all day, hoping she'd had a better time spent with the ladies than she had the day before. He'd also worked with Abram in the barn and had a crutch to measure up against Ben.

He opened the door and immediately paused, looking at the clean floorboards. He stepped inside, then leaned back against the closed door and took off his boots, putting them side by side against the wall. Voices from the kitchen pulled him through the house in his stockinged feet.

"Are you sure that's how Mrs. Steele said to cook the onions?" a skeptical Madeline asked as Chris entered the kitchen.

He took in a deep breath and immediately liked what his nose told him was cooking. Onions. Peppers. Garlic. "Smells mighty good in here," he said aloud.

Ben twisted in his seat and grinned. "Frosty's home!"

The two girls and Evelyn stood at the stove, all of them looking into a large frying pan, but they turned around when they saw him. Chris drank in the expressions on their faces as an empty place in his heart filled right up with contentment. Laura sent him a big smile, no trace of the sullen expression she had worn for the first two weeks he'd had the children. Madeline came away from the stove with arms outstretched for a hug. He bent down to accept her embrace and a kiss on his cheek.

Then there was Evelyn. She looked beautiful. Her nose and cheeks were a trifle pink, telling him she'd spent a good part of her day outside. Her deep red hair was still in the long braid, trailing down to her waist. Her lips turned up in welcome, but her eyes remained dark. They searched his as she spoke her simple greeting. "Welcome home, Chris."

Home. Had he called this little house by that name yet? It hadn't felt like a home until Evelyn had come, reading stories to the three children and filling the rooms with her presence, chasing away the gloom the same way light chased away shadow.

"Thank you." Those two brief words held a lot more than simple gratitude. Maybe someday he'd be able to tell Evelyn all that she meant to him.

"Is that for me?" Ben asked from his place at the table.

Chris still held the crutch, and he cleared his throat as he turned to face Ben. "Sure is. This here is what we call a prototype. It's a test to see what works and what we need to change to make your crutch just right."

"Good. Because I'm tired of being carried around." Ben's chin came up, along with a hint of stubbornness in his eye that imme-diately reminded Chris of Ben's father.

"Clark had to give him a ride on his back." Madeline slid into a chair across from Ben. "And he teased him the whole time."

Ben lifted one shoulder. "I didn't mind that so much." He looked up at Chris, his smile returning. "He kept braying like a donkey."

"That right?" Chris chuckled and leaned the crutch against the table. "I've always liked those Bolton kids."

Ben's eyes brightened suddenly. "We have a surprise for dinner."

"You'll never guess what we're having," Laura announced proudly. "We aren't going to give you any hints, either."

Madeline's nose scrunched up. "I don't really want to eat it, but Mrs. Steele says we must."

Leveling Madeline with a half-serious, half-playful glare, Chris intoned, "If Ruthie says to eat something, you can bet you'd better follow her instructions." Chris walked over to where Evelyn pushed around sizzling vegetables and fried pieces of meat warmed in another pan.

"Ruthie made those." Evelyn pointed with the wooden spoon in her hand to the fried food. "She just brought them over a few minutes ago and told me to keep them warm. And she said when the onions are translucent, the vegetables are done." She scooped up some onions and held them up, pursing her lips as she studied them.

They were pretty lips. Rosie from being pressed together. And they were smooth and soft as satin. He knew thanks to the kiss she'd pressed to his cheek before.

"Do these look transparent to you?" She glanced at him with her eyebrows drawn sharply together, but when their gazes met, her eyes grew large. What did she see when she looked at him? Did she know that she captivated him?

His eyes darted to the onions on her spoon, then down to the peppers and other vegetables in the pan. "I think they look fine."

He didn't step away. He met her eyes again, and he moved in a little closer so that their shoulders brushed. "Let me try a bite, to be sure."

"Be my guest, sir." She held the spoon up to her lips and blew on the food, chasing away the steam in what had to be the most attractive way he'd ever seen, then held the wooden utensil up to his lips with a quirk to her smile. "Your sample, sir."

Why had his mouth gone dry? And the sudden heat rolling through him from head to hoof had nothing to do with the green peppers on the tip of that spoon. Chris tried to concentrate on the vegetables, and Evelyn thrust them closer to him. He opened his mouth, not feeling at all as ridiculous as he probably should, and accepted the bite.

"Mm." He nodded his approval, though the food could've tasted like ash and had the consistency of gravel and he probably would've responded the same. "Seems done to me."

Evelyn tapped the spoon against the pan, gave everything another stir for good measure, and then nodded. "Splendid. Dinner is served."

It took another few minutes of shuffling plates and pans before everyone was at the table with helpings of vegetables, cornbread muffins, and fried-something-or-other in front of them. Madeline had found the smallest piece of fried meat for her plate, and Evelyn had followed suit with the second-to-smallest. Laura and Ben, however, seemed eager to eat whatever hid beneath the golden cornmeal batter.

"Frosty gets the first bite," Laura declared, watching him with unconcealed glee. "You have to guess what it is."

Chris sliced a piece of meat off and examined the coloring. "Hm. It's not flaky, so fish is out of the question."

"Where would we even get fish around here?" Evelyn asked, eyebrows shooting upward.

"Fair point. Nearest fishing hole is quite a ways away." Chris studied the color. "It's white. So I'm guessing chicken or pork." Since both of those options were safe enough, he popped the food in his mouth and started chewing. The cornmeal covered the taste at first, but then he started sorting out a gamey flavor that meant wild meat. "Quail?"

"Nope," Ben and Laura chorused. Madeline watched him with wide eyes and her mouth slightly agape. What food would make a little girl with a normally adventurous character so uncertain?

"Some kind of lizard?" The texture seemed right. "It's a lizard or a snake." He gave a shrug. "That's probably the closest I can get to a guess."

"Tell him, Ben," Evelyn said, calmly slicing into her fried reptile, though he didn't miss the wrinkle above her nose as she examined the meat.

"It's a rattlesnake," Ben announced with undisguised glee. "A big one, too. Mrs. Steele showed me before she had to clean it."

Madeline went a touch green and put her fork down on the table again. "It was horrid," she whispered, scowling at her plate.

Laura looked to Madeline, then up at Chris. "It was in the garden with us."

Chris's gaze darted to Evelyn, his insides went cold, and he swallowed the too-large bite of fried rattlesnake. "You were in the garden when the snake showed up?"

"Perhaps three feet from where I stood." She continued to examine her food rather than meet his gaze. She finally closed her eyes and put the food in her mouth. She went pale as she chewed, but her color returned when she swallowed. She released a large sigh. "That wasn't all that terrible, actually."

Chris had wanted someone to teach Evelyn what to do if she came across a snake, but he didn't think the lesson would come so soon or so dangerously. And he hasn't even been nearby when she'd run into the creature. "I'm sorry, Evie."

Finally, her eyes met his. "Ruthie was there, and she took care of it as though nothing was even amiss. I think it's a good thing it happened as it did." She went on slicing another piece of food. "The children learned a valuable lesson, and I don't intend to step out of doors without something sharp in my hands ever again. I didn't realize until today how dangerous it can be simply to walk through a garden."

A guilty weight pressed against his heart. "Evie." He stretched out his arm and laid his hand over hers. The children went quiet, and he felt their focus on the two adults responsible for their care. Their parents, from here on out. "I'm sorry you weren't prepared. I promise to help you and the children learn how to keep safe out here on the ranch."

She turned her hand over and curled her fingers around his. "Thank you for that." Then her chin came up, and her eyes met his. "Do you intend to go out again tonight, to try to catch the rustlers?"

Chris glanced over at the children, noting their wide eyes. He put on a smile, squeezed Evelyn's hand, and then released it. "Sure am. Me and my posse of ranch hands. Likely, it'll be a quiet night. I'll make sure Gus is on the porch again, and I'll be back nice and early. Maybe we can make breakfast together again. Would you kids like that?"

Their expressions lightened, and the children started talking about their day. The girls giggled over trying mousemelons for the first time, and Ben had played checkers with Lee enough times to win at least one of their games. The cheerful chatter surrounded Chris, and the children's smiles relieved him of more burdens than he knew he carried. They were safe and happy.

He steadily avoided looking Evelyn's way until the kids cleaned their plates and went into the main room to prepare for the evening's book. At that point, he finally met Evelyn's gaze. He sat at the table still, and she stood beside the sink. Turned to face him.

"Ruthie had an interesting perspective on what you and the men are doing to catch the rustlers."

Chris crossed his arms and leaned back in his chair. "That a fact? Abram helped me come up with our plan, you know. And where we stationed everyone."

"She also reminded me that Abram isn't one of the men out there." Evelyn approached the table, hands clenched at her side though her countenance remained calm. "Ruthie even made it seem like *you* shouldn't be out there, since there is danger and you have a family dependent on you."

He came down onto all four legs of the chair abruptly, and the resounding clunk made Evelyn wince. "I also have a job to do. I'm the foreman, Evelyn. Do you know what that means?" He kept his seat and narrowed his eyes at her. She didn't understand, and he obviously needed to explain things to her. "It means I'm responsible for my boss's cattle and my boss's men. The cattle are getting stolen, right out from under my nose. The men are needed to do something about it, and I'm the one telling them what to do."

Wrapping her arms around herself, Evelyn rocked back on her heels. "King isn't going out for *his* men and cattle."

"Because he pays me to see to things."

"Dangerous things," Evelyn retorted, her trim frame winding tighter. "Chris, we've been married a matter of days, and you're already running off to do things that might get you killed. You might have a job to do for the ranch, but you've got a job to do for the children, too. You promised you'd provide for us and keep us safe." She lowered her voice, darting a glance at the door between the kitchen and main room. "How can you do that if you get shot by a rustler?"

Though her words pierced his heart, leaving him buck-shot with guilt, Chris had to shake his head. "I can't provide for any of you if I don't do my job." Then he rose to his feet, slow and steady. He wasn't angry, but he sure was frustrated. "What about you? You nearly stepped on a rattler today. What about your promises to care for the children? Being snake-bit is as dangerous as getting shot. Maybe more so. We can dig out a bullet. We can't do a thing for venom. Every time any of us step foot out the door, we're taking a risk."

Her chin came up. "That isn't the same thing at all. I didn't go out looking for trouble."

"You think that's what I'm doing?" He came closer to her, hands out and words gentler. "Evie, I'm doing everything I can to stay safe. I'm not running out the door to challenge anyone to a duel. I'm protecting livestock and the livelihood of everyone on this ranch. Losing cattle is losing money, and the means to keep this place going. You had as much chance of getting run over by a runaway horse in England as you do of being snake-bit out here. That's all I'm trying to say."

She looked down at his hands but didn't take them. Instead, she glared up at him again, and this time he saw a glimmer of something other than anger. It wasn't quite fear, either. Before he could put a name to the emotion, she turned away. She put her hands behind her back and started untying her apron.

"Fine. I suppose if you get yourself shot, I'll still have access to your bank account."

She might've meant for the words to sting, but Chris had the feeling Evelyn fought not to cry. Like a cornered puma, she was ready to strike out however she could to avoid getting hurt.

Her fingers twisted at the apron strings, and he saw she'd made a mess of the knot. Chris sighed, letting out his exasperation, before stepping closer and gently knocking her hands away. "Let me do this. You've turned it into a walnut-sized ball of twists."

She put her hands on her waist and stood still, and as he concentrated on the apron strings, he couldn't help but feel sorry for getting her riled up. "Evie," he said, keeping his eyes on his work as he tugged one of the strings through the snarl. "This is how things out here work. Every time you step outside, you're taking your life in your hands. And we can either choose to live in fear of everything that lurks in canyons and under rocks, or we can choose to have some faith and practice a lot of common sense."

He gave one last tug. The strings fell to her sides. But rather than step away, he put a hand on her shoulder. Carefully, he turned her to face him. The tears had escaped her pretty eyes, and her nose had reddened with her attempts to hold everything back.

She hastily pulled the apron off over her head, then wiped her eyes with the corner of the cloth. "What do I do if something happens to you?" she asked, and his heart twisted at the pain in her voice. Did the idea of his death hurt because she'd lose his protection, or because she'd lose *him*? The answer to that question didn't matter right then. What mattered was the lost look she wore, the plaintive way she'd asked the question.

"Evie." He put both hands on her shoulders. "You crossed an ocean and half a continent with your daughter and almost nothing but the clothes on your back. You're the most determined woman I've ever met. If anything happened to me, you'd have money, friends, and time to figure out what came next." He spoke truly enough, though he hoped with every ounce of strength he had that she'd never have to face a day like that.

Maybe he should've said something along those lines. Maybe he should've told her that he intended to spend the rest of his life with her. That he felt like a little bit more of his heart belonged to her with every day that passed. Instead of saying any of that— words that took time, and words that didn't do justice to the complex things in his head and heart—Chris drew her closer. Slowly, and only into a careful embrace. Though he wanted so much more.

Holding her and offering comfort this way felt right. Natural. Like he'd done it all his life. Chris closed his eyes and tried to memorize exactly how it felt, even though he'd much rather kiss her.

The thought startled him. It was too soon. He'd promised he wouldn't force her into anything. He hadn't even tried to court her yet.

She deserved so much better.

He ended the embrace before she could respond. It'd hurt too much if she pulled away. So he released her and stepped back, his neck and face going warm. He cleared his throat and looked away before he could see her expression. He ran one hand through his hair while shoving the other in his back pocket.

"I'd better get going. The men will be ready to ride out soon." He took one step back, then another, then turned and went up the steps without looking back.

"Chris?"

Pausing near the top of the steps, Chris glanced over his shoulder. Evelyn was looking down at the floor. "Yes?"

"Mrs. Harper came by this afternoon. She said there's a picnic at the church in two days. The children and I would like to go. Will you accompany us?"

His heart flipped. It wasn't a rejection, a demand, or a plea. Only an invitation for him, for the two of them, to make their family a part of the community.

"I wouldn't miss it for all the silver in the Territory." That said, he went on up to gather his things for another night sleeping out in the desert.

CHAPTER TWENTY-ONE

The night of their disagreement, Evelyn bid a polite farewell to Chris after he told the children goodnight. But that didn't dispel any of the tension she felt growing between herself and her new husband. She tried not to think about the look in his eyes when they'd spoken and what it meant, reassuring herself that Chris hadn't placed any demands upon her. Yet there was little else to do but think when she lay down at night, listening to the sounds of wind against the house and the far-off lowing of cattle.

When she finally fell asleep, she dreamed of England. She dreamed of walking along a grassy hill, her hands out to catch the long wispy stalks. Everything was green and beautiful. But she realized she couldn't find the children. Or Chris. And she woke up, unable to catch her breath, to the sound of a dog barking. She stilled and listened, waiting. Remembering where she was.

The dog stopped. The door downstairs opened, and she heard nothing else until a pair of footsteps came up the stairs. They paused before her door.

And then she heard the barest tap on the wood. "Evie? Just wanted you to know that I'm home." The rustlers hadn't come, then.

Should she answer him? Let him know that she had woken, that she had slept terribly, waiting for his arrival? She opened her mouth, then closed it again. What if he took her response as an invitation to come in? Instead, she pulled the blankets up all the way to her chin. She wasn't ready for that.

His footsteps receded into the room across the hall. The room where he slept on the floor, atop and beneath a pile of blankets. He hadn't complained once about sleeping there, either.

You're being ridiculous, Evelyn. She rolled over and glared at the empty half of the bed. Though meant to hold two people, it was smaller than the beds she had slept in when she had been married before. Yet she couldn't bring herself to take up the whole of the mattress. Instead, she kept to one half. Reminding herself again and again that she wouldn't have the room to herself forever.

When will Chris stop being patient? Would it be better to be the one to invite him in? That would only be clinging to the illusion that she had any control over the matter.

Except. Chris had told her that she had control. He'd never treated her with anything other than respect.

But the thought that he might've kissed her in the kitchen— brief as it was—had made her stomach twist and her heart gain speed faster than a locomotive. What if, instead of that comforting embrace, he'd leaned in and pressed his lips to hers?

It was all she thought about as she fell asleep again.

When she awoke that morning, she came down the stairs with her hair coiled up at the top of her head and wearing a blue-striped dress. She'd taken extra care with her appearance, though she couldn't explain why.

And she felt almost eager to begin her day.

First, she had to take care of the beans she had soaked the evening before—at Ruthie's insistence. Evelyn had stared at the dried beans as they'd tumbled out of the bag and into a pot of water, convinced the pebble-like little things would never be edible. But this morning, she'd rinsed them, keeping the water to pour on the seedlings Ruthie had planted the night before. They were softer. Ready to be boiled.

Evelyn hadn't ever had beans for breakfast. But then, she'd never eaten rattlesnake before, either. When she'd consulted Dannie's book on the subject of bean preparation, it had proven less than helpful. Demonstrating once more how far-removed from her old life Evelyn had become.

The girls came into the kitchen not long after Evelyn rose, still yawning but dressed for the day. They had braided each other's hair. Madeline had two braids behind her ears and hanging across her shoulders while Laura's fell down her back in one thick, dark rope. Would a day go by without Evelyn thanking heaven that the two girls had become such fast friends?

Ben came in next, a hand on the wall to help him keep his balance as he hopped on one foot from room to room. He scowled as he sat, propping his injured foot up on the chair across the table from him.

"Good morning, Ben." Evelyn brought him a cup of cool buttermilk and placed it on the table before him. "Sweetheart, is your foot hurting?"

He shrugged one shoulder. "A little."

A deep voice from the stairs drew everyone's attention. "I think that's boy-talk. Let me interpret it for you, Evie." Chris came down, sliding his suspenders over his shoulders as he talked. "I'm betting his foot bothered him throughout the night. Maybe he even kicked it against something, making the injury throb." He jumped down the last step and went to kneel beside Ben. "Am I right?"

Ben's bottom lip stuck out, but he quickly sucked it back in. "I kicked the wall. It still hurts."

"I'm not surprised." Chris looked up at Evie, wearing a smile so devoid of worry that she wondered if he even remembered their disagreement the night before. Or how he had ended it with his gentle reassurances. "I'll take a look at our injured soldier."

Didn't he feel the tightness between them? A nearly tangible, twisting rope pulled Evelyn toward him while she fought so hard to stay at a safe distance. Maybe he didn't notice. Or maybe... maybe he wasn't fighting it like she was.

Evelyn backed away. "Thank you." She gave her attention to the beans again, wrinkling her nose at the brown things in the pot. She'd eaten kidney beans before, of course. And Windsor beans. But not whatever these strange, drab colored things were. But if a former countess could eat rattlesnake, surely she could enjoy brown beans. With a dash of salt or two.

By the time she had food on the table, Chris had re-bandaged Ben's foot. The girls had set the table and were eagerly discussing another visit to the barn after they completed their chores.

Evelyn broke into their eager conversation. "Mathematics, then kittens."

"Schoolwork comes first," Chris said at the exact moment Evelyn spoke. Their eyes met over the table while the children all groaned. Then Chris winked at Evelyn. "I don't know what all the belly-aching is about. There's a wide world out there, kids. More to see and do than you can even imagine. The best way to prepare for that world, and all the adventures you'll have, is to gain an education."

"Like Jim Hawkins," Ben murmured, head bent over his plate.

Evelyn raised her eyebrows. "Exactly right. The ship's officers were teaching him how to do mathematics in order to navigate a ship."

"Maybe I'll do that. Someday." Ben appeared thoughtful as he started eating his breakfast.

"Women don't get to sail ships," Laura muttered, crossing her arms and glaring at her plate. "All we do is stay home, do chores, and raise babies."

Evelyn's jaw dropped open. "And who, dear child, has taught you such a terrible falsehood? Certainly not any of the women on this ranch. And I'd imagine your own mother wouldn't have said such things."

Laura blushed and sank lower in her chair. "Boys at school. Before—before we came here to live."

"Was your schoolteacher a man or a woman?" Chris asked in his usual unhurried way.

"A woman." Her cheeks turned red.

"Right. And what did your mama do before you came along? You've gotta know all about that." Chris's smile ticked upward.

Laura rubbed at her arms. "Mama went to school to be a nurse."

Evelyn leaned forward, eyes wide. "I didn't know that about your mother, Laura. How wonderful."

The little girl shrugged and looked to her side, where Madeline stared back at her with a serious frown. The girls obviously had spoken of this already. "It didn't do her much good," Laura whispered. "She just stayed home with us most of the time. Then she went to help the Grady family, and she got sick, and she died. So did my dad."

"Influenza and diphtheria," Chris said when Evelyn looked to him. Her heart sank. Terrible illnesses on their own, but together? Horrible. "Your mother's schooling did many people a lot of good, Laura. In fact. You wait here just a minute." He rose from the table and turned to the stairs, then spun around to meet Evelyn's eyes. "Mind if I get something out of the room?"

She slowly shook her head, wondering what he was up to. He went up the stairs, and she turned her attention to Ben. He'd gone still during the conversation. She put her hand on his shoulder, and when he looked up at her, Evelyn cupped his cheek in her hand. "It's hard to talk about your mother and father sometimes, isn't it?"

He nodded, and his eyes glimmered with tears. "I miss them. So much." Then he was crying, and Evelyn moved her chair next to his to wrap her arms around him.

"It's all right, Ben. You can miss them, and you can cry about it." Her eyes grew wet, but she held him more fiercely and met Laura's gaze with a watery smile. "I want you both to know that you can talk about your mother and your father whenever you wish. It will help keep their memories alive in your hearts, and it'll help you both remember all the stories about them."

"My mama does that," Madeline added in her sweet voice. "She tells me stories about my grandparents, even though she misses them. Her papa worked at the biggest bank in London."

"That's right." Evelyn's heart squeezed tighter. "Some days, the memories and stories might make you cry. Other days, those memories will fill you with joy. I promise."

Chris came down the stairs again, holding a thick leather-wrapped sheaf of letters. "Here we go." He put the packet on the table and untied the strip of leather keeping it all together. "These are all the letters your dad wrote to me over the years. I'm happy to share them with the two of you. Every single one. For today, I've got a special one in mind." He shuffled through the well-worn stack of envelopes and folded papers. As Evelyn watched his eyes, she realized he had to know what was in each letter by sight.

How many times would a man need to read a pile of letters to know them so well? Had he missed his dear friend or just been lonely? How had he managed to keep all the letters?

He pulled out an envelope that looked older than most and opened it. He sat back in his seat, cleared his throat, and read aloud.

"Dear Chris, I can't tell you how hard it is to write this letter. I thought about not telling you what's happened, so I can forget it. But then I figure I'm doing wrong by my darling wife. She saved Laura today, and I just stood by like a fool. I didn't know what to do. Laura stood right next to me, choking. Her little face went blue. I grabbed her shoulders and shook her. I was near ready to turn her upside down. But then Maria came into the room and, with great calm, made Laura bend over while she delivered a series of had thrusts to Laura's back. Laura gasped in a breath, and then Maria reached down our baby girl's throat and pulled out a nickel."

Chris paused here and looked up. "Your mother knew just

what to do to save you, Laura. She learned while she trained to be a nurse."

Laura blinked and sniffled. "I didn't know Mommy saved me like that."

Chris handed her the letter, and she took it reverently in both hands. Then he looked from Ben to Laura, and he pointed at the stack of paper. "There are lots of mentions of your mother helping other people, all through those letters. Your dad was proud of her, of how much she knew and how quick she was to help. So don't you say anything against her nursing, or her education. Be grateful for both, if you can, and try your best to be just like her."

The room went quiet, but Laura nodded quickly before pressing the letter to her chest. "I promise I will, Frosty."

Ben sniffled again. "Me, too."

"Good." Chris looked down at his plate of breakfast. "Maybe we oughtta mention our gratitude for all the good people in our lives this morning." Then he did just that, while Evelyn kept her head ducked down and her eyes closed tight.

Perhaps she didn't need to fight so hard against Chris's charm. Because more and more evidence piled up, reaffirming his goodness in ways she'd never expected.

But that goodness wouldn't matter if he risked himself in a way that might steal him from her, the way a desire to help others had stolen Laura and Ben's parents away from them. Could she risk opening her heart to him when she might lose him? How much worse would it hurt to let herself care for him than to fight the growing feelings in her heart?

THE THIRD NIGHT OF THEIR WATCH, THE MOON STILL BRIGHT enough to tempt a crooked cowboy to come hunting cattle, was as quiet as the previous two. Chris worked the situation over in his mind as he rode back to the bunkhouse with the ranch hands.

They were all tired but didn't grumble. They knew as well as he did how important it was to keep their boss's cattle where they belonged.

Perhaps the rustlers had finally moved on. Or they'd caught wind that Chris had set his trap, though he couldn't think how. All the men had sworn to keep silent. Even Travis and Clark were under orders not to mention their ambush to anyone outside of the ranch.

Whatever the case, three nights of all the men swapping watch duty had gone by, and they needed a change.

The sky turned lavender in the east, though sunrise remained a way off. When they arrived at the edge of the paddock, Chris started barking his orders. "Everyone gets a few hours of sleep. If you want to go to the Sonoita picnic later, that's all right by me. I need three men to stay behind. One watching the canyon to sound the alarm if the rustlers show, two to keep watch on the buildings. Sort it out amongst yourselves, if you can. For now— get that shut-eye."

A chorus of "yessir" and "yes, boss" met his ear as he dismounted. A quarter of an hour later, Chris made his way to his front porch. Gus gave his customary greeting, and Chris tossed him the last of a biscuit he'd taken with him for the night in the desert. Snapping the treat from the air, the dog issued one of his usual rumbling-growls that sounded more like talking than an animal's warning. Then he jumped off the porch and went on his way.

One of these days, Chris wanted to lay claim to a cattle dog of his own. He'd seen Ben playing with the litter of Gus and Fable's puppies and figured the boy might like an animal, too. The problem was, trying to keep a working dog as a pet might be hard on a kid. Then there were the girls, bringing barn cats into the house and fawning over half-wild kittens.

Animals on a ranch all had jobs to do, if they wanted to earn their keep. But why couldn't an animal's job include making a passel of kids happy?

He grinned to himself as he walked through the door. Seems he was the kind of man to want to spoil the children under his care. Pets. Books. Toys. He'd started working on a dollhouse for the girls with Abram, who'd then suggested a small barn for Ben for his toy animals.

If he could find something to give to Evie to spoil *her* a bit, he'd be especially happy. He sat quietly on a stool near the doorway—it had appeared the previous day, right next to the spot where he left his boots before creeping upstairs at night. Evelyn had put it there, he'd be willing to bet on it.

He pulled off the heavy, dusty leather boots. Still thinking.

What would make Evelyn smile? There's gotta be something that she misses about her old life that I could give her.

It wouldn't be wealth. He might make a decent living for an Arizona cowboy, but that wasn't nearly the same thing as being an English lord. Evelyn hadn't said much about her life before, or how she had filled her days as a countess. Maybe he needed to ask more questions. Though he hadn't wanted to pry at first, now that they were married, there were things he probably should know about her and her past.

Ready to climb the stairs up to another night of sleeping on the floor, Chris rose to his feet and stretched his arms high above his head with a groan. Movement on the couch caught his eye, and he stilled. Narrowing his eyes, Chris tried to make out the shape of what or who had shifted. He approached as quietly as he could, not wanting to wake the children.

The shadows in the room were still thick enough that he had to stand directly over the couch before he realized the person curled up there was Evelyn—with knees and elbows tucked in since she was too long for the furniture. What was she doing on the barely padded bench? She had a cushion under her head—one that Mrs. Bolton had embroidered for him when he'd moved in that said "Home Sweet Home" in blue-stitched lettering. And she had a thin fabric covering her shoulders. Her shawl?

There wasn't a fire in the hearth, and October nights at the ranch were always cold enough to merit one.

He needed to wake her up and send her to bed. Except, now that he stood there, so near her in the dark, he hesitated to touch her. The sun would be up soon. Would she be capable of falling back to sleep so soon after waking?

Chris debated with himself for too long. Evelyn shifted again in her sleep. Her arms went over the side of the couch, and then—

Iron hit Chris hard enough across one leg that he yelped and stumbled backward, and instinct alone kept him moving that way to avoid the next swing of his attacker. Something caught his shirt and nearly dragged him away with it. Chris's feet tripped him up, and he fell backward and down to the ground, hard.

"Evie," he gasped out, somehow remembering three children remained asleep in the house. "It's me! It's Chris." She stood over him, her outline barely visible. She held a rod in her grip out to one side, the way he's seen baseball players hold up a bat.

"Chris?" Evelyn lowered her arms and then knelt beside him. A solid "thump" on the floor implied she'd dropped her weapon. "Oh, my goodness, I'm terribly sorry. I had the worst dream, and then I woke, and you were standing over me—" Her hands were on his arm and chest, running over his clothes as though looking for an injury. "I panicked. All I could think about were rustlers, and I didn't hear Gus bark like he usually does when you come home." She leaned over him, the white of her nightgown picking up the dim morning light coming through the window. Her braid fell over her shoulder. "Did I hurt you?"

"Evie." His voice had gone hoarse. Likely because he'd caught the warm vanilla and sugar scent of her. She was so close, and he was still mostly on his back. "I'm fine. Maybe a little bruised." He pushed himself up to sitting, slowly enough that she had time to withdraw her hands and rock back on her knees. "You've got a good swing."

"Thank you?" she squeaked. "I feel terrible."

"Don't." The sky grew lighter as they spoke, the room around them turning a blue-gray color. "If I'd been a no-good cow-thief you'd have driven me into the ground like a stake." He kept his voice light, trying to ease whatever guilt she still felt. "Those kids are lucky they have you watching over them. What'd you hit me with, anyway?" He rubbed at his thigh just above his knee. At least she'd whacked the good leg. He wasn't sure the other one could take another injury so soon after healing up from a break.

"A fire poker."

A shudder went through him. Hit a person in the right place with that, and they'd be dead. Even if a woman was the one swinging the metal. "Clever." He squinted through the morning gloom at her. "Why were you sleeping on the couch? It can't be comfortable."

"Oh." She wrapped her arms around herself. "I over-excited myself. I was thinking about rustlers and rattlesnakes before falling asleep." Her tone sounded light, but he didn't miss the tremble in her quiet laugh. "Then there was a dream...and I just wanted to be near the children and the doors."

"I see." Chris rested his elbows on his knees, tracing her features with his eyes as the light allowed. "You were afraid." He didn't blame her. "I wish I knew what to say to help, but the truth is, there's not much reassurance I can give you. There's always something out here to be afraid of. But isn't it the same in England? You never know when a lightning bolt will fall out of the sky, or when illness will fall on you or someone you love." He wanted to touch her, to offer reassurance somehow. Holding her hand, putting an arm around her shoulders, or cupping her soft cheek in his hand....

Instead, he cleared his throat and kept right on talking. Like a fool. "All we can do is our best, Evie. And pray that God makes up the rest."

"I'm beginning to understand that," she murmured. Evelyn shifted where she sat, and Chris realized the floor couldn't be comfortable for someone wearing nothing more than a nightgown.

That knowledge struck him again in a way that closed his throat right on up past the point of speaking. Instead, he pushed himself up to his feet and then held out his hands to her, silently. Her slender hands slid into his, and as he closed his fingers around hers, Chris felt warmth tingling through him from head to toe. He lifted her to standing.

"Thank you." Her soft voice barely reached his ears. Then she shifted and stumbled—her foot had caught the hem of her gown—directly into his chest. He caught her against him, holding her steady and keeping them both upright. His hands had fallen naturally to her waist. The warmth of her skin seeped through the material of her nightgown. She tipped her chin up, and the air between them blazed with all the heat of the summer sun.

Chris had wanted to kiss her more than once. She couldn't doubt that he'd welcome her lips against his. But he wasn't about to take advantage of this moment. She'd set the pace, even if his heart wanted to race clear across the desert and back for her.

Evelyn drew in a deep breath that he couldn't help feeling, given that they were near plastered together from her fall. She let it out with a control that impressed him, even as the soft hint of her breath tickled his neck.

She stepped away, and his fingers nearly tightened as they grazed the fabric of her gown one last time. Ten types of disappointment closed around Chris's heart. He disguised it as best he could, chuckling. "The kids will be up soon." Pretending nothing had happened seemed best. "If we want any rest, we'd better get on up to bed."

"What?" Her startled gasp jerked his mind back where it belonged. Far away from imagining her kiss and going right back to practical matters.

"Our own beds," he amended quickly. Heat crept up his neck. "Your bed, my bedroll." He snapped his mouth closed. He'd developed a reputation for being a man of few words. Because he thought things over carefully before speaking. Except when it came to Evelyn. With the countess, his mouth let escape whatever foolishness was in his head.

"All right." She turned around and leaned over, finding her fire iron. He saw the flash of her sheepish smile in the semi-darkness. "Let me put this away." That accomplished, the two of them went into the kitchen together. Chris let Evelyn precede him up the stairs, following behind her one step at a time. He noticed her hand brushing the wall as she went.

He needed to add a handrail to the staircase. Prioritize it, even. He'd talk to Abram about making something pretty for the supports, too.

They reached the landing, and Evelyn's hand was on the door latch.

Chris added a door handle to the list of things his wife deserved. She ought to have a nice one. Brass, maybe.

He turned to go into his room, his exhaustion heavy enough that he'd likely have no problem sleeping on the floor for the few hours he allowed himself before waking for the day's work. And the picnic. The first picnic he'd attend as a married man. With three kids in tow.

"Chris?"

He spun back around, already halfway in his room. It sounded like she'd said his name more than once. "Sorry, Evie. I'm tuckered out. What'd you say?"

She stood in her doorway. "I'm glad you returned safely."

He smiled to himself. "Me too."

She lingered, as though she had more to say, but then she pressed her lips together good and tight. Her door closed quietly behind her. Chris made himself as comfortable as he could, and he closed his eyes with high hopes for a restful nap. With one hand tucked behind his head, he'd nearly slipped to sleep. Then an image of Evie in the dark, wearing a nightgown and standing in his arms, delayed his plans for a time.

CHAPTER TWENTY-TWO

The large hamper didn't feel like it held enough. Evelyn had piled in tin plates, cups, jars of tea and lemonade, and as much food as she had that would travel well. Which wasn't all that much, really. Dannie had promised to bring food to share, too. She'd even offered to make a mince pie the two of them had found a recipe for in the large English cookbook.

Evelyn peered into the top of the hamper, then closed it with a sigh. She brushed her hands off on her apron before untying it. She'd been much more careful with her knots and bows after the incident with Chris in the kitchen. She hung the apron up and went in search of the children.

Madeline and Laura were playing marbles, wearing their second-best dresses that nearly matched. Both were made of a chocolate brown cotton with darker stripes on them. They'd even done their hair the same.

"We want everyone to know we're sisters now," Laura had explained. "Even though we look and sound different."

"Dannie says my British accent is charming," Madeline had said with a frown. "But I'd much rather sound like everyone else."

Evelyn had tried not to laugh, even if the idea of her daughter losing some of their shared dialect pricked at her heart. "Sounding like yourself is perfectly acceptable."

Now she took in their happy play with an easy smile. "Are you girls ready?"

"Is it time?" Laura asked, making ready to leap to her feet.

"Almost. When Chris and Ben come back, we must be on our way." She ran her hands down the skirt of her gown self-consciously. It was one of the first she'd made with fabric she'd purchased for that purpose. She'd finished it late the evening before, after the children had gone to sleep and prior to retiring to bed herself.

The deep blue fabric, patterned with sprays of tiny white roses, had been too lovely to ignore where it sat upon a shelf. It only occurred to her when she slipped it on that morning that perhaps it was too fine for life on a ranch. She'd seen Ruthie and Beth wearing blouses of soft pink and yellow. Dannie tended toward blouses and split skirts most of the time and wore plain dark skirts with light colored shirtwaists otherwise. The one exception for Dannie to dress in more colorful clothing was Sundays.

Still. Maybe she'd been a bit vain when she'd chosen this dress and asked for Beth's help selecting and cutting a pattern. She'd used more fabric on the sleeves and added white buttons to the back that Madeline had to help her do up.

She went back to the stairs now, hesitating at the bottom. Though most of the community had met her now, only the Harpers had come to the ranch since her marriage. Ruthie had assured Evelyn that the word of her marriage had likely spread faster than a prairie fire—however rapid those were. That made today the first time Evelyn would be introduced in a company of people as Mrs. Morgan.

The wife of a foreman—did that hold any importance in her new community? She couldn't be sure. Not without sounding odd when she asked. But she wanted Chris to be proud of her, whatever the case, when they appeared together at the picnic.

"We're home," Chris called from the front room. "And your brother's already an expert with his crutches."

"Yep," Ben said with confidence. "Look how fast I can go."

Evelyn stepped aside as he barreled into the kitchen, swinging his hurt leg while supporting himself with a crutch beneath each arm. He grinned up at her when he caught her eye.

"Look, Mama. I raced Frosty home and I—" His words stopped suddenly, and he looked at Evelyn with a frown. "Is something wrong?"

Evelyn put a hand to her heart, realizing he hadn't called her "mama" on purpose. He'd likely been excited, and the word had slipped out without his knowing. But for one moment, she'd felt her heart respond with pure elation. And motherly pride.

"You surprised me," she said with a truthful smile. "Look at how well you manage those crutches. I am most impressed."

All children were easy to love, in her opinion. Ben and Laura especially so, given how much she wanted to fill the empty places in their hearts with happiness and light. Not that she would ever wish to replace their mother. And in that moment, though she wondered if it was blasphemy to do so, she sent a thought to heaven. *I promise, Maria. I'll honor you in every way I can while I look after your little ones.*

Ben's chest puffed up with pride and he swung out the door again, telling his sisters about racing Chris home from the Steeles' house. Chris himself appeared in the doorway a moment later, leaning one shoulder against it. His eyes were soft around the edges, matching his smile.

"I heard," he said, the words meant to stay between them. "Are you all right?"

"A little taken aback." She didn't want to discuss it yet. Though, given Chris's response to Madeline calling him papa, he knew well enough how she felt. Instead, Evelyn lowered her gaze from his and smoothed her hands from her waist down to her hips. "Is this dress all right? I thought I might change."

"Don't. Please."

His response made her head come up swiftly. And she saw the softness in his expression had melted away, and his eyes held heat in them instead. His lips crept slowly upward.

"You're beautiful, Evie. That dress is perfect for you." He spoke the words with a simple sincerity she hadn't heard from another man. Ever. Before she formed a response, he rolled down the sleeves of his faded blue work shirt. "Give me a few minutes to get prettied up to match. I've done enough this morning that I need to clean up a bit. Then we'll get on our way." He disappeared up the stairs.

Evie cleared her throat and touched her hair, checking the twists of curls she'd teased out to frame her face. She brushed her cheeks with her fingertips, too, feeling the heat of a blush upon them. A woman married three times probably ought to be beyond blushing at compliments. But there was something about the way Chris looked at her when he said such things. An honesty that took her by surprise, and a way of making her feel like he meant to compliment something deeper than her appearance.

She heard his step overhead and pulled herself from her fanciful thought. "Children? Let's tidy up the marbles. Girls, get your shoes buttoned up."

Not ten minutes later, Chris reappeared in the doorway wearing dark gray trousers with a matching suit coat in his hand. His shirt was a clean white, and he wore a pair of suspenders that somehow brought all Evelyn's attention to the pleasant physique beneath them. He tightened a thin string tie around his collar, then pulled on the coat. "Everyone ready for some fun?"

The children cheered, and soon they were out the door and in the wagon. Dannie and Evan were on horseback, along with Dannie's younger brothers. Clark moved his horse closer to the buckboard wagon, letting the children lean out to pat the animal's neck while he talked about picnics of the past.

Evelyn had climbed up on her own while Chris was busy with the mules. His help, with his touch at her waist, wouldn't do her any favors that day. Her mind already felt muddled whenever she looked at him. And her heart kept doing strange acrobatics without her permission.

Beth and King Bolton rode in a buggy that Evelyn hadn't seen before. It looked like it would be of more use in a town than in the middle of a desert. But they looked quite pleased to be perched on the small seat together. The Steele family sat in their own wagon laden with chairs and crates of food. A few of the cowboys milled about on horses of their own, waiting for a signal from King to lead their party out.

Once their wagon fell in line behind the rest, Evelyn watched as Chris handled the reins with an easy confidence she couldn't help admiring. But then, that was how he handled just about everything. Even when she felt the world turn upside-down, Chris would give her an easy smile and speak in that measured way of his that calmed her.

Of course, she'd always found Chris attractive. Objectively, she admitted he had a strong jaw, well-placed nose even if it looked like it had been broken once, high cheekbones, and those glorious eyes....

Glorious eyes? Something must be terribly wrong with me. Evelyn shook her head at herself. "Get hold of yourself," she muttered aloud.

"What was that?" Chris asked, turning to regard her from beneath the brim of his hat. "Something wrong?"

"No. Everything is right as rain." She batted her eyelashes at him, then bit the insides of her cheeks and looked away. Focusing on the mule's backside, in fact. Surely, she couldn't entertain any more ridiculous thoughts or feelings if she kept her eyes upon the animal's hide.

Except a large butterfly fluttered past, drawing her eyes away to the meadows surrounding them. And then the mountains, and then the beautiful expanse of light blue sky. The cool breeze teased at the ribbon of her straw hat, and she couldn't help but smile when Madeline and Laura sang a rhyming-game song that Laura had taught Evelyn's very proper British daughter.

Sonoita appeared on the other side of a rolling hill. Only a handful of buildings huddled along the path. A church, a trading post, a blacksmith and carpentry, and a few houses. A crowd had gathered in the empty field beside the church, with children running around tables and picnic blankets, laughing and calling to one another. Women were putting food out, and men were leading horses to a large cistern of water or talking with one another around their wagons.

Her stomach spasmed nervously, and Evelyn's mind went back to the first appearance she had made on Lord Tyneham's arm. She'd been a countess. The highest ranked woman in the room. Yet every eye had turned upon her with unkind criticism. Sneers had appeared on some faces while others had smirked. Everyone had known she didn't belong, yet she'd carried herself with enough grace that a few had turned green with envy.

Here she was once more, about to arrive on the arm of a man in a place where everyone must realize she didn't belong.

"Don't run off right away." Chris's sudden words made her startle as he guided the mules to the cistern. When her gaze snapped to his, she wondered if he sensed her panic. His hand fell to where hers gripped the edge of the seat, covering her fingers with his. "I'll help you carry things to the table and pick the perfect spot for our blanket. If you don't mind."

She cocked her head to the side, trying to sound unconcerned. "Are you especially particular about where you sit on the ground, Mr. Morgan?"

He kept his eyes ahead of him, but a grin appeared on that handsome face of his. "Not especially, though I'm particular about keeping my wife company at a picnic."

Her heart fluttered, and some of her worry fell away. Chris didn't want to show her off. He just wanted to be near her.

Evelyn released her hold of the bench and took his hand in hers instead. "In that case, I'd appreciate your assistance."

Somehow, his grin stretched wider. "Most kind of you, Mrs. Morgan." He didn't let go of her hand until he had to leave his seat.

∼

THOUGH CHRIS DIDN'T MISS THE NUMBER OF JEALOUS LOOKS SENT his way, he kept his attention on Evelyn from the moment he helped her down from the wagon until they had laid out their blanket and weighed it down with stacks of plates and their basket. The children had run off the moment they'd left the wagon, to play a game in the field.

Evelyn watched them, chewing her lower lip between her teeth. "Do we need to worry about snakes?"

"Some of the men mowed the grass short yesterday," he told her, wrapping her arm through the crook of his. "Snakes don't tend to come out into an exposed area with short grass. And see there—" He pointed at a dog at one corner of the field. "That's Sparky's terrier. He'll let us know if he smells so much as a whisper of a snake."

"Sparky?" she asked, raising her eyebrows with sudden interest. "Evan told me about him. He's from England, too, isn't he?"

Chris smiled at the eagerness in her tone. He doubted Evelyn had ever met someone like the old miner before. "Let's go say hello. He's usually guarding the pie table at these events."

The old man delighted Evelyn, doffing his hat to her and at once making fun at Chris's expense. "Can't say I ever thought this fellow would marry," Sparky said, squinting in Chris's direction. "He seemed a confirmed bachelor, given the way all the young ladies would flirt, and he'd never take notice."

"Oh, really?" Evelyn looked up at him with mischief in her brightened eyes. "I had a suspicion our marriage would lead to at least a few broken hearts."

"Did you?" Chris wanted to tug her a little closer, to tease her as he reassured her. "I can't say I ever noticed any of the girls around here paying me any attention. I think you imagined it, Sparky."

Hooting with laughter, the former miner slapped his knee. "There's a thing to say to your elders. I'll pay you the compliment of saying this fine lady is too pretty for the likes of you, Frosty. An English noblewoman. First the son of a marquess, now a countess. What's next, do you figure? Think Queen Victoria herself might come to pay a call on us?" He waggled his graying eyebrows, making Evelyn laugh aloud.

"I highly doubt Her Majesty would go to such trouble. Especially at her advanced age." Evelyn waved away that topic, as she usually did when anyone brought up English high society. "It amazes me to find two fellow countrymen in this place, so far from our native shores."

"There was a lot more of us for years and years, all in Tombstone and Bisbee. Miners from Wales, Cornwall, and engineers from the north. All working to make our American bosses rich." He winked. "But it was a lot easier to do that work here than it was back there. Even if the ground is a bit different."

Sparky abruptly shifted to talking of England and all that he didn't miss about his home country. "The blasted weather, for one," he said, while Evelyn's eyes sparkled with delight. "It rained every blessed day and night, it seemed. A man could never dry out his socks."

Evelyn laughed. "Whereas here, everything is dry all the time."

"I've come to appreciate it, with my old age. It's rare my rheumatisms give me trouble." He leaned forward as he spoke. "Not that you young folk need to worry about that. But tell me, Mrs. Frosty, have you had much call to miss anything from our soggy isle?"

Every muscle in Chris's body tightened, and he held his breath as he waited for her answer. What was it she missed that he could return to her? Or did she long for England to the point that he'd never fill that desire?

"Sometimes, I miss the music," she admitted, a wistful smile curving her lips upward. "I played piano, and I attended musical performances as often as I was invited. But otherwise, I cannot think on much that I should trade for what I have found here." Was it Chris's imagination, or had her hand tightened upon his arm? "I never liked fish, which we had an abundance of in England. I cannot say I am fond of the rain and cold. Or the crowds. I feel as if Arizona goes on forever, with more than enough room for everyone."

"Aye, I know precisely what you mean." Sparky held his arms out wide to demonstrate his point. "This country goes on forever. I own my farm here. In England, I'd be a tenant, if I ever worked my way out of the mines at all." He shrugged and rubbed at the patch on his elbow. "As to the music, just you wait. We've got some musicians here who know how to play, and you'll yearn to dance until the stars come out."

"There's a piano in the church." Mrs. Harper had been standing on the other side of the table, laying out a plate of cookies. "If you'd like to play sometime, Mr. Mason is in charge of the building. He'd loan you its use anytime." Then she nodded to Dannie. "The Boltons used to talk about ordering a piano from San Francisco. Whatever happened with that, Daniella?"

"That was a very long time ago, when I enrolled in school." She shuddered. "My dad thought I'd want to practice piano when I was home for the holidays, but I begged him to let me be. Piano playing isn't for me."

A piano.

Chris's smile tightened. He'd wanted an idea of what would make his house a home for Evelyn. Now he knew. He couldn't imagine the expense of bringing even the smallest of those instruments out here. But then. With the railroad, maybe it wouldn't be terrible.

Evelyn took in the well-laid table, then looked up at Chris with raised eyebrows. "How is it that there aren't any insects to bother the food? I feel like every time I open the kitchen door, I have a new intruder buzzing around my head."

Dannie snorted. "It's an old trick, and maybe one you don't want to know."

When Evelyn looked more curious, Mrs. Harper pointed toward the end of the table. "It's not a mystery, my dear. We make the first round of boys who arrive put together a more tempting meal for the flies."

When his wife still appeared curious, Chris tugged her gently to the end of the table and pointed to an elevated pile of manure. "There. The flies like the smell of that more than they do the desserts."

Her eyes rounded, then she looked up at him with that wrinkle in her nose. "What if someone steps in it?"

"Generally, no one does. But I'm betting if some poor soul forgot to look where he was going, he'd find himself short on dance partners." He grinned when she gaped at him in silence. "You have to admit that its innovative."

"I suppose so. If it keeps the insects away from the chocolate cake Ruthie brought, I cannot disapprove."

One of the younger couples, new to the cattle business and the valley, approached next. Before long, Evelyn conversed with an ease that made Chris proud of her. She'd conquered the nervousness he'd sensed that morning.

Mr. Harper called the informal gathering of friends to order, announcing a blessing on the food. Then he bid the friends and neighbors gathered to make up their plates and enjoy a meal before the children went back to their games in the field.

Ben, Laura, and Madeline returned to their picnic spot. All three had rosy cheeks and eyes bright with happiness. They'd joined the ranching and farming children at their games and made fast friends in the way only children could do. Then the three of them talked excitedly though the meal, barely giving Chris or Evelyn the chance to say a word. More than once, Chris met Evelyn's gaze over the children's heads and shared a knowing smile.

When Ben swung upward on his crutches, the girls joined him in hurrying back to a knot of children already finished with their meals.

"They didn't eat enough," Evelyn murmured, voice soft and expression thoughtful. "I suppose they'll be hungry again in minutes."

"Doubtful." Chris leaned back on his elbows and stretched his legs out in front of him on the blanket. He tipped his hat down to shade his eyes. "Didn't you ever play like that as a kid? You'd fill up on air and sunshine and wouldn't need anything else. They're too busy to even think about hunger." He chuckled. "And I've seen them nip more than a few cookies from the dessert table."

"I don't think I ever played that way." Evelyn looked down at him, her posture perfect with her legs tucked daintily beneath her. Sparky was right. She was far too good for Chris. Elegant and beautiful to his gracelessness and lankiness.

But he was falling for her, faster and harder with each passing day, and he'd make up his lack somehow. Even if it meant getting a piano from San Francisco and carrying it back to the ranch on his back. Somehow, he'd show Evelyn how he felt. And soon.

The neighbors Chris had come to know during his time on the ranch were a good sort. They didn't question Evelyn's presence among them, and he hadn't heard any disparaging words about their quick marriage.

People out west knew better. The days of mail order brides weren't all that far in the past.

A few of the men came together between the field and the picnic area, carrying instruments with them. Chris grinned. "I know our music isn't as fine as what you're used to hearing," he said as the fiddlers started warming their strings. "But maybe you'll like it."

"I like all sorts of music." Evelyn leaned forward, her eyes on the musicians. "Is that a banjo? I haven't ever heard one, though I've seen them."

"A banjo, a mouth harp, and a harmonica will round out the fiddlers." Chris listened as the music began, the song lively and well known to many. Travis Bolton, with a grin only a boy of seventeen could wear, took Jessica Harper by the hand and started dancing. A polka, by the looks of it.

Chris chuckled. "That girl isn't going to know what to do with herself when he goes away to university. They've been sweet on each other longer than I've been around."

Evelyn put her hand on the ground near his and shifted so she sat more on her hip, leaning toward him. "I think they're adorable. You can tell he dotes on her, and she obviously thinks the world of him. It's in their eyes."

Studying her profile, Chris gave an easy shrug. "Young love."

"Yes. Untested. Untried." She met his gaze, and the whimsy of her smile made his heart skip a beat. "Full of hope for the future."

He'd missed out on something like that. On youthful adoration and holding hands with a sweetheart. He'd been too set on making his own way in the world, on going out West. Chris had dedicated himself to his job, determined to be the best drover, then the best foreman that anyone knew. He was honest and loyal. He'd never had time for the girls or women who'd had marriage on their minds.

He was married to his work, maybe. At least, that's how it had been. Until the kids had needed him. And then he had needed Evelyn.

"What are you thinking?" she asked, her voice low. Her cheeks had turned pink, and that sprinkling of freckles across her nose made him unaccountably think of stardust in the Milky Way.

But he couldn't tell her that. Instead, he went with something slightly more dangerous when he answered.

"I'm thinking I'd like to dance with you."

Evelyn's blush deepened. "Here? Now?"

"Yep." He sat up and held his hand out to her. "Would you like to dance with me, wife?"

Her lips formed a silent "oh" before she slipped her hand into his. "Yes."

Others had already followed Travis and Jessica Harper's example, Dannie and Duke among them, dancing while sharing a secretive smile. In that moment, Chris envied the two of them. They'd met, fallen in love, and married. Sure, there'd been uncertainty between them a time or two, but everything had worked out.

The musicians changed to a waltz, played with more spirit than such a dignified dance called for, but it still meant holding Evelyn closer. It meant not having to share her with anyone else. No changing hands or partners.

Evelyn put one hand near his shoulder, at the top of his arm, and held the other up and out, and Chris realized her form was different. There was a grace in the way she held her wrists. Not at all like the other women he'd danced with in the past. He had to dart another glance at Duke and Dannie, guessing that the son of a marquess and former wife of an earl would have similar dance training.

Instead of putting his hand on her waist, he followed Duke's example and put his right hand on her left shoulder blade, near the center of her back. And that changed everything. Instead of dancing as he'd done all his life, moving in time to the music with a vague notion of how to get his partner from one side of the floor to another, there was a sudden purpose to his movements.

Evelyn followed him effortlessly. With a contended lift of her lips, and her eyes half closed. Awareness of his wife's beauty and gentility settled more firmly on his heart. Along with the knowledge of how good it felt to hold her, and how much he hoped for more opportunities to crop up soon.

Maybe he needed to ask Duke about how the English danced. He liked it a lot better than what he'd been taught. And Evelyn— well, he wouldn't mind practicing with her, if she'd let him.

The music came to an end, and Stretch Robertson, the farmer playing the banjo, called out, "This here's our favorite square dance. Y'all get ready. Jake's gonna call it." He nodded to one of the fiddlers, who grinned like a madman. Even some of the children squealed and came to form the rows several adults had fallen into.

Evelyn's content expression had changed to one of confusion. "A what?"

"It's a folk dance." He squeezed her hands and tugged her gently into one of the rows, lining her up between Dannie and Jessica Harper. "We'll help."

Dannie put her hand on Evelyn's shoulder. "It's like an old-fashioned country dance. Jake will call out the steps. It's a lot of fun."

"This here's the one we call the Barrel Cactus." Jake, a thin-whiskered cowboy employed at another ranch, started his calling as soon as the music started up. "Gentlemen, bow to your ladies, ladies show your courtesy. Now, allemande right."

Evelyn leaped forward a half second after the other ladies had moved, raising her right hand to meet Chris's. They walked around in a circle until Evelyn stood where she'd started.

"Do-si-do."

"Oh dear," she said aloud, a flash of worry in her green eyes. "I haven't the faintest idea what that is."

Dannie interpreted for the very alarmed Englishwoman. "Don't touch, just forward, around, and backward."

"Then again, the other direction," Chris explained.

"Join hands and bow to your neighbor!"

With Chris and Dannie helping, Evelyn soon had gone through each step twice. Then, when everyone joined hands to form a circle, Evelyn's wide-eyed confusion melted away.

With long strands of coppery hair coming loose from the elegant knot at the top of her head, Evelyn danced as light on her feet as a fairy. She wore a wide grin the likes of which he'd never seen on her before. "This is incredible."

"Do-si-do with your neighbor, and put your lady on the right," Jake called, dancing in a circle as he played his fiddle. "Now take your lady by the hand, spin her around—ain't that grand?"

Chris had both her hands clasped in his as he spun her around, and Evelyn put her head back and laughed. He wanted very much to capture that moment somehow, tucking it forever into his heart. The music stopped abruptly, as it nearly always did, and she fell forward into his arms. Both her hands pressed against his chest, and she breathed deeply as though she fought to catch her breath. All around them, the other dancers clapped to show their appreciation for the caller and musicians. But Chris only had eyes for Evelyn.

CHAPTER TWENTY-THREE

T he sun had set by the time the mules stopped in front of their house. Evelyn sighed deeply, looking over her shoulder into the wagon bed where the children yawned and looked about blearily. Ben and Madeline had both fallen asleep during the drive back to the ranch, but now all three peered up at her with tired eyes and smiles.

Chris jumped down from his seat and held his hands out to Evelyn. She stepped into them without reservation. Given how much she'd danced, Evelyn didn't trust her feet to stay steady enough to get her down safely. Besides. It was high time she admitted she liked it when Chris put his hands on her waist.

Her hands landed lightly on his arm. "Thank you, Chris."

"Papa?" Madeline leaned over the side of the wagon. "Do we have to go to bed n-n-now?" The last word barely escaped through a wide-mouthed yawn the girl couldn't suppress.

Chris chuckled and looked down at Evelyn, his hands still on her waist. "You'd better ask your mama. We've gotta get the wagon unloaded and the mules to bed, still. Maybe you could help with that?"

All three children groaned, and Evelyn had to bite back a smile. "I think your papa needs the help. Everyone climb down and bring something inside. Ben, we can drape the picnic blanket over your shoulder so you can help, too."

When Chris released her to help the children down from the wagon, it took Evelyn a moment to regain enough of her senses to cover her own yawn and walk up to the front door. She opened it for the children, who came in laden with an empty hamper, picnic blanket, and a few other odds and ends. Chris brought in a crate filled with small gifts from the neighbors who'd wanted to congratulate them on their marriage.

The kindness of the near-strangers in their small community had altered something within her. When she'd arrived, she'd thought the Boltons and Steeles were a rare find. But now, she wondered. Perhaps she'd always been surrounded by kind people and simply never known how to find them. A tiny corner of a North American territory couldn't possibly be the only place such gentle people congregated.

Evelyn went inside the house and helped the children put things away, while Chris disappeared to take care of the livestock and the borrowed ranch wagon. He returned by the time the children had cleaned up and put on nightgowns and, in Ben's case, a long nightshirt. They were all sitting in the main room when Chris came into the house. Evelyn stood, reading to them. The children were on the couch, the girls curled over either arm and Ben leaning against Laura.

She'd chosen a passage from the beginning of *Through the Looking Glass*. Chris leaned against the door as she read the last stanza.

> *And though the shadow of a sigh*
> *May tremble through the story,*
> *For 'happy summer days' gone by*
> *And vanish'd summer glory—*
> *It shall not touch with breath of bale*
> *The pleasance of our fairy-tale.*

"I love big words," Ben said quietly, his eyes drooping. "Mommy and Daddy did, too. They used to read poems at night." He snuggled closer to his sister, then he said softly, "Do you think they miss us like we miss them?"

With all the love a mother's heart could hold, Evelyn went on her knees before him and touched the little boy's cheek. She saw Laura's eyes open, too, watching her. "I know they must, darling. I'm certain they know that you're safe, too. They know we are looking after you and that we love you very much. I hope that makes your mommy and daddy happy."

Ben's eyes flickered from hers to look over her shoulder. "You love us?"

"Very much." There wasn't even the slightest hesitation in Chris's deep voice, and then he was standing beside her. "And we're going to look after you the way they'd want us to. I promise."

Laura sat up and looked over at Madeline. "I like having a sister. And today...we were like a real family." She yawned again. "I like the way Maddie calls you mama and papa. Do you think—could we maybe do that, too? Or—maybe just try, for a little while?"

Evelyn looked up at Chris, and she knew she didn't imagine the way his eyes glowed with emotion. He spoke with a gentleness that always made her heart turn tender toward him. "I'd like that a lot, Laura. Ben, too, if he wants. You can try it, and if you change your mind, you can switch back. Whatever you decide, though, you should know that I've decided to raise you—all three of you—as my son and daughters. No matter what."

"Papa," Ben said, trying the title out with care and an approximation of Madeline's accent that made her giggle. "I like it."

"*Mama*." Laura grinned. "Do I sound British when I say it like that? Mama."

"Very British," Madeline responded. "I like having a sister and brother, too."

"You two are lucky." Ben picked up his crutches. "I already

SALLY BRITTON

had one sister, now I've got two. Do you think I'll get a brother someday?" he asked with all the innocence of a child, his eyes on Evelyn's. "Can we get another boy in the family?"

Evelyn's cheeks blazed and she didn't dare look at Chris, though she could have sworn she felt his gaze on her. She answered as tactfully as she could, but as quickly as she dared to avoid hearing Chris try to answer that oh-so-complicated question. "You have Lee to play with, and Travis and Clark, too. They'll have to do for now." She stepped back. "We had better go to bed. Girls, I'll tuck you two in first and hear your prayers."

She'd had an aunt who used to do that. Listening to her children say prayers at night. Evelyn had always thought the practice sweet, though her mother found it "insufferably religious."

Chris suddenly scooped Ben up, crutches and all, and the boy squealed in surprise. "I'll help Ben to bed, then we can swap rooms and goodnights."

"That sounds like a marvelous plan." Evelyn stuck both hands out, one for each little girl, and walked them to their room. The girls knelt together by Laura's bed while Evelyn sat at its foot, head bowed. Together, they recited the Lord's Prayer. Their sweet voices blended together beautifully. Evelyn tucked them into their respective beds, kissing first Laura and then Madeline on the forehead.

"Mama?" Madeline whispered before Evelyn withdrew.

Evelyn sat on the edge of her bed, brushing a bit of loose hair off her daughter's forehead. "Yes, darling?"

"I'm glad you're Laura and Ben's mama, too." She leaned into Evelyn's touch. "I don't know what I'd do if you died. I've been thinking about it. A lot. It makes me so sad for both of them. I told Laura we could share, that you'd love all of us. Because you always wanted lots of children."

Evelyn's throat closed, making it difficult for her to respond to her daughter's words with more than a nod. She'd told Madeline of her secret wish years ago, when Madeline asked why she had no brothers or sisters. The truth had hurt too much, and Madeline had been too young to understand fully. So Evelyn had wrapped her little girl in her arms and said, *"I used to wish for a whole house full of children. Now I have you, and you are such a wonderful daughter. How could I be so selfish to want more?"*

Madeline had seemed content with that answer at the time. She'd never asked about siblings again. But, as was often the way with children, she'd carried her mother's words in her heart.

Leaning closer, Evelyn touched her nose to her daughter's. "You are a very selfless and sweet person, Madeline. And you're right. We can all share each other. When you share your heart with others, it never diminishes the love you give. It only grows to fit even more people inside." She kissed Madeline's forehead. She rose and looked to Laura's bed, seeing the little girl already sound asleep. Worn out from her long day.

Then she turned to the doorway and froze. Chris was there, leaning against the doorframe, watching her with arms crossed and blue eyes reflecting the lamplight. How long had he been there?

"Ben's probably already asleep," Chris said, his voice low, though not quite a whisper. "I promised him you'd be in, though, so you'd better at least go take a peek at him." Chris pushed away from the doorway, and his shoulder brushed hers as they passed one another. He went to Madeline first.

"Here's my Maddie. What did you think of your first square dance?" he asked, and as Evelyn left the room, she heard Maddie's gleeful answer.

Ben wasn't quite asleep, but he was close. He smiled when she gave him a kiss on the cheek, then he snuggled his sawdust horse closer. Evelyn combed her fingers through his dark hair, his place in her heart growing with every breath.

Evelyn rose and took the lamp out of the room with her, its soft glow making the shadows dance cheerfully along the walls. She put the lamp on the table, then went to light the single candle on the mantel. With the sun gone and the seasons changed, the front room was beginning to grow too cool for her liking.

She knelt to start a fire. Beth had taught her during their first week at the ranch. While she prepared the kindling, her mind lingered over Ben's request to call her mama instead of mommy. A slight alteration in the manner he addressed her made it all right for him to love her, to let her love him, without replacing his mother.

The strength of children always surprised her. She'd been lost when her mother died, when she'd found herself alone in the world.

Evelyn lit a taper with the oil lamp, and she touched her small flame to the kindling in the hearth. A soft glow began deep in the wood, then grew. Slowly, the warmth of the flame seeped into her clothing. Her cheeks. Her hands.

Laura and Ben were quite lucky to have Chris. Chris, who was so ready to give them protection and safety, a home, and his devotion.

Chris came into the room, still wearing his boots and suspenders, though he'd cast off his hat, tie, and jacket some time ago. He pushed his hand through his hair, leaving it a tidy wave instead of the rumpled mess it had been when he'd removed his hat. "May I join you?"

"Of course." Evelyn sat on the couch, sinking against the pillowed back. With her heart yet tender from the conversation with the children, unnecessary busy-ness lacked appeal.

Chris was nearly to his rocking chair when he snapped his fingers. "Oh. I have something for you. I nearly forgot." He spun around on his heels to face her. "Don't go anywhere." He went back into the kitchen, with Evelyn's eyes following his long-legged stride. The man's walk ate up the ground faster than any dignified Englishman's ever would. She smiled to herself, trying to imagine Chris dressed in the fine suits of an English gentle-man, with a tall black hat and snowy cravat. She completed the mental image with a monocle and giggled to herself.

"What's made you laugh?" Chris had re-entered the room, one hand behind his back. "Me?" His eyebrows rose high.

That expression would certainly cause him to lose his monocle. That made her giggle again, and she hurried to cover the sound with her fingers.

A corner of his mouth hitched upward. "I'll take that as a yes. I don't mind, though. You have a kind laugh."

"A kind laugh? I am not certain I know how such a thing sounds." She folded her hands in her lap and sat straighter, but as she corrected her posture, a hairpin at the back of her neck pulled horribly, making her wince. Evelyn reached up and pulled the horrid thing out and placed it on the arm of the chair.

Chris had kept his hand behind his back and picked up a stool with the other, bringing it to sit in front of her with only an arm's length of space between their knees. "Sure. You never sound like you're laughing *at* anyone. You're not making light of anybody or laughing at their expense. You're laughing because something brought you joy. I like it."

Evelyn felt her cheeks warm. "Thank you." His blue eyes studied her with a softness to them that made her heart thrum contentedly. "Did you say you had something for me?"

"Yep." He made no move to reveal whatever he had tucked behind his back, though his gaze lingered on her features. "I'm starting to think it was a foolish idea."

"Now I am most curious." Evelyn leaned forward. "What is behind your back, Mr. Christmas Morgan?"

With that he laughed, though she saw the way his ears reddened. Perhaps because she had used his full given name. "Fine, but only because I sense you'd be more than willing to blackmail me after that." He drew from behind his back a wooden frame, and he handed it to her with a sheepish smile. "I asked Madeline to pick her favorite of the drawings you've been making. We can replace it with whatever you want, but this is what she chose."

Evelyn held out her hands and accepted a wooden frame, the

smooth wood already polished, the corners fitted together perfectly. And in the frame, without glass to protect it, one of her sketches of the windmill with rolling, grassy hills and the Mustang Mountains, as Dannie called them, in the distance. She'd been teaching the children about landscapes in between mathematics and penmanship practice.

It wasn't a frame-worthy piece. At least, it never would be in England. Not when there were oil paintings and watercolors and artists with talent and skill far beyond hers. But she had enjoyed the exercise and found it pleasing. In fact, she had noticed the picture was missing from her stack of sketches that same morning.

As she gazed at the picture in the frame, her thumb caressing the wooden edge, her eyes filled with tears. Perhaps she hadn't recovered sufficiently from the children's sweet words of hope and love. More likely, Chris had touched her heart with a simple gesture of thoughtfulness.

"You didn't need to do this." She looked up from the frame to her husband.

Chris stared back at her, his expression calm and thoughtful. "It's only the start, Evie. I know I haven't got all that much, compared to what you're used to, but I want you to love our home. So I'll do what I can to make it perfect for you."

Her throat closed up, and the tears spilled over, though she smiled through them as she wiped her cheek. "Thank you." She stood, and he leaned back as she put the picture in its frame upon the mantel. Evelyn adjusted it carefully, trying to keep her hands busy long enough to get hold of her emotions. "This isn't my best, you know. Though I am not an accomplished artist, I could certainly make something more worthy of the mantel."

"If it's your work, whatever it is, it'll be plenty worthy." The sincerity she heard made her turn around to regard him with open surprise.

"I have never met a man like you, Chris."

His infectious grin appeared across his striking face, but she knew him well enough to catch the uncertainty in his blue eyes. "I suppose you didn't have a chance to meet any cowboys before we met in Bisbee."

She stepped closer to him, his upturned expression sobering when she stood near enough for her skirt to brush his boot tips. "That isn't what I mean. You are the most kind, generous, and compassionate man I have ever encountered. Here or anywhere."

Evelyn put her hand upon his cheek, and she heard his sharp intake of breath as her fingers grazed the light stubble along his jaw. He didn't move. His eyes didn't drift from hers. Her heart urged daring, but her head made its case for caution.

Where she trod now, she had never stepped before. She had never felt as vulnerable, as lost, as she did as she bent closer to Chris. Moving with deliberate slowness, watching as his crystal-blue eyes darkened, Evelyn risked her heart by placing her lips upon his.

WITH MUSCLES AND BONES, THE VERY SINEWS OF HIS BODY, ACHING to enfold Evelyn in his arms, Chris fought hard to stay still. He wouldn't startle her or rush her. Not now. Not now that Evelyn finally moved toward him with lips parted and eyes full of yearning.

Her lips brushed his, tentatively, and then she pulled back enough for a breath to escape from him before she kissed him again. This time, though the touch of her lips to his remained tentative, he felt her courage rising. She put her hand on his cheek, and Chris took that as permission to kiss her in return.

With his chin lifted, he cupped her cheek and brushed at the still-damp tear track upon her cheek. She kissed as though she wasn't certain how much daring to permit herself. Her grace and gentility extended even to this, with her movements hesitant and her lips a light touch as they parted from his and met them again.

Chris wanted more for Evelyn. If that meant showing her how to be bold, he was willing. More than willing, truth be told, to help her learn. He put one hand around her waist, tugging her forward and into his lap. Once she sat there, both her arms slid around his neck, and he held her steady at the waist. Then he left off kissing her lips to place tokens of his affection, sharing pieces of his heart, by leaving kisses on her cheeks. Her forehead. Her temple, as he tucked her closer to him.

Evelyn's hands slid down from behind his neck to rest against his chest, and she breathed deeply while resting her head against his shoulder.

"I don't understand." Her whispered words tickled the hollow of his throat where he'd left his collar unbuttoned. "I've never felt this way before."

How could those words both sadden and elate him? As beautiful as she was, inside and out, how had she never known the tenderness and love that he wanted to give her? Two marriages. One of which had produced a marvelous child. And yet, Chris knew, no one had ever treasured her as he did.

He spread his palm against her lower back while his other hand stroked her hair. "It's new to me, too, Evie." He'd never held a woman close. Certainly, never as he held Evelyn. Sitting on a stool before a low-burning fire, the house peaceful and still around them, Chris could've stayed right there forever.

Wanted to, in fact.

"Evelyn?" His heart squeezed when she pulled back enough to look up at him, her eyes flickering with honey-colored flames. Everything about her, the sweet scent of her hair, the touch of her skin, made his mind spin and his soul tremble.

How had a practical solution to their problems resulted in such intensity of feeling? Not that he minded. In fact, falling in love with his wife was the best thing that had ever happened to him.

If he spoke his feelings to her right then, with the glow of the fire and the children asleep, would she think he expected something in return? He could see the confusion in her eyes, and he d felt the hesitation in her first kiss. By her own admission, Evelyn was lost in the growing affection they had for one another. But he knew she felt it. She couldn't kiss him like that without feeling it.

Maybe they needed more time. Since they were married, living in the same house, raising the same children, working together constantly, they had all the time they needed. Didn't they?

He cleared his throat. "I think I need to get some sleep. There wasn't much chance to last night, and I've got to get an early start tomorrow...."

In two blinks, the soft expression melted from her face. Her whole body went stiff, and her hands left his chest. Her words came out with a halting stutter, as though she wanted to say something entirely different. "Of course. You must be exhausted."

She had her feet beneath her and left his lap with a suddenness that had him reaching for her before he caught himself again. Keeping her back to him, Evelyn smoothed her dress. "I need to turn in as well. The children have lessons tomorrow morning, and chores, and I promised Beth I would help her air her bedrooms tomorrow so I can learn how to take care of ours." The words continued to pour out of her, coming faster and faster as she walked away from him.

Chris's heart sank. He'd spoken carefully but hadn't put enough thought into her reaction. He hurried across the room to her before she could slip through the door and disappear upstairs. He took her hand and tugged her gently back to him, and as she turned with her face tilted upward, he read the hurt in her eyes.

"Evie." Chris gathered her close, her skirts brushing either side of his legs and her hips in his hands. "If I don't let you go, if we don't say goodnight right now, there's a real possibility we'll end up in the same bed together tonight." His gaze lowered from her wide, enchanting eyes to her kiss-swollen lips that parted in a gasp. "And I'm not sure either of us is ready for that just yet." Though he very much wished they were.

Her eyelashes lowered, and her cheeks darkened. "I see."

But he didn't know if she approved. Because Evelyn whirled away from him. She darted up the stairs like a doe fleeing into the mountains, never looking back. Too intent on her escape.

With a groan, Chris leaned against the kitchen door frame. He scrubbed at his face, then his hair, and worked at not thinking of how near Evelyn remained. How she slept in a bed meant for both of them. And how incredible she felt in his arms.

Instead, he took off his boots and put them by the door. Then he extinguished the lamps, the single candle, and banked the fire. His eyes lingered on her framed drawing until it grew too dark to see the details. Finally, he made his way up the stairs and to his bedroll.

Where he tried, in vain, to banish Evelyn's kisses from his mind before he fell into a fitful sleep.

CHAPTER TWENTY-FOUR

Though Evelyn knew she'd acted the part of a hoyden the evening before, she didn't regret a single moment of her time spent near the fire with Chris. She wanted to give him her trust. And her heart. Every day with him, watching him with the children, gave her greater reason to believe he wasn't going to hurt her.

That morning at breakfast, they'd steadfastly avoided looking at each other until she served him coffee. Then he'd looked up to say thank you, as he always did, and when their eyes had met, they both smiled. And blushed.

Which, Evelyn reflected later as she helped the children with their spelling, was ridiculous. In fact, she made that one of their spelling words for the new week.

R-I-D-I-C-U-L-O-U-S.

"What does that mean?" Ben asked when he'd written the whole thing out. "Does it mean silly?"

Evelyn picked up Chris's copy of *Webster's American Dictionary* to read aloud. "From Latin. It means laughable, funny, or absurd. It says here it can also mean 'outrageous.'" Absurd felt the most accurate for her current circumstances.

Chris and she were husband and wife, and a wife enjoying

her husband's kisses ought to be perfectly acceptable. Perhaps her mother hadn't prepared her for such enjoyment, and in fact all Evelyn's previous experience had taught her wifely duties were a chore rather a pleasure. But she had taken to watching the other couples on the ranch, each in a different stage of marriage and love. The tenderness they showed one another had her yearning for the same.

She blushed again, standing there with the dictionary in hand. Until Laura said, "You're turning red, Mama."

Evelyn snapped the dictionary cover closed. "It must be warm in here." She kept them working another half-hour on academic matters, then had the children tidy up so they could go visit the main house after luncheon.

Even there, she remained distracted. She went from room to room with Beth, taking hold of the feather mattress toppers and shaking them out before laying them in the open windows. Thankfully, such work didn't require much mental prowess. And Beth wasn't inclined to speak overmuch. The woman seemed lost in her own thoughts, humming to herself while occasionally laying a hand across her abdomen.

When they went downstairs again for tea, Beth let out a sudden gasp.

"Is something wrong?" Evelyn rose from the chair she'd only just relaxed into. "Beth?"

"Oh, I am terribly sorry, Evelyn. I completely forgot to give this to you." She hurried to the mantel where she picked up an envelope. "Whiskers was visiting, when he crossed paths with Mr. Holloway. Whiskers didn't come home until late last night, and he dropped the mail off here."

She presented the envelope to Evelyn. "I thought about bringing it over last night, but the lights were already out. And then it slipped my mind completely this morning. I don't know what's come over me, lately—"

Evelyn crossed the room to take the envelope from her friend, then she gave Beth a warm hug. "You needn't worry a bit, Beth.

When I was pregnant with Madeline, I forgot everything. I left my house without my gloves, I misplaced my husband's spectacles, I made appointments I forgot to keep." She laughed as she pulled back, meeting Beth's gaze squarely. "I think growing a child is a reasonable excuse for having your thoughts on other matters."

"You have no notion how much I needed to hear that." Beth lowered herself into her chair. "I've been wandering from room to room, forgetting entirely what I'm looking for only to find that I'm already holding it. Like my good sewing scissors."

Evelyn laughed with her friend, then looked down at the envelope in her hand. She went cold inside, and her lips parted in a soft gasp. "It's from Boston."

"I did see that postmark," Beth murmured, raising her eyebrows. "I thought it might be from one of those schools you wrote during your first week here." Somehow, Beth managed not to sound as curious as Evelyn thought she must be.

Turning the envelope over, Evelyn broke the seal and tugged out two pieces of thick paper. The first was covered in handwriting, and the second was typewritten. Evelyn read the handwriting first.

"It's from the school Dannie attended. The headmistress answered my letter." She read to herself, her eyes rapidly taking in the letter from salutation to the extravagant signature at the bottom. "They are offering me a place, starting in January. With a cottage on the grounds for Madeline and me to live away from the school." They looked at the typewritten paper. "This is a form for Madeline's application and entry as a student."

Slowly, Evelyn lowered herself onto the edge of the couch. She looked again at the paper, where a starting salary that made her heart jump in surprise met her eyes. "It's such a generous offer." She stared at the paper in shock. Here it was. An answer to her providing for herself, and her daughter, without depending on the sympathy of anyone else.

"I don't suppose it's too late to accept."

Beth's quiet words made Evelyn's body tense. "I'm married," she said, her voice too soft. Almost uncertain. She raised her gaze to her friend's and shook her head. "It's too late."

"Annulments exist for a reason, Evelyn." Beth stared at her, expression smooth. Her body quite still. She spoke slowly. Carefully. "You married Chris because you didn't see another way. Everyone here knows this. Now, here is your opportunity to choose."

"There isn't any choice," Evelyn protested, her hand trembling. "Unless you think—do you think I should go? That I don't —we don't belong here?" She had struggled with that thought herself, from the moment that rattlesnake had appeared in the garden. But she had learned. She could learn more. "Do you think Chris would want me—"

And there it was. The only reason she would consider leaving. If Chris *didn't* want her. Yet he had seemed to care for her. Treating her with tenderness and respect. Trusting her. Patiently waiting for her to understand things. For her to accept him as her husband.

"I don't think it matters what Chris Morgan wants." Beth spoke with a steadiness, a motherly tone, that made it impossible to be angry at her. "What matters is what *you* want. You've told me, Evelyn, how both of your first marriages came about. You married because you had no other choice. I worried for you when you accepted Frosty's proposal. But I understood." Beth rose from her chair and came to sit next to Evelyn, putting her arm around her shoulder. "This is your chance, right here, to make a choice. Do you want to be a wife to Chris and mother to his children? Or do you want independence in a way you've never had it before?"

Her hand stopped trembling. Evelyn looked down at the papers in her hand again. Beth was right. Evelyn could pack her bags and leave. She could go to Boston, giving Madeline new opportunities. Making her own way without dependence on anyone else for the first time in her life. Chris would help her get an annulment. She knew that.

But she was more than just Madeline's mother. She was Laura's and Ben's, too.

And Chris...he was unlike any man she had met before. The thought of leaving him now, when she had a chance at love—

Evelyn folded the letter and dropped it into her lap. *Love.* That word had never passed between them. She couldn't possibly know if she loved him. Or even what it meant to love someone other than Madeline.

She looked up at Beth, even as her shoulders dropped. "I care about Chris."

Beth's eyebrows nearly met her hairline. "Isn't that a good thing? If you want to stay, that is."

"Only if he feels the same about me." Evelyn rubbed at her eyes, then let her hands fall into her lap. "What if he doesn't, Beth? What if he only sees me as a mother for the children, a housekeeper—though a very poor one. How could I live the rest of my life with a man who doesn't see me as more than a business partner?" She shivered.

"It sounds as though you need to have a talk with your husband." Beth laid her hand over Evelyn's. "As your friend, while I would do anything to keep you here, I know enough about you to see that this letter matters. Your decision regarding it matters, too."

"Thank you." Evelyn squeezed Beth's hand, tears prickling at her eyes. "Your friendship is important to me, Beth. I've learned so much from you. I don't think I've ever had a friendship like yours before." She sniffled. "I'll speak to Chris. But...but I want to stay. If he wants me to stay."

Beth nodded, a look of relief in her eyes. "Here. Have some tea. Get your strength up a bit." After Evelyn had nearly downed the whole cup, Beth settled in the chair across from her. She tilted her head to the side. "Forgive me for asking, Evie. But since we're speaking of difficult subjects today, I have wondered. Did you hope to have children with Frosty?"

Evelyn's face flamed hot, and the rest of her body flushed with heat immediately after. "We haven't discussed the possibility. Or lack of it." She put a hand to her cheek. "It was difficult for me, with Madeline. I was dreadfully ill. Then there weren't any more pregnancies. My doctors couldn't tell me why."

Beth nodded slowly. "I'm sorry. I shouldn't pry. But know that I hope for the best for the two of you, no matter what that means for your future. I can already see how happy you've made Frosty, and how much happier you are now than you were when we met. If your path takes you elsewhere—"

Evelyn's heart filled with gratitude. And the question of future children. Quite suddenly, that was more pressing than the letter in her hand. Did she want more children? Did Chris? She'd wondered, more than once, if it wasn't her body to blame for the lack of children. She felt healthy. Her body behaved as a healthy body ought. But there was no way to know for certain.

At present, she had three children under her care, taking up her heart, and a new husband she had true affection for. The letter in her lap crinkled when she leaned to put the cup on its saucer. She folded the papers and put them both in her apron pocket.

She didn't want to leave.

At that moment, a knock sounded at the front door. Both women rose from their chairs.

"I'll get it," Clark called from the study. He and his brother were working on a history course together and had agreed to teach the three younger children about Russia while they reviewed what they learned. Clark went to the door and threw it open wide, then turned to announce, "It's just Frosty."

Evelyn's stomach flipped forward and back again. She met Beth's gaze, her eyes wide. It was as though their conversation had summoned him.

"Just Frosty?" Evelyn's husband repeated, sounding amused.

"Sorry." Clark turned back around. "How do you want to be announced? Maddie's been teaching me English etiquette, you know." He sounded on the verge of laughter. "I'd make a great master of ceremonies at a ball, she says."

"It's the loud voice," Beth supplied as she stepped into the hall in front of Evelyn. "What brings you by way of the front door, Frosty? Do you need King?"

"No, ma'am." Chris had stepped inside, and his blue eyes darted to meet Evelyn's gaze when she came up behind Beth. "I've come with a request, and to take my wife away with me."

Clark grimaced. "I'm going back to studying with the kids." He went through the study door and shut it behind him with a snap.

Beth chuckled. "Someday, that boy's mind will turn to romance, just like his brother's." Then she looked over at Evelyn. "I'm imagining this husband of yours wants us to look after the children while he kidnaps you. We would love to keep them for dinner tonight."

"Oh—are you certain?" She tried to put an extra meaning in her expression. "I know it might be inconvenient, with your condition."

The rancher's wife stuck her nose up in the air. "If you don't think I can handle three little children for one evening, Evelyn Morgan, you are seriously underestimating me. Now, off with you. Enjoy some time with your husband. We'll walk the children home at nightfall."

With a thankful smile, Evelyn squeezed her friend's hand and walked by, untying her apron strings as she went. "Is this really a kidnapping?" she asked Chris as he held the front door open for her.

"I prefer to think of it as *absconding*."

"Ah, an excellent word. I'll add that to our spelling list."

He looped his arm through hers, a familiar motion now. One that set her at ease—though Evelyn came to a stop when she saw two saddled horses waiting in front of the house at the bottom of the porch.

"Chris, I'm not dressed for riding." She lifted the edge of her skirt, looking up at him with wide eyes.

"Let's get you home and in a split skirt, then. Probably a hat, too. Sun's still hot this time of day." He tugged her forward, leading her down the steps, then he lifted her onto the back of the horse. "It'll just take a minute, and then I have something I want to show you."

Evelyn squeaked when he mounted up behind her, bringing the horse around to take her back to their house. The other horse followed when Chris whistled. "These two are my personal cutting horses," Chris said as they rounded the main house to make for their own. "Your smartest horses should always be the cutting horses. They've gotta want to work and follow orders to do a good job."

"That is understandable," Evelyn murmured, her head spinning with his nearness. "Do they have names?"

"Of course they do." He chuckled, and his breath tickled the back of her neck. "We're on Trigger, and that's Phoenix, named after one of our bigger cities right here in Arizona."

"It's a pleasure to meet them both," she said, somewhat unsteadily. Her husband's chest rumbled with amusement behind her.

When they arrived in front of their house, Chris dismounted first, putting his hands up to catch Evelyn as she slipped down from the saddle. His hands lingered on her waist, and Evelyn resisted leaning into him for a kiss. They weren't alone. There were men milling about all over the ranch. And did she have any business showing him such affection before they talked?

"I'll only take a moment. Do I need anything other than proper riding attire and a hat?" she asked.

"Nope. I've got everything we need."

Curious as to what he meant, and how long he had planned whatever it was he had in mind, Evelyn hurried inside with a giddiness she hadn't felt in years. Possibly not since childhood. She ran up the stairs while unbuttoning her shirtwaist. She'd put on something sturdier for a ride, along with the single split skirt Dannie had insisted she sew during her second week at the ranch. Then all she needed to do was put on her straw hat and stab it through with a hatpin. She hadn't bought proper boots yet, but her shoes would do well enough.

Evelyn was out the door again in less than a quarter of an hour, and pleased with herself, too. "Where are we going?" she asked again as Chris knelt to turn his knee into a mounting block for her.

"You'll have to wait and see." Once she'd settled in the saddle, Chris stared up at her an extra moment, a grin wide as the Arizona sky across his handsome face. "You make a pretty cowgirl, Evie."

Her cheeks went warm, and her insides curled with pleasure. "Thank you, kind sir." Then she took up the reins. "Lead the way, Mr. Morgan." She'd be happy to follow, no matter where he went.

CANYONS STRETCHED NORTHWARD IN SEVERAL DIRECTIONS, BUT Chris didn't take Evelyn down the same route he'd ridden with the men when they'd hoped to find evidence of rustlers. Instead, he took her eastward, toward the mountains and into the mouth of a shallow canyon. Really more of a gully, given that it only held water during the rainiest monsoon seasons.

Along the way, they talked. About everything. She told him about the morning with the children, and the things she'd learned about keeping house. She asked about his day, and he told her about tracking down a sick calf and bringing it back to the barn where they could keep an eye on it. They talked about the children wanting puppies and kittens, and how they might bring a furry beast into their home as a pet.

In fact, Chris felt as though they'd been a team for far longer than the five weeks they'd known each other. Evelyn's lilting alto, echoing off the stone and dirt walls of the canyon, was as familiar to him as the birdsong he heard every day on his rides in the desert.

Before long, he was telling her about his first job in the Territory. A story he hadn't told often. "I worked for a family in the western part of the territory. The Hintons. The boss was a troublesome sort. He owned a saloon, the general store, and a ranch in their little town. I think he aimed to own the whole thing before long, given the way he bought up property. He paid well. But he had a way about him..." Chris cringed. "I saw him pistol-whip a *vaquero* once. I heard him yelling at his wife and kids. She was a young thing, too. Not much older than me when I worked for him. I was seventeen."

"He sounds like a terrible man," Evelyn said, her expression grim. "Why did you take a job with him?"

"I was a boy from Missouri with little practical experience." He shrugged. "I found another cowboy at the station in Phoenix, and he told me he knew a man who needed more hands. But working for Hinton, I learned real quick to keep my head down and my mouth shut. He was a hard man. As soon as I'd saved enough to get together my own horses—because his men all had to use his—I left. I heard tell later that someone shot Hinton while he sat at a card table, drinking and gambling in his own saloon."

Evelyn shuddered. "That's terrible."

"I've heard worse. Seen a little of it, too." Chris wondered how much to tell her. Arizona Territory wasn't as wild as it had been thirty years before, or even in the twelve years since he'd arrived. Things were getting better. They had a university, now, and marshals. Sheriffs. Votes. Trains. Things were turning more and more civilized with each passing season.

Then again, they did still have rustlers to deal with. Where decent folk tried to eke out a living, there'd always be a few snakes hiding under rocks. But that wasn't what today was about. He'd brought Evelyn out into the desert with a different end in mind.

They turned up an incline, the canyon narrowing, and water showing beneath their horse's hooves.

"The thing about our Sonoran Desert," he said, looking over his shoulder to watch her eyes, "is that it's full of surprises. Danger? Sure. Mountains and rocks? Of course. But occasionally, you find a real treasure out here. Like this one." He watched her as they rounded the last bend, and everything around them changed as they emerged into a glade of trees. Evelyn's widening eyes reflected the beauty of the hidden grove. Tall, spindly trees that only grew in small clusters around the ranch. Pockets of earth with water, where cool air collected and rested between rock and branch, creating an oasis that felt like it didn't quite belong in the same land that grew cactus and mesquite.

Water from two springs in the mountain above flowed into a three-foot-deep pond, with an outlet somewhere under the ground and rocks. The ground beneath the trees had soft soil, from years of leaves falling and turning to dirt, but the oasis lacked the troublesome, choking weeds of the desert since all the critters who came through for water nibbled at the growth, too.

Evelyn looked around with wonder, putting her hand out to cup a leaf changing from green to gold. "Is this part of the ranch?"

"Sure is." Chris dismounted and came around her horse to help her down. This time, when her feet touched the ground, he kept his hands upon her waist with a purposeful grin. "Do you like it?"

"Yes." Her hands rested on his forearms, and she peered around them again before her gaze settled on his. With a slight tilt to her head, she offered him a curious smile. "Thank you for bringing me here. It's glorious. And...almost cold." She shivered, the tremor of her body flowing through his hands, into his arms, and touching his heart.

"Our elevation is higher, and the trees and water form their own environment." He took her hand and led her to the edge of the crystal-clear water. "This comes from the mountain, all along rocky streams, so it's clean and cold water." He brought her to the only man-made structure in the grove. The Boltons had formed a small dam directly beneath one of the springs, letting the water spill out first into a basin the size of a large bowl before it tumbled out to the main body of water. Chris cupped his hands in the water and brought it to his mouth, taking a sip. "Try it. It's fresher and cleaner than any water you've had before."

Evelyn cupped her hands together and dipped them in, shivering again with the cold, then brought it to her lips and drank. She closed her eyes as she sipped, then hummed with pleasure. "That is incredible. This came from the ground, here?"

"Amazing, isn't it?" He took her cold hand in his and led her to a large, flat stone, gesturing for her to take a seat. Then he did the same and pulled off his boots, then his socks. "Now you need to dip your toes in. It'll cool you off after that ride."

She squinted at him. "I assure you, I am perfectly cool this very moment. The stone is cold." She laid her palm on the rock between them. "The air here is chilled. I have no reason to remove my shoes and stockings."

He chuckled and stretched his feet out into the water. "Suit yourself. This is my favorite place to come in the summer. July. August. It's harder to get to, because the monsoons fill up the creeks in the canyons, but it's worth the trip. I thought we could bring the kids up here sometime. After Ben's foot gets better."

"They would enjoy that." Evelyn pulled the pin from her hat, taking that off and setting it beside her. Then she produced a handkerchief from a pocket in her skirt and dipped it into the water before dabbing at her neck with a delicacy he'd never seen another woman use.

When she spoke again, it was with a hesitancy he hadn't expected. "Chris. I need to tell you something."

"All right. I'm listenin'."

He watched his lovely wife fidget and her bright expression dim to something far more solemn. He sat straighter, and he gave her his full attention. Waiting patiently.

Finally, not looking at him, she said, "I received a letter from the school in Boston. They offered me a position, with a generous salary, and a home of my own for myself and Madeline."

His heart dropped clear to his feet. The world tilted. "Oh." He stared at her, uncertain. What did she want him to say? Probably not the protest that rose to his lips. That he squashed down. His voice dropped as he asked, "Do you...do you want to leave?" More the fool him, if she did. Here he was, ready to proclaim his intentions toward his wife—to court her, to love her for the rest of their lives, and she could cut and run.

Her eyes shone, and then her eyelashes trembled with the first sign of tears. "I don't," she admitted, but the devastation in her voice kept him from feeling any kind of relief. "But I don't want to be trapped again. Chris. I've come to care for you, and the children, and this place. Madeline and I are happy here. And I thought that would be enough. But I've already lived through two awful marriages, with husbands who didn't care a fig for me. I can't do it again. So if you don't want me here, or if you can't see your way to feeling more, I need to know." She raised her eyes at last, and one hand crept to her cheek to dash at her tears before falling to her throat. Her chest heaved once. "I need to know what you think of me."

And Chris said the first thing that came to his mind. "You're a wonder, Evie."

Her hand stilled against her throat, and she raised her eyebrows at him. "I beg your pardon?"

He tilted his hat back as he took her in, from the tip of her freckled nose to the curling ends of her lustrous copper braid. Then down to her pointed shoes. "You've come across the world to a new place, a new way of living, and I don't think I've ever heard you complain. You haven't cursed your luck. You haven't whined about your circumstances, even though you've every right to be upset by what's happened. You just keep on pushing forward, tackling each day with a determination that leaves me in awe of you."

He felt genuine pleasure when her cheeks pinked, then

reddened, and her eyes lowered. "I haven't borne everything with grace, though I appreciate your compliment." She shook her head, her gaze lingering on the water. "I rose beyond the station that Society thought belonged to me. To everyone back in England, it likely seemed that I received exactly what I deserved for presuming to rise above my station." Her smile turned somewhat rueful. "And yet, for all their jealousy and bitterness toward me, I never had the things I truly wanted."

Chris covered her hand with his, her skin cool from the rock as he threaded their fingers together. "Tell me exactly what you want, Evie."

"Happiness. To be loved and cared for." She studied their joined hands, and a long strand of her hair slipped from her braid to graze her neck. She didn't seem to notice. "Having Madeline helped. Otherwise, my life in England was so empty compared to what I found here in less than a month. Friends. Purpose. I want to stay," she whispered.

His heart thundered in his chest, and Chris knew the time had come to tell her he wanted to give her everything she longed for. If she would let him. Raising their joined hands to his lips, Chris brushed a kiss across her knuckles.

There was no one here to interrupt. There were no chores to see to. No bed to tempt him to take things farther than what his wife was ready to accept. The sound of water trickling over rocks and lapping at the ground beneath their feet created a sense of calm that finally gave him the ability to form the right words. At least, what he hoped were the right words.

"Evelyn. When I proposed we marry, I was being practical. I wanted to help you, and I knew I needed help, too." He watched as she raised her gaze to his, and he noticed the careful way she watched him. Feeling as uncertain as he did. "The minute you said yes, giving me permission to plan a future with you and Madeline in it, everything changed. My world shifted, putting you right there at the center. Not a day, not a minute, has gone by without me thinking about you. Without me trying to find ways to make you happy. I can't explain it." He chuckled, his gaze falling from hers as he tried to get hold of an emotion closing off his throat. He had to get through this. Now. Because this might be the most important speech of his life.

"I've never had a sweetheart before. I don't know the first thing about courtship, except to know I'm doing this backward since we married first. But I need you to know that this—" He used his free hand to gesture from her to him. "This isn't a practical arrangement for me anymore. It's more meaningful than that. You've become my friend. My partner. My wife." Her eyes glowed up at him, her expression growing soft and tender. "I want you to stay. Because I'm falling in love with you, Evelyn."

He let his declaration linger in the air, watching as his wife flushed and she lowered her eyes with a flustered, demure expression. He squeezed her hand. "I know that my feelings aren't part of the deal we made. I'm not asking for anything to change. You don't have to feel the same way, either. But you should know. Please don't leave now. Give me a chance to prove myself to you."

"I can do that, Chris." She looked up at him, searching his eyes, and he watched as she parted her lips to speak, only to press them together again. Rather than make her feel like she had to say more, Chris relaxed and grinned at her. Telling her relieved a weight he'd carried around in his heart for some time. She knew how he felt. And he had no intention of letting her go without a fight.

"We can stay here as long as you want. I brought some food for a picnic. Are you hungry?" He rose before she answered and rolled up the legs of his trousers. Chris waded through the water to where the horses had wandered to graze. He started whistling, watching carefully where he put his feet, until he'd made it to the saddlebags and the wrapped-up hand pies and cookies he'd brought along for their supper. He turned around to bring everything back and saw Evelyn rolling down her stocking.

The shapely, fair-skinned leg he glimpsed nearly made him

drop everything he held. She'd pulled her dress up to knees, too. She rolled down and removed the other stocking as he watched, then stretched both feet in front of her to ease her toes into the water.

Her gasp was loud enough for him to hear it, then she looked up at him with eyes as big as an owl's. "It's *freezing*. How did you bear to walk through it?" But she kept her toes in the water, and he grinned back across at her.

She might not be ready to love him yet. But he was going to love her with his whole heart. Just see if he didn't.

CHAPTER TWENTY-FIVE

They left the beautiful glade with enough time to make it home by sundown. Evelyn let Phoenix do most of the work, holding the reins loosely in her hands. The horse knew to follow Chris and Trigger. That left her with plenty of energy to think and overthink everything Chris had said to her. Not just his confession, which had come as the most pleasant surprise she'd ever had, but all the things he'd said to her since their first meeting.

As self-assured as he was when it came to his work and life on the ranch, the man had a humble nature. He didn't swagger the way she'd seen some of the cowboys swagger, nor did he look down his nose at anyone the way her second husband had done. The respect he showed to her, a former countess, he used in his treatment of everyone else. He had an easy smile now that he wasn't alone in his work with the children. And he had a laugh that made her stomach flip and her heart ache.

Did she love him?

Possibly.

She certainly cared for him more than she had cared for. . well, thinking on the other men in her adult life seemed so fruitless now. Comparing them to Chris Morgan was like comparing dust to diamonds. Chris was the diamond.

That letter she'd left in her apron might as well have been dust, too. Because she couldn't imagine leaving. Not now that she knew what was in Chris's heart. Not if she could trust him with her own.

When they arrived back at the house after returning the horses to the paddock, the Boltons were sitting on the front porch in the rocking chairs.

"These are mighty fine, Frosty." Mr. Bolton rocked forward and back. "Hope you don't mind Beth and me trying them out. We ought to get you a rocking chair, Beth." His eyes twinkled at his wife, who blushed prettily. "It'd be a fine thing for the nursery."

"I ordered these from Missouri." Chris put his hands in his pockets and leaned against the column supporting the porch cover. "There's a man there who makes them by the dozen. My family had six of these lined up on their front porch at home."

"Seems like mighty fine craftmanship." Beth ran her hands over the arms of her chair. "What do you think, Evie?"

"I quite like them. They're comfortable, especially if you put a cushion down first." Evelyn lingered near the door, both wanting to go inside to check on the children and stay with the adults.

As though sensing Evelyn's hesitance, Beth nodded to the front door. "The children are playing with the barn Abram delivered to Ben while you were away."

"A barn?" Evelyn raised her eyebrows.

"With animals," King added, still enjoying his rocking back and forth. He was a tall man, with legs stretched out farther than Chris's reached in the same chair. He was fine looking, too, even if he was in his fifties. He looked like he had years and years of good health ahead of him. He'd already proven himself a fine father. His new little one couldn't ask for better.

Evelyn looked up at Chris. "A barn and animals for Ben."

He looked a little sheepish as he shrugged. "I was going to

wait for Christmas. We're making a dollhouse for the girls, too. But with Ben laid up until that foot heals, I thought it'd be a good idea to go ahead and give him something to do inside the house."

The care he showed the children had quickly grown to be one of her favorite things about him. Evelyn extended her hand to take his, and though he looked a bit confused he accepted the touch.

"Thank you, Chris. That was sweet of you."

His mouth twitched upward in the start of one of those wide grins she loved, but before it could reach its widest, Gus started barking from the paddock.

Mr. Bolton rose to his feet, peering into the distance. "Whiskers is riding in faster than a greased eel."

Evelyn turned around to see a cowboy coming toward them at speed, making straight for their front door. He pulled up on his horse so abruptly that the creature reared back, whinnying in protest.

"The rustlers are back," the man said, his eyes blazing above his wild beard. "I saw four of 'em. They cut a dozen out, at least. Must've come in from some other place, but they're riding 'em toward the north canyons."

Mr. Bolton muttered a curse and slapped the rail in front of him, but Chris immediately went into action. First, he barked at Whiskers, "Get the men mounted and my horse saddled." Then he stormed into the house, flinging the door open with enough force that it bounced back, closing behind him.

Evelyn met Beth's eyes, finding them as wide with worry as her own. She opened the door and went after her husband, hearing his boots tromp loudly up the stairs.

She glanced to Ben's room and was relieved the door was closed. The children were laughing and talking, from what she could hear. She rushed to catch up to Chris, her heart pounding against her ribs.

"Chris?" She ran up the stairs, holding her dress out of the way. "Chris, what are you going to do?"

He came out of his room with a rifle in one hand and a belt full of ammunition in the other. He leaned the gun against the doorway and slung the belt around his hips, just below the belt that already held a holster with his six-shooter. They'd ridden out with a shotgun that afternoon, and he'd left that somewhere in the barn when he'd put up his saddle.

How many guns did the man need to go out after cattle thieves?

Her heart went cold. "Chris. What are you doing?" she asked again, feeling dizzy.

"I need to round up the men and go after the rustlers. King, Duke, and Abram will stay here with their boys. They'll keep a watch on the homestead to make sure no one circles back for the horses we keep here."

"But Chris—"

"This is my job, Evie," he said sharply, his blue eyes as cold as his nickname. "One that I've been failing ever since those no-good wolves started picking at our herds this spring. King pays me to get his cattle to market, not to let them get stolen right out from under my nose." He picked up his rifle, pointing it down and away from her.

She put her hand on his arm, stilling him. "This isn't safe."

"No, ma'am. It isn't. But it's part of the work." He bent and pressed a kiss to her lips. "I love you, Evie. I've gotta go." He pulled away before she could protest or say another word, the cloth from his shirt slipping through her grasp like flour through a sieve.

His boots pounded down the stairs, the sound jolting Evie into following him once more. She made it to the porch just as his feet hit the ground. He was barking orders at Whiskers while King and Beth stood next to each other, arm-in-arm, on the porch.

"Get the men together. Every cowboy who expects his pay at the end of the season is riding out. We're putting a stop to this and getting our cattle back. Get a move on."

Whiskers tipped his hat and then spurred his horse into a gallop, despite the short distance to the bunkhouse and barn.

Chris whirled on his heel. "We'll get them this time, King."

King gave a slow nod. "I trust you'll take care, Frosty."

Evelyn waited to hear her husband make a promise to his boss that he hadn't made to her, but Chris only gave a tight nod before hurrying off to where the men were already rushing. Evelyn took a step, as though to go after him, her lips parted to call him back.

The men he meant to pursue wouldn't want to be caught. Cattle thieves still hanged in Arizona Territory. Would they run or fight? That she didn't know what Chris would find if he caught up to them made her blood run cold. She turned to look at Beth.

"They'll be safe, won't they?" she asked, her voice hoarse.

Beth exchanged a look with King, who's lips now formed a grim line beneath his mustache. Then Beth looked back at Evelyn, a smile on her face that didn't quite reach her eyes. "Frosty is the best foreman this ranch has ever had. He's smart. I'm sure he'll be just fine."

But no one could make Evelyn any promises.

She hadn't even had the chance to say goodbye to him. Or to tell him—tell him what he really meant to her.

Evelyn turned around, ready to march down the steps and straight to the barn. But the men were already riding out. She saw them go through the *zaguán* and heard the echoes of hooves striking the ground.

It was too late. Her husband was gone.

A DOZEN CATTLE STOLEN MEANT HUNDREDS OF DOLLARS LOST. FOR most spreads, that many cattle missing meant a financial hit that wouldn't be something easily recovered from. Given the precarious position of the KB Ranch for the last few years, the loss wasn't acceptable.

Chris didn't need to shout orders to his men. They'd prepared for this. Half of the men broke away and rode north to the pasture where Whiskers had spotted the cloud of dust. Their job was easy. They needed to spook the rustlers into leaving the cattle behind to flee.

Two men rode hard, making for the wide northern split from Middle Canyon to the north. That was the least likely direction for the rustlers to head, given it would take them away from the Mexican-Arizona border.

Chris, Ed, and Dominó went for the southwest fork of Middle Canyon, just before it branched. They'd try to get ahead of the rustlers. If the thieves had already driven the cattle ahead of them, Chris and his men would stop the cattle from emerging through Middle Canyon and into the maze of smaller, southern canyons.

If the thieves abandoned their prize, as Chris hoped, it would mean a confrontation.

Less than an hour of daylight remained. If it went full dark before they had the men in hand, they'd get away. Again. Chris wasn't about to let that happen.

He'd trust his men, and everything would work out just fine.

They arrived at the southwest branch of Middle Canyon a quarter of an hour after leaving the ranch. Chris didn't hesitate to ride down into it, Ed with him, while Dominó stayed on the southern embankment.

Chris slid his rifle out of its sheath. His side of the little canyon, more like a twig than a branch of the main canyon, was six feet above the canyon floor. He pointed his rifle the direction they expected to see the rustlers.

Chris stayed right there, smack in the middle of the dried-out wash, mounted and holding his position with a casual posture. Ed rode up the other side, positioning himself on the opposite embankment directly across from Dominó. All three remained silent, listening.

They didn't have long to wait before the echoes of horse

hooves sounded, and Chris rested his hand on his revolver's handle.

Dirt sprayed upward in the distance. Not enough to be men *and* cattle, he'd wager. Good. The other men had done their job and rescued the cattle. The debris kicked up by the fleeing thieves came onward like an approaching dust devil, until Chris knew the fleeing rustlers had one last bend to turn to come into sight.

He lowered the brim of his hat and squared up.

There were a dozen ways this could go wrong.

But there was one very big motivation to make sure everything went right.

It wasn't just the job. Though that's all Chris had needed in the past.

The rustlers came around the corner and pulled up when they saw Chris, cussing up a storm.

Chris continued sitting there like he'd been waiting for hours. "You're trapped," he shouted over the din of their horses' shuffling as the men tried to calm their jittery animals. "Throw down your weapons and come along peaceful-like."

One of the riders twisted in his saddle, and when his gaze collided with Chris, the rangy-looking man shouted hoarsely. "Frosty? That you?"

The other riders stilled, and Frosty's gut clenched. He knew the voice, and after a moment, he recognized the rest of the man. He cracked the man's name like a whip. "Buck."

He wasn't all that surprised, it turned out. Buck had been a hand with the ranch the year before. Dannie had humiliated him by spurning his advances, and King had sent him packing when the boastful cowboy had proven dishonorable.

"How long have you been part of this outfit?" Chris asked, sparing a quick glance up at Ed. The three of them had shared a bunkhouse, meals, jokes, and a lot of time in the saddle. Ed had always been arrogant, but he'd been good at his job. He'd earned Chris's respect a time or two with how he handled the animals.

Chris's gaze darted to the other men, trying to pick out the leader. There was always a hierarchy in groups like this, and the sooner he took down the real threat, the sooner the danger would be over.

The horses had calmed, and the rustlers were looking at Chris, hands hovering over holsters.

Chris met the eyes of one of the men whose hand crept too close to his pistol. Except he didn't see a man when he peered closer. Dirt on the boy's face had disguised his age. The kid couldn't be older then sixteen or seventeen. "I've got men with their guns trained on you, son. Draw it out slow and drop it in the dust. Now."

Three of the riders with Buck were boys. The other full-grown man might've been Buck's age. It was hard to tell with his dirty beard and scowl.

"Do what he says," Buck snapped. "Slow." He glanced up, catching sight of first Dominó and then Ed. He tipped his hat back when he saw the latter. "Ed. Been a while."

"Not long enough, Buck," Ed snapped from his position. "Get your piece out and drop it."

Slowly, and with a wide grin, Buck pulled his gun and tossed it to the ground.

It wasn't time to relax just yet.

"Now you're all going to dismount." Chris watched Buck and the other full-grown adult. The men who should've known better. Dragging kids into rustling? It was worse than the act itself. These boys were likely down-on-their luck farmers' sons. Maybe orphans, looking for a place to belong and finding trouble instead.

It didn't matter. They'd done something stupid. Because someone—maybe Buck—had told them it was easy money.

Dominó jumped into the culvert, still holding his rifle, and collected up the guns from the ground while Ed covered him. Then Dominó backed away, arms full, until he was behind Chris.

Chris gave his next command. "I want all of you on your

stomachs. Flat cn the ground." The three youngsters started to obey.

"Now hold on a minute." Buck raised both hands on the air. "You're not planning on taking us in, are you?"

"That's up to King Bolton, since it's his cattle you've been stealing." Chris let his gaze rest on the uncertain boys. "I imagine he'll let the first-time offenders go." One look at these kids wou_d remind King of his own sons and how easy it'd be to lead a boy astray. He wouldn't want boys punished for following lesser men. One of the boys visibly slumped in relief, then lay down on his stomach without another word.

"You don't know that." Buck scoffed and came a step closer. "You know as well as I do, a man's as likely to hang for this as he is to do prison time."

Chris ground his teeth together. He needed Buck to shut his trap before he made the others frightened enough to fight or run. "You know as well as I do that no one has actually hung for cattle thieving in years."

Dismounting, Chris took the rope out of his saddle. "Get on the ground, Buck."

Buck puffed his chest out. "No."

Chris looked at the still-standing boys and the other man. "You three. Move on over where the only smart member of your little gang is on the ground. Now." When he barked the last word, the two boys jumped to obey. The other man just raised his hand and grinned, taking a step back.

"Ed?" Chris asked.

"I'm watching him."

"Dominó, you get those boys tied up." Chris stepped closer to Buck. "Don't make this harder on yourself," he warned, dropping his voice lower. "Give me your hands."

Buck smirked and held his hands together in front of him. Chris approached, cautiously. When he had the rope around Buck's wrist, Buck balled both hands into fists and rammed them upward into Chris's jaw, knocking him back. The other man tackled Dominó with one quick, flying leap when Buck's movement distracted Ed.

Chris launched himself up again, tucking his shoulder to barrel into Buck's stomach, knocking the thief to the ground. Buck, his hands still free, knocked a fist into the back of Chris's head, making him see stars.

They rolled, and Chris's head slammed into a rock.

"Stop." With that shout, Chris's eyes darted briefly to see that the other fellow had Dominó as a shield, a knife pressed to his neck. "Let him go, or your friend gets stuck."

Chris released Buck, who rolled away and to his feet. Before Chris could get up, Buck turned on him and aimed a booted kick right at Chris's ribs. Once. Twice. The third time, Chris was sure something inside his body had snapped.

Absurdly, all he could think in that moment of pain was that Evelyn wasn't going to be happy with him.

Especially if he didn't come home at all.

"Leave him," the man shouted at Buck. "I'm not adding murder to cattle-thieving, if'n I can help it."

"Drop the knife," Ed shouted from his place above them. "I've still got a bead on you, you dirty sidewinder."

The man holding Dominó laughed. "But you'd have to go through your friend here to get me, wouldn't you?"

Where were Chris's men who'd come up from behind the rustlers? Taking the cattle all the way back to the ranch?

Chris rolled onto his knees, arms wrapped around his midsection. He was hunched over, and in the fading light, he saw Buck swipe one of the guns from the ground.

"Ain't gonna kill him." Buck casually spun the revolver in his hand. "Just gonna maim him a bit. Now. Which leg was the bad one?" Buck started to turn around again, and Chris took a chance to dive at him.

The gun hit the dirt, and Chris landed on top of Buck's midsection. In a brief scramble, he planted his fist into Buck's right cheek, then drew his own revolver and held it to Buck's forehead.

"I don't have to go through anybody," he said through his teeth, meeting Buck's wide eyes. Fervently praying Buck would stop. Chris hadn't ever killed a man. But if the lives of good people were on the line, including his own, he wouldn't hesitate to protect them. "Tell your man to drop the knife."

Buck's voice trembled. "Drop it, Gator."

The man with the knife—Gator—swore a whole Bible's worth of curses. "This isn't going to end well for me."

A new voice, brisk and accented, spoke from behind Dominó and his captor. "You can either take a chance with a bullet here, or a chance with a judge later." Duke had joined them, though where the Englishman had come from, Chris couldn't say. He hadn't ridden out with them.

Gator hissed, much like his namesake, and threw his knife aside. Dominó whirled around and threw a punch into the other man's face, knocking him down. The cowboy had the knife-wielding rustler trussed up like a calf during branding in a handful of seconds.

Chris let loose a long breath, his eyes still on Buck's. "We're both getting up. And you're done trying to surprise me. You got that?"

"Yeah. I got it."

Chris rolled away from Buck and onto one knee—then all the way up. He wrapped one arm around his midsection and the gun trained on Buck. Dominó had finished tying up the boys and now came to do the same to Buck. Once all the thieves were secured, Duke came down the embankment, a rifle slung over his shoulder.

"I can see dust coming this direction. I think the other gentlemen from the ranch are finally going to join the party."

"A party you weren't invited to attend," Chris grumbled, checking the boys for other weapons. He removed a knife from one kid's boot and a smaller pistol from the belt of another.

Duke heaved the first kid to his feet and helped Dominó throw the kid over his saddle, like a sack of potatoes. "I did wonder about that. Why, exactly, was I not informed of this plan?"

"You're part of the family." Chris and Ed heaved Gator over his saddle the same way and tied him to it. "And a newlywed."

A mirthless chuckle followed that statement. Duke paused and turned around. "I hate to point out the obvious, Frosty, but so are you. A newlywed, I mean. We both still have jobs to do."

"This wasn't one of yours." Frosty looked eastward, hearing more horses approach. At last. He turned to find Ed's hands free. "Ed, why don't you go get the men we sent to the north canyon?"

"Sure thing, Frosty." Ed saluted and climbed back up the shallow wall to his horse.

Duke approached, gun in hand, and gave Chris a hard look. "The more men you bring on these things, the better. Obviously. And as you said, I'm part of the family. That means I have a vested interest in keeping our ranch, men, and cattle safe. The same as you."

Dominó stood with his arms folded, staring at their row of captives. "*Tiene razón*, Frosty."

"I know he makes sense." Chris glared at the hand but didn't have time to say more. His men had finally arrived. He spent the next quarter of an hour giving instructions, checking rope, and getting everyone out of the canyon and back to the ranch. Mounting proved a painful task. His head was pounding, and his mid-section was well-bruised.

Dusk was swiftly turning to dark when Duke rode up beside Chris. "You take a lot of burdens on yourself, Frosty."

Chris stiffened up, then bit back a groan when his ribs protested. He didn't look at his friend. "It's my job. I'm the foreman."

"And I am the rancher's son-in-law, with a stake of my own in the land and cattle. Yet I knew nothing of what you had planned should the rustlers come back." Duke shrugged when Chris finally glanced his way. "One of the first things I learned when I came to the ranch was that we all have to look out for each other. We cannot do so if we do not know where to look."

Chris gave a tight nod. "True enough." They rode in silence for several minutes before Duke spoke again.

"Did your wife at least know your plan?"

"No." Chris fought the urge to cough when dust caught in his throat. His ribs couldn't take much more. "Didn't figure she needed to."

The Englishman laughed, making his horse dance to the side. "I can only imagine the trouble you'll be in, then."

"Trouble?" Chris glanced at the other man, confused. "Why? You figure she wanted to ride out with us, too?"

"Not at all." Duke smirked. "But to her, it likely appeared that you did no more than arm yourself and take off riding across the desert, like you were on your way to a shootout rather than a well-laid plan. I can't even imagine what Dannie would do to me if I behaved that way." Appearing highly amused with himself, Duke nudged his horse with his heels and got far enough ahead that Chris felt perfectly justified in grumbling out his complaints about the nosy Englishman.

Except he had the sneaking suspicion his friend was right.

CHAPTER TWENTY-SIX

Evelyn heard the men come in while she sat near the front window, reading to the children. She stopped mid-sentence and put the book in Laura's lap. "Continue, dear, to the end of the chapter. I'll return shortly." She picked up her shawl and wrapped it around her shoulders, then went out the front door and down the steps.

The men rode steadily, a line of horses carrying bundles barely visible in the half-moon's light. None of them came her way, though two men broke off from the group and rode to the main house. Perhaps to report on what had happened.

Evelyn left the porch, her steps slow as her eyes tried to pick out what she was seeing. Why were there so many animals and so few men? She made it to the paddock, leaning against the fence and squinting until she realized men had been slung across the backs of the horses like baggage. She covered her mouth with her hand. Were those men wounded, making them incapable of riding upright?

They kept going to the road, so she needed to get to the house to intercept whoever had gone there to speak to King. She climbed the paddock fence, startling several horses, and ran across it to climb the other fence into the stable yard. She made it to the first step on the back porch when the door opened.

A tall man with a lean build stood silhouetted in the doorway, and Evelyn's heart cried out in relief. She stumbled up the steps and flung herself at her husband, wrapping her arms around his middle. Burying her face in his chest, she fought back tears, but her body trembled with the release of her fear.

"Evie—" Chris groaned, his arms falling gently across her shoulder and wrapping around her waist almost gingerly. "Evie. I'm fine. We're all safe."

The tears won the battle, falling down her cheeks. "You're not hurt?" She lifted her chin to look up at him.

He winced. "A bit bruised and banged up, maybe."

"Bruised?" She stepped back and looked up at him. There was an angry red and purple swelling along his jaw. Scratches along his face. She brushed his cheek with her fingertips, and he leaned into her touch. "What happened? Did anyone else get hurt? Shot?"

"Thankfully, no." Chris covered her hand with his and turned to kiss her palm. "Though I'll admit, we had a moment when I thought the worst might happen. Evie, I promise we were careful. We had a plan."

She wiped at her eyes with the back of her hand, then stepped away from him. "A plan? To run off with guns when it was almost dark, to track down and surprise desperate men?"

A step in the kitchen made her look away from her husband before he could answer her, and she saw King standing there. "Sorry to interrupt you, ma'am." He smiled at Evelyn but seemed to know enough to keep it a tame grin. "Frosty, Duke says you want to let the three boys go and take the others to Tombstone to await trial."

"Maybe not let go," Chris said, one arm still around her waist. Almost as though he'd forgotten he held her. "I think we oughtta hold them here and talk some sense into them. Maybe find some jobs for them to do around the ranch."

"Ah, rehabilitation. I am all for it, for the young people." King nodded once. "Very well. Duke and I will ride out with the rest of the escort. You go see Ruthie, then keep an eye on this place while we're gone."

Chris frowned and opened his mouth, an objection clearly on his tongue.

Evelyn covered his mouth with her hand, and he looked down at her with wide eyes. She smiled sweetly at King. "I'll make certain your foreman follows *orders*, King."

The old cowboy chuckled. "Thank you, my lady." He bowed, and Evelyn had to smile that now, of all moments, he remembered the title she no longer made use of. Then King left the room, chuckling and calling out, "Duke, let's catch up to the men and pay that visit to the Tombstone Sheriff."

Chris looked down at her, his eyebrows pulling together while a wrinkle appeared in his forehead. "Evie." Her hand muffled his words. "I should go with them."

She moved her hand but fixed him with the most furious glare she could muster while still recovering from her tears. "Why do you need to see Ruthie? You said you just had a few bruises."

He tried to step back, but she grabbed him by his suspenders and pulled him closer—making him grimace and groan again. "Evelyn. Please, be gentle."

Glowering at him, Evelyn raised up on her toes so they were eye-to-eye. "*Why?*"

Chris's ears turned pink. "I might have a broken a rib. Or cracked one, at least. I don't know."

Evelyn's jaw dropped open without her permission. She took his hand and pulled him out the back door. "We are going to see Ruthie this very minute. I thought you said you only had a few bruises? When are you going to stop telling me half-truths?" She pulled him down the steps, listening to him gasp in pain. She hardly felt guilty at all. "And here I am, turning down a teaching position in Boston for you."

He stopped dead in his tracks, necessitating she whirl around to glare up at him again. His eyes were wide, glowing with hope.

"Evie—"

"Or you don't tell me *anything* until someone tells me first. Like the rattlesnakes, and the danger surrounding rustlers. I am not a delicate English flower to be blown over by a desert breeze."

"I know that, Evie."

She jabbed a finger into the center of his chest, making him wince. "Then stop treating me like you can't trust me with things."

"Yes, ma'am." For the first time, he appeared contrite. "I didn't want you to worry—"

"And yet, that's all I've been doing, it seems." She turned around with a huff and tugged him after her.

"You've decided to turn down the school?" he asked, and her heart spun around before springing wildly up against her chest.

"That's not important right now." She wasn't about to speak to him on such matters until he'd been bandaged up.

They arrived at Ruthie's back door. Evelyn knocked on it as politely as she could.

Lee opened the inside door and looked through the screened door at her. "Mrs. Morgan."

"We need to speak to your grandmother, please, Lee." The boy nodded and opened the door to let them in. Evelyn marched her husband to the Steeles' kitchen table and pointed to it. "Sit."

He did as he was told, grinning up at her. She nodded, pleased that he had finally chosen to act with intelligence. He wrapped one arm around his middle and glanced to the back door. "Maybe you should go home and be with the kids?"

Evelyn narrowed her eyes at him and tipped her chin upward. "The children are perfectly fine. My husband, on the other hand, needs a great deal of watching at present."

Ruthie came in on that note, already tying an apron on. "Good evening, Evie. Frosty. You catch the troublemakers?"

"Sure did. Without firing a shot." He gave Evelyn a quick

smile that she most certainly didn't return. From the moment he left her at the house, she'd felt fear's grip around her heart, squeezing and squeezing until she could hardly breathe.

What if she'd lost him? What if Chris had died?

She couldn't lose him so soon after finding him. Her heart would break into a thousand pieces, and she'd never put it together again. Evelyn hadn't even told him yet what he meant to her. But the moment he'd ridden away, she'd known she could never entertain the idea of leaving. She'd made her choice.

"Sounds admirable." Ruthie put her hands on her hips. "So, what do you need old Ruthie for, hmm? That bruising on your chin? Did you lose a tooth?"

Chris worked his jaw and winced. "Don't think so. But, ah—I took a few kicks to the ribs and gut." He removed his hat and put it on the table behind him.

"*Kicks?*" Evelyn covered her mouth with her hand when she heard the shrillness in her voice, then she shook her head. "How were you kicked if you were on horses, and *they* were on horses?'

For a moment, her husband looked less pained and more concerned. "I promise, I'll explain all of it to you, Evie."

"Later," Ruthie said, hands on her hips. "Let me get some bandages. And boil some water to make a poultice for the bruising. Evie, get your husband's shirt off, then I'll get to work on him. I'll settle my menfolk and be back in a moment." She left the kitchen, muttering to herself. "Bruised and broken cowboys, and I have to put them all back together again."

Evelyn crossed her arms and glared at her husband. "You heard her. Suspenders off, first."

"Yes, ma'am." He winced as he raised a hand to slide the suspender off one shoulder, then sucked in a deep breath as he tried to lift the other.

Taking pity on him, Evelyn came forward. "I suppose I had better help." She slid the suspender off the other shoulder for him. He raised his hand to unbutton the top of his shirt and winced. "Stop." Evelyn covered his hands with hers, lowering them to his lap. "Let me." She undid the top button of his shirt, noting the frayed bits of cloth and dirt streaking the front. "I'm sorry you're hurt."

"I'm pretty sure I deserve it," he muttered, the warmth of his breath tickling her skin.

She undid the next button, and the next. His breathing grew more ragged, and Evelyn couldn't tell if it was from pain or her proximity. Her fingers slowed the farther down she went, and her cheeks flooded with heat. She hadn't yet seen her husband wearing less clothing than what he wore when leaving the house.

Halfway down his shirt, she changed tactics. For both their sakes. "I'm going to untuck this, now. If you'll stand?" He did, not saying a word, and she took hold of either side of his shirt. She pulled upward until she had the hem and the last three buttons in sight. With him standing, she made quick work of those last buttons, then slipped behind him with her eyes still lowered to help him remove one arm at a time from the clothing.

Evelyn's mouth went dry at the sight of his broad back. She saw a clear line upon his neck marking where his shirt protected him from the sun. There were a few freckles on his shoulders. His back, broad and strong, tapered into a narrower waist. Then she circled around to his front, clutching his shirt in her hands, and let her gaze admire him.

Apparently, Chris had a shyness of character she'd yet to see. He crossed his arms over his chest, pain etching lines in his face. And she saw the flush spreading upward from his neck into his face. That made her smile. "I've seen a man's chest before, Chris."

He raised his eyes to the ceiling, as though asking heaven for strength, before lowering his gaze to hers. "This isn't exactly how I thought you'd see mine."

Evelyn nearly laughed, but her eye caught the bloom of bruising along his midsection. "Oh, Chris—"

Ruthie came back into the room, a basket in her hands. "Lay back on that table, young man, and let's see if you're bruised or broken." She put the basket on the table, and Evelyn saw the long strips of cloth inside.

Biting her lip, Evelyn sidled closer as Ruthie started to gently press upon Chris's sides. "How can I help?" she dared to ask.

"Your part comes when you take this stubborn cowboy home. He'll need to rest, either way, and keeping a man like Frosty out of the saddle for a few days will take some work. The foreman's as mulish as they come."

"I'm not that bad—" Chris's words stopped abruptly as he yelped in pain.

"Bruised." Ruthie shook her head. "Maybe a fracture. You'd holler a lot more if it was broken. What about your head?"

"My head?" He winced again.

"I saw the back of that head when you came in." Ruthie held her hand out and helped Chris sit up, groaning in agony. "You've got some blood on it. See. Look at your hat." She held it up for him and pointed to the inside at the back. Sure enough, streaks of blood were on the band.

"I guess I hit it on a rock." Chris glanced at Evelyn, looking sheepish. But all her frustration had melted away for the moment. Instead, she began to feel a deep and abiding gratitude. He'd come home, injured but alive.

She might cry all over again.

Ruthie had his head wound, small as it was, cleaned and bandaged in no time. She debated wrapping up his ribs, but she didn't want to hurt his ability to breathe. "That's the danger, you see," she told Evelyn. "If he can't breathe properly, it could lead right to pneumonia."

Evelyn shuddered and held Chris's shirt and hat to her chest. "Thank you, Ruthie. I'll make sure he rests."

"Make it at least a week, Frosty."

Her grimaced. "I'm the foreman—"

"And even the foreman gets laid-up sometimes," Ruthie snapped. "Evie, you mind what I said and keep him as still as you can."

"Thank you, Ruthie." Evelyn impulsively hugged the older woman. "Thank you."

"Now, now." Ruthie hugged her back, then she whispered, "He'll be as lively as a jackrabbit in no time. You'll see."

Evelyn tucked her husband's things under one arm, and when they made it outside under the starry sky, she slid her arm around his waist as though to offer him support. He put an arm around her shoulder as they walked down the well-worn path from one house to the other.

~

EXHAUSTION BEAT A DRUM IN CHRIS'S HEAD, AND HIS LIMBS FELT heavier with each step he took home. But he held Evelyn to his side, and that made things much less terrible. When they walked in the front door together, the children were nowhere to be seen. The oil lamp still flickered on the table.

"Don't you move," Evelyn told him sternly, leaving him standing by the door. "I'm going to look in on everyone." She hurried from the girls' room to the boy's, her shoulders relaxing as she closed Ben's door behind her. "They all went to sleep. On their own." Her lips turned upward. "I can hardly believe our luck."

"They're good kids," Chris said, bending as though to remove his boots.

"Chris, don't you dare." Evelyn hurried to his side and took his hand. "Stop that. Come on, let's get you upstairs so you only have to sit down once."

Grimacing, Chris followed his wife as she took down the lamp and led the way upstairs. A night on the floor, feeling as he did at that moment, sounded awful. Maybe he could sleep sitting up in his rocking chair. That might be better than stretched out flat on a few blankets and floorboards.

Evelyn stopped at her door and pushed it open, then stood back and gestured for him to go inside.

Chris froze where he stood, one foot on the landing and the other still on the top step. He gazed through the open doorway. "Evie."

"You need a bed tonight, Mr. Morgan. Stop trying to argue with me and do as I say. Please." She gestured for him to follow her.

First the shirt, now this. But it meant nothing. She was being thoughtful. Compassionate. Looking after him while he was injured. She had a nurturing instinct that he admired, even if she meant to use it on him.

Chris limped along inside, his formerly broken leg aching. Maybe he'd hurt that during the tussle with Buck, too. He lowered himself onto the edge of the bed, but before he could work on his boot, Evelyn had bent and taken it in hand. Bracing himself, Chris bit the insides of his cheeks to keep from making a sound while she tugged off one boot and then the other. She stood them up, side by side, near the wall.

"What else do you need?" she asked, resting her hands on her hips. As though she helped grown men get ready for bed every night.

His neck and cheeks went warm. Chris scratched his knuckle. "I think I can manage. But Evie—where are you going to sleep?"

She pointed to the bed. Specifically, to the pillow on the opposite side from where he sat. "Right there. Like I always do." She went to the chest of drawers, opened it and removed white, folded clothing, talking all the while. "Don't get any ideas. You are injured. And I'm taking care of you, like Ruthie said. Prepare for bed. I'm making tea to help you sleep. I'll return shortly."

She left with a newly lit candle in one hand and what he assumed was her nightgown in the other.

For several minutes, he sat there, completely still and horribly confused. "Don't get any ideas," he repeated to himself. "Don't get *any* ideas, Chris Morgan." He went to her wash basin and poured water from the pitcher into the large bowl. He washed up as well as he could. Then he took off his pants and looked down at his long drawers. They didn't look bad. He'd put on clean outer and underclothes before taking Evie on their ride that afternoon.

Was it only that afternoon? It felt like days ago rather than hours.

Aching both inside and out, Chris climbed into the bed and pulled the quilt up until he could tuck it beneath his chin. He closed his eyes and grumbled to himself. "This is fine. We're married. It's fine. Evie knows what she's doing."

"Do I, though?" her voice asked, and Chris sat bolt upright, and then gasped in pain as he fell back again. He heard his wife giggle, a nervous sound, and raised his head just enough to glare at her.

In the soft glow of the oil lamp, his wife looked like an angel in her white nightgown. She'd taken her hair down, too, and left it in one long braid across her shoulder. The nightgown covered her from neck to toe, with long sleeves edged in lace. Beautiful. He'd never seen a prettier sight in all his life.

She approached the bed slowly, not meeting his eyes, and put the candle on the table at her side of the bed. Then she held a mug out to him. "Your tea."

Chris pushed himself up enough to accept the cup and press it to his lips. He knocked back the tea, noticing nothing except that the liquid was hot. Every sense not attuned to the woman standing on the other side of the bed didn't matter. He held the empty cup out to her, falling back to the pillow with a groan.

Even if she hadn't warned him about *ideas*, he wasn't in any position to have them. Everything hurt. And it hurt more each passing moment.

Evelyn blew out the candle. He felt it when she lifted the edge of the quilt and slid inside, the bed creaking and the mattress dipping toward her.

Their shoulders brushed.

Chris stared up at the ceiling in the dark, clenching his jaw as tightly as he could.

The pain was nothing to the torture of finally sharing a bed with his wife, but in exactly the wrong circumstances.

"I'm sorry for this," he finally said aloud.

Evelyn shifted. Turning on her side. *Toward* him. "For what? Being in my bed? Getting injured? Not telling me about your plan?"

He grimaced. "All of it, I suppose."

"You can make it up to me by telling me everything that happened tonight. I want to know it all, please."

"Evie," he protested. "They hurt no one but me. Do you really need to know more?"

She shifted, and then her hand was upon his bare arm. "Yes, Chris. I do."

Chris covered her hand with his, twining their fingers together. Then he closed his eyes and started talking. But he started back when he and Ed had laid out the plan for the other men, making certain to explain how they'd decided to plan their confrontation with the rustlers. As he recounted the events of the night, Evelyn's grip on his hand tightened. When he told her how he'd been thrown to the ground, she gasped and moved closer, wrapping her arm through his and thoroughly distracting him. Enough so that he didn't speak again until she asked, "And then what happened?"

By the time Chris finished his story, Evelyn had her cheek pressed to his shoulder, their arms and fingers linked, and he could feel her hip against his. Everywhere they touched, his skin felt like it had been lit on fire. Yet he had to lie perfectly still and pretend to be unaffected.

"Oh, Chris." She turned her cheek and pressed her lips to his shoulder. The touch on his skin made his heart thud all the harder in his chest. "I'm grateful that you're all right. I don't know what I would've done if you'd been hurt more...or if something worse had happened." She sounded adorably sleepy. He wished he could see her. Or that he could move enough to put both arms around her and hold her close.

"Even if something had happened to me," he said, voice softer than before, "you and the children would've been fine. I promise. We made sure of that."

She yawned and snuggled closer to him. "That's not what I meant."

His breath stilled. He considered her words. Then his question. "It's not?"

But Evelyn's breathing had changed, growing deep and long. She'd fallen asleep.

Despite his exhaustion, Chris tried to stay awake longer. Just to enjoy the sensation of having his wife by his side.

CHAPTER TWENTY-SEVEN

"Chris Morgan, Ruthie had no idea how right she was when she said you were stubborn."

Chris yelped in surprise at his wife's words, then spun around.

Evelyn planted her feet firmly in the bedroom doorway two days later. "You aren't leaving this house. Abram, Cookie, and the cowboys have the chores well in hand. You're going to rest until King and the others return."

Chris had gotten out of bed, frustrated and irritable, and dressed. Without Evie knowing while she worked with the children downstairs. She'd brought him breakfast in bed two days running. Slept with him—and *only* slept—in that cursedly beautiful nightgown two nights in a row while he lay awake wishing for more, while his whole body protested if he breathed too deeply.

"Evie, darlin'." He'd taken to calling her darling, too. If she minded or noticed, she hadn't said. "I can't stay here forever. I'm fine." He stood and looked around the room again. "Have you seen my boots?"

"Yes." She said nothing more, only crossed her arms.

"Well? Where are they?" he asked, stepping closer to her.

"I gave them to Madeline and told her to hide them." She smiled brightly at him. "And she isn't here right now, so don't bother shouting for her."

He grimaced and came closer. He didn't necessarily want to go tromping around the ranch, with every step jolting through his leg and up to his ribs, but staying still didn't agree with him. "You listen here, Mrs. Morgan—"

"I do enjoy when you call me that." She batted her eyes at him in a mockery of flirtation. Then she spun on her heel and left the room, saying over her shoulder, "Ruthie said you'll have pain in those ribs for a month, and that you shouldn't ride for two weeks, and you shouldn't work at all for a week. What do you think she'll do to you if you go against her orders?"

He'd followed her out of the room and then paused mid-step. "Nothing good," he muttered, going down the stairs one at a time, hand on the wall for balance. "Maybe I'll see if Abram can help make the rail for these steps."

His wife's laughter drifted up from the kitchen. "Now *that* would make Ruthie truly upset. Enlisting her husband to defy her orders."

He made it to the table before his midsection ached too much to keep on moving. Maybe it was a good thing Evelyn had taken matters into her own hands to keep him home. Still, he wasn't about to go get back in bed like an invalid. Eying the stairs, he decided he wasn't ready to tackle those yet, either.

"Go read," Evelyn said, her back to him as she fiddled with the teakettle. "I know you want to start that H.G. Wells novel."

Standing in the kitchen and watching his wife sounded more appealing, but his leg protested. So did his head. Pretty much every part of his body wanted rest. He sighed, then grunted in pain. "I guess that doesn't sound too bad." He made his way to the bookshelves in the front room, finally noticing how quiet the house was. "Where'd you say the kids went?"

"They're helping Clark and Lee with those puppies again. Apparently, they're ready to find homes for the little ones, and they want to make a good impression on the farmers and people who've said they might take one."

Chris found the hardcover novel with an image of a sphinx stamped on its cover. He shuffled over to the rocking chair but thought better of using his favorite chair with the knowledge that it moved far too much. And moving hurt, at the moment. So he settled on the couch, tucking a cushion between him and the hard arm of the furniture.

Evelyn came in a few minutes later, just as he turned another page in the book. She set two mugs of tea on the short table by his arm, then settled down next to him. "Would you read to me?" she asked. "You don't need to start over. I already read through the first chapter."

Chris glanced at her with some suspicion, but she'd tucked her legs up on the couch and leaned in close. Then her cheek rested on his shoulder, her eyes on the pages of the book. "All right. If that's what you want."

"Yes, please."

He read to her, at first too conscious of the weight of her head upon his shoulder, the scent of her hair, and the way her body brushed against his. But soon the awareness shifted, growing comfortable, and Chris took her hand after turning the page. There they stayed, sipping at their cooling tea occasionally, reading about the impossible ordeal of traveling through time.

Later that evening, after the children had bid Chris goodnight and Evelyn went to tuck them in, he stood at the window examining the new curtains Evelyn had pinned up. He needed to make her a curtain rod, too. Or hooks. Something to make the curtains easier to open and close.

Evelyn came up next to him, the whisper of her skirts brushing against his ankles. She still hadn't returned his boots to him. She had sworn she wouldn't until he promised he'd do exactly as Ruthie had said. And he refrained from making the promise, just so she'd keep teasing him about it.

"What are you thinking about?" Evelyn asked, standing next

to him and brushing his hand with hers. He took that as an invitation to hold her hand. She'd been gentle and quite at ease with touching him for the last several days. He dared to hope it was a sign of her growing affection for him.

"Lots of things. Like how I need to get you a curtain rod for these curtains. I like them. They're pretty." She'd chosen a thick fabric, almost canvas-like, in a light blue. They'd block the heat from coming in during the summer, but the color was pleasant. "And then I started thinking about how much has changed since you've come into my life. There are the little things, like curtains. And the big things, like Ben, Laura, and Maddie calling me papa." He pronounced it like Evelyn and Madeline, the British accent making him smile. "I didn't think Ben and Laura would ever want to call me anything but Frosty. Like everyone else."

"You make a wonderful papa." Evelyn leaned her head against his shoulder. "You love the children very much. They know it and love you in return."

He squeezed her hand, the peace of the moment seeping deep into his heart and soul.

In the gentle silence, with only the sounds of the fire crackling in the hearth, Evelyn murmured, "I love you, too."

Chris moved maybe a little quicker than he should when he turned to look down at his wife, but the twinge of pain was nothing to the building elation in his heart. He put a hand on each of Evelyn's shoulders and looked down into her deep green eyes, reflecting firelight at him in copper bursts. "Evelyn. What did you just say?"

She returned his gaze with a smile that made his knees go weak. "I love you, Chris Morgan." A teasing glint appeared in her eyes. "*Christmas* Morgan, I suppose I should say, to make it a proper confession."

He slid his hands down her arms, then put them around her waist and pulled her closer. She tipped her chin up just enough to keep their gazes locked. "You can call me whatever you like,

Evelyn Agnes Morgan. For the rest of our lives, all that matters is that I'm yours."

The kisses they'd shared before, tentative and searching, cautiously affectionate, were nothing to the way he kissed her then. He poured his heart into the embrace, holding his wife close, while she returned his affection with a fervency that left him undone. And hungry for more. Much more.

When her arms went around him and she leaned against his chest, Chris yelped and pulled back, though his lips lingered near the corner of hers. "Ouch," he muttered by way of complaint.

Evelyn's eyebrows drew down, concern appearing upon her lovely face. She brushed his lips with hers again. "You have been out of bed too long. You need to rest."

"By all means," he said, unable to stop his crooked smile. "Let's go to bed."

She scoffed, and he had the pleasure of watching her cheeks turn a dark shade of red. "To rest."

"Yep. Eventually." He grinned and kissed her again while she laughed, forgetting all about his injuries in favor of holding his wife. Secure, at last, in her love.

Theirs might not have been a traditional courtship and marriage. They'd still done everything backward. But he'd have it no other way. Even if no one would've ever believed a countess could fall for a cowboy.

EPILOGUE

CHRISTMAS MORNING, 1895

The Morgan House, KB Ranch,
Arizona Territory

E velyn sat on the rug before the fire, leaning against
Chris, watching as the children played with the toys
Father Christmas had brought them. The girls had their
dollhouse with several pieces of tiny furniture, and new dresses
Evelyn had sewed for their dolls. Ben had a row of tin soldiers,
half of them in blue (American Revolutionaries, Chris had insist-
ed), the other half in red (the tyrannical redcoats—or British
Loyalists, as Evie called them).

On Evelyn's left hand, she wore a new ring made from
Arizona silver inlaid with small green garnets found in the Bisbee
mine. Chris had presented it to her with a flourish and refused to
say exactly when he'd had it made. The piece was small and
dainty, and Chris swore the stones brought out the golden glints
in her eyes.

"I wanted to get you a piano," he'd said, sounding a little
apologetic. "Maybe next year?"

"My darling, this is perfect. Oh, I love it." She'd kissed him thoroughly while Ben groaned and the girls giggled.

She'd presented Chris with several new shirts she had sewn herself and a quilt made up of bits and pieces of all the extra fabric she had accumulated from her projects since arriving in Arizona.

But there remained one more thing she had tucked away for him.

"All right, children. It's time to go to the Boltons' house," Chris said as the clock on the mantel struck ten. The families of the ranch had agreed to come together to read the Christmas story and have luncheon.

Chris and Evelyn walked together, arm in arm, down the porch steps. Though when Ben leaped down all three steps with his growing cattle dog barking at his heels, Evelyn had to lean into Chris to keep from falling over. She laughed.

"Slow down, Ben," Chris called, wrapping a protective arm around Evelyn's middle. "I think he's still making up for the lost time with crutches."

"I think he's a happy little boy." Evelyn looked over her shoulder to see the girls following behind demurely, each cradling a doll and talking excitedly about the new books they'd received and which they would read first.

The winter wind in Arizona ruffled their clothes and coats, but the sun shone brightly enough that Evelyn didn't feel the usual biting sting in the air. The day was quite perfect.

"We'll get snow, come January," Chris predicted, looking toward the mountains. His breath puffed out in front of him in a little cloud. "Then I'll take the kids up to the foothills for sledding."

"I'm sure they'll love that." Evelyn examined the ring on her hand, having left gloves behind for the purpose of enjoying her gift in the sunlight. It was quite perfect. More precious to her than any of the jewels she'd left behind in England.

They arrived at the Boltons' home and filled the parlor with talk and laughter. They had exchanged family gifts the evening before, but now the children compared what they had received and passed compliments all around. Travis had a new set of luggage, since he was leaving on January second for Texas and University. Clark had a similar gift, even though he wouldn't be joining his brother until the fall, when he turned seventeen.

As King read the story of the nativity, he had one arm around his wife. Beth rested both hands on her mid-section, which had started to grow round. Dannie and her brothers had been delighted with the news that their stepmother was increasing their family by one more. And given the way Dannie's eyes went misty during the Christmas story, and her hand briefly brushed across her midsection, Evelyn had the feeling that the Rounsevell family would make their own announcement soon.

When they returned to their own home that evening, and after they tucked the children in bed with kisses and prayers, Evelyn snuggled up next to her husband on the couch. He held a new book in his hand, one he'd insisted she needed to read. Written by a woman, Louisa May Alcott, the story was about a family of girls during America's War Between the States.

"Before we begin." She took the book from him and set it aside. Chris raised his eyebrows and leaned closer.

"Yes, darlin'?"

She loved when he called her that. "I have one more gift for you." She reached into the pocket she'd sewn into the folds of her skirt. "I wanted to wait and give it to you when I could explain without being interrupted."

He chuckled, though his eyes held curiosity as he studied her. "The children were pretty enthusiastic this morning."

She grinned back at him. "Hold out your hand and close your eyes."

He did as she commanded, and she placed the gift in his palm. She'd accompanied Chris to Tombstone, along with Dannie and Evan. The men had had business to see to, on behalf of the ranch. So she and Dannie had enjoyed time on their own. Evelyn had visited a watchmaker.

"Open your eyes."

Chris looked down at the watch and let out a low whistle. "Wait a minute. That's not—?"

She'd had a watch made for her husband, with a particular copper penny set into the outer casing. "The same one," Evelyn assured him, leaning into his shoulder again. "The penny you dropped when we first met."

"The penny you *think* I dropped. You've still never proven it fell out of my pocket," he said, kissing her temple. "What do you think? Did it bring you good luck?"

"The very best. Which is why I'm returning it to you. To make sure it brings both of us more of the same. I love you, Chris."

Chris took great delight in showing her how much he felt the same way about her.

IF YOU ENJOYED FROSTY AND EVIE'S STORY, BE SURE TO ORDER THE third (and final) book in this American Victorian series, *A Lady's Heart of Gold*. My favorite cowboy, Ed, gets to meet his match in a feisty English reporter.

When a determined English newspaper reporter arrives in the Arizona desert, she expects to find the lawless and the illiterate. Instead, she meets a well-spoken and handsome cowboy who's ready to prove to her there's more to the Territory than cattle and cacti.

HISTORICAL NOTES

The term "Indian" for Native American and First Nations people is inappropriate. However, it was applied here with historical accuracy in mind. The term was used sparingly, and in reference to the characters' understanding of the Native peoples of North America.

Buffalo Soldiers were stationed at Fort Huachuca for several years, and many retired in Arizona. There is a museum there you should go see if you're ever down that way.

Cattle Rustlers ran on both sides of the national border with Mexico. A border which was invisible at that point in history in almost all respects.

Sonoita is a real town, but all I borrowed from it is its name and general location.

The KB Ranch is loosely based on the Empire Ranch, which was founded by an Englishman and his Canadian partners in the 1870's and is a working ranch to this day. The letters written by the Englishman home are still available to the public today, and they were immensely helpful in writing this book. I had the opportunity to tour the working ranch and several original buildings, including the adobe structure that served as the bunkhouse in this book.

Many thanks to the Empire Ranch Association for their upkeep of the land and houses. This ranch hosted several Old West style movies and television shows over the years, including those starring film cowboy John Wayne.

I lived in the area where I based this novel, in a little town called Sierra Vista, for five years. Unlike a lot of Arizona, Sierra Vista rarely hit triple digit temperatures in the summer, and it was a wonderful place to live throughout the year. The Empire Ranch is in an even better position, up in the mountains, with tall grasses and biodiversity you wouldn't expect to find in the middle of the desert state. So if it doesn't exactly fit your mental picture of Arizona, know that I did my best to be accurate to my own experiences in the area.

ACKNOWLEDGMENTS

Thank you to my loving family. For their patience and love, for their help.

Many, many thanks to Jenny and Emily at Midnight Owl Editors. Jenny set me straight on more than a few things this time around, and Emily stepped in to proofread my novel at the last moment.

I will forever be grateful for my dearest friend and designer, Shaela Kay of Blue Water Books. She created this lovely cover, but also acted as my alpha-reader and helped me shape this story.

I'm also grateful to Jacob of DabbleWriter.com who created the absolute best writing app that I have ever used.

Thank you to all my Regency readers, who trusted me enough to follow me to the American West. Thank you to all my new readers who found me through Duke and Frosty. I couldn't do this without y'all.

ALSO BY SALLY BRITTON

CASTLE CLAIRVOIR ROMANCES

Mr. Gardiner and the Governess | *A Companion for the Count* | *Sir Andrew and the Authoress*

HEARTS OF ARIZONA SERIES:

Silver Dollar Duke | *Copper for the Countess*

THE INGLEWOOD SERIES:

Rescuing Lord Inglewood | *Discovering Grace*

Saving Miss Everly | *Engaging Sir Isaac*

Reforming Lord Neil

THE BRANCHES OF LOVE SERIES:

Martha's Patience | *The Social Tutor*

The Gentleman Physician | *His Bluestocking Bride*

The Earl and His Lady | *Miss Devon's Choice*

Courting the Vicar's Daughter | *Penny's Yuletide Wish*

STAND ALONE ROMANCES:

The Captain and Miss Winter | *His Unexpected Heiress*

A Haunting at Havenwood

ABOUT THE AUTHOR

Sally Britton, along with her husband, their four incredible children, their tabby Willow, and their dog named Izzie, live in Oklahoma. So far, they really like it there, even if the family will always consider Texas home.

Sally started writing her first story on her mother's electric typewriter when she was fourteen years old. Reading her way through Jane Austen, Louisa May Alcott, and Lucy Maud Montgomery, Sally decided to write about the complex world of centuries past.

Sally graduated from Brigham Young University in 2007 with a bachelor's in English. She met and married her husband not long after and started working on their happily ever after.

Vincent Van Gogh is attributed with the quote, "What is done in love is done well." Sally has taken that as her motto, writing stories where love is a choice.

All of Sally's published works are available on Amazon.com and you can connect with Sally and sign up for her newsletter on her website, AuthorSallyBritton.com.

www.ingramcontent.com/pod-product-compliance
Lightning Source LLC
Chambersburg PA
CBHW030555180626
46816CB00005B/1545